One Woman's War

Also by Rosie Goodwin

The Bad Apple
No One's Girl
Dancing Till Midnight
Tilly Trotter's Legacy
Moonlight and Ashes
The Mallen Secret
Forsaken
The Sand Dancer
Yesterday's Shadows
The Boy from Nowhere
A Rose Among Thorns
The Lost Soul
The Ribbon Weaver
A Band of Steel
Whispers
The Misfit
The Empty Cradle
Home Front Girls
A Mother's Shame
The Soldier's Daughter
The Mill Girl
The Maid's Courage
The Lost Girl

The Claire McMullen Series
Our Little Secret
Crying Shame

Dilly's Story Series
Dilly's Sacrifice
Dilly's Lass
Dilly's Hope

The Days of the Week Collection
Mothering Sunday
The Little Angel
A Mother's Grace
The Blessed Child
A Maiden's Voyage
A Precious Gift
Time to Say Goodbye

The Precious Stones Series
The Winter Promise
An Orphan's Journey
A Simple Wish
A Daughter's Destiny
A Season for Hope
A Lesson Learned

The Flower Girls Collection
Our Fair Lily
Our Dear Daisy
Our Sweet Violet

The Rags to Riches Trilogy
The Rag Princess

Rosie Goodwin is the four-million-copy bestselling author of more than forty novels. She is the first author in the world to be allowed to follow three of Catherine Cookson's trilogies with her own sequels. Having worked in the social services sector for many years, then fostered a number of children, she is now a full-time novelist. She is one of the top fifty most borrowed authors from UK libraries and has sold over four million copies across her career. Rosie lives in Nuneaton, the setting for many of her books, with her husband and their beloved dogs.

Rosie GOODWIN
One Woman's War

ZAFFRE

First published in the UK in 2026 by
ZAFFRE
An imprint of Bonnier Books UK
5th Floor, HYLO, 105 Bunhill Row,
London, EC1Y 8LZ

Copyright © Rosie Goodwin, 2026

All rights reserved.
No part of this publication may be reproduced,
stored or transmitted in any form by any means, electronic,
mechanical, photocopying or otherwise, without the
prior written permission of the publisher.

The right of Rosie Goodwin to be identified as Author of this
work has been asserted by her in accordance with the
Copyright, Designs and Patents Act, 1988.

This is a work of fiction. Names, places, events and
incidents are either the products of the author's
imagination or used fictitiously. Any resemblance to
actual persons, living or dead, or actual
events is purely coincidental.

A CIP catalogue record for this book is
available from the British Library.

ISBN: 978-1-80418-308-3

Also available as an ebook and an audiobook

1 3 5 7 9 10 8 6 4 2

Typeset by IDSUK (Data Connection) Ltd
Printed and bound by CPI (UK) Ltd, Croydon CR0 4YY

The authorised representative in the EEA is Bonnier
Books UK (Ireland) Limited.
Registered office address:
Block B, The Crescent Building
Northwood, Santry
Dublin 9, D09 C6X8
Ireland
compliance@bonnierbooks.ie

www.bonnierbooks.co.uk

This one is for my dear life-long friend Cheryl and her family on the sad passing of her lovely husband Phil, a devoted husband, father and grandfather.

Phillip Keen 2.2.1952–13.9.2025

He really was a truly lovely man. R.I.P Phil, you will be sadly missed by all who knew you.

Prologue

France, October 1914

Her eyes were adjusting to the darkness now as she peered ahead into the gloom. In the sea of mud that seemed to stretch for as far as her eyes could see, she could just make out the shapes of bodies slumped on the ground, and the sound of men screaming in pain echoed around her. It was like being trapped in a nightmare and tears poured down her pale cheeks as the stretcher-bearers raced onto the field. They stopped at each shape they came to, moving on to the next if the person was dead. They would be the last to be brought from the field if they were lucky. If not, they would be swallowed up by the mud where they had fallen. Those that were still alive were hastily put onto the stretchers and brought back to be loaded onto the back of the truck. The minutes stretched into an hour and then two until at last, Jim reappeared and climbed in beside her. He was covered in mud from head to toe with only the whites of his eyes showing and he looked weary.

'Time to go, Nurse, there's no more room in the back till the next trip.'

Annie nodded and with shaking fingers she started the engine and turned the truck around. The screams that were coming from behind her were unnerving and her heart ached as she thought of how much pain the men must be in.

'It's been bad today,' Jim confided as he felt in his pocket for his cigarettes. He offered one to her and when Annie shook her head, he lit one and took a deep drag on it to steady his nerves. It didn't matter how many times he did this job it always upset him to see young men no older than himself with limbs blown off. Many of them bled to death before they could get to the hospital.

When they arrived, nurses helped get the injured inside, and then it was back to the battlefield to search for any remaining survivors. There were far fewer this time, despite the men scouring the field. Many were already dead, and they would be brought back on the final trip of the day and laid in the tent that served as a morgue.

By the time the last trip was over, Annie's nerves were in shreds. Never in her wildest dreams had she imagined such carnage and it had shaken her badly.

'Well done, Nurse Lilburn,' the kindly ward sister said. 'Go and get a hot drink and some rest now. And in the morning, you can go into the morgue with another nurse and collect the dog tags from the corpses so that we can get them buried.'

'Yes, Sister.' Annie shuddered at the thought. It had been bad enough to have to see their poor broken bodies piled into the back of the truck but the thought of having to touch them filled her with dread.

On legs that seemed to have developed a life of their own Annie walked to the canteen, the smell of death still in her nostrils. It had been a long, long day.

Chapter One

Nuneaton, February 1914

'Come on, let's get you upstairs so you can have a lie-down.' Annie took Maggie Lilburn's elbow and helped her to rise from her seat. She had just come home after closing the second-hand shop she ran in town to find Maggie sitting in a chair. She had suffered with mental health problems ever since losing her daughter some years before and recently it seemed she was getting worse.

Annie helped Maggie towards the door that led into the spacious hallway of the house in Swan Lane. There was no sign of a meal being ready so once she had settled her upstairs, she would have to make a start on preparing one.

Annie had lived with Maggie and her husband Levi for some years after Maggie had taken her from the local workhouse when she was a child. Levi and their son Charlie would soon be home from work and hungry for their supper.

She gently placed Maggie on her bed and put a blanket across her legs. As she turned to head for the door, she gasped. Just for a moment she could have sworn she saw the outline of a little girl standing close to the bed, but when she blinked and looked again there was nothing there. Her heart thudded with shock. She often found Maggie chatting to Penny, her daughter who had passed away, but was it possible that Maggie *could* actually see the little girl? Were there really such things as ghosts?

Once back downstairs, Annie sank onto a kitchen chair and took a deep breath to calm herself. But dinner wasn't going to cook itself, so after a minute she went to the sink and started to prepare some vegetables.

She had just put some pork chops into the oven when Charlie came in and put his hat and coat over the back of a chair. He worked in an accountant's office in the town and was the brainy one of Maggie and Levi's three sons. When they were both at school, Charlie had been the one who helped Annie with her schoolwork and he had even taught her to speak French.

'Had a good day?' he asked politely.

She nodded. 'Busy, and yourself?'

He shrugged as he crossed to fill the kettle at the sink. 'Same as always.'

As Charlie measured some tea leaves into the pot they heard Levi's old horse, Dobbin, plod down the side of the house and, glancing out of the kitchen window, Annie saw him leading the horse to his stable.

'Better make a full pot,' she told Charlie; Levi loved his cup of tea when he first got home. It was no wonder, really, after he had been working out in the cold all day. The rag-and-bone round could be pleasant in the summer when the sun was shining but it wasn't much fun during the winter months, not that Levi ever complained. Until not so long ago Annie had gone out on the rounds with him but she now ran the shop they had opened in town, selling some of the second-hand goods Levi collected.

Outside, Levi unharnessed the horse and led him into the stable where he gave him a brisk rub down and threw a warm blanket across him. Then after feeding him, he made his way into the kitchen.

'Hello, you two,' he greeted Charlie and Annie cheerfully as he dragged his flat cap off and hurried over to hold his hands out to the fire. 'Are Davey and Spirit not back yet?'

Davey Froggett worked alongside Levi and had recently wed Annie's close friend Eve.

'Speak of the devil, 'ere they are now,' Annie told him as Davey appeared in the yard outside and led Spirit into the stable.

Once he'd got her settled, he popped his head round the door and winked at Annie. 'All right are you, love?'

'I'm fine,' Annie said with a smile. 'Will you come in for a cup of tea afore you get off?'

He shook his head. 'No, I won't, ta, I'd best get 'ome to me wife.' He chuckled. 'I still can't get used to sayin' that. Ta-ra for now.' Then with a cheeky grin he closed the door and was gone.

'Have a good day, did you?' she asked Levi, as she laid the cups out.

He shrugged. 'So-so. It's allus quieter in the winter, as you know. But where's Maggie? Havin' a lie-down, is she?'

Annie nodded as she strained the tea into the cups. 'Yes, she's, er . . . not 'ad a good day from what I could see of it.'

'Oh.' He frowned. 'Chattin' to Penny again, is she?'

Annie nodded as she handed him his drink.

Levi had caught her doing it himself a few times lately and was sorely concerned. 'Hmm, I reckon she's gettin' worse again. I wonder if I shouldn't get Dr Brain in to have a look at her?'

'No, don't do that,' Annie said quickly. 'What I mean is, he'll just say she needs to go to Hatter's Hall again an' you know that does her no good. It makes her worse if anythin'.'

Maggie had already had one stay in the local mental asylum, and it had taken her a long time to get over it.

Levi looked unsure, so Annie rushed on, 'Look, I could cut my hours at the shop down through the winter. Peggy or Eve could manage on their own and then I'd be here more an' the missus wouldn't 'ave to be on her own so much.'

'But you already do more than yer fair share,' Levi pointed out.

Annie shrugged. 'I'm not complainin', am I? I could keep on top o' the book work while I'm 'ere an' give Maggie a hand wi' the household chores. *Please*, mister . . . Don't call the doctor in again just yet. Let's give 'er a bit longer an' see 'ow she goes, eh?'

Levi nodded. 'All right, so long as yer sure.'

Charlie drained his cup and stood up. 'I'm off to get ready then. I'm going to Coventry tonight.'

'But what about your dinner?'

'Oh, don't bother wi' anythin' fer me. I'll get somethin' while I'm out,' he said, avoiding Annie's eyes.

'Is, er . . . everythin' all right atween you an' Charlie, Princess?' Levi asked when he had left the room. 'Only I can't 'elp but notice there seems to 'ave been a bit of an atmosphere atween you two fer the last few weeks.'

'We're fine.' Annie felt her cheeks flame as she busied herself at the cooker, and thankfully no more was said. Until recently, Charlie had been her hero and she'd been quite smitten with him. That was until she'd found out about his friend Peter and he'd confessed that he was a homosexual. Annie didn't know what to think. She dreaded how Maggie and Levi would react when he told them and just hoped that it wouldn't push Maggie over the edge mentally.

Half an hour later, after Levi had washed and changed and fetched Maggie from upstairs, they sat down to eat together.

'Mmm, this looks delicious, hinny,' Levi said as he forked a piece of juicy pork chop into his mouth. He glanced at Maggie who was pushing her food about the plate and urged her, 'Come on, pet. Eat up. You ain't as far through as a line prop.'

'It's fashionable to be skinny now,' Maggie told him dully, and he chuckled. No matter how ill Maggie was she was still a slave to fashion. She had to have the latest gowns and the best of everything. It was a far cry from when they were first married and barely had two ha'pennies to rub together. Moving to Swan Lane from the little courtyard in Abbey Street some years before had been a huge step for them and Levi had hoped it would satisfy Maggie. But then she had insisted that the house be furnished to a high standard too, and over time he had lost count of how much she had spent fulfilling her dream. Sadly, none of it had compensated for the loss of their only daughter, Penny, who had been killed in a road accident at just four years old. At the time Levi had feared Maggie would not survive it, and she had suffered ever since, speaking regularly to the dead child as if by doing this she could cling on to her.

'So,' Annie said brightly, hoping to keep the mood light, 'Davey and Eve certainly seem very content in the rooms above the shop.'

Levi smiled. 'When you marry someone yer love – *really* love – yer'd be happy livin' in a shed, wouldn't yer, Maggie? Why, we were poor as church mice but it didn't bother us back then.'

When she didn't reply he lowered his head and concentrated on his meal in silence. Annie was glad when it was over.

'I think I'll pop round to Peggy's an' tell 'er that I'll be finishin' at lunchtime each day now fer a while,' she told Levi when she had washed and dried the dinner pots. She still felt shaken after the strange vision she had seen in Maggie's room.

He looked up from the newspaper with a frown. He was greatly concerned about all the trouble abroad and was praying that it wouldn't affect the family, but he forced a smile as he told her, 'Aye, you do that, pet.'

Some minutes later, as Annie walked down the side of the house, she noticed someone standing at the bottom of the drive. When she saw that it was Reggie, their neighbours' son, smoking a cigarette, her stomach sank.

'Ah, I thought you'd be out if I waited long enough,' he said, flashing her a smarmy smile. 'I thought perhaps we could go for a drink or something?'

'Thanks, but I 'ave things to do, and I'm seeing Monty later,' Annie answered shortly and strode straight past him. Monty was Reggie's younger brother and Annie was very fond of him, but Reggie was a different matter entirely. He made her feel uneasy with his constant pursuit of her. She often wondered how two brothers could be so different.

Scowling, Reggie dropped his cigarette and ground it out with the heel of his boot. Jumped up little bitch. Who did she think she was anyway? She was just a kid from the workhouse, a nobody, the lowest of the low, yet she wouldn't give him the time of day! It didn't stop him wanting her, though. In fact, the more she rejected him the more of a challenge she became and one day he'd have her, by God he would, by fair means or foul. Thrusting his hands deep into the pockets of the expensive overcoat he stormed away.

Chapter Two

'Peggy . . . can I ask you something?'

Peggy glanced up from the skirt she was repairing and looked at Annie. They were seated in the tiny living room of the little two-up, two-down cottage, Levi and Maggie's former home, where she now resided.

'Now what sort of a question is that, me girl?' She frowned. 'Ain't yer known me long enough to know yer can ask me anythin'?'

Peggy, who had formerly worked at the workhouse when Annie was living there, was the only person who had ever shown her kindness until the Lilburns had adopted her. She was also a very long-standing friend of Maggie and Levi and now worked in the shop with Annie.

'Well . . . I was just wonderin' . . . an' I know it's a funny question, but do you believe in ghosts?'

Maggie blinked in surprise. 'To be honest it ain't somethin' I've ever given much thought to,' she admitted. 'Why do you ask?'

'Oh, nuthin' really.' Annie looked embarrassed as she flicked her long black hair across her shoulder, but Peggy could read her like a book.

'Would this be somethin' to do wi' Maggie? Yer know, her thinkin' she can see Penny all the time?'

'I suppose it would,' Annie admitted.

'Hmm, well, all I can say is, I ain't ever actually *seen* a ghost meself, but just after my Frank died, I remember one night I was lyin' in bed an' was so low I were cryin' an' I begged 'im fer a sign to show me that he were still near.'

'And did he come?'

Peggy shook her head sadly. 'No . . . I didn't actually *see* 'im, but all of a sudden, I smelled 'im. Yer know 'ow each of us 'as our own special smell? Well, suddenly I smelled him an' then the next minute I felt calmer an' more peaceful, so who am I to say that ghosts don't exist? There's a lot more between 'eaven an' 'ell that we mere mortals don't know about.'

'Yes, I suppose there is,' Annie answered in a small voice. 'Reggie from next door were waitin' fer me when I came out again this evenin'. He asked me out,' she said, changing the subject.

'Did 'e now? I hope yer told him to sod off. He's bloody bad news that chap is,' Peggy declared.

'Of course I did. I wouldn't go out wi' him if he were the last man on earth,' Annie stated firmly.

'Good, I'm pleased to 'ear it. An' what's happenin' wi' Charlie now? I've noticed that you two ain't seemed quite right together fer some weeks but you an' young Monty seem to be gettin' closer.'

Annie blushed and lowered her head and Peggy nodded knowingly.

'You've found out, ain't yer?' she said quietly. 'That Charlie's . . . yer know?'

Annie's head snapped back up. 'How long have you known?'

Peggy nodded. 'I've known fer some time, luvvie. These things 'ave a habit o' gettin' around. That's why he's been takin' so many beatin's. Folks round 'ere don't like them that are different. But I couldn't tell yer, could I? Yer'd never 'ave believed me. Yer had to find out fer yerself. I'm so sorry, I know yer had a soft spot fer him.'

Tears welled in Annie's eyes. 'I realise now why you always tried to steer me away from 'im,' she said in a choked voice.

'Try not to blame 'im,' Peggy said softly. 'He can't help 'ow he were made. But I dread to think what's goin' to 'appen when Maggie finds out; yer know what a snob she is an' in her delicate mental condition this could be the end of 'er.' She stared at Annie thoughtfully for a moment before suggesting, 'I'm glad you're finally payin' Monty some attention. He's a good lad, but it wouldn't be a bad idea if yer got somethin' else to give yer an interest other than workin' all the time an' all. Yer know what they say, all work an' no play makes Jack a dull boy!'

'Oh yes, such as what?'

Peggy shrugged. 'I don't know. You could do night classes or per'aps join the Red Cross to learn basic nursin', they're allus cryin' out fer staff at the local hospital an' you've allus said you had a yen to be a nurse. If things abroad go as Levi keeps on about an' we do end up at war there'll be a need fer more nurses.'

'But what about the shop?'

Peggy chuckled. 'Me an' Eve 'ave got it down to a fine art now. An' anyway, if yer did an evenin' course yer could still do what yer wanted in the day.'

Annie stared thoughtfully into the fire. 'You know, that's not a bad idea,' she agreed. 'I'll 'ave a think about it.'

Levi thought it was an excellent idea when she put it to him over breakfast one morning. He was always telling her that she didn't get out enough. And so, after he'd left for work and Annie had seen that Maggie had everything she needed, she set off to enrol for the course at Chilvers Coton Church Hall.

'I'm pleased to 'ear it,' Levi praised when she told him over dinner that evening. 'It'll do you good to get out an' about a bit more. Yer might make some new friends an' all.'

Maggie said nothing, but Annie hadn't really expected her to. She had never shown much interest in anything she did.

The following evening, as Annie was preparing to dish out the evening meal before going off to her first class, Levi appeared and one glance at his face told her that he was not in a good humour, which was unusual for him.

'Is Charlie in yet?' he barked as he slung his cap onto a chair.

'Er . . . I don't think so. I haven't been back from the shop for long and since then I've been cookin' the dinner. Why . . . is there something wrong?'

'Nowt fer you to worry about, hinny.' He removed his coat and crossed to the sink to wash his hands.

Annie watched him from the corner of her eye. It was so unusual to see Levi in an ill humour that a bad feeling started in the pit of her stomach. Minutes later, as she began to mash a panful of potatoes, Charlie walked in, and Levi immediately confronted him. 'I want a word wi' you, me lad!'

Charlie looked mildly surprised. Like Annie, he wasn't used to seeing his father in a bad mood. 'Oh aye, what about? Do we need to go into another room for privacy?'

'No point,' Levi ground out. 'Cos if what I've 'eard is right, everybody'll know about it soon enough anyway.'

'So go on then, spit it out,' Charlie told him with a bravado he was far from feeling. He had a horrible idea what was about to come, but then he'd been expecting it for some time.

Levi looked towards Annie and Maggie before he turned back to Charlie. He'd had his own thoughts about what might be happening with him for a while, but he'd been praying he was wrong. But now he could ignore them no longer. 'A little bird whispered to me today that you . . . that you're a . . .' He faltered, as if he couldn't get his words out. Eventually, he took a deep breath before spitting out, 'That you're a *fuckin' shirt lifter*!'

The colour drained from Charlie's face but he straightened his back and stared at his father.

Maggie looked on in horror. Levi never normally swore in front of her. He knew that she didn't approve of it! 'Levi . . . what a *terrible* thing to say,' she began.

Charlie held his hand up to silence her. He had always known that this moment would come and now that it had he almost felt a measure of relief. At least now there would be no more hiding what he was from them.

'It's all right, Mam. If what Dad means to say is that he's heard I'm homosexual, then he would be right.'

Levi's face crumpled as he hung on to the back of a chair. 'Yer mean . . . *it's true?*'

'Aye, Dad, it's true,' Charlie answered with tears in his eyes. 'An' I'm right sorry if it upsets yer, but I can't help who I am.'

'H-how long 'ave yer known!' Levi had almost come to blows with the man who had told him, even though he had a suspicion he was telling the truth. But it just didn't bear thinking about that a son of his could be . . .

'I've known since I were knee-'igh to a grass'opper,' Charlie told him. There didn't seem any point in lying now.

Maggie had never made a secret that she thought people like him weren't normal, and now she was openly crying. 'B-but you *can't* be,' she stuttered. She had pinned all her hopes on Charlie now that his brothers Barney and Harry had left home and she could hardly believe what she was hearing. 'We could get you help . . . take you to a doctor or—'

'Mam, I ain't got an illness,' Charlie barked.

'B-but what you are . . . it's unnatural and not to mention *illegal!*' She choked, covering her mouth with her hand. She had always had suspicions that Annie had feelings for Charlie and had prayed that nothing would ever come of it, but even that would be preferable.

'I am what I am,' he said miserably as his temper subsided. He'd always known it would be like this if it ever became known.

'So what can we do about it?' she pressed, as if she could wave a magic wand and make it go away.

He shook his head. 'Nuthin', which is why I'm thinkin' o' movin' away to save causin' you any embarrassment.'

'Moving away . . . to *where?*'

'Yer may as well know it all now,' he mumbled. 'I have a . . . a friend, an' we're thinkin' of goin' to live in France.'

'A *friend*? What sort of friend? And *France*?'

'All right, he's more than a friend if yer must know.' Charlie hung his head as his mother started to sob and Levi dropped heavily onto a chair. He'd dreaded having to deal with something like this.

'And what would you live on in France?' his father asked, his voice somewhat calmer.

'Peter, my friend, is older than me and has a very good job. He's a barrister,' Charlie informed him. 'He'd soon find work there and so would I. We can both speak fluent French. It might . . . well, it might be for the best to save you an' Mam any embarrassment.' He turned and went to his room without another word, leaving Levi and Maggie to stare at each other while Annie busied herself at the sink.

'Whatever will we do now word of this is out? We'll never be able to hold our heads high again,' Maggie whimpered.

Levi's eyes widened. 'Is what people say all you care about at a time like this, woman?' He could hardly believe his ears.

'Well . . . we *do* have our reputations to maintain.' Maggie sniffed and dabbed at her eyes with a wisp of handkerchief, and looking towards Annie she snapped, 'And I hope we can trust you not to mention this to anyone.' When Annie didn't immediately answer she frowned. 'Unless you already knew . . . *Did you*?'

Annie turned to face her and nodded. 'Aye, I did as it happens.'

'*What*? And you didn't tell us! How long have you known?'

'Since shortly before Christmas,' Annie admitted.

'Why didn't you tell us?'

'Cos it weren't my place to,' Annie told her with her chin in the air. 'And what you 'ave to remember is, Charlie is a grown man now. What he does is 'is own affair.'

Maggie sank back and wrapped her arms about herself as all the hopes and dreams she'd had for Charlie crumbled to dust.

Levi suddenly rose from his seat and, snatching up his coat, he made for the door. 'I'm goin' out,' he said shortly and left, banging the door behind him so loudly that it rocked on its hinges.

Maggie looked up in alarm. It wasn't like Levi to storm out like that. He was usually the one who tried to calm difficult situations. But instead of staying there and challenging Charlie, he was running away. She glowered. If Levi hadn't been so soft with the boys as they were growing up this would probably never have happened. Standing, she stamped away to their room. She'd have something to say to him when he decided to come back, and he wouldn't like it!

Chapter Three

Peggy glanced up in alarm from the gown she was ironing as her front door flew open and she was shocked to see Levi standing there.

'Why what are you doin' back, man? Forget somethin', did you?' It hadn't been long since Levi had dropped the day's load off to her to sort through. Then, sensing that something was amiss, she glanced towards her daughter, Ellie, who was doing her homework at the table and told her gently, 'Go an' find somethin' to do upstairs fer a bit, would yer, pet? Yer can finish that later.'

Ellie needed no second bidding. Anything was better than doing homework, especially sums, so she skipped away quite happily. Levi, meanwhile, sank into the fireside chair and, resting his elbows on his knees, buried his head in his hands.

Without a word, Peggy went to fill the kettle at the sink and put it on to boil before measuring tea leaves into the teapot and preparing two mugs. Levi was clearly very distressed about something and she had a horrible idea what it might be, but until he was ready to tell her, she wouldn't ask any questions.

When the tea was ready, she carried a steaming mug across to him and, settling in the chair opposite, she silently sipped at hers.

'Oh Peggy . . . I heard sumthin' today,' he said eventually, sounding broken. Still, she remained silent and he went on, 'It concerns our Charlie . . .'

With a sigh, she nodded. 'An' I reckon I know what it is.' Her voice was soft. 'I wondered 'ow long it'd be afore yer found out.'

His head whipped up. 'You *knew*?'

She nodded. 'Yes, I think 'alf the town does.'

'So why didn't yer warn me?'

She shrugged. 'How could I? You'd not 'ave thanked me fer interferin'. Have yer spoken to Charlie about it?'

'Yes.'

'An' he didn't deny it?'

When he shook his head, she sighed and, reaching out, she laid her hand gently on his arm. 'Well, it ain't the end o' the world, yer know. He's still Charlie, the son you love an' raised. An' if you're honest wi' yourself I reckon you'd 'ave to admit that deep down you had an idea.'

'Suspectin' it an' knowin' it are two different things. But now he's actually admitted he . . . he admitted he's . . .'

'Homosexual?"

He nodded miserably and she sighed again. 'I know it must 'ave come as a bit of a shock but the signs 'ave always been there 'ad yer looked fer 'em.

'Didn't you ever find it strange that Charlie never showed any interest in girls or never had a girlfriend? No, cos he were allus tucked away inside readin' or writin', weren't he? The thing is, though, now that yer know why, what are yer goin' to do about it?'

'I don't know,' he admitted. 'I've got to try an' get me head round it all. Charlie is on about goin' to live in France wi' his . . . his friend!'

'Perhaps that ain't such a bad idea.' Peggy took another sip of her tea. 'They're a lot more broadminded out there from what I've read. How 'as Maggie taken the news?'

'Huh! As you can imagine. She seems more worried about what the neighbours will think.'

'Sod the bloody neighbours!' Peggy tossed her head. 'What you 'ave to remember is, Charlie is still yer flesh an' blood, fer better or for worse. If you turn yer back on 'im now an' he does go to France yer may never see 'im again. Is that what yer really want?'

Levi rubbed his forehead. His thoughts were all in a whirl and at that moment he didn't know what he wanted.

'I wonder if he's realised that if 'e goes down this path he'll never be a dad or 'ave a family of 'is own?' he mused. 'Wherever 'e goes if word gets out, he'll be ostracised.'

'But that's 'is choice. He obviously thinks this friend of 'is is worth it,' Peggy pointed out. 'I reckon what you need to do now is calm down an' give the matter some serious thought. Maggie should an' all.'

'You're right,' Levi admitted and after draining his mug he rose to leave. 'Thanks fer listenin', Peggy.' It was strange, he thought, that recently he found it easier to talk to Peggy than his own wife. Peggy didn't give a toss about what other people thought, she only worried about the people she cared about, and she had a heart of gold. 'I'm sorry fer disturbin' you. Happen things will look a bit better in the mornin'.'

'Yer didn't disturb me,' she assured him as she followed him to the door. 'But think on what I said, eh? I'd hate to see yer have regrets.'

'I will,' he promised.

Peggy watched him go with tears in her eyes. He had tried so hard for his family but it was unravelling around him. First, he had lost Penny, his only daughter; as for Maggie, she was never satisfied, no matter what he did. Then his oldest, Barney, the wanderer, had run away from home to live with the circus, followed by Harry, the womaniser, who had been forced into a marriage he didn't want. Finally, there was this latest revelation with Charlie. Of all of them it seemed there was only Annie, who wasn't even blood related, who didn't let him down, and sometimes she felt sorry for her as well. There must have been times when the girl had wondered if she would have been better off staying in the workhouse, because ever since going to live with the Lilburns she had been drawn into the family's problems. Not that she ever complained. She was a good girl was Annie, one of the best! With a sigh she went to call

Ellie down to finish her homework before going back to what she had been doing before Levi arrived.

Back at the house, Annie had put the dinner out, but Maggie just pushed the food around the plate and Annie had suddenly lost her appetite as well. She was keeping Levi and Charlie's food warm over pans of hot water on the hob.

By the time Levi reappeared, Maggie had left the table and gone back to her usual seat. Annie served him his meal without a word, but he hardly ate a thing either.

'Charlie still in, is he?' he asked.

She nodded. 'Yes, he's up in his room. Should I take him 'is meal up on a tray? It'd be a shame for it to go to waste.'

Levi nodded. 'Aye, if yer wouldn't mind, pet. And, Annie . . . Thanks, lass.'

She loaded Charlie's dinner onto a tray and went upstairs. But before she could knock at his door, it opened.

'Oh . . . I was just bringin' yer meal up.'

He smiled, but it didn't quite reach his eyes. 'Thanks Annie, but I reckon I'll give it a miss this evenin'. I'm goin' to Coventry.'

'To see Peter?'

'Yes, I reckon it's time we made some plans. I don't wanna cause me ma an' da more pain than I have to.' He marched past her and disappeared off down the stairs.

Annie felt as if her heart was breaking but she could see the sense in what he said. By the time she returned to the kitchen, he had already left, and Levi and Maggie looked as if the end of the world had come. His news had clearly shaken them both to the core and she couldn't help but feel sorry for them. She made a large pot of tea and gave them each a cup before tackling the dirty dishes and, when she was done, she set off for her first Red Cross lesson, glad of the distraction.

Chapter Four

May 1914

'How is the trainin' goin', luvvie?' Peggy asked one evening early in May when Annie called in to see her on her way home.

'I've finished the course an' I passed the test with flying colours. The medical practitioner who trained us 'as recommended I should do my VAD training,' Annie answered proudly. 'Of course I won't be a fully trained nurse – I'd be doin' the more menial jobs, like scrubbin' the wards, changin' bandages, doin' bed baths. But I must admit I love it. I'm even wondering if I should enrol to become a fully qualified nurse.'

Peggy beamed with pride. 'Then well done you. It's a very worthy profession, although if you do decide to become a full-time nurse we'll miss yer. And Monty would too.'

'I know.' Annie frowned. She knew how heavily Levi relied on her and how much Monty thought of her and the one thing that was stopping her from going ahead with full-time training was the thought of letting them down. 'I think I'll just go ahead with the VAD training for now, so I won't be off anytime soon.'

In actual fact, the training course and the time she spent with Monty had proved to be a welcome distraction from the tense atmosphere back at the house. Monty was so loving and kind that he always managed to cheer her up. Charlie was still at home, but ever since Levi and Maggie had learnt of his sexual preferences the mood had been fraught. Maggie had done nothing but cry and insist he seek medical attention for what she termed 'his ailment', and Levi hadn't come to terms with it either, although he'd said no more on the subject. Charlie had confided to Annie that he and Peter still intended to live abroad but Peter had some cases to conclude before they could leave.

'Between you an' me I'll be glad to go,' he'd told her.

His words had been like a stab in her heart. Not so long ago she had imagined they would have a bright future together and now here she was preparing to say goodbye to him, for she had a feeling that once he left, he would never come back.

She spent another half an hour with Peggy before setting off for home and she had just left the courtyard and entered Abbey Street when she saw Harry walking towards her with his hands thrust deep in his pockets and his head bowed. She waited for him to come abreast of her before saying cheerfully, ''Ello there, Harry. Everythin' all right, is it? Yer look like you've got the weight o' the world on yer shoulders.'

'Oh, 'ello, Annie. Sorry, I were miles away. I'm just off to the Pig an' Whistle fer a few pints. Anythin's better than stayin' in an' listenin' to that wife o' mine whingein' an' the baby screamin' its bloody 'ead off.'

'Oh dear.' She fell into step beside him. 'Things not so good at 'ome?'

'Good?' he snorted. 'I'll tell yer, gettin' wed were the worst thing I ever did. I wish I'd just done a runner.'

'Oh, I'm sure it can't be that bad,' she answered, hoping to cheer him up. 'Becca is probably just touchy cos she's not long had a baby. I bet she'll soon settle down.'

'I doubt it!'

It was hard to believe that this was the same footloose and fancy-free young man he had once been. He looked thoroughly miserable, but he only had himself to blame. He was now the father of a baby girl, who they had named Matilda, but he didn't seem to be enjoying being a new parent very much.

'I noticed that the circus is settin' up in the Pingles,' he told her. 'So I dare say you'll all be gettin' a visit from our Barney any time soon. Lucky bugger! At least he can come an' go as he pleases. An' what about our Charlie, eh? Who would 'ave thought that he'd turn out to be a queer! I bet me ma is gutted.'

'Well, it wouldn't do if we were all the same, would it?' Even now Annie found herself forced to defend him.

As they reached the Pig and Whistle, Harry smiled at her. 'Right, I'm away in. Take care now, Annie, an' tell me ma I'll be round to see her soon.' And with that he swung the door to the pub open, releasing a waft of cigarette smoke and stale ale.

She had taken no more than a few steps when someone else shouted her name and, glancing over her shoulder, she groaned. It was Reggie and he was hurrying towards her.

'Annie, how are you?'

'I'm all right, ta.' She started walking again but he fell into step beside her and her heart began to thud.

'It's unusual to see you out and about of an evening.'

'I've just been to my first aid course and called in to see Peggy,' she told him, although she really didn't see why she should have to explain her whereabouts to him. She wished now that she'd allowed Monty to come and meet her as he'd wanted to.

'That's lucky because I was just going to see if anything is on at the cinema. Do you fancy coming?'

'No thanks,' she said tartly. She was beginning to wonder if he was following her again, for lately he seemed to turn up everywhere she went. 'I have to get back now. I have things to do.'

'But surely it would do you good to have an evening off?' he wheedled.

Annie suddenly stopped so abruptly that he almost collided with her and, hands on hips, she faced him. 'Look, Reggie, once and for all. *I. do. not. want. to. go. out. with. you*! Have I made myself clear now? To be honest you're gettin' to be a bit of a nuisance! It seems like every time I turn around yer there! An' anyway, after what yer tried to do to me a while back I wouldn't care if I never laid eyes on yer again! You must know that I'm seein' Monty. I wonder what he'd think if he knew yer were followin' me about!'

An ugly red colour seeped up his neck and into his cheeks as he took a step back. 'All right, there's no need to get shirty!' He glared at her with narrowed eyes. 'I was drunk and I told you I was sorry, didn't I? You've done me a favour really. I can just imagine what my friends would say if they saw me out with a bastard maid from the workhouse. I just felt sorry for you, but you can go to hell. Our Monty is welcome to you!'

They were facing each other like two opponents in a boxing ring and for one awful moment Annie thought he was going to hit her. But instead, he smiled, a spiteful, malicious grin that sent a shiver running down her spine. 'You're all weird, the whole lot of you,' he snarled. 'Especially your beloved *Charlie boy*! Oh, don't think that everyone didn't know you'd set your sights on him. Pity you hadn't realised he was a queer, eh? Huh! Now why don't you creep back to my baby-faced little brother. He's about the best you'd manage!' And with that he turned and stamped away.

Shaken, Annie turned and headed for home, praying she wouldn't encounter anyone else she knew that night. She'd had enough for one day what with one thing and another.

It was nearing lunchtime two days later as Annie was preparing to go to the shop when Barney breezed into the house on Swan Lane.

Maggie had had a particularly bad morning, crying and chatting to her dead daughter, but at the sight of him she perked up and held her arms out to him.

'Oh *sweetheart*, it's so lovely to see you.'

Barney nodded towards Annie as he crossed to his mother and allowed her to kiss his cheek. 'Hello, Ma, all right, are you?'

She certainly didn't look it. She had lost more weight since he had last seen her and there were dark circles beneath her eyes.

'Oh, you know, I get by.' Maggie grabbed his hand and manoeuvred him into the chair opposite her. 'Annie, make Barney some tea.'

Annie sighed. She had been about to leave but she did as she was told.

'I suppose you've heard the news about Charlie?' Maggie stared at her son who looked bewildered.

'Heard what? He's all right, ain't he?'

'It all depends what you mean by all right.' Maggie shook her head. 'He . . . he's confessed to us that he's a . . . a homosexual.'

'*Oh!*' Barney didn't know what to say.

'And he has a *friend*. A special friend who he is talking of going to live with in France!'

In truth Barney had had his suspicions about his brother for some time but when it came to it, Charlie was still family.

'We're so ashamed,' Maggie rushed on. 'I hardly dare show my face outside for fear of what people will say when it becomes common knowledge. If he doesn't go to France, I've no doubt he'll be run out of town anyway. Or worse still, he'll be locked up!'

'But he's still our Charlie, Ma,' Barney pointed out.

Maggie wrung her hands and shook her head. 'I just can't understand what I did wrong with him. Neither you nor Harry are like that.'

'From what I know of it, you ain't done nothing wrong. People like Charlie can't help the way they are,' Barney said compassionately. Then hoping to lighten the mood he looked towards Annie. 'An' how are you?'

She smiled and nodded as she poured boiling water over the tea leaves in the pot. 'Oh, busy as usual. And you?'

'Oh, I'm all right,' he replied.

But Annie wasn't so sure he was. She'd noticed that he didn't seem to be his usual cheery self. All the sparkle seemed to have gone out of him since Mercy, the girl he loved, had gone to prison; clearly the circus no longer held the same attraction for him as it once did.

Hoping to cheer him up, she said, 'I dare say the missus will tell you your dad has bought a motor car. He fetches it from Coventry this week and we're all quite excited about it. He's goin' to give me some drivin' lessons.'

Barney grinned and looked back at his mother. 'Ooh, you are goin' up in the world, Ma. What sort is it?'

Maggie perked up instantly. 'It's a Swift Wagonette,' she told him proudly. 'I've been on at your da to get one for ages and he finally agreed. Quite right too! The Taylor-Lloyds have had one for some time now.'

'An' of course yer can't be outdone,' Barney laughed.

Maggie sniffed indignantly. 'It's nothing to do with that but we have to keep up with the times.'

Barney winked at her as Annie took their tea to them. He knew what a snob his mother could be.

Shortly after, Annie finally set off for the shop, leaving mother and son to have some time together. She was running late but wasn't overly concerned. Eve and Peggy were more than capable of coping without her and lately Annie was beginning to feel a little restless. It wasn't that she wasn't grateful for the opportunities Levi had given her but lately she'd been thinking about what she was going to do with the rest of her life. The unrest had started after she had begun her Red Cross training, and now she was wondering what it would be like to become a fully trained nurse. She somehow couldn't imagine herself just settling down with Monty and having one baby after another, not for a while at least.

That weekend, there was great excitement when Levi drove carefully up to the house in their new motor car. He'd taken some driving lessons prior to buying the car, although he was still a little nervous behind the wheel – it was very different to driving his horse and cart.

Maggie demanded that he take her for a ride straight away. She dressed regally for the occasion and insisted that Levi wear his one and only suit. They set off with Annie in the back seat and Levi drove them around the town, amused to see how Maggie waved to everyone they passed. Her moods were so inconsistent. One day, like today, she could be fine, then the next in the depths of depression. Still, he was heartened to see that the motor car had given Maggie a lift.

'When will you teach me to drive?' Annie questioned. She was almost as thrilled as Maggie with their new acquisition.

'Oh, give me a few days to feel a bit more confident, then I'll give you some lessons,' he promised.

Maggie scowled. 'Is that a good idea? What if she were to scratch the paintwork?' She stared proudly at the bright red exterior and the black running boards that ran the length of the car on either side.

Levi chuckled. 'I've no doubt after a few goes she'll be able to drive better than me,' he assured her.

Maggie sniffed. She would have liked to argue but didn't want to spoil the day.

On the way home, they stopped outside the courtyard for Peggy and Ellie to see their new purchase and Ellie danced with excitement.

'Can I come for a ride in it, Uncle Levi?' she begged. Maggie had taken both Ellie and Annie from the workhouse on the same day. Ellie had been just a baby then, but sadly the novelty of having her had soon worn off so when Maggie had considered returning her to the workhouse, Peggy had stepped in and had treated her as a daughter ever since.

Levi laughed and lifted her to sit beside Annie on the back seat. 'Of course, madam. Where would you like to go?'

'To see the circus in the Pingle Fields,' she answered excitedly. And so they set off again.

It was one of the most pleasant afternoons they had spent together in a long time, although Annie didn't join them at the circus. She preferred to stay and guard the car.

Later, Levi dropped Ellie back with Peggy and they drove home and parked the new car next to the stables.

'Next weekend, you can have a go,' Levi promised. Annie could hardly wait.

Chapter Five

The following week, as he had promised, Levi began to give Annie driving lessons and she loved it.

'You've took to it like a duck to water,' Levi praised. 'Another month or so an' there'll be no more I can teach yer.'

They had left Maggie at home having a visit from her daughter-in-law and her baby granddaughter. Maggie still wasn't overly keen on Becca but she doted on Matilda and their visits always seemed to cheer her up.

Another new pastime of Annie's was working for a few hours a week at the cottage hospital. It had been her tutor's suggestion and Annie loved that too, although because she wasn't a fully trained nurse, she was given only the very mundane jobs, such as cleaning the wards and serving the patients their meals. In no time at all she'd become very popular with both the patients and the staff alike because of her cheerful disposition. However, working there seriously limited her free time, and sometimes she felt there were never enough hours in the day. Monty wasn't keen on it either as she never had time to see him. She was either at the hospital, in the shop or working on Levi's books, and most nights she dropped into bed exhausted.

'You're doin' too much, me girl,' Peggy scolded her one day when Annie dropped in to see her. 'When did yer last 'ave time to go to the theatre wi' young Monty, eh?'

They were fortunate in Nuneaton to have Mr Leon Vint's Picturedome where they could watch films, and where vaudeville acts also came to perform. There was also the Prince of Wales Theatre. A few years before, she and Monty had seen Charlie

Chaplin in *The Humming Birds*. They'd also seen Gilbert and Sullivan operettas, Shakespeare and Victorian melodramas and Annie had loved every one, although they were a distant memory now as she seldom had time to do anything but work.

'Not recently,' Annie admitted. 'But I will make time soon, I promise.'

'Hmm, well see as yer do.' Peggy wagged a finger at her. 'It ain't natural fer a young gel like you to be workin' all the hours God sends. If you ain't workin' yer runnin' round after her ladyship in Swan Lane. You should be out enjoyin' yerself. Yer only young once, yer know. Why, most of the lasses round 'ere your age are settlin' down an' gettin' wed.'

Annie pulled a face. 'Good luck to them. But that ain't what *I* want to do, not yet at least,' she said firmly, and seeing that she had annoyed her, Peggy wisely changed the subject.

In no time at all it was the end of June and Levi was even more concerned about the unrest abroad.

'I wouldn't be surprised if this didn't escalate into a war,' he fretted. 'An' me biggest fear is that we'll get dragged into it.'

'Don't be so ridiculous,' Maggie snapped. 'How could we possibly get involved?'

Levi said no more. He knew she didn't worry about things like this, but he was gravely concerned. And his worries only escalated when he bought a newspaper with the headline:

Archduke Franz Ferdinand of Austria and his wife Assassinated!

'This is it; we'll get dragged into it now, you just mark my words,' he whispered to Annie out of earshot of Maggie.

Annie was well aware of how well read Levi was on world affairs but on this score, she silently prayed that he would be wrong.

On the fourth of August, however, Levi's prediction came true when war was declared on Germany. The town was shocked.

Suddenly recruitment centres were springing up everywhere and young men flocked to sign up, as if they would be embarking on a great adventure.

'You're not thinking of enlisting, are you?' Annie asked Monty that evening as they went for a stroll together. It was one of her rare nights off and although she wasn't ready to fully commit to him, she was very fond of him.

He shrugged. 'I'm not sure yet to be honest. Mother is dead against it and has forbidden me to. But I'm old enough to make up my own mind.'

'And what about Reggie?'

He snorted. 'Huh! I can't see him volunteering to go. It would be too much like hard work, and work is a dirty word to him. Between you and me I've heard whispers that he's got his fingers into all sorts of pies, most of them illegal. He's certainly never short of money, although he doesn't turn in to work very often.'

Annie chewed on her lip. 'Well, as you say, it's up to you . . . but I hope yer don't go. I don't know how we'd all cope if anythin' were to happen to you.'

He squeezed her hand gently. 'Let's just wait a while and see what happens, eh? They're sayin' that it should all be over by Christmas.'

She nodded, but she was still troubled.

The next day, as she made her way to the shop with Peggy, she was shocked to see lines of young men laughing and joking as they queued outside the recruitment centre.

Peggy shook her head sadly. 'Silly young buggers,' she commented. 'I don't reckon they know what they're lettin' 'emselves in for.'

Within days the same young men were being given a grand send-off by a brass band and their concerned relatives at Trent Valley Station. Many were bound for the Isle of Wight, but others were sent to training camps across the country. Within twenty-four hours over seven hundred men from neighbouring Coventry had signed up and by August the seventh the number had swelled to a thousand, although the numbers were less for the smaller town of Nuneaton. Amongst them were clergymen and doctors who would be called on to help the injured and the dying. There were men from the police force and the railways as well as groups of men from the large car factories that were thriving in Coventry.

And then one morning Barney came home to Swan Lane and dropped a bombshell. The circus was due to move on, and he had decided not to go with them. 'I've signed up fer the army,' he told his shocked family.

The colour drained out of Maggie's face as she stared back at him horrified. 'You've done *what?*'

He looked sheepish as he shrugged. 'It makes sense, Ma. There ain't gonna be much call for circuses till this lot is sorted out, so I thought I may as well make meself useful.'

'You bloody young *fool*!' Maggie was almost beside herself. 'You could have come here and worked with your da if you were afraid of being out of work.'

'Oh yeah, an' get called a coward! No, I felt it were the right thing to do but I wanted to come an' see yer before I go off to start me trainin'. I shall be joinin' one o' the Warwickshire regiments.'

'Oh *Barney*!' Maggie dropped heavily onto the nearest chair. She was clearly shaken and her face was the colour of putty. 'Wh-when do you leave?'

'Tomorrow.'

'An' I'll be goin' with him.' Maggie spun around to see Harry had entered the room and she began to cry.

'You too? But *why?* It's so irresponsible. You have a wife and baby to consider.'

Harry could have admitted that this was part of the reason why he wanted to go but instead he shook his head. 'Well, they'll be all right, won't they? Becca's mam an' dad will see to that.'

Maggie felt as if the bottom of her world had fallen away as she clutched at the arm of the chair and tried to get her breath. Very soon two of her sons would be fighting for King and country and she didn't know how she would bear it. It had been hard enough to cope with the loss of her daughter and the news about Charlie's sexuality, but should she lose Harry and Barney as well she knew she wouldn't want to go on.

Up until this point Annie had merely looked on but as an awkward silence settled on the room she said tentatively, 'I, er . . . think yer both very brave.'

Maggie's eyes flashed fire as she turned to glare at her. 'Brave . . . *Brave*, you say! You don't know what you're talking about, you *stupid* girl. They could be *killed*.'

'Now calm down, Ma. None o' this is Annie's fault.' Barney could see that Annie was blinking back tears and he hurried over to place a comforting arm about her shoulders. 'You're lookin' at the worst that could happen an' yet we could well be home fer Christmas.'

'What time are you leaving tomorrow?' Maggie's voice was dull, as if all the stuffing had been knocked out of her.

'Eleven o'clock from the train station,' Barney told her soberly.

'Aye, me an' all. We'll be on the same train then,' Harry told him.

'I'll be there to see yer both off,' Annie promised in a shaky voice.

'And so shall I. I'm proud of yer, boys,' Levi cut in and received a glare from Maggie.

'So will I, although I still don't agree with what you've both done. You should have spoken to me and your da first,' Maggie said peevishly. And then a thought occurred to her. 'And what about Charlie? He's been talking about going to live in France.'

'I'm afraid I can't see that happenin' now.' Barney shook his head. 'That would be about the worst place he could think o' goin' at present.'

'You don't think he'll sign up as well, do you?' Maggie's voice was fearful. If Charlie did decide to enlist that would be all her sons at risk.

'That'll be somethin' he 'as to decide fer 'imself.' Barney patted his mother's hand. 'But like I said, even if he did, we could all be back in no time. No one seems to think this war will go on for long.'

'Then let's just pray they're right.'

The next morning found Maggie, Annie and Levi, who had taken the day off from his rounds, standing on the station platform to see the boys off to war. There was an almost carnival atmosphere in the air with a brass band belting out popular tunes and the men all had looks of great excitement on their faces as their terrified mothers clung to them. Annie noted that neither Becca nor any of her family had come to see Harry off, and as if he could read her thoughts, he told them, 'Becca didn't come cos she 'as the little 'un to look after. We said our goodbyes at home.'

'Hmm!' Maggie sniffed her disapproval. She had gone to great trouble with her appearance and in her grand dress and bonnet she stood out amongst the more modestly dressed townspeople.

The train pulled in and lifting their kitbags the young men began to clamber aboard, opening the carriage windows so they could speak to the people on the platform. Harry and Barney were amongst them and Maggie clung on to their hands until the very last minute.

'Take care,' she shouted above the cheering. 'I don't want either of you to be heroes! And make sure you write to me often.'

The guard walked along the platform, slamming the doors, and when it was done, he blew his whistle and the train chugged slowly into life, covering the platform in steam that rose to float above them in the rafters.

As the train pulled away Maggie, Levi and Annie stood waving until it was lost to sight. Then, looking bereft, Maggie allowed Levi to lead her out to the car, while Annie set off to the shop with a heavy heart.

As an abandoned child in the workhouse she had constantly wondered who her birth family might be. All she had of them was a small bundle of the clothes she had been wearing when she had been left on the workhouse step. Amongst them was a beautiful shawl and every time she touched it she would close her eyes and try to imagine the woman it had belonged to. For years she had been convinced that her mother would come back for her and they would live happily ever after, but she never had.

Annie had watched other children chosen to go to new homes, but it had never been her until Maggie had turned up. At first, living with the Lilburns hadn't been what she'd hoped, as Maggie had never treated her as a daughter, but Levi had always been kind and, somehow over the years each and every one of the Lilburns had become her family, even though she still dreamt of finding her real one. As she walked along, she prayed silently that the boys would return safely. She dreaded to think what effect it would have on Maggie if they didn't.

Chapter Six

The next evening, as Annie was putting the finishing touches to the evening meal, Charlie appeared and she knew instantly that something was wrong. Even so she knew better than to question him. Charlie had withdrawn from all of them since making his confession and she knew that if he needed to talk, he would do it in his own time. That time came a short while later as they were eating. He suddenly laid his knife and fork down and told them, 'Peter has enlisted.'

'Oh . . . I see,' Maggie answered, not quite sure what she should say, although she was secretly relieved. Surely with the dreadful man out of the way Charlie would come to his senses and realise that he wasn't homosexual after all. 'So, what are you planning to do now? You're not thinking of enlisting too I hope?'

'I haven't decided yet,' he admitted as he pushed his chair back from the table. Suddenly he had no appetite, no anything if it came to that, without Peter. He had been his whole world but now he was painfully aware that the lovely life they had planned to share in France may never happen. Without another word he quietly left the room. Levi frowned. Like Maggie, he was finding it difficult to accept what Charlie had told them.

'Do you think he'll go?' Maggie asked her husband.

He shrugged. 'I've no idea but whatever he decides I'll abide by it. He's a grown man after all.'

Annie stood up and began to clear the dirty dishes away. She had promised to do a couple of hours at the hospital that evening so the dirty pots would have to wait until she got back, unless Maggie did them, but that was highly unlikely.

She quickly changed into her Red Cross uniform and left the house.

When she arrived at the hospital, she found the matron waiting for her in the entrance foyer.

'Ah, Nurse Lilburn. May I have a word?'

Annie followed her into her office, wondering if she had done something wrong. Once the door had closed behind them the matron told her, 'I'm afraid some of our nurses and doctors have enlisted to work in the field hospitals that are being set up abroad and that has left us with a shortage of staff, so I was wondering, would you be prepared to work longer hours for the duration of the conflict? I only ask because although you are not fully trained you are excellent at what you do, and your help would be invaluable to us.'

Annie blushed at the praise and smiled. 'I'd love to, Matron, but I couldn't manage full time.'

'Any hours you can spare would be greatly appreciated,' the matron replied. 'I'm afraid that when this war gets properly under way, we can expect a lot of casualties. Meantime, it will help to further your training, so thank you.'

Annie went away with a spring in her step. Maggie had never been one for handing out praise so it was nice to feel appreciated, although she wasn't sure how Peggy and Eve would feel about it. It would mean she spent less hours in the shop helping them.

The next morning, she set off for the shop early but the minute she entered she saw that Eve had been crying, and she guessed what was wrong immediately.

'Oh no . . . Davey's joined up, 'asn't he?'

Eve nodded as she mopped at the tears that had started again. 'Yes . . . he just went off an' did it yesterday wi'out warnin' me. He says he don't want to look like a coward an' he felt it were 'is duty to go.'

Annie didn't know what to say to make Eve feel better so she simply gave her a hug. It was then that she suddenly realised that when Davey left, Levi's rounds would be cut in half. Levi had bought another horse and cart to provide Davey with work but with the way the young men of the town were flocking to join the forces it was doubtful he would find anyone to take his place. Unless she started to work with him again. She bit her lip in consternation. She had promised matron she would put more hours in at the hospital but how could she if she had to collect rags and bones all day?

She said as much to Peggy as the three women had a tea break later that morning and Peggy sighed. 'I shouldn't get worryin' too much about that just yet, pet. Think about it, things are goin' to be harder to get if there's a war on, includin' clothes, so people ain't goin' to be so keen on gettin' rid of 'em. It's highly unlikely there'll be enough pickin's for just Levi, let alone two o' you. An' if there's less comin' into the shop we won't be as busy, so you'll still 'ave time to do yer bit at the hospital.'

'Does Levi know that Davey is goin' yet?' Annie asked Eve.

The young woman sniffed. 'He was goin' to tell 'im this mornin', so I've no doubt he will know by now.'

'Well, this'll certainly curb her ladyship's spendin' a bit,' Peggy said with a wry grin and even Eve managed to raise a smile at the thought of that. They all knew how many demands Maggie made on Levi, but if the money wasn't coming in, he wouldn't be able to pander to her anymore. The way things were going it seemed everybody was going to have to tighten their belts.

Monty was waiting outside for Annie that afternoon when she finished at the shop. He often walked her home and she always enjoyed his company but today he seemed very quiet, and as they walked along hand in hand, she glanced at him and said softly, 'You've signed up, ain't you?'

Her stomach sank as he nodded. 'I just came from the recruitment centre. I leave for training the day after tomorrow.'

'Oh Monty . . . does your mother know yet?'

He gave a rueful grin. 'Not as yet, and I don't mind admitting I'm not much looking forward to telling her. I've no doubt I'll get a good old ear bashing, but still, it's done now. I've signed on the dotted line and there's nothing the old dragon can do about it. I just wouldn't have felt right staying here while everyone else was going off to do their bit.'

'I can understand that,' Annie admitted, but it didn't make the hurt any less. All she could do now was pray that the rumour the war wouldn't last for long was true.

'I'm sorry to leave you,' Monty said quietly. 'But we'll have all the time in the world once this war is over.'

'Of course we will.' She just hoped he was right.

Two days later, she found herself once more standing on the platform at the train station. Both Monty and Davey would be travelling on the same train and Eve was there sobbing broken-heartedly as she clung to Davey. Mrs Taylor-Lloyd was there too.

'I didn't expect to see *you* here,' she said, staring disdainfully at Annie.

'*Mother!*' Monty glared at her and she looked away as if there was a bad smell under her nose. She couldn't see why a mere servant, as she thought of Annie, should be there to wave her son off, but she said no more. She didn't want them to part on bad terms.

'Now you just look after yourself,' he said, turning back to Annie.

'I think it should be *me* telling *you* that,' she replied tearfully.

'And you *will* write to me, won't you?'

'Of course I will,' Annie promised as the men began to board the train. 'Goodbye, Monty, I'll be thinking of you. Stay safe.' She pecked his cheek then turned and hurried away, leaving Monty to say his goodbyes to his mother in private.

Once outside the station she waited for Eve to join her. The poor girl was sobbing and Annie felt helpless to say anything that might ease her distress, so she merely gripped her hand and gave it a comforting little squeeze.

Three weeks later Barney and Harry were home again. They had been given overnight leave to see their families before being shipped out to France. Barney looked so different that Maggie almost didn't recognise him when he first entered the kitchen. His lovely dark hair, which he usually wore on the long side, was now cropped close to his scalp, and in his army uniform he suddenly looked much older.

'How was the trainin'?' Annie asked him later that evening when Levi and Maggie had gone to bed.

'Harsh,' he admitted, flicking a cigarette end into the fire.

Annie could well believe it, he looked exhausted. 'When will you get leave again?'

'How long is a piece o' string?' He shrugged. 'I suppose it'll all depend on what happens out there.'

'And how is Harry bearin' up?'

He grinned. 'Not so good. I'm used to hard work, what wi' erecting the big top an' movin' the fairgrounds round all the time, but he's really struggled. Bein' a butcher ain't quite so physical, see. He's gone to spend the night wi' Becca an' the baby but he's callin' fer me in the mornin' so he can see you all afore he leaves. We're both goin' to be in the Royal Warwickshire Regiment so I'm hopin' we'll stay together but we won't know for sure till we get over there.'

'Monty an' Davey have joined up,' she told him with a frown. 'Poor Eve is heartbroken. Charlie told us that his friend Peter 'as gone as well an' it's knocked him fer six. I wouldn't be surprised if he weren't the next to enlist.'

'Huh! Our Charlie wouldn't last five minutes,' Barney snorted. 'He's a pen pusher not a fighter an' I doubt he'd even get through the trainin'. Though sayin' that they seem to be takin' everyone they can get at the minute. But that's enough about that, tell me what you've been up to an 'ow the new shop is doin'.'

They spent the next hour chatting of other things before going to their rooms. It was hard for Annie to sleep that night as she thought of how different their lives were going to be for the foreseeable future. Nuneaton was like a ghost town with hardly any young men to be seen and already different companies and businesses were asking women to step forward to do the jobs the men had done previously. Annie herself was due to do her first full shift at the hospital the next day, so she'd need to say her goodbyes to Barney at home before she left.

A few days later Annie arrived home early one evening to find Levi upset. 'We've been told that they're takin' any horses that are young enough to go to war, so that'll mean our Spirit will have to go.' He shook his head sadly. 'She's such a gentle soul. I just thank God our Dobbin is too old to be any use to 'em.'

Annie was sad to hear it. She had come to love Spirit but there was nothing she could do to stop it happening. The army came for her a few days later and there were tears in Levi's eyes as he led her out from her comfortable stable.

'Take care an' stay safe, me little lass,' he said softly as he stroked her silky mane. He watched as she was led away and returned to the house with a heavy heart.

Despite many young men going to war and the horses being taken, along with the atrocities they were all reading about in the newspapers each day, Nuneaton still felt relatively war free. Annie had a horrible idea that it wasn't going to stay that way for much longer though. And all too soon she would be proved right.

Chapter Seven

On the 23rd August, the British Expeditionary Forces met the Germans at the Belgian town of Mons. At first, they managed to hold them at bay, but the German offensive drove back the French leaving the British flanks exposed and they had no choice but to abandon their positions and retreat to the Somme with the French. Here they hoped to halt the German rush on Paris.

Harry and Barney were amongst these men and already they were weary and felt as if they were a million miles from home. As they had soon discovered, practising with dummy targets at a training centre with the Lee Enfield rifles they had been issued with was totally different to having to use them on human targets. It was far worse for Harry than Barney. He wasn't used to hard physical work and his hands had been smooth when he joined the army, but already they were calloused and sore, and no matter how much he washed them he was convinced he could still smell blood on them. One night, as they sat resting in one of the many deep trenches that had been dug, he broke down as he remembered the first German he had shot.

'He were only about my age,' he told Barney tearfully. 'An' all of a sudden he just seemed to come out o' nowhere. Fer a minute we just pointed our rifles at each other but then I suppose me self-preservation kicked in an' I knew it were either him or me so I . . . I pulled the trigger.' He screwed his eyes up as in his mind's eye he saw the spurt of blood that had gushed from the young German's chest. 'Fer a moment he just looked shocked an' then he went down like a sack o' potatoes. An' I remember thinkin', he were somebody's son, or brother or lover . . .'

'I know, mate.' Barney slapped him on the shoulder. 'But as yer said, if you hadn't o' pulled that trigger *he* would 'ave. Now come on, pull yerself together an' let's go an' see if we can't find us sommat to eat, eh? We can't fight on empty stomachs.'

Harry swiped the tears from his cheeks with the back of his grimy hand before following his brother along the trench through a sea of mud. The war had barely begun but already he had had enough.

In Nuneaton, Annie had popped in to see Peggy after yet another long, gruelling shift at the hospital. Extra beds were being shipped in daily to deal with the many casualties that they feared may soon be arriving. As yet there had been none, but posters of Lord Kitchener with the words *Your Country Needs You!* on them had sprung up all around the town and now even men who'd had no intention of volunteering were joining the queues at the recruitment centres.

'There'll be no young men left in the town at the rate we're going,' Peggy commented glumly to Annie as they sat together over a cup of tea. Her own sons had also joined up and she had cried on the day she waved them off, wondering if she would ever see them again.

'They'll be home before we know it,' Annie assured her, although she wasn't so sure. Nothing was certain and the townsfolk were living in fear. Almost everyone had someone – a husband, a brother or a son – who had gone to fight, and every day they dreaded someone knocking on the door with a telegram telling them that they would not be coming home.

'Anyway, how is Maggie?' Peggy asked.

'Not good to be honest,' Annie admitted, draining her cup and putting her nurse's cape back on. They were well into September now and there was a bite in the air. 'She seems to 'ave gone off into her own little world again an' she chatters to Penny non-stop.

I dread to think what she'll be like if anything 'appens to Harry or Barney. It'll tip 'er over the edge. How are things at the shop?'

Eve and Peggy had been running the shop alone for the last couple of weeks while Annie worked at the hospital.

'About as we expected. Now that there's only Levi out collectin' the amount o' stuff we've got comin' in 'as gone down by over 'alf! I think folk are hangin' on to things they'd normally 'ave got rid of in case o' bad times ahead.'

Annie nodded; it was understandable. As yet there had been no shortages but they all knew there would be if the war went on, and people were making provision for it, stocking up wherever they could.

Levi was already at home when Annie got back a short time later and he smiled at her. ''Ello, pet.' He pointed to a pan of potatoes bubbling on the stove. 'I peeled some spuds and put some sausages in the oven. I thought it'd save you a job when you got in.'

She gave him a grateful smile as she glanced at a pile of ironing waiting to be done. She had washed the clothes a few days before but Maggie had made no attempt to iron them. There was no surprise there – Maggie still liked to act the part of a lady. She had had a terrible tantrum the Sunday before when Levi had refused to take her for her usual Sunday afternoon drive.

'No, lass, there'll be no more joy ridin' fer a while,' he had told her gently. 'I 'eard there's likely to be a petrol shortage soon, so best to keep a full tank in case it's needed fer somethin' important, eh?'

'But we *always* go for a ride out after church on Sunday!' she had cried indignantly. 'Why should we have to give up our few pleasures in life?'

'Fer the same reason as our lads an' thousands more like 'em are givin' up their freedom to try an' keep us safe.' His harsh tone had shocked her and she had stormed out of the room to sulk in her bedroom for the rest of the afternoon.

Tonight, she was curled up in her chair with a warm shawl wrapped around her. There was a vacant look in her eyes and Annie couldn't help but feel sorry for her. Since glimpsing Penny some time before, Annie had not seen the dead child again, but it had made her wonder if perhaps there could be such a thing as ghosts.

She hurried upstairs to get changed out of her uniform and the rest of the evening passed in a blur as she attended to the ironing and any other jobs that needed doing. Maggie retired early and just before Annie and Levi went to bed, he made her a cup of cocoa, which they drank in front of the fire.

'If things don't pick up soon, we're goin' to have to tighten our belts,' he said worriedly. Thankfully, he had managed to pay off the mortgage on the house some time before, but even so the running costs of such a large place were high.

Annie nodded. 'Do we really need such a big house now? There's only the four of us,' she said sensibly. 'I wonder if Maggie would consider movin' to somewhere a little smaller.'

Levi snorted derisively. 'There's about as much chance o' that happenin' as hell freezin' over.' He sighed. 'Maggie loves this house an' I reckon I'd 'ave to drag her out kickin' and screamin'.'

'Then perhaps we should give the shop up?' she suggested. 'We could always go back to working in the clothes shed at Peggy's.'

'It just might come to that,' he admitted. 'But we'll be all right fer a while. Let's just hope this war ends quickly then we'll get by.'

Annie couldn't have agreed more.

In the middle of September, the British Expeditionary Force played a large part in the battle to stop the German's from entering Paris when they blocked them at Marne, forcing them to retreat from the battlefield. However, the victory came at a high price with many British lives lost. The first casualties of war, or at least those that were deemed well enough to travel, began to filter into the hospitals while the ones who were more seriously injured were forced to stay in the field hospitals. The sight of the telegram boy pedalling his bicycle along the roads delivering the dreadful news that a loved one was missing or had been killed became a common sight and something everyone feared.

When the first victims of the war arrived at the hospital, Annie was horrified at the sight of them. There were young men with limbs missing, others with raging fevers and some who had lost their sight. Some of them were so traumatised by what they had been through that they cried piteously for their mothers, and Annie spent as much time as she was able to at their bedsides, comforting them as best she could. It was heartbreaking seeing such young men cut down in their prime and everyone prayed harder than ever for the senseless war to end.

By late October there were swirling lines of trenches stretching from the sea in France as far as the Swiss border. Fierce battles were raging all along them with the British Expeditionary Force holding on to the Flanders town of Ypres. Aircraft, Zeppelins and submarines were now also playing important roles. Paris had been bombed and a German U-boat had sunk three British cruisers.

The mood of the men who had gone so valiantly to fight for their country was grim. It was now bitterly cold and they were fighting and living in appalling conditions with no respite. The trenches were cold and muddy and full of as many rats as men.

One morning, as Annie turned in for her shift at the hospital, she was met once again by the matron who asked her into her office.

'Nurse Lilburn, I have been asked to volunteer some of my Red Cross and fully trained nurses to go and work in the field hospitals in France,' she told her without preamble. 'Obviously only the best will be of any use to them. And of course, you immediately sprang to mind. I've seen how compassionate you are with the patients and believe that you would be an invaluable asset to them out there, especially as you once mentioned you can speak French.'

Annie nodded. 'Yes, Matron, I can. My brother taught me.'

The matron nodded. 'Excellent. However, you are under no pressure whatsoever. It is up to you whether you wish to go or not. I realise you will need some time to think about it, and to speak to your family, as will the other nurses I have in mind. But I would appreciate it if you could give me an answer tomorrow.'

Annie was shocked. It was the last thing she had expected. 'Yes . . . of course, Matron,' she mumbled.

'Thank you. You may go about your business now, Nurse.'

Annie left her office in a daze, her mind whirling. She clearly had a lot to think about.

'So, what do you think?' she asked Levi that evening after she'd told him what Matron had said.

He scratched his head. 'Hmm . . . I can't say as I like the idea,' he admitted. 'It's bad enough lyin' awake every night worryin' about the lads. But then I'll understand if yer decide to go, so the decision must be yours, pet.'

'In that case, if you're sure you can all manage 'ere without me, I think I'll go.'

He blinked back tears and forced a smile to his face. 'Now 'ow did I guess you were gonna say that?' He reached out and tenderly stroked her hair. 'You've got more pluck in yer little finger than most women twice yer age 'ave in their whole body. I just ask that you don't take any risks, pet.'

'I won't,' she promised.

Chapter Eight

Annie was due to be shipped out to France along with a number of other Red Cross and VAD nurses at the end of October. Two days before her departure, she went into town to buy a few last-minute things. She was in Wash Lane when she saw Reggie striding towards her and she instantly stepped behind a group of women and pretended to be looking in the shop window.

She couldn't help but overhear the women speaking of their loved ones who were away fighting the war.

'I ain't slept a full night since my Johnny went,' one lady said. 'An' every time I see the telegram lad it's all I can do to remain standin' fer fear he's comin' to me.'

Reggie was almost abreast of them now and Annie fixed her eyes on the window, hoping he wouldn't spot her. But one of the women had seen him and angry colour rose in her cheeks as he drew level. He was dressed in an expensive overcoat and a pin-striped suit and the woman almost pounced on him and pressed something into his hand.

'Here, take that,' she stormed. 'How can a young 'ealthy bloke like you 'ave the gall to walk about town when all our lads are away doin' their bit fer the war, eh? Yer should be ashamed o' yerself, so yer should. Yer nowt but a yeller-bellied *coward*!'

From the corner of her eye, Annie saw the colour drain out of Reggie's face as the group of angry women surrounded him. And then he opened his palm and a white feather floated on the wind. Pushing his way past them he took off as fast as his legs would carry him, their jeers ringing in his ears.

'The idle young bugger should be *ashamed*,' the woman who had given the feather to him shouted after him, shaking her fist. 'They should make all o' them that's fit go whether they want to or not!'

Annie knew the same thing had recently happened to Charlie and beat a hasty retreat in the opposite direction. She could understand him not wanting to go, he was such a gentle-hearted soul, but she couldn't help but agree with the woman and had no sympathy for Reggie whatsoever. She quickly made her purchases before making her way to the shop where she found Peggy and Eve dusting the shelves with not a customer in sight.

'It's slow again today,' Peggy moaned. 'An' Levi barely brought anythin' back from his rounds yesterday. But what are you doin' 'ere? Why ain't you at the hospital?'

'Matron gave all the nurses going to France a couple of days off before we leave so I thought I'd come and see if there was anything I could do to help you,' Annie explained.

Peggy tutted. 'There's nowt that me an' Eve can't do so you just get yerself back 'ome an' 'ave a rest afore yer go,' Peggy scolded. 'There's barely enough to keep us two busy let alone three of us. 'Ow is young Charlie by the way?'

The week before Peter, Charlie's friend, had come home briefly from training to say his goodbyes before being shipped out. Charlie had insisted that Annie should meet him, and so she had somewhat reluctantly accompanied him to the station.

Levi had not mentioned Peter's name since the fateful night Charlie had told them about his relationship, whereas Maggie had prattled on about him to the point that Annie had almost expected him to be some sort of monster with two heads. It had come as a pleasant surprise to find that he was actually very nice. He was handsome and well spoken and it was obvious from the way the two men gazed at each other that they were very much in love. Annie had only stuck around long enough to be introduced and share a cup of tea in the station café before she had left them to have their last precious moments alone together.

Charlie had been bereft ever since and now Annie had a feeling that he would be enlisting soon as well. It was only the fact that his mother had begged him not to that had stopped him doing it before.

'He's not good,' Annie admitted.

Peggy shook her head. 'It's a cryin' shame. We can' 'elp the way we're born an' it wouldn't do if we were all the same, would it? I just wish Maggie would go easy on the lad.'

'So do I, but anyway, if you're sure there's nothing I can do, I may as well get back an' try an' get the house into some sort of order before I leave. I dread to think what it'll look like wi' Maggie runnin' it.'

'She'll just 'ave to pull her finger out the way the rest of us do,' Peggy said unsympathetically. 'But yer will come an' see us again afore yer go, won't yer, pet?'

'Of course.' Annie felt a lump in her throat as she realised just how much she was going to miss Peggy – all of them, in fact. For although Maggie had never been the mother figure she had hoped for, she and the rest of the Lilburns were the only family she had ever known.

Before Annie knew it, it was the morning of her departure. Levi had taken the morning off work to say goodbye, but Maggie had stayed in bed. Annie wasn't surprised. Maggie had never pretended to love her – or perhaps she just couldn't face another goodbye.

As they sat drinking their last cup of tea together, Levi asked Annie for at least the tenth time in as many minutes, 'Now, are yer quite sure you've packed everythin' yer need, hinny?' He seemed more nervous than Annie was.

'Quite sure. I'm not going to need much. I can't see us 'avin' a lot of time off. Try not to worry, I'll be fine.' Annie reached across the table and gently squeezed his hand, before glancing at the clock and rising hastily. 'But I really should go now. We 'ave to be at the station by nine o'clock.' She was dressed in her Red Cross uniform and as she slipped her cape around her shoulders Levi thought how smart she looked.

'I wish you'd let me come to the station wi' yer to see yer off.'

She shook her head. 'No, honestly, I'd rather say bye 'ere.'

Seeing the tears in his eyes she gave him a quick peck on the cheek and, lifting her bag, she hurried away. Prolonging the goodbyes could only make things worse as far as she was concerned.

The station was teeming with nurses when she got there, all looking as nervous as she felt. Then she saw another nurse, who looked to be about her own age, hurrying towards her. Annie had seen her briefly at the hospital a few times, although they had never been properly introduced.

'Hello, I'm Beulah Malton-Smythe.' When Annie raised an eyebrow, she grinned. 'I know – it's a right mouthful, isn't it? I don't know what Mummy was thinking when she landed me with it, but you can just call me Belle Malton. I think I've seen you at the cottage hospital?'

Annie smiled and held her hand out. 'That's right, I'm Annie Lilburn.'

'Nice to meet you, Annie. Do you reckon we could stick together on the journey? I'd feel better if I were with at least one familiar face.'

'Of course. Do you 'ave any idea where we're goin'?'

Belle shook her head. 'I haven't got a clue. I don't think they've told anyone; all I know is it'll be somewhere in France.'

They heard the train approaching and minutes later they were herded aboard like sheep. Unfortunately, they were unable to find two seats together in any of the carriages, so they chose to sit on their bags in the corridor.

As the train chugged away from the station, Annie glanced at her new companion from the corner of her eye. She was tall and attractive and had lovely green eyes, but it was her hair that was her most striking feature. It was a mass of fiery red curls, whereas Annie's was jet black and, as Maggie was fond of saying, 'as straight as pump water'.

'I don't mind this part of the journey but I'm not looking forward to going on the ship,' Belle confided. 'I've never been on one before, have you?'

Annie shook her head. 'No I 'aven't, and atween you an' me, I'm not much relishin' the thought of it eithers.'

'So where are you from?' Belle asked.

'Swan Lane.'

'Really?' Belle chuckled as she wiggled about trying to get comfortable. 'So am I. My father is a doctor. What does yours do?'

Rather than go into lengthy explanations, Annie answered without hesitation, 'He's a rag-and-bone man.'

Belle blinked with surprise but kept any comments she might have made to herself. 'So, what made you volunteer for this?'

'To be honest, Matron asked me if I would be prepared to come, so I agreed. What about you?'

Belle giggled. 'I had a horrible feeling that Mummy and Daddy were pushing me towards their friend's son and I can't stand the sight of him, so I took this as the easy option. I must admit I'm a terrible flirt and I don't feel ready to settle down just yet.'

Annie couldn't help but like the girl, her giggle was infectious, and she was glad they had met. It would make the long journey so much easier having someone to talk to.

By the time they drew into Euston Station some hours later they were both stiff from sitting in uncomfortable positions, but they didn't have long to think about it before they were hurried across the platform and out to a large military truck with bench seats in the back of it and a canvas top. This would take them to the port, and from there they would board a ship to France. As they clambered aboard, someone handed each of them a pack of cheese sandwiches and a small flask of water.

Belle sighed as she looked at it. 'Hardly lunch at the Ritz, is it?' she said ruefully, but they were hungry by that time so they ate every bit of the sandwiches.

When they eventually drew into the port, they both stared in amazement at the enormous ship they were being ushered towards.

'Crikey, it makes you wonder how anything this big and heavy could possibly float, doesn't it?' Belle whispered. 'I hope she's watertight. I don't fancy taking my chances in Davey Jones's locker!'

The nurses streamed aboard and were led down a steep staircase into the bowels of the ship where there were rows of benches, but no windows, so it was dark, gloomy and very damp.

'Brrr!' Belle pulled her cape more tightly about her. The girls were both suddenly very conscious that soon they would be leaving their homeland far behind them and they wondered if they would ever see it again.

Chapter Nine

The crossing was choppy and many of the nurses were seasick and had to use buckets to vomit in. Before they were even halfway through their journey the smell was appalling, and everyone was keen to get back onto dry land.

By the time they docked in France, Annie felt as weak as a wrung-out dishcloth. She and the other nurses emerged onto the deck to find it was getting dark. They were ushered towards the gangplank and onto the dock where they found yet another open-backed truck waiting for them.

'Oh, my backside is so sore after sitting on these hard seats all day,' Belle complained once they set off.

Annie could only nod; she felt too weak to say anything, and it seemed the other nurses felt the same as the final leg of the journey was made in near silence.

Back in Nuneaton they'd had some distance from the war, but as they drove through the villages of France, they saw the carnage that had already taken place. Whole houses had been burnt to the ground and the smell of smoke and destruction hung on the evening air. Far off they could hear gunfire and it struck terror into their hearts as they realised they were nearing the fighting.

After what felt like hours they came to a stop in front of a motley array of tents and an army sergeant greeted them.

'Welcome, ladies.' He saluted them as they clambered down from the back of the truck. 'Your barracks are over here. If you'd like to follow me. Please leave your bags by your beds and go to the canteen where I'm told there will be a meal waiting for you. After this, you are free to rest, but you must report to the hospital tent for six o'clock tomorrow morning where you will be told what your duties are to be. The latrines and showers are in that tent at the end, but be warned, there is a shortage of water so we are having to restrict everyone to one shower a week, and even then, I cannot promise the water will be warm.'

Belle and Annie glanced at each other. Neither of them had expected the place to be luxurious but this was so much worse than they could ever have envisaged. The ground beneath their feet had been churned into a sea of mud and duckboards had been laid down across it.

They followed the sergeant to the first tent where twelve of the nurses disappeared inside. Annie and Belle found themselves in the second tent and once the sergeant had left, the twelve nurses stared around in dismay, shocked to see how basic their living accommodation was. There were six beds lined up on either side with a small locker to each of them and a potbellied stove to one end, which was belching out smoke. This, it seemed, was to be their only form of heating.

'Right, come along, girls,' one of the nurses said. 'We're here now so we have to make the best of it. Choose which bed you want and drop your things on it then we'll go and get us something to eat. I don't know about you lot but I'm so hungry my stomach thinks my throat's been cut. I wonder what culinary delight they'll have ready for us.'

After her recent bout of seasickness just the thought of food turned Annie's stomach and she stood aside as the others stampeded towards the back of the tent, each girl hoping to get the warmest position beside the stove. Soon after they all trudged out into the darkening night. The canteen was positioned beside the large hospital tent and was lit with oil lamps. The unappetising smell of boiled cabbage and burnt sausages greeted them as they entered, but most of the girls were so hungry they would have eaten anything, and they queued up with their plates held ready.

'Shall I get you something?' Belle offered as Annie sank down at one of the tables.

Annie shook her head. 'Thanks, but I couldn't eat a thing. A cup of tea would be nice though.'

Belle was back soon after with a tray of food for herself, which looked just as unappetising as it smelled, and two mugs of stewed black tea. The tea was lukewarm, but Annie sipped it anyway and started to feel a little better. When they'd finished, they visited the toilet block, which proved to be small cubicles with wooden seats inside. The smell was rank and they got out as quickly as possible. Back in their tent, they undressed hastily and after slipping into their nightdresses they jumped into the lumpy beds and pulled the thin, scratchy blankets over them.

'I'm not so sure I'd recommend this as a holiday from what I've seen so far,' Belle said wryly. 'And this mattress is as hard as a rock!'

'So is mine, but I'm so tired I reckon I could fall asleep on a clothesline,' Annie told her, and as if to prove her point she was fast asleep seconds later.

'Wakey wakey, girls, it's time to use the toilets, get breakfast and report to the tent for duty,' a loud voice barked the next morning.

Annie startled awake and, glancing down the tent, she saw a sister in a navy dress and a starched white cap standing at the entrance. The girls quickly lifted their towels and made for the toilets and the shower block where they washed as best they could in the icy cold water. It was still dark outside and by the time she was finished Annie's teeth were chattering.

It was no better for Belle, but her voice was still cheerful as she urged, 'Come on, let's go and get into our uniforms and see what's on offer for us in the canteen this morning.'

They were faced with a choice of porridge or toast. It was edible and filling, although not very appetising. Still, both Belle and Annie were hungry, so they ate their fill as they stared around at the people in the tent. As well as the other new arrivals, there were a number of nurses and doctors who looked almost dead on their feet. They had clearly just finished shifts in the hospital tent and couldn't raise a smile amongst them.

'Poor devils,' Belle whispered as she battled to pin her cap over her unruly curls. Her hair seemed to have a life of its own and the cap kept springing off. 'Some of those doctors look rather dishy, though, don't they?'

Annie grinned. As she was soon to discover, Belle was indeed a terrible flirt.

She was just finishing her second cup of tea, which was nice and hot this morning, when a sister appeared in the doorway and clapped her hands to draw their attention.

'Could the new recruits follow me, please.'

The young women stood and followed her out into the darkness and shortly after she led them into the enormous hospital tent where all chatter ceased as they got their first glimpse of the true horrors of war.

Rows of beds were lined up along each side, occupied by men, some looking so sick they might already have been dead, while the nurses dashed from one bed to another tending to them. There was an overpowering smell of vomit, disinfectant and stale blood that made Annie want to gag, and there was a coarsely laid wooden floor of planks stretching from one side of the tent to the other, which was awash with mud.

The sister broke them up into groups. One group were given mops and buckets and set to washing the floor to try and make it a little less slippery. As they were soon to discover it was a never-ending task, for before they had even gone the length of it the people coming and going were bringing more mud in.

Annie and Belle were consigned to the sluice to wash the bed pans, and their first sight of the huge pile waiting for them made them gasp with horror. A large Belfast sink with a pump had been erected in the tent, but the water, which was fed from a well, was icy cold and soon neither of them could feel their fingers.

They had almost finished the first lot when some nurses appeared bringing them yet more to clean. They were beginning to think they would never escape, but eventually the sister came back to ask, 'Have either of you ever given a bed bath?'

Annie's face flamed as she shook her head, but Belle just smiled.

'I think that's a no from both of us,' she told their superior. 'But I'm willing to give it a go if Annie is?'

When Annie nodded the sister smiled her approval.

'Good. Then each take a bowl of water, a towel and a bar of soap and follow me.'

Once they had everything they needed they followed her back into the ward where she drew curtains around a young soldier's bed. There was a large frame holding the covers off the bottom part of his legs and the sister explained, 'Corporal Radcliffe has had an amputation. He is still very weak as he lost a lot of blood, but he's been extremely brave, haven't you?'

The young man, who looked barely old enough to be there, nodded, his face completely devoid of colour.

'Nurse Malton, you attend to him and you, Nurse Lilburn, come with me.'

Annie noticed that the curtains were also pulled around a number of other beds close to the nurses' desk at the top of the ward. Seeing where Annie was looking, the sister explained in a low voice, 'They are the unfortunates who we don't expect to survive. The least we can do is give them a little dignity and allow them to pass in private.'

Annie swallowed and blinked. She had seen some sad sights at the hospital in Nuneaton but never in her wildest dreams had she imagined it would be as bad as this; she almost felt as if she had walked into hell.

She gave her first bed bath to a young corporal who had bad burns across his torso and face. Annie guessed that he might have been quite handsome before but now he was horrifically scarred. He lay as still as a corpse while she tended to him as gently as she could, his eyes staring up at the roof of the tent. She blushed a deep brick red as she undid his pyjama top with shaking fingers, but by the end of the morning she had gone past that stage.

It was well after one o'clock when the sister allowed them to break for a short lunch and even Belle was quiet as they picked their way along the muddy duckboards to the canteen. In the distance they could hear gunfire and explosions, and Annie shuddered.

'I wonder how many more poor devils are goin' to cop it today?'

'I don't know, but Sister just told me there'll be another influx of patients later this afternoon or this evening.'

'But where will they put them?' Annie questioned. The ward was already full to bursting.

'Apparently those that are fit enough to travel will be taken to hospital ships and sent home later on,' Belle told her.

They each had a light lunch of soup and bread rolls washed down with two cups of tea before returning to work. When they got to the tent, they found the doctors and nurses preparing the patients due to be transferred to the hospital ships. Annie didn't think any of them looked well enough to be sent anywhere, but now she knew there would be more soldiers coming in that day, she understood that the beds were needed.

She was sent to help a young private who was crying broken-heartedly. 'I don't wanna go 'ome like this.' He gestured to the empty sleeve of his pyjamas with his one good hand. 'What's me girl gonna think when she sees me?'

'I'm sure she'll be very proud of you and realise how brave you've been,' Annie answered in a wobbly voice as she packed his few possessions into a bag. 'And at least you're still alive.'

'Huh! More's the pity.' He clenched his fist. 'What good am I gonna be to anybody wi' just one arm? How am I supposed to get a job an' earn a livin' now?'

Annie was at a loss what to say to comfort him so carried on in silence until two ambulance men appeared and bore him away. The next two hours continued in the same vein, and by the time the last of the patients had been taken away there were a number of empty beds, which they then had to make up with fresh sheets. The day was already beginning to darken by that time and soon after the sound of the explosions and gunfire ceased.

'Hopefully that's it until tomorrow,' the ward sister said wearily. 'The stretcher-bearers will be venturing onto the battlefield now to collect the injured and then they'll go back for the dead bodies.'

'Wh-what will happen to the bodies, Sister?'

'There's another large tent behind this one which serves as a temporary morgue. But before the bodies are taken for burial we have to remove their dog tags so their relatives can be informed. Not a nice job, but it has to be done.'

Annie shuddered at the thought as she remembered the day she had seen Barney and Harry off at the station. There had been an almost carnival atmosphere then and she wondered how they were faring now.

They were led into the morgue almost an hour later to collect the dead men's identity discs and the sight of all the lifeless bodies laid out in rows brought a lump to her throat. They were almost all covered in mud and blood from their wounds and Annie knew it was a sight that would haunt her for the rest of her life. After the identity discs had been removed, the male nurses then manhandled the bodies into body bags ready for burial.

'Don't they even get washed?' Annie asked a nurse.

The woman shook her head. She had been there from the first and was hardened to the sight now. 'Unfortunately, there's no time. It seems disrespectful, I know, but we have to focus on the living.'

By the time they left the morgue tent, both Belle and Annie were as white as sheets and wondering what they had got themselves into. But there was no time to dwell on it, for the first of today's patients were being carried in and doctors and nurses swarmed around them trying to determine who needed treatment first. Those that were grievously injured were whisked away to the operating theatres while the others were found beds and settled.

It was almost nine o'clock that night before Annie and Belle were finally dismissed and as they made for the canteen their spirits were as low as they could be. The sister had informed them they would be working during the day for the rest of that week, but then they would take it in turns to work the night shifts too.

In the canteen, there were large pans of beef stew simmering, but after the sights they had seen neither of them could stomach it. Their first shift had been so much worse than either of them could have imagined.

'I feel dirty,' Belle said wearily as she sipped at a large mug of tea. 'I'd do anything right now to sink into a nice hot bath.'

'I know exactly what you mean. I've washed me 'ands at least half a dozen times,' Annie answered. 'But I can't seem to get rid of the smell of blood.'

They finished their drinks and started off for their tent. 'I was goin' to write 'ome tonight but I think I'm too tired,' Annie said quietly.

'It'll wait until tomorrow.' Belle stifled a yawn as they entered their tent. The stove was lit and it was surprisingly warm. Some of the nurses who had worked that day were already fast asleep, so not wishing to disturb them the two young women changed into their night clothes and quickly hopped into bed.

'That's our first day done,' Belle whispered.

'Hmm, let's just hope we've already seen the worst.'

'I hope you're right, but I've got a horrible feeling we haven't,' Annie whispered.

Chapter Ten

The following day, which again began at six o'clock in the morning, Annie discovered from one of the other girls in her tent that they were just outside the village of Ypres.

'Our lads are just about 'anging on to it,' she told Annie in a broad cockney accent. 'But Paris 'as been bombed. I'm Cissie by the way.' She was short and plump and had a kind face and mousy brown hair.

'Please to meet you, Cissie. Although I could 'ave wished fer it to be under better circumstances. I'm Annie an' that's Belle over there.'

The three girls smiled at each other as they dragged their uniforms on and so another day began.

Annie wrote to the family and Peggy the next day adding a PO box number where any return mail would reach her, although Cissie warned her that apparently it could take some time and was very hit and miss. 'The nurse who told me reckons she can get three or four letters all in one go, then nuffin' fer ages,' she sighed.

By the end of the first week, both Annie and Belle were exhausted and after taking advantage of the one shower a week they were allowed, they spent their first Sunday afternoon off sleeping.

Every day when the new patients were brought in, Annie anxiously scanned their faces to make sure that no one she knew was amongst them, even though there was every chance that Barney, Harry and Monty were off fighting somewhere else. The war had spread to almost every part of the world, it seemed, and the hope that they would all be home for Christmas was becoming more unlikely with every day that passed.

As Annie and some of the other nurses entered the ward for the beginning of the second week, the sister approached. 'Can any of you drive?'

Annie and one other nurse held their hands up.

'Excellent. You others get to work and you two come with me.'

The sister led them into a small office – no more than a curtained-off corner of the ward – and told them, 'I'm afraid we are desperately short of drivers and stretcher-bearers.'

'You mean the ones that fetch the injured and dying off the battlefields?' the other girl asked.

The sister nodded. 'I'm not going to lie to you. It can be a very dangerous job, hence the shortage of volunteers. Some of the men who've done it previously have been injured, so you are in no way obliged to do this. Sadly, although each side agreed to a ceasefire at the end of the day so the injured and the dead could be collected, the Germans don't always stick to it. But if you could see your way to volunteer, I'd be most grateful. You wouldn't be expected to carry the injured and the dying yourselves. The men will do all the heavy lifting. You would just drive them back to the hospital.'

'I'll do it, Sister,' Annie said without hesitation. She doubted there could be anything worse to see out in the field than what she had already seen in the hospital.

'And so will I,' the other girl, who Annie later learnt was called Veronica, said more uncertainly.

'Wonderful.' The sister looked relieved. 'In that case neither of you need report for duty until eight o' clock each morning. I'm afraid the field runs can go on until quite late, depending on how many are injured.'

'When would you like us to start?' Annie enquired.

'This evening, when the ceasefire begins. For now, though, go about your duties.'

Almost as soon as they had returned to the ward, a nurse appeared from the curtains drawn about a bed and beckoned to

Annie. Then in a low voice she asked, 'Could you go in there and stay with him? He'll not last much longer. I don't like any of our men to die alone but I have medication to give to other patients.'

Annie nodded and stepped through the curtains. She was confronted by a young man who she was sure would have been very handsome before he'd had one side of his face blown off, along with an arm and a leg. The doctors had done all they could for him, but he had lost so much blood that his body was shutting down and there was nothing more they could do. His eyes were feverishly bright and as they tried to focus on Annie, he gave her a lopsided smile and held his hand out to her. 'Will me mam be here soon?' he asked piteously.

Annie realised that his mind was wandering. She saw from his notes that his name was David and, sitting close beside him, she gripped his hot hand in hers.

'She most certainly will,' she told him in as cheerful a voice as she could muster.

He sighed contentedly. 'Y-you'll like me mam. Sh-she's kind.'

Annie knew that his end was near. He closed his eyes for a few minutes and when he next opened them, he smiled the most beautiful smile as he looked at Annie. 'Ma, yer came, I knew yer would.'

'Well, I wouldn't let yer down now, would I?' There was a catch in Annie's voice as she realised he thought she was his mother. Leaning forward she gently stroked the damp hair from his forehead with one hand and gripped his remaining clammy one in her other, and soon after his eyes closed. Annie knew that he could probably still hear her so she kept up a gentle stream of chatter so he wouldn't feel alone. He took his last breath almost an hour later and as Annie looked down on his still form a tear trickled down her cheek at such a useless waste of a young man's life. Gently she pulled the sheet across his face hoping that she had at least brought him a small measure of comfort in his last minutes.

*

That afternoon, one of the stretcher-bearers gave Annie a lesson on driving the large truck that would transport the injured and dying later that day. It was a huge vehicle, far bigger than the modest car Levi had taught her to drive, but Annie was a quick learner and was sure she would soon get the hang of it. It was nothing more than an open-backed truck with a canvas roof, and she felt it was quite inadequate for transporting injured soldiers, but, as she was fast learning, they had to make the best of what they had.

By the time the evening ceasefire began, Annie was a bag of nerves. It had been hard enough having to listen to the gunfire and the fighting in the distance, but now she would be going to the very edge of the battlefield and she felt apprehensive. One of the stretcher-bearers, a tall, thin young chap from Birmingham, climbed into the cab with her to give her directions while the others all clambered into the back.

'Nice to meet you, I'm Jim.' He introduced himself cheerfully.

'Annie,' she answered as he pointed her in the direction they were to go.

'I haven't seen you driving before. First time, is it?'

She nodded. 'Yes, and I must admit I'm a bit nervous.'

'Hmm, it is a bit dauntin' till you get used to it,' he admitted with a shake of his head. 'I'd be out there fightin' with 'em if it weren't for these.' He stabbed at the glasses perched on the end of his nose. 'I didn't pass the medical cos of bein' short-sighted so I opted to do this instead. At least this way I feel like I'm doin' me bit.'

'I'm sure you are,' she assured him as the truck picked up speed on the bumpy roads. The closer they came to their destination the murkier the air became. The smell of gunfire and smoke hung in the air and the ground became like a mud bath. At one point Annie feared they would get stuck in it but somehow, she managed to keep the large vehicle going. And suddenly they were there on the perimeter of the field and she drew the truck to a halt.

'Right, you stay here an' keep your head down,' Jim told her as he climbed out. 'The Jerries don't allus stick to the ceasefire an' we've had more than a few stretcher-bearers mowed down.'

Annie felt terrified as the men left the truck, but she didn't regret agreeing to come. Her eyes were adjusting to the darkness now and she peered ahead into the gloom. In the sea of mud that seemed to stretch for as far as her eyes could see, she could just make out the shapes of bodies slumped on the ground and the sound of men screaming in pain echoed around her.

It was like being trapped in a nightmare and tears poured down her pale cheeks as the stretcher-bearers raced onto the field. They stopped at each shape they came to, moving on to the next if the person was dead – they would be the last to be brought in, if they were lucky. If not, they would be swallowed up by the mud where they had fallen. Those that were still alive were hastily put onto the stretchers and brought back to be loaded onto the back of the truck. The minutes stretched into an hour and then two, until at last Jim appeared and climbed in beside her. He was covered in mud from head to toe with only the whites of his eyes showing, and he looked weary.

'Time to go, Nurse, there's no more room in the back till the next trip.'

With shaking fingers, Annie started the engine and turned the truck around. The screams coming from behind her were unnerving and her heart ached as she thought of how much pain the men must be in.

'It's been bad today,' Jim confided as he felt in his pocket for his cigarettes. He offered one to her and when Annie shook her head, he lit one and took a deep drag on it to steady his nerves. It didn't matter how many times he did this job it always upset him to see young men no older than himself with limbs blown off. Many of them bled to death before they could get to the hospital.

When they arrived, some of the nurses helped get the injured inside, and then it was back to the battlefield again for any remaining survivors. There were far fewer this time, despite the men scouring the field. Many of the remaining were already dead and they would be brought back on the final trip of the day and laid in the tent that served as a morgue.

By the time the last trip was over, Annie's nerves were in shreds. Never in her wildest dreams had she imagined such carnage and it had shaken her badly.

'Well done, Nurse Lilburn,' the kindly ward sister told her. 'Go and get a hot drink and some rest now. And in the morning, you and another nurse can go into the morgue and collect the dog tags from the corpses so that we can get them buried.'

'Yes, Sister.' Annie visibly shuddered at the thought. It had been bad enough to have to see their poor broken bodies piled into the back of the truck, but the thought of having to touch them filled her with dread.

On legs that seemed to have developed a life of their own Annie walked to the canteen, the smell of death still in her nostrils.

Chapter Eleven

'So, how are things?' Levi's sister-in-law Flo asked one dark evening in mid-December. They were racing towards Christmas and the weather was bleak, with severe frosts coating everything each morning, although they'd not yet had any snow.

Levi shrugged; his hands were covered in soap suds as he scrubbed the dirty pots at the sink. 'Obviously they could be better,' he answered shortly. There had been no letters from Barney, Harry or Annie, and every day he was eaten up with worry about them. He'd said as much to Maggie but as she'd pointed out, had anything happened to them they would have heard.

Flo batted her eyelids at him, but it had no effect on Levi. He had become used to his sister-in-law's advances and wasn't very happy that, since the war had started, she'd become a frequent visitor.

'Yer know, if I were to move in I could see as all this were done for yer when you got home of an evenin'. It don't make sense just you an' Maggie rattlin' round in this great place. An' I'd be company fer Maggie durin' the day.'

Levi had heard this what seemed like a million times over the last couple of months, but he couldn't think of anything worse than having Flo and her tribe living here full time. Even so he didn't want to be rude and hurt her feelings, so he just shook his head.

'We do still have Charlie here,' he pointed out. 'An' he usually pitches in an' helps wi' owt Maggie ain't managed to do.'

Flo frowned but noticing that he was looking at her, she quickly plastered a smile back on her face. 'Well, just think about it,' she encouraged. She had never been one to give up easily. 'How's the new job goin' anyway?'

Levi had been forced to close the rag-and-bone yard and was driving for a living, collecting ammunition from the former car factories that were now busily making rifles and bullets for the troops. The shop had also had to be temporarily closed, and Peggy and Eve were working in one of the same munitions factories.

'I wonder you haven't got yourself a job,' he said drily. 'There are thousands of women who are having to do the jobs the men can't do while they're away.'

Flo looked horrified. She hadn't done a day's hard work in her life and had no intention of starting now. Ignoring the implied question, she leant over to fill the kettle, making sure her ample bosom brushed against him. She had just set the kettle on the hob when the back door suddenly opened letting in a blast of icy air and Susan, Maggie's other sister, appeared.

Flo looked less than pleased to see her. 'Well, well, look what the cat's brought in. It's Miss Susanne. What brings you 'ere all the way from London?'

'I've come to stay for Christmas, and while I'm here you may call me Susan,' Susan told her curtly. Glancing at Levi, she added in a softer tone, 'If that's all right with you, of course?'

'You know you're always welcome,' Levi told her warmly. He had always got on better with Susan, despite her dubious reputation.

Susan dropped her heavy carpet bag onto the floor and began to take her gloves, coat and bonnet off. 'Where's our Maggie?'

Levi pointed to the ceiling. 'She's upstairs havin' a lie-down. She's got a ragin' 'eadache.'

'How has she been?'

'Not good. Worse if anythin' since our Barney an' Harry joined up. She gets all into a tizzy if she so much as glimpses the telegram boy.'

'Any news from them yet? Or from Annie?'

He shook his head. 'No, we did 'ave one letter from Annie shortly after she left but nothin' since.' He dried his hands on a large piece of huckaback and sighed.

'How did she sound? Where is she?'

'She weren't allowed to tell us where she is and you know Annie, she sounded fine, but she wouldn't tell us if she wasn't. She's a brave little lass.'

Flo sniffed as she prepared the teapot. Levi always seemed to have more to say to Susan than he did to her.

'And how is Theo?' Levi asked. 'I'm surprised you won't be spending Christmas in London with 'im.'

Susan flushed as she took a seat at the table. 'Oh, he's, er . . . gone away for the holidays on business,' she said evasively – she wasn't going to tell her brother-in-law that he had turned tail and gone into hiding for fear of being called up. Theo was the love of her life, and she had never stopped hoping that one day he would make an honest woman of her. It was he who had set her up in a grand apartment in London and trained her to be a high-class prostitute, known as Miss Susanne.

'In that case you're welcome to stay fer as long as yer like,' Levi said cheerily. With Susan here he wouldn't have to worry about Maggie being on her own all day.

The three of them had just sat down to drink their tea when Charlie appeared, but he didn't look as Susan remembered him. He had lost weight and there were dark shadows under his eyes.

'Hello, Auntie Susan, Auntie Flo, Da.' He nodded towards them and walked across to the hall to go upstairs.

'Hold on, son, I've got some dinner keepin' warm for you in the oven,' Levi told him.

Charlie shook his head. 'Thanks, Da, but I've already eaten. Why don't you have it for your supper?' And with that he disappeared.

Susan raised her eyebrow. 'Good grief. Is he all right?'

It was Flo who jumped in to tell her, 'He's pinin'.' She gave a wicked little titter. 'Fer his *boyfriend*, ain't that so, Levi? His boyfriend is away fightin'. Yer did know he's a queer, didn't yer?' she asked, feigning innocence.

Angry colour spread up Levi's neck and into his cheeks. If looks could kill the one he gave Flo would have done the job in seconds. She was a wicked gossip was Flo. It was no wonder she had no friends.

However, Susan took it all in her stride and continued to sip demurely at her tea before saying, 'Well, it wouldn't do if we were all the same, would it? And they're not doing anyone any harm. Poor Charlie must be worried sick. And how is your Jim, Flo? Has he thought of joining up to do his bit yet?'

'Huh! It'd be a cold day in hell afore that idle sod would do that,' Flo snorted. 'It takes me all me time to kick 'im outta bed each mornin' to turn in to his job at the bookies, the idle bugger!'

Now that Susan had turned up Flo knew the chances of Levi letting her and her crew move in with him before Christmas were gone and she wasn't pleased, so standing up she collected her hat and coat and yanked them on.

'I dare say I'd best get back. I've no doubt I'll see you both before Christmas.' And with that she headed for the door and after slamming it resoundingly behind her, she disappeared into the frosty night.

'Oh dear. Why do I get the idea she isn't too pleased to see me?' Susan gave a wry smile.

'Ah, take no notice of her. She's just put out cos I've been ignorin' her hints to move herself in here.' Levi shook his head. 'Can you imagine what it'd be like? She'd drive me mad! All her seven 'ave flown the nest now so she's on 'er own. Most o' the girls 'ave got married an' the lads are away fightin'. Between you an' me I reckon they couldn't get away quick enough. She's allus been a slovenly devil. Her an' Maggie would be at each other's throats in no time cos yer know how Maggie likes everythin' just so.'

Her face serious, Susan asked, 'And what about Charlie? Is what she said true?'

Levi flushed. 'Aye, it is, lass, more's the pity. It's him I worry about. Lookin' back the signs were all there right since he were a nipper but I chose to ignore 'em. He's never shown any interest in a lass. I just hoped he were a slow starter an' hadn't met the right girl yet. Just goes to show how wrong yer can be, don't it?'

'Aw well, it's not the end of the world, is it? He's still Charlie, and you'll just have to accept him as he is. It's either that or lose him.'

'I know yer right,' Levi admitted. 'An' I've got me head around it now, but I can't say the same fer our Maggie. She were devastated when he told us.'

'Hmm, more worried about what people would say more like,' Susan answered. She could read her sister like a book and knew all too well what a raging snob she was. 'But how is she really? Does she still talk to Penny?'

He rubbed his chin and nodded. 'Aye, she does . . . all the time now. She tries to hide it, but I hear her an' to be honest I don't know what to do about it.'

'Have you thought about getting a vicar in to talk to her about the afterlife?' she suggested. When he raised an eyebrow, she rushed on, 'What I mean is, if he could perhaps persuade her that Penny is in heaven now, in a better place, it might comfort her enough to let her go.'

He thought on her words for a few moments before shaking his head. 'No, I 'adn't thought o' doin' that, but I don't think it'd do any good.'

'Aw well, it was just a thought.' Susan lapsed into silence and Levi looked at her carefully.

'And how about yer tell me why yer really here, lass. I know you wouldn't just leave Theo alone fer Christmas fer no good reason, an' what yer said about him bein' away don't quite ring true.'

Susan stared into the fire before answering quietly, 'Theo was afraid of being called up, if you must know. He doesn't believe in fighting so he's gone to ground. But it's not just that . . .' She took a deep breath. 'I'm going to have a baby, Levi. It's due in June sometime.'

'Why that's *wonderful*,' Levi said, genuinely pleased. 'Happen this will be the time fer him to make an honest woman of you.'

She sighed. 'He doesn't know yet,' she admitted tentatively. She could hardly tell him that she didn't want Theo to know until it was too late for him to persuade her to get rid of the baby, as he had the last one. Sometimes the guilt about what she'd done weighed heavily on her. She still had nightmares about that unborn baby, and wondered often what it would have been like had she let it live. She couldn't take the life of this little one as well, she just couldn't.

'I see.' Levi patted his chin, unsure what to say. He knew only too well the stigma that was attached to a baby born out of wedlock, even though times were changing. 'All I can say is yer welcome here fer as long as yer want to stay. Fer good, if need be, an' the little 'un when it comes, so don't fret on that score . . . but what I would advise is to tell 'im. It is his child when all's said 'an done, ain't it?'

Susan nodded. She was sure of it this time because she had made her clients take precautions. 'We'll see, but thank you.'

Maggie was pleased to see Susan when she got up the next morning and almost immediately burst into tears. 'They've all gone except Charlie,' she sobbed on Susan's shoulder.

'I know, Levi told me.' Susan patted her arm. She wanted to tell her sister about the baby but didn't know how. Maggie was nowhere near as broadminded as Levi so instead she said quietly,

'But you have to try not to worry. They're both sensible lads. I'm sure they'll be fine.'

'Everyone said it would be all over by Christmas.' Maggie wrung her hands as she began to pace the floor. 'But here we are with Christmas almost upon us and there's no sign of it stopping.'

'It will; it can't go on forever and our lads are doing a grand job out there,' Susan told her optimistically. 'Now tell me how Peggy, Eve and little Ellie are getting on. Are they still working at the shop?'

Maggie shook her head. 'There's not enough stuff being collected to keep it open so it's had to be closed for now, as have half the other shops in Nuneaton. It's like a ghost town, and Peggy and Eve are both working in a munitions factory. Most of the women hereabouts are.' It had never occurred to Maggie that she could be there too; she was too used to being waited on and playing the lady. 'Even Annie's gone, working in some field hospital in France, so keeping this place going is down to me now,' she ended bitterly.

'I dare say you could look around for somewhere smaller,' Susan ventured, but Maggie glared at her and so she quickly changed the subject.

Susan made them both a light breakfast of boiled eggs and tea and once she had tidied the pots away, she made an excuse to go out for a while. She needed to clear her head. Despite what Levi had said she decided it wouldn't hurt to have a word with the vicar about Maggie so she made for the vicarage next to St Mary's Church.

The vicar's housekeeper, a small plump woman with a friendly smile called Mrs Bee, answered her knock and Susan gave her her warmest smile. 'Good morning, I'm so sorry to trouble you, but I wondered if it would be possible for me to have a few words with the vicar?'

The woman frowned, considering her. She had to admit the young woman in front of her was impeccably dressed and very well spoken. 'He's working on his sermon in his office at present, but I can always ask him if he can spare you a few minutes if you'd like to come inside, dear.'

Susan stepped into a large hallway and waited while the woman disappeared into a room, which she supposed must be the office. She soon returned to tell her, 'He has to go out to see one of his parishioners in half an hour, but he can spare you a few minutes.'

Susan was shown into a book-lined office in the middle of which stood a large, highly polished desk. An elderly man with grey hair and a rather large red nose was seated behind it and he rose to shake her hand.

'How do you do? How might I help you, Miss . . .?'

'Morris,' Susan answered as she took his hand. 'I've come to see you about Mrs Lilburn.'

'Ah, the Mrs Lilburn that attends the church each Sunday?' he enquired.

'Yes, I'm her sister.'

He motioned to a chair in front of the desk and once she was seated, she began to explain her concerns about Maggie.

He listened closely with his hands steepled on the desk. 'I was aware of her daughter's death,' he said when she'd finished. 'But I wasn't aware that she was still grieving so badly. She always seems so self-assured when I see her.'

'Unfortunately looks can be deceptive and it's got to the point where myself and the rest of her family are gravely concerned about her mental health. She has already had one stay in Hatter's Hall a few years ago, but I fear another might be detrimental so I wondered if there might be anything you could say to her to help her come to terms with Penny's death?'

'Hmm.' He stared through the window for a few moments. He was run off his feet at present visiting wives and mothers who had lost loved ones to the war, but even so he didn't like to think of

Maggie suffering, so he nodded. 'I shall call in to see her as soon as possible,' he promised. 'And rest assured I will do all I can to convince her that Penny is at peace now.'

Susan breathed a sigh of relief and left, happy to leave it in the vicar's capable hands. There was no more she could do.

Chapter Twelve

'I can't believe it's nearly Christmas,' Belle said as she placed a kettle on the stove in the tent. The nurses often made their own tea if they could scrounge the tea, milk and sugar from the canteen. 'If I were at home now, I'd be all dolled up at a dance or somewhere nice.'

Annie gave a weary smile as she stifled a yawn. She had not long got back from the battlefields and after what she had seen the last thing she felt like doing was celebrating, even if they could have.

'I've heard they're calling a truce for Christmas Day,' Belle went on.

Annie nodded. 'Yes, I heard the same.'

'Then we might have an easier day.'

'I doubt it after the number of casualties I fetched back today,' Annie said sadly. 'The hospital tent is bulging at the seams, so there'll be plenty to do, whether we get more casualties or not.'

'Aw well, at least we have a Christmas dinner to look forward to,' Belle said, ever the optimist. 'Apparently some of the French people from the village will be bringing some nice plump turkeys to the cookhouse for us.'

Annie couldn't help but smile as she watched Belle go to the tent flap and peep out.

'I don't suppose you're hoping for a glimpse of the new doctor who's just arrived?'

Belle quickly dropped the flap and came back inside. The kettle was almost boiling so she spooned some sugar into their mugs. 'Well, Dr Howard is rather dishy, isn't he?'

'You're quite incorrigible,' Annie told her. 'I think you've been flirting with half the male staff here.'

'And why not?' Belle pouted prettily. 'There's not much else to do with our time off, is there? Not that we get much of that. I was rather hoping they'd let us go home for a few days at Christmas. Still, I suppose we'll just have to make the best of it.' She made the tea and while Annie lay on her bed drinking hers, Belle started to brush her hair and apply a thick layer of scarlet lipstick. 'I don't suppose I can persuade you to come to the NAAFI for an hour? Word has it that some of the troops will be coming.'

Annie groaned. After a hard day on her feet every limb ached and she couldn't think of anything worse. 'No, sorry, I'm afraid you'll have to go on yer own. Me feet are throbbin' an' all I want to do is sleep.'

Belle giggled as she fluffed up her curls. 'Suit yourself and don't wait up for me.'

Annie grinned as she watched Belle trip from the tent. No matter how bad things got Belle always managed to put a smile on her face and she was grateful that she had her for a friend. With another yawn she struggled into her nightgown, pulled the blankets up to her chin and was asleep almost before her head hit the pillow.

When Annie arrived at the ward the next morning, the sister beckoned her to follow. Annie was led into an office tent a short way from the hospital where they could talk more privately and she was surprised to see a Frenchman waiting there. He was dressed in a beret and an old overcoat and looked like a farmer.

'Bonjour, Mademoiselle.'

'Bonjour, Monsieur.' Annie nodded towards him as he removed his beret and gave a little bow and at that moment a man in army uniform also joined them.

Annie gazed from one to the other, confused.

'Have you had time to speak to her, Sister?' the officer enquired.

The woman shook her head. 'No, sir, I thought I'd leave it to you to explain.'

'I see.' He looked Annie up and down before asking, 'And you can assure me that she is totally trustworthy?'

'Nurse Lilburn is one of the most hardworking, dedicated nurses I have ever had the privilege to work with, sir,' the sister assured him with her nose in the air. 'Furthermore, she can speak fluent French. Otherwise, I would never have recommended her to you.'

Annie's knowledge of the French language had come in handy on more than one occasion as a few of the doctors and nurses were French. Sometimes those that couldn't speak very good English had called on her to translate for the patients and Annie had always been happy to help.

'Very well.' The officer, who Annie noticed was very handsome, smiled at her. 'In that case I shall explain what this is all about. But first you must swear to me that nothing you are about to hear will leave this room.'

When Annie nodded, he went on, 'I'm sure you will have heard of the French Resistance workers? They work tirelessly to smuggle our more important men out of here and safely back to England. Unfortunately, they have one such man who was badly injured hidden at Monsieur Jacques' farm.' He indicated the man with the beret. 'We have arranged to have him sent back to England this evening. However, because of his injuries he will need a nurse to travel with him, which is where, I hope, you will come in. But before you make a decision, I must inform you that this will not be without risk. Should the Germans capture you your life will be in grave danger.'

'May I ask why he can't just be admitted to the hospital to be treated?' Annie asked innocently. She had heard about the French Resistance fighters, but this was the first time she had actually met one.

'Let's just say that he is privy to information that must be relayed to England as soon as possible.' He waited for a few moments as Annie mulled over what he had said before asking, 'Do you think it is something you would consider doing?'

'But what will we do with the injured man if we make it back to England?'

'That has all been arranged,' he assured her. 'There will be a car waiting for you at a point in Dover, and once there your job will be done.'

'And 'ow will I get back here?'

'The same way as you go, by boat with Monsieur Jacques here.'

'And what will I tell my friends? They're bound to notice I'm missin'.'

'They will be told that you have been sent to help out at another field hospital. So, what do you think? There will be no repercussions if you decide you would rather not do it, of course.'

Annie nodded. 'I'll go. Tell me exactly what I 'ave to do.'

A look of relief swept across the young officer's face. 'Monsieur Jacques will be waiting for you at the back of the hospital in a covered cart at nine o'clock this evening. Once well away from here you will be met by a car that will take you to the coast where a boat will be waiting for you. There will be men there to lift the injured man in and all you will have to do is tend to him on the journey and then return with Monsieur Jacques.'

'Yes, sir.' Annie stood tall. She felt a little apprehensive, but she was determined to go through with it.

Once the officer and the Frenchman had left, the sister told her, 'I suggest you finish at two o'clock today, Nurse. Try and get a few hours' sleep because it looks as if you have a very long night ahead of you. Oh, and if you have any civilian clothes with you, I suggest you wear them this evening. It will look less conspicuous than your uniform.'

Annie found that the rest of the morning seemed to pass interminably slowly, but even when the sister sent her to rest at two o'clock, sleep eluded her.

Thankfully, both Belle and Cissie worked late that evening, so Annie was able to change into the one civilian outfit she had brought with her and slip away into the darkness without being seen. She waited behind a tree a short way away from the hospital tent, her teeth chattering from the cold. At last she heard a horse and cart trundling towards her.

Not a word was exchanged as Monsieur Jacques pointed towards the covered back and she clambered in. The cart immediately started moving again and as her eyes adjusted to the darkness, she saw a mound covered with sacks behind the seat. She crawled towards it and peered down into two feverishly bright eyes.

'Y-you must be Nurse Lilburn?'

Annie nodded. 'That's right, but you can call me Annie if you like.' The poor soul looked ghastly pale.

'I'm Alex Gordon.' He held his hand towards her and she shook it, alarmed to feel how hot it was. He looked to be somewhere in his mid- to late twenties with fair hair, but because of the gloom she couldn't determine what colour his eyes were. However, she could see that he was very attractive and her heart did a little flutter. It was funny because it had never done anything like that for anyone other than Charlie.

'May I ask what injuries you have?' she asked, feeling all at sixes and sevens.

He pointed towards his stomach. 'I got shot and the bullet is still in there,' he told her with a wry grin. 'Happen I'll be dead meat if they don't manage to get it out soon.'

'Why didn't they bring you to the hospital to have the bullet removed?'

He tapped the side of his nose and winced. When he managed to get his breath back, he told her, 'Too risky. I'm on the Germans' most wanted list. I'm afraid I can't tell you more than that.' The effort of talking had made fresh blood appear on the bandages wound about him.

'You just lie still and try and rest,' she told him, although she knew there would be little chance of that. Every time the cart went over a pothole he gasped, and she knew he must be in a lot of pain.

They seemed to drive for a very long time but at last she thought she saw a glimmer on the sea, and a few moments later they turned a corner in the road and there it was, spread out before them.

'We weel 'ead for the beach now, monsieur,' the driver told them in a strong French accent. It was quite late and the roads were deserted as he turned the cart down what appeared to be little more than an overgrown farm track. It was particularly bumpy there and Annie kept a fresh dressing pressed to Alex's wound to try and stem the bleeding, wondering how he was going to survive a sea crossing . At last, they drew onto a beach in a small cove.

'Where are we?' Annie asked.

The Frenchman shook his head. 'Eet is better that you do not know, mademoiselle. But 'ave no fear, one of our men will be 'ere shortly with the boat.'

Sure enough, some fifteen or so minutes later they heard an engine, and a boat turned into the cove. It was steered in close to the beach and the engine died as two men jumped out and splashed through the waves to them.

They greeted the driver in French before turning to Alex and Annie. 'We will carry you both out to the boat, yes? Do not fear, we are very strong.' With no more ado the shorter of the two lifted Annie and her small medical bag, as if she weighed no more than a feather, while the other man lifted Alex. They were both deposited in the boat, which was much smaller than Annie had expected.

So small, in fact, that she wondered how it would fare if the sea was rough. There was a wooden shelter at one end of it and Alex was placed in there on a bench seat with just enough room for Annie to sit beside him, while the two men sat up front.

It was achingly cold and she was pleased to see that they had thought to bring a pile of blankets, which she immediately tucked around the injured man. The last thing Alex needed was to catch pneumonia on top of everything else. Seconds later they were off. Thankfully the sea was as calm as a millpond and as the moon lit its surface it looked as if it had been sprinkled with diamond dust. One of the men was keeping a close eye on the disappearing land with a pair of binoculars but no one appeared to be following them. Annie was all too aware of what could happen if they did. It would almost certainly mean death for all of them. Sensing her fear, Alex gripped her hand and again she got a little flutter in her stomach.

'You're very brave to risk this. Thank you,' he said quietly, and she squeezed his hand. She just wanted the journey to be over and for him to be in safe hands. She changed his dressing twice in the next few hours and offered sips of water to keep him hydrated, but other than that there was little more she could do for him. At one stage he fell into a fitful sleep still clutching her hand, and she dozed too, until she started awake and became aware of the men talking. In the distance she could see the white cliffs of Dover. Never had a sight been more welcome and she could have cried with relief. Glancing at Alex she saw that he was still asleep so she sat quietly as the men steered the boat towards the beach, where she could see a car waiting in the darkness.

'Alex, we're here,' she whispered, and when he opened his eyes and looked at her, he smiled. Despite the bitter cold, he was still drenched in sweat and Annie was seriously concerned for him. 'You'll soon be on your way to a hospital where you can get the care you need,' she told him in a wobbly voice.

'Thank you ... you've been an angel,' he whispered. 'And, Annie ... I hope we meet again one day, in better circumstances.'

'So do I.'

The Frenchmen steered the boat into the cove now and she saw two men in hospital uniforms waiting on the sand.

'This is it,' she told him. 'Goodbye and good luck, Alex.'

He squeezed her fingers one last time before the larger of the Frenchmen lifted him and bore him away. The night was eerily quiet with only the sound of the waves lapping on the beach to be heard. Annie watched as Alex was carefully placed in the back of the car and then it pulled away, the engine sounding startlingly loud in the cold night air.

'Now we must get you back safely, mademoiselle,' the large Frenchman told her as he splashed through the waves and climbed back into the boat. 'I would ask when we are safely out to sea if you would please discard all the soiled dressings over the side of the boat. We want no evidence of anyone injured 'aving been in here. If we are stopped say nutting please. We are merely fishermen trying to earn a living and you are my daughter, yes? You see, I 'ave a net to add truth to my story. I am Andre by the way, and this is Francois.'

Annie nodded and began to gather up all the bloodied dressings. Twenty minutes later, when there was nothing but sea to be seen in every direction, Annie tossed the dressings overboard and curled up beneath the blankets that had kept Alex warm, and as she slid into a fitful sleep it was with his face before her eyes.

Chapter Thirteen

'Mademoiselle, mademoiselle!'
At the gentle pat on her arm, Annie sprang awake. She was stiff from lying on the hard board, cold and disorientated, but as she looked up into Francois' face, she remembered where she was and hastily pulled herself up onto one elbow.

'We are 'ere, mademoiselle,' he told her gently. 'And now you must get safely back to the 'ospital, *oui*?'

She knuckled the sleep from her eyes and looked towards the small cove they had set off from.

'First I carry you ashore,' Francois went on. 'And then you must climb to the top over there and 'ide amongst the trees. Soon the cart will come to take you back. Do not show yourself to anyone else.'

She nodded and collected her things together and pushed them into her small medical bag. Francois hopped out of the boat, lifted her over the side and carried her to the sand, where he gently put her down. Removing his cap, he gave her a little bow. 'Many thanks for your 'elp, mademoiselle. You are a very brave young lady and eet was a pleasure to meet you. Goodbye for now.'

He turned and splashed back to the boat and as Annie began the steep climb up the hill, she heard it pull away. It had been too dark to see much the night before but now as she reached the top, she saw a huddle of burnt-out cottages. Clearly the Germans had done their worst here and she shuddered to think of how may innocents might have perished. These had once been people's homes but all that remained of them were piles of rubble and ashes. She headed for a clump of trees and hunkered down behind one, shivering. She had not eaten since lunchtime the day before and was hungry so she hoped when she got back to the hospital there might still be some food going in the canteen. But first she would have to report to the sister to tell her that the escape had been successful. She thought of Alex and wondered if he'd had the operation to remove the bullet inside him yet. She hoped so, they had got on well and she wondered, if they had met under different circumstances, what might have developed between them. There had certainly been an attraction there, but she would probably never know.

At last, she heard the clip-clop of a horse's hooves and peeping out from behind the tree she saw Monsieur Jacques anxiously looking around from his seat on the cart.

'I'm here!' She stepped out from behind the tree and smiled to see the look of relief that lit his face.

'Ah, *mon cherie*, thank goodness. All went well, *oui*?'

'Very well.' She threw her bag into the back and clambered up beside him. 'We landed safely and a vehicle was waiting to transport Mr Gordon to hospital, so hopefully he'll get the help he needs to make a full recovery.'

'Ah, *parfait*!' He patted her arm but there was no time to waste, so he set off for the hospital.

Once there she went straight to report to the ward sister.

'Well done, Nurse Lilburn.' The sister looked relieved to see her back. 'Now, perhaps you would like to take a few hours off to get some rest?'

Annie shook her head, 'Thank you, but I managed to grab some sleep on the way back so I'll just go and get some something to eat, freshen up and I'll be back.'

Belle was in the canteen having a quick tea break when Annie entered. 'Ah, so you're back.' She looked genuinely pleased to see her. 'Sister said she'd sent you to the next hospital to help out for the night because some of the nurses were ill. How did it go?'

Annie felt herself flush. 'Oh, you know ... busy!' She hated lying to her friend but she didn't have any choice.

'I'll see you later.' Belle gave her cheery smile. 'Bye for now, sweetie.'

Half an hour later, after grabbing a sandwich and a cup of very hot, sweet tea, Annie reported for duty again and another long day began.

That evening, Annie set off with the stretcher-bearers to recover the injured from the battlefield. She was bone tired, as were all the hospital staff as they struggled to cope with the influx of patients. The only bright spot on the horizon was that the Christmas Day truce had been confirmed. A whole day without fighting. Already Annie was thinking how strange it would be not to have the noise of guns and explosions in the background. When she had first arrived, the constant drone had set her nerves on edge, but she had become so used to it now, she didn't notice it so much.

She and the other nurses had done what they could to make the hospital wards look festive, with bunches of holly dotted here and there, and as she set off that evening, she was looking forward to getting back and joining Belle in the NAAFI for a little Christmas Eve party. Some of the soldiers were being invited and although Annie wasn't much of a partygoer, she supposed it would be better than sitting in the tent on her own.

She was helping the stretcher-bearers to load the injured into the back of the truck when a soldier caught her eye. His face was grey and he was covered in blood, but there was something vaguely familiar about him, although for the life of her she couldn't think why.

When the back of the truck was fully loaded, she headed back to the hospital and as always, doctors and nurses were waiting to help carry the men into the wards. One young man, who didn't even look old enough to be there, was crying piteously for his mother, and Annie felt a lump form in her throat as she gripped his hand and spoke soothingly to him. His other arm was missing and he was bleeding profusely. He was rushed straight into theatre but Annie knew his chances of survival were slim. By the time the new patients had been taken inside, Annie was exhausted and the last thing she felt like doing was getting ready for a party, but she had been looking forward to it and so she went back to their tent and changed before letting her hair down and brushing it.

On entering the NAAFI, she smiled as she saw Belle surrounded by a group of young soldiers. She wasn't surprised. Belle was extremely attractive, and she knew it. An old wind-up gramophone was belting out Irving Berlin songs while some of the nurses and soldiers danced. They had managed to get hold of a few bottles of wine from somewhere and although Annie didn't usually drink, she helped herself to a glass and took a seat at the far side of the room. It was nice to sit down after being on her feet all day, but soon Belle spotted her and hared over, closely followed by her admirers.

'Gentlemen, meet my good friend, Nurse Annie Lilburn.'

Finding herself the centre of attention, Annie blushed as the soldiers began to hound her to dance with them.

'Perhaps later,' she mumbled, taking a big sip of her drink, and eventually they got the message and turned their attention back to Belle.

Suddenly she remembered the soldier who had looked so familiar to her that evening, and as she sat there wracking her brains as to who he might be and how she might know him, it came to her, and she felt the colour drain out of her face. He looked remarkably like Peter, the man Charlie was in love with.

Glancing across at Belle, who was still flirting outrageously, she put her drink down and slipped out into the bitingly cold air. As tired as she was she knew there would be no sleep for her that night if she didn't put her mind at rest one way or another.

Entering the admissions ward, she scanned the sea of faces in the beds, until she found the one she was looking for. She approached him quietly. There was a large cage over his legs and he looked so pale that he might have been dead. The nurses had prepared charts which hung on the ends of the beds of each patient and as she glanced through his, her heart sank. He was indeed Sergeant Peter Fellows.

As she stood there trying to take it in, one of the night nurses approached her. 'What brings you here tonight, Nurse Lilburn?'

'I thought I recognised this man earlier,' she explained. 'And now I've remembered where from. How is he?'

The nurse frowned and took Annie's elbow, gently leading her away from the bed out of earshot of the patient.

'He's due to go down to theatre anytime now. He stepped on a mine and his left foot was blown off. Between you and me I think his chances of surviving are slim. It looks like he already had foot rot from standing ankle-deep in the cold mud and what's left of his leg is badly infected. Poor chap. How do you know him?'

'H-he's a friend of my brother's,' Annie told her in a shaky voice. She could only begin to imagine what it would do to Charlie should anything happen to his beloved Peter.

'That's sad.' The nurse patted her arm. 'But there's nothing you can do here so go and enjoy a break with the others. I wish I could.' And with that she was off to tend to another of the patients who was clearly delirious.

Despite being tired, Annie slept little that night and at first light on Christmas Day, she reported back for duty.

Sister looked mildly surprised to see her. 'You're an early bird. You're not due to come on duty for at least another hour.'

'Oh, I couldn't sleep so I thought I might as well come in.'

'Well, we never say no to another pair of hands. Perhaps you could start the bed baths?'

Annie nodded and headed to the sluice room to collect a bowl and some clean towels. She peeped at Peter as she passed his bed, but it was hard to see how he was as he hadn't properly come round from his operation yet.

Sometime later, the nurse she had spoken to the night before passed her as she went off duty. 'That man you know, the friend of your brother . . .'

'Yes.' Annie stared at her questioningly.

'He's had his operation but as I thought things aren't good. They think he has gangrene in his leg.'

Annie bit her lip and when the nurse moved on, she approached Peter's bed again. He was as white as lint and she knew he was going to be in a lot of pain when he woke up.

In the rest of the ward the men who were able to were sitting up and in fine spirits: they had a turkey dinner to look forward to as well as a glass of wine that the local villagers had kindly supplied to have with it. The sister usually forbade alcohol but because it was a special day she had decided to relax the rules a little.

Word had reached them that because of the one-day truce their men and the Germans had actually joined together and sung Christmas carols to each other across no-man's-land and it made everyone realise that a lot of the enemy soldiers probably didn't want to be there either. No matter where they were from, they were someone's son, lover, husband or brother and their families were probably missing them just as much as the British soldiers' families were.

Peter came around just before lunchtime to find Annie sitting at the side of his bed holding his hand. He blinked at her, confused.

'It's all right, Peter, you're in hospital, and you've 'ad an operation,' she soothed.

He licked his dry lips and she reached for a glass of water and helped him to have a few sips.

'D-don't I know you from somewhere?' And then, as he realised who she was, his eyes stretched wide. 'It's Annie, isn't it? . . . Charlie's sister.'

'That's right. I recognised you when they brought you in so I've been keeping my eye on you. Charlie would want me to.'

As she laid his head gently back on the pillow, he asked, 'What sort of an operation have I had?'

Annie had dreaded him asking but she steeled herself and answered, 'I'm afraid you've lost part of one leg. You stood on a mine, an' if what the rest of your men are sayin' is right, you're quite the hero. You knocked another soldier out of the way and took the blast yourself.'

He screwed his eyes tight as he tried to take in what she had told him. 'Lost . . . leg. But how will I be able to fight now?'

'There'll be no more fightin' fer you. You'll be sent back 'ome to recover when you're well enough to travel.'

'But . . . I can still feel both my legs,' he argued as he looked towards the cage covering them. 'I can't have lost one.'

'It's normal to think you can still feel it,' she assured him. 'But the main thing is, you're still alive. You could 'ave been killed.'

Tears sprang to his eyes. 'But what am I supposed to do with one leg? I'm a cripple.'

'There are lots of things you'll be able to do. Especially once you've got a prosthesis.'

The sister approached the bed and Annie was relieved that the conversation was stopped from going any further.

'Ah, you're awake, Sergeant Fellows,' the sister said cheerily. 'Just in time for a Christmas dinner. How are you feeling?'

'I'm fine.' Peter made to pull himself up the bed a little and winced with pain.

'Nurse Lilburn, go and fetch the doctor to check the sergeant, please.'

Annie was only too happy to do as she was asked as the sister swished the curtains about the bed and began to examine the patient's leg – or what was left of it.

'You've been a very lucky man, old chap,' the doctor told him when he arrived.

But once he was alone with the sister, he shook his head. 'I'm afraid I had to take more of the leg than I wanted to because, as I suspected, he has gangrene. If we can stop it from spreading any further, he has a fine chance of a full recovery, but if not . . .' There was no need for further words. They both knew what the outcome of that would be.

Chapter Fourteen

'Merry Christmas everyone! To absent friends and loved ones!'

Levi raised his glass, and all seated at the table duly lifted theirs. Peggy and Ellie were there, as well as Susan, Eve, Charlie and Maggie, but despite Levi's best efforts, none of them were really in the mood for celebrating. All their thoughts were with the ones they were missing.

'Right, I'll carve, shall I?' Levi sliced into the enormous turkey he had fetched from one of his former customers the day before. Peggy had arrived early that morning to prepare and cook the meal, and now everything was done to perfection. There were crispy roast potatoes, brussels sprouts, winter cabbage, buttered potatoes and a delicious sage and onion stuffing – Eve's contribution – along with a large jug of thick gravy.

It was a wonderful feast but only Ellie really did it justice. The others merely picked at their food, their thoughts far away.

Following the main course, there was a Christmas pudding that Peggy had had soaking in brandy for weeks and to go with it she had made a large jug of creamy custard, but again most of it went untouched.

'I wonder what my Davey is 'aving for 'is dinner?' Eve mused as she took a sip of wine. 'I 'ad a letter from him two days ago, did I mention?'

Levi grinned. 'Only about ten times. Try not to worry, I'm sure even the troops will be given a day off today.'

Charlie suddenly pushed his chair back from the table and headed for the stairs. He had been sick with worry about Peter for days now since having a terrible premonition that something was wrong.

'Charles, come back here, it's rude to—'

Levi held his hand up to silence his wife. 'Leave it, lass. The lad is worried about . . . his friend.'

Maggie snorted. 'Friend indeed,' she muttered, lifting her spoon and pushing her pudding about the dish.

Peggy turned to Eve. 'Shall we get this clearing away done, love? The pots ain't goin' to wash 'emselves.'

'No, Peggy, you've done enough,' Levi protested. 'I can do them later. Sit yourself down an' put yer feet up fer a while.' He was hoping his words would shame Maggie into offering to help, but she merely went and settled herself in the chair by the fire, spreading her silk skirts decorously around her as if she was the lady of the manor.

'I'll help,' Ellie offered, and jumping up she began to carry the dirty pots to the sink.

Much to Maggie's disgust, Levi had insisted they should dine at the large kitchen table rather than in the formal dining room. As Levi had pointed out, being in the dining room would have meant having to light yet another fire and he was trying to economise on coal. On everything, if it came to that. Sometimes he wondered if Maggie even realised there was a war on, for she was still trying to carry on as they had before.

Once the table was cleared, Levi and Ellie settled down for a game of chess. He had been teaching her to play for some time but she still hadn't quite mastered it, so it was fairly one-sided. Meantime, Eve and Susan tackled the mountain of dishes, one washing and the other drying and putting away.

Suddenly Ellie asked the question that was on all their minds, 'I wonder what the rest o' the family are doin' now?'

'Hopefully they'll all be tuckin' into a dinner as good as the one we just had,' Levi said with a grateful smile at Peggy. He shuddered to think what they might have sat down to had it been left to Maggie.

Peggy smiled back as she filled the kettle and put it on to boil. 'This fancy wine is all well an' good but yer can't beat a cup o' tea,' she said as she warmed the teapot, and Levi couldn't have agreed more. He had never been much of a drinker.

It was mid-afternoon when the snow began to fall and soon everything outside was coated in a thin white blanket, making it look brand new.

'I reckon we might make tracks in a minute,' Peggy remarked, eyeing the window. 'At the rate this is comin' down we might get snowed in.'

Levi chuckled. 'But yer only live round the corner,' he pointed out. 'But I'd better go an' feed old Dobbin. I was gonna let him out of his stable for a couple of hours this afternoon but lookin' at the weather I reckon he'll be better off stayin' inside.'

'I'll come an' 'elp,' Ellie volunteered, dashing after him, leaving the women alone.

In France, as the afternoon darkened, a hush fell in the hospital tent as suddenly the sounds of the soldiers singing 'Silent Night' wafted to them on the air from the edge of the battlefield. When they had finished, the German soldiers then sang a carol in their native tongue and all along the edges of the trenches candles were lit that shone like Christmas trees in the darkness, a sight that brought a lump to everyone's throats. During the afternoon they had had a game of football with the British soldiers.

'If only this truce could go on,' the sister whispered to the young doctor standing beside her. 'War is such a useless waste of young lives!'

'I agree,' the doctor said soberly before turning to go and tend to one of his patients, who he doubted would last the night.

Annie was seated at the side of Peter's bed. He was in a lot of pain and his temperature had risen alarmingly.

'How was Charlie when you left?' Peter croaked as she sponged his forehead with cool water. She had already answered the same question at least six times.

'He was well, although 'e were missin' you terribly,' she told him once more.

'I hope he doesn't go and do anything rash like signing up,' Peter fretted. 'Charlie isn't cut out to be a fighter.'

Annie saw the way Peter's eyes would soften each time Charlie's name was mentioned and she knew in that moment just how much he loved him. 'You just 'ave to concentrate on getting well so you can go home and begin your lives together.'

Peter nodded. 'Yes, I know, although I feel we'll have to rethink where we go. Did Charlie ever tell you that we were planning to live in France? I'm not sure where we can go now. Do you think you might write him a letter for me tomorrow if I tell you what to say? I'd happily do it myself but for some reason I have the shakes and I doubt he'd be able to read my writing.'

'Why don't we do it now?' she suggested. 'I'm sure Charlie will love knowing you wrote to him on Christmas Day. Just wait while I go and scrounge some paper and a pen off Sister.'

She had written countless letters to loved ones for the men who were unable to do so, but she knew this one was going to be particularly difficult.

She was back in no time and as she settled down, Peter began,

My darling Charlie,

It's Christmas Day and I'm wondering if you are thinking of me and missing me as much as I am missing you. Can you believe I am in a field hospital and Annie is here with me as my nurse. What are the chances of that happening? I'm sorry

to have to tell you that I have lost a leg after stepping on a landmine. I don't know how you will feel about that? I hope it won't affect your feelings for me, dear boy.

Annie tells me that once I am on the road to recovery I will be shipped home and I can be measured for a prosthesis. At least we can be together again then, it's all I dream of. Charlie, I've never been a great one with words but I hope you know that you are, and always will be, the love of my life. I cannot imagine living without you, being here has shown me that.

I don't know how long it will be until I manage to get home but know that I am counting down the hours until we can be together again. Meanwhile, promise me you will keep yourself safe for me. Life would not be worth living without you, my love.

Love always,
Peter xxxxxx

Annie steadied his hand as he wrote his name at the bottom of the page and then she popped it in an envelope and addressed it.

'Promise me you will see that it's posted?' he implored.

She patted his hand. 'I shall take it to the mail sack myself,' she promised in a shaky voice. 'Although I can't promise how long it will be until Charlie receives it. The post is very hit and miss.'

He stared at her for a moment before saying in a low voice, 'Thank you . . . for not judging us, I mean.'

'Love is love when all's said and done. But now I'd best go and get this in the mail sack. I'll be back later.'

As she headed out of the tent, she found herself thinking about Alex Gordon and wondering how he was faring. She hoped he was recovering and decided that as soon as she got the chance, she would ask the sister or one of the doctors if they had heard anything of him.

*

The next day the fighting resumed and the nightmare began all over again. The hospital staff were running dangerously low on medical supplies as the ship bringing the last lot of medical equipment and medicine had been sunk by a German U-boat and there was no way of knowing when the next lot might arrive, which was gravely worrying, but the wounded continued to be brought in, so they just had to do the best they could.

The New Year came and went uncelebrated. The nurses and doctors were far too busy doing what they could for the patients, but because of the shortages the mortality rate was higher than ever.

Shortly after the New Year, Annie was asked if she would be prepared to do more sea trips with injured soldiers, and over the next few weeks, she crossed the Channel three times. The crossings were treacherous in the bitterly cold weather and many of the patients she attended on the trips perished before they reached their homeland, but Annie did all she could for them and cried for those who didn't make it.

'You're a very brave young woman,' the sister told her gratefully after one such crossing but Annie shrugged.

'I'm only doin' my bit, Sister.'

'Even so there aren't many nurses that I would entrust the patients with,' the other woman insisted. 'Most of them would run a mile if I suggested they should risk their lives as you have.'

Peter was still at the hospital, but as the doctor had feared, the gangrene was spreading. He was far too ill to move and Annie feared it was just a matter of time before he passed away, unless a miracle occurred.

'Is there nothing more we can do for him?' she asked a young harassed-looking doctor late one afternoon. She was mopping Peter's fevered brow with cool water and she had a bad feeling. Peter didn't seem to know where he was half the time now and frequently called out for Charlie, which broke her heart.

'I'm afraid not.' The doctor sighed as he swiped a stray lock of hair from his forehead. He hadn't slept for almost twenty-four hours and was dead on his feet. 'I think we should prepare ourselves for the worst.'

Later that evening, Annie left Peter's side to go and collect the wounded and when she returned, she saw the curtains drawn about his bed. Her heart sank as she headed towards it just as the sister came from behind them.

'Is he . . .?'

'No, not yet, but I fear it won't be long. You have my permission to stay with him unless you want to go and rest.' The sister knew Annie had grown close to Peter and she touched her back gently as she passed. Annie took a deep breath and went to sit beside him. He was lying very still and his breathing was shallow.

She took his hot hand in hers and as she held it to her cheek her tears dripped onto it. 'Try and fight it, Peter,' she urged. 'For Charlie's sake. He'll be devastated if he loses you.' But her words fell on deaf ears and Peter passed away just over an hour later.

Chapter Fifteen

February 1915

Peggy was round at Maggie's one day early in February when there was a knock on the door, and when she opened it, her heart dropped at the sight of the telegram boy standing there.

'Telegram for Mr Charles Lilburn.'

'H-he's at work at present but I'll see he gets it,' Peggy mumbled, taking the telegram from him with a shaking hand.

'Who was it, Peggy?' When Maggie spotted the brown envelope that everyone dreaded in her friend's hand, the colour drained from her face and she dropped heavily onto the nearest chair.

'It's all right,' Peggy hastily assured her. 'It's fer Charlie.'

Relief flashed across Maggie's face. For a terrible moment she had feared it could be news of Harry or Barney.

'It must be about that *friend* of his,' Maggie said bitterly. 'And if it is, perhaps this will be an end to all this nonsense about him being . . .' Her voice trailed away and Peggy shook her head. Maggie could be so heartless at times. 'Queer, were you going to say?'

'Well . . . yes! I'm sure it was only that friend of his who made my Charlie think he was that way inclined. If something has happened to him Charlie will hopefully find himself a nice young lady and get on with his life.'

Peggy sighed as she went to prop the telegram up on the mantelpiece. There was no point arguing with her, but if the telegram contained what she feared it did, her heart ached for Charlie. He was going to be heartbroken.

Peggy decided to stay until Charlie got home that evening and when he did, she gazed at him for a moment before saying quietly, 'Th-there's a telegram for you . . . It's on the mantelpiece.'

A muscle twitched in his cheek as he looked towards it, and for a moment he just stood there as if he had been turned to stone. Then without a word he went towards it and stared at it as if it might bite him before slowly lifting it.

'You'd best open it, lad,' she said gently.

He took a deep breath and did as she suggested. As his eyes scanned the page, every ounce of colour seemed to drain out of him and he began to shake.

'Is . . . is it bad news?' Peggy's voice was so low he could barely hear it.

Up until then Maggie had said not a word but now she asked scathingly, 'Is it something to do with that . . . *friend* of yours?'

'Yes, it is, Ma. And Peter wasn't my *friend* as you call him . . . he was my whole world.'

Maggie had no chance to comment before he turned and quietly left the room.

'Well, *really*, I don't think there was any cause for him to speak to me like that,' Maggie said indignantly. 'I was only asking!'

'Aye, you were.' Peggy shook her head as she reached for her coat. She had already stayed much longer than she'd intended. 'But it was the way you asked it. I'd advise yer to go easy on 'im tonight else yer likely to lose 'im for good.' And with that she tugged her coat on and left.

'Charlie not in yet?' Levi asked when he came home a short time later.

'Oh, he's in all right,' Maggie fumed. 'Locked himself in his room, he has.'

Levi frowned. 'Why is that?'

'A telegram arrived for him and once he'd read it there was no talking to him.' She pointed to the sheet of paper on the table and after reading it Levi sighed. It was from Peter's mother, who had sent the telegram to inform Charlie of Peter's death. Peter must have given her Charlie's address before he went to war and asked her to inform him should anything happen to him.

'Poor lad, his friend Peter has died of injuries he sustained in battle. Charlie must be devastated.'

'Perhaps he'll see sense now and steer away from *those* sorts of people in future,' Maggie sniffed.

Levi stared at her hard for a moment before heading for the hall door. He had to admit that he had been no happier with Charlie's choice of partner than Maggie. But he had come to terms with it now and accepted Charlie for who he was. He was still his son after all.

Outside Charlie's bedroom door he paused before knocking gently. 'Charlie . . . I just found out what happened. I'm so sorry, lad. Is there anythin' I can get fer you?'

When no reply was forthcoming, he knocked again before trying the door. It was locked.

'Charlie, I know yer must be hurtin' but it won't do no good to lock yerself away. Why don't yer come downstairs an' let me make yer a nice cup o' tea, eh?'

He waited, but again there was only silence so with a sigh he went back downstairs. No doubt Charlie would come out in his own time, and when he did, he would do what he could to comfort him.

After eating the meal that Peggy had prepared for them, Levi took a tray of food up to Charlie and left it outside his door before going to bed, but when he got up the next morning it was still where he had left it, untouched, so he quietly took it back down to the kitchen and got ready to go to work.

When he got home that evening, he found Maggie sitting alone by the dying fire in the kitchen. 'How was Charlie today? Did he get up and go to work?'

Maggie shrugged. 'I have no idea. If he did, he must have left before I got up, I haven't seen him.'

'What? And after the news he got yesterday you mean to tell me you ain't even been up to check on 'im!' Annoyed, he headed for the stairs and once outside Charlie's bedroom door he tentatively tapped on it. 'Charlie . . . it's me, Da. How yer feelin' today, son?'

When there was no reply, he tapped again before trying the door, and to his surprise he found it was unlocked, so he quietly entered the room. The bed was neatly made but there was no sign of Charlie. A cold finger chased down Levi's spine as he crossed to the wardrobe and opened the door. It was quite empty and Levi groaned aloud. 'Ah, lad, where 'ave yer gone?' he said to the empty room. Turning, he made his way back down to the kitchen with a heavy heart.

'How is he?' Maggie questioned.

'If you'd 'ave bothered to go up an' check on 'im you'd 'ave known that he's gone,' Levi answered shortly as he lifted the kettle and began to fill it at the sink. Peggy was working that day so it would be up to him to make them an evening meal.

Maggie scowled. 'What do you mean he's gone? Gone where?'

'Who knows? In the state o' mind he were in, he could 'ave gone anywhere.'

'Then we must find him and bring him home!'

'Oh yes, so you can put 'im down again?' Levi said angrily. 'An' anyway, how are we supposed to find 'im if he doesn't want to be found, eh? He could be anywhere. It'd be like lookin' fer a needle in a haystack.'

Suddenly, Maggie looked distraught. 'But he *must* come home!'

'Why? When he needed yer support the most, yer turned yer back on 'im. It's my bet he's gone fer good an' atween you an' me I can't say as I blame him.' Levi shook his head, his heart heavy.

He made Maggie a light meal and when she sat down to eat it, he shrugged his coat on. As yet, he hadn't even washed but sensing his mood Maggie hadn't commented as she normally would have.

'Why are you putting your coat back on?' she asked with a quiver in her voice. 'Where are you going and how long will you be?'

'I'm goin' out an' I'll be as long as it takes,' he said shortly and left, slamming the door behind him.

Outside, Levi pulled the collar of his old coat up and set off with his head bent and his hands thrust deep into his pockets. He'd had no idea where he was headed when he left the house, he just knew he had to get away from Maggie for a while, but now his footsteps led him to Peggy's cottage.

Peggy was standing at the stove stirring a large pan of stew for herself and Ellie when he walked in, and she looked up surprised.

'Levi . . . is everything all right?' She wondered why she was bothering to ask, for one glance at his set face told her that it wasn't.

'No, things are not all right,' he answered shortly. 'It's our Charlie . . . he's gone wi'out so much as a word. He's taken his clothes an' all.'

'Oh dear. I feared sommat like this might 'appen. Come an' sit down fer a bit. Have yer eaten?'

He shook his head. 'No, but I made sommat for Maggie afore I left.'

Peggy secretly thought that Maggie should have had a meal ready for him to come home to, but she kept her thoughts to herself. 'In that case you'd best sit down an' 'ave some o' this. There's far too much here fer me an Ellie.'

He shook his head, but Peggy wasn't going to take no for an answer and gave him a stern look. 'I said sit down. If you don't get sommat inside yer then I won't eat either.'

Meek as a lamb, Levi removed his coat and sat down just as Ellie appeared from upstairs. 'There, now eat that.' Peggy slammed a plateful of stew and dumplings down in front of him before fetching her own and Ellie's. Most of the meal was eaten in silence save for the ticking of the clock on the mantelpiece and the cracking of the logs on the fire. Ellie had picked up on the tense atmosphere and wisely stayed quiet, and as soon as she'd finished her meal, she shot off upstairs to finish her homework. She was doing very well at school and was already thinking about what she might like to do when she left.

'Any idea where he might have gone?' Peggy asked in a softer tone as she went to make a cup of tea.

'No, he didn't even leave a note . . . nuthin'.'

'Then all yer can do is wait to see if he gets in touch an' respect his need for some time to 'imself,' she said sensibly. 'Charlie's a grown man an' he's got his head screwed on. He'll not go doin' anythin' daft, I'm sure.'

Levi shook his head. 'I don't know, Peggy. I thought when I bought the 'ouse in Swan Lane that it'd be the start o' better times fer all of us but nuthin's worked out as I'd planned. Barney an' Harry are away fightin'. Annie's away nursin', an' now Charlie's gone an' all. An' as fer Maggie . . . I sometimes feel as if I don't know her anymore. Oh, I know she took our Penny's death hard, we all did, but life 'as to go on. She just can't seem to move past it an' accept that Penny won't be comin' back.'

'Grief takes everybody different,' Peggy pointed out. 'She will come to terms wi' it eventually. An' as fer the kids . . . Well, this bloody war can't go on forever, can it? An' then God willin' they'll all be back safe an' sound.'

'I 'ope yer right,' he muttered. 'Cos I don't think Maggie could take losin' another of 'em.'

Chapter Sixteen

October 1915

In October, newspapers reported that the nurse Edith Cavell, who had been accused of spying, had been executed by a German firing squad, and Levi was sick with worry.

'For them to kill a woman like that in cold blood,' he ranted to Peggy. 'It means none of our nurses out there fightin' are safe, includin' our Annie. God above, when is this bloody war ever goin' to end? Our troops are out in Gallipoli now an' heaven knows how many of 'em will come back. It's turnin' into a bloodbath.'

'I know,' Peggy soothed. 'But there's nowt any of us 'ere can do about it.'

It had been a hard year for everyone as food became scarcer. Most of the imported food could no longer reach the British ports and everyone was feeling the pinch. Many people, Levi included, had transformed their lawns and flowerbeds into vegetable plots and were growing whatever produce they could to make their meals go further.

Although he no longer needed to, now that he wasn't doing his rounds, Levi was calling into Peggy's each evening after work. It was impossible to talk to Maggie about anything important. Her mental health had deteriorated further over the last months, and she now spent most of her time chatting to her dead child, seemingly locked away in a world of her own. It hadn't been so bad while Susan was staying with them, but after she had returned to London early in February, Maggie was left alone for long spells of time, which did her no good at all.

Susan had waited until she was sure her pregnancy was too far advanced for Theo to talk her into getting rid of the child before going home, and in June she had given birth to a baby girl. While staying with them the only one who had known she was having a baby was Levi – no one else had noticed her thickening waistline as Susan had hidden her condition beneath baggier clothes.

Soon after she had left, Levi had called the doctor in to assess Maggie and it had been suggested that she should spend another spell in Hatter's Hall, but once again Peggy stepped up to the mark and offered to help out with her more. The vicar had also called and tried to speak to her about life after death and how Penny was now at peace, but it had seemed to do no good whatsoever.

It was this that Levi wanted to talk to her about and so once she had made him a hot drink he said quietly, 'Peggy, I've been thinkin' ... I were wonderin' how you an' Ellie would feel about movin' into Swan Lane? Just till this war is over, o' course. It would make things so much easier fer all of us, an' that place is far too big fer just me an' Maggie. At the moment, yer back an' forth helpin' us as well as tryin' to hold yer job down. There's no reason fer you to be here anyway, till I can resume me rounds an' you can open the shop again. What do yer think?'

'I, er ... the idea 'ad never occurred to me,' she admitted as she put some scones fresh from the oven onto a plate. 'But I dare say it would make sense. Just give me a bit o' time to think on it, eh?'

The conversation went no further, for at that moment the door banged open and Eve appeared. She was breathless and as white as a ghost and had obviously dashed out of the rooms above the shop without even stopping to put her coat on.

'Why, luvvie ... whatever's the matter ...' The words died on Peggy's tongue as she saw the dreaded brown envelope Eve was gripping, and her hand flew to her mouth. 'Oh *no*! ... Is it Davey?'

Eve nodded and then the tears came. 'It says he's . . . *missin'* in action, *presumed* dead,' the poor young woman choked as Peggy and Levi looked helplessly on.

'Oh, pet, I'm *so* sorry.' Levi was out of his seat in a flash and gathered her into his strong arms as she sobbed her heart out. 'Try an' hold on to hope,' he urged. 'After all it says he's missin', *presumed* dead! That don't mean he is. He could 'ave been taken prisoner by the Germans or managed to get away somewhere.'

Eve clung to him like a leech. Davey had been sent home three months previously to recover after a nasty gash to his leg had become infected and had made him unfit for action. They had spent a blissful three weeks together until the doctor had announced he was fit enough to return to the front, and now she had yet more shocking news to tell them.

'H-he *has* to be alive,' she whimpered. 'Otherwise he'll never get to meet his son or daughter. The doctor told me this mornin' I'm almost three months pregnant!'

'Oh pet, that's *wonderful* news,' Levi told her. 'Just think how proud Davey'd be if he knew.'

Peggy hurried over to kiss Eve's pale cheek and add her congratulations to Levi's. 'Yes, it's a blessin', so you just cling on to hope, girl. This little one will meet its dad, you'll see.'

Levi left Eve to Peggy's tender ministrations soon after and went home with a heavy heart, carrying the meat pie Peggy had made for his and Maggie's dinner. He really didn't know what he would have done without her lately. She had been his rock and he hoped that she'd give thought to his suggestion of moving in with them. It would make it so much easier for everyone if they were all under the same roof and it wasn't as if they didn't have the room. He also wondered if he should ask Eve to come too. She could hardly stay on her own once the birth was imminent, and having a new baby in the house might be just the thing to bring Maggie out of her depression.

There had been no word from Barney, Harry, Annie or Charlie for months but then Levi knew this was to be expected. They could go for months without hearing from any of them and then suddenly two or three letters would arrive at once. It didn't stop him worrying, though. The town was already in mourning, for many people had received word that their sons or husbands had been killed in action and it seemed such a pointless, useless waste of precious young lives!

'Ah, sweetheart, here's Daddy now,' Maggie told the empty seat at the side of her when Levi walked in, and he sighed as another long night stretched ahead of him.

The next evening, when Levi called in to Peggy's cottage after work, she informed him that she had decided to take him up on his offer for her and Ellie to move in. He sighed with relief. With more people in the house, it would mean that Maggie wouldn't have to be on her own quite as much and surely that could only be a good thing.

And so that weekend he harnessed Dobbin and set off in the cart to help Peggy move her belongings. She had filled some carpet bags with all her and Ellie's clothes, as well as Ellie's many books. It had been decided that the cottage would remain just as it was until Peggy hopefully returned to it after the war.

From the very first evening it was obvious that the new arrangement was going to work well, and suddenly Levi didn't feel quite so lonely. It was nice to come home to a friendly face and someone who asked about his day, and he enjoyed having Ellie back.

The following week, Peggy suggested to Eve that she might like to join them too, at least until after the birth of the baby, and Eve readily agreed. And so once again, Levi harnessed Dobbin and went to fetch her and the few belongings she wished to bring with her.

Suddenly the house was full again. Everyone got on well together and Peggy had endless patience with Maggie, who didn't even seem to realise they had moved in. Sadly, because of Peggy and Eve's work in the munitions factory, Maggie was still alone for most of the day, so Levi suggested that Peggy should perhaps go part-time.

She frowned, but as he pointed out, there was more than enough to keep her busy with looking after the house and washing, ironing and cooking for them all, and so she had eventually agreed. The new arrangement was working well and a few days later, when a letter arrived from Annie, Levi's spirits lifted even more.

'What does she 'ave to say?' Peggy asked as he read the letter while she was dishing the dinner up. She missed Annie almost as much as Levi did.

'Just the usual really,' Levi told her with a shake of his head. 'It sounds as if they're rushed off their feet with all the casualties. She must be exhausted, but I've yet to hear her complain.'

'That's our Annie,' Peggy agreed proudly. 'I can still remember her when she were nowt but a nipper in the work'ouse. That housemother were fair cruel to the child but Annie never let her get her down. She's got spirit that girl has. I just wish they'd let her come home for a bit of leave.'

'I wish they'd let them *all* come home for leave,' Levi sighed, but they both knew the chances of that were slim unless, God forbid, one of them was injured. The war was escalating. Despite everyone predicting that it wouldn't last, there was still no end in sight.

Chapter Seventeen

'Nurse Lilburn.'

Annie looked up from the patient she was tending. 'Yes, Sister?'

'A word in my office, if you please?'

'Of course.' Annie straightened her apron and followed her down the rows of beds. She had a good idea what was coming. Once they were alone, she asked, 'Is it another sea crossing, Sister?' She had done six now.

The sister nodded almost apologetically. 'I'm afraid it is, and the person who needs help has asked for you specifically.'

When Annie raised an eyebrow, she went on, 'It's Captain Gordon. I believe you saw him safely back to our home shores some time ago?'

Annie's heart did a funny little flutter as a picture of Alex Gordon's face flashed before her eyes. She had often thought of him and wondered how he had fared. Neither the sister nor the doctors had been able to tell her when she had asked them.

'He isn't injured again, is he?'

The sister shook her head. 'Not him, no. But the person he has been working with is.' She paused for a moment before lowering her voice. 'I feel that you have earned my trust now, Nurse, and I'm sure you are aware that the people we ask you to escort back to Dover are not your average soldiers. Captain Gordon and his team are highly trained to go behind enemy lines and gain valuable information from the Germans, which is then relayed back to London. They work closely with the French Resistance and are amongst the most wanted men in the country. Should they or anyone accompanying them ever be captured they would face death by a firing squad. Captain Gordon believes that you saved his life when you did the crossing with him, which is why he has specifically asked for you. Even so, I would quite understand if you would rather not do it. Should you decide to, this crossing will be slightly different as it will involve you going ashore with the men when they reach Dover. You will stay in London for approximately two to three days while Captain Gordon reports to his office and then he will make the return journey with you.'

'I see, and where would I stay?' Annie queried.

'All that has been arranged,' the sister assured her.

Annie nodded. 'In that case I'd be happy to do it.'

The sister looked relieved. 'Very well, as before I shall inform the other nurses that you are needed at another hospital for a few days and, needless to say, it is of the utmost importance that you say nothing to them about where you have really been.'

'Of course. When do we leave?'

'This evening. Do you still have civilian clothes you can wear?'

'Yes, Sister.'

The woman nodded. 'Then good luck, Nurse Lilburn. The cart will pick you up to take you to the port at the usual time and I shall pray for your safe return . . . and thank you.'

Annie left the room with a little bubble of excitement in her stomach. She knew what a risk she was taking but she was looking forward to seeing Alex Gordon again.

That evening she hid once again in the small copse on the borders of the camp until the cart appeared, and Alex Gordon jumped down to help her into the back.

'I'm glad you agreed to come,' he told her, indicating towards another man who was lying on a pile of sacks, his face ghastly pale and his leg heavily bandaged. Even in the gloom she could see blood seeping through the bandages. 'This is First Lieutenant Leonard

Fairbrother and I'm afraid he's in rather a bad way. We came within a whisper of being captured and he took a bullet in his leg. Perhaps you could take a look at it when we're aboard the boat.'

'Of course.' Annie's heart was beating like a drum and she was glad that the darkness hid her blushes. She patted the small carpet bag she had brought with her. 'I brought some dressings just in case.'

They were under the canvas cover of the cart, but it was raining steadily and bitterly cold, so she guessed that it wasn't going to be a very pleasant crossing. They fell silent until the sea came into view and once again the cart turned off the lane onto a track that led down into the small cove.

Ten minutes later the boat appeared and came in as close as it could to shore. Alex lifted his colleague and splashed out to the boat with him before coming back and doing the same for Annie. She had told him she was quite happy to wade out herself, but he wouldn't hear of it. 'No point in all of us having to sit in wet clothes,' he pointed out, so she wisely agreed.

Within minutes of the boat pulling out of the cove, it began to bob alarmingly. As soon as they were far enough from shore to be certain they hadn't been seen, Annie braced herself as best she could and unwound the bandages on the injured man's leg. The bullet had entered through the kneecap and Annie could see that it had done extensive damage and needed urgent surgery. Alex helped her to tie a new bandage as tightly as he could just above the wound to try to stem the bleeding. It must have been incredibly painful but thankfully the man was only semi-conscious.

'So 'ow are you? Did you make a full recovery?' she asked Alex when they had done as much as they could for the patient, including Annie giving him a large dose of laudanum from her medical supplies.

'Yes, thanks to you I did.' He stared at her for a moment. He had thought of her often and now he understood why. With her jet-black hair and huge blue eyes, he found her very attractive – although some would have argued she wasn't conventionally so. She was slightly too tall and slim than was fashionable, but it wasn't just her looks that he was drawn to, it was her kind nature.

'I didn't do much really,' she answered, embarrassed.

'Oh, believe me, you did. You didn't just see to my wound; you kept my spirits up.'

'Did they send you 'ome to recover after your operation?'

He stared out to sea. 'Yes, they did. Have you had any leave?'

She shook her head. 'Afraid not. The hospital's so busy no one 'as 'ad any leave yet.'

'That's too bad . . . is there anyone special at home waiting for you?'

She briefly thought of Monty, before shaking her head. 'No . . . not really, just my family. Well, my adopted family. They took me from the work'ouse when I was little.'

'Really?' He listened enthralled as she began to tell him about her life. By the time the white cliffs came into view Annie had poured out her heart to Alex. It was strange, she was usually quite a private person, but he was so easy to talk to.

The crossing had been rough and despite the small shelter at the back of the boat, they were all soaked to the skin.

'I'll be glad when we can get this poor chap to 'ospital,' Annie fretted. 'He's frozen through and the last thing 'e needs is to catch a chill on top of everything else.'

They became silent as Alex kept watch on the approaching cove. Thankfully there was no sign of anyone watching them, so eventually he nodded to the Frenchman who was steering the boat and he manoeuvred it in as close to the beach as possible.

'If we're all going to return together in a couple of days, where will the boatman stay until we go back?' Annie questioned.

'For your own safety it's better that you don't know,' Alex told her in a low voice. 'But rest assured we have safe houses here as well as in France and he will be quite all right until I send for him.'

By the time they had got the injured man ashore, the car that would drive them into London had appeared. The Frenchman turned the boat and disappeared off into the sea mist, leaving no sign that it had ever been there.

Annie made the patient as comfortable as she could in the back of the car while Alex climbed into the front beside the driver and began to speak to him in a low voice. It was much warmer in here and once Annie had changed the dressings on Leonard's wounds for the last time, she fell into a fitful doze. She woke when the car drew up outside a hospital and realised that they were in London where a doctor and a nurse were waiting for them with a trolley and once they had whisked the patient away the driver turned the car and headed into the city centre.

Even though it was now the early hours of the morning there were still people around. Annie was shivering with cold and was thankful when the car at last came to a stop again, this time outside a small hotel. Alex had a final word to the driver before helping her out and whispering, 'Don't say anything when we get to the desk. Just leave the talking to me. I'll explain when we get to our room.'

Annie looked slightly worried. He had said *our room*, but surely, he had meant *rooms*?

A tired-looking young man with a very spotty face and slicked-down hair was on the reception desk and when they approached it, Alex told him, 'I have a double room booked for my wife and I. Mr and Mrs Smith.'

'Ah yes, sir. I'll just get you your key,' the young man said.

Annie could have sworn she saw him smirk, and she blushed. He clearly didn't believe a word Alex had said.

'Why did you tell 'im we're married?' she hissed as Alex took her elbow and led her towards a lift in the foyer.

Alex grinned. 'So that we appear respectable. But it's wartime. How many couples do you think they have booking in under the name of Smith? He'll be so used to it by now that he won't give us a second thought. He'll just think we're another couple trying to make the most of the time they have left. But don't worry, I'm not going to leap on you, I promise. You'll be quite safe with me.'

They reached a door on the first-floor landing and after unlocking it, Alex ushered her inside and she blushed an even deeper shade of red as the first thing she saw was a double bed.

'I suggest you get out of those wet clothes, have a warm bath and try to get some sleep. I'm afraid I have to report to my headquarters and don't know how long I'll be.'

'*Must* you go tonight?' Annie was nervous at the prospect of being left alone.

'I'm afraid so, but I'll be back as soon as I can. And don't worry, I'll sleep in that chair over there so feel free to use the bed. I'll have a pot of tea and some sandwiches sent up on my way out.' He paused as if there was something more he wanted to say, but clearly thinking better of it, he nodded and quietly left the room.

Annie crossed to a door that led into an ensuite bathroom with a large claw-footed bathtub, much like the one Maggie had had installed in Swan Lane, and she smiled. She couldn't even remember the last time she had been able to have a proper bath and wash her hair, and despite being bone tired she stripped off her wet clothes and slipped into the dressing gown that hung on the back of the door. A little while later, as the bath was running, there was a tap at the door and she opened it to find a young girl there balancing a tray of sandwiches and a pot of tea.

Annie took the tray from her, thanked her and tucked into the sandwiches, which were full of very tasty ham. She ate everything and helped herself to two cups of steaming hot tea before at last sliding into the bath. Once immersed in the steamy water, she sighed with ecstasy. After the cold showers they were forced to endure back at the hospital, this was pure luxury. She washed her hair until it was squeaky clean and after slipping into the nightgown she had packed, she went back into her room to rub it dry in front of the fire, then she brushed it until it gleamed like polished coal.

It was then that the nerves kicked in as she thought of Alex returning. He was the only person she had ever felt attracted to apart from Charlie, and then there was Monty. As she thought about Alex, she realised that while she had opened her heart to him about her past, he had told her very little about his apart from the fact that he lived somewhere in London. She suddenly wondered if he had a sweetheart and was shocked when she realised she didn't like the thought of that.

Crossing the room, she hopped into bed and pulled the blankets up to her chin, watching the door warily. Would he stick to his promise of sleeping in the chair? She was shocked again when she admitted to herself that she half hoped he wouldn't. Alex had awakened feelings in her that she had never known she had, and that she had certainly never felt with Monty. Just a touch from Alex could make her tingle all over and she found herself wondering what it would be like to kiss him and feel his hands on her body.

Angry with herself, she turned onto her side and snuggled down. Dawn was fast approaching by that time and before she knew it the soft feather mattress and the plump pillows ensured that she drifted into a dreamless sleep.

The sound of someone knocking on the door made her start awake and she was surprised to see that daylight was streaming through the gap in the curtains. She was even more surprised to see Alex go to answer it and return with a loaded tray, which he placed on the small table by the window. She hadn't heard him return and guessed that he must have stuck to his promise and slept in the chair.

'Come on, sleepy head. Breakfast's up,' he told her cheerily as he began to pour them a cup of tea each. 'I wasn't sure what you'd like so I ordered us each a full English, I hope that's all right?'

His hair was damp and he was in fresh clothes so she guessed he must have had a shower or a bath. He had shaved, too, and looked so handsome that her heart gave a little leap as she went to join him, very conscious that she was clad only in her nightgown.

'This is lovely,' she told him as he pulled a chair out for her. 'But I'm not even dressed yet. Sorry, I didn't 'ear you come in.'

She stared in awe at the fat juicy sausages and crispy rashers of bacon in front of her. It was a far cry from the lumpy porridge she was used to back at camp.

'I didn't want to wake you,' he answered. 'And by the way, you look beautiful. Did you enjoy your bath?'

'Oh yes, very much.' The words spilled out as she flushed with pleasure. 'Did, er . . . everythin' go all right at your headquarters, and 'ave you 'eard how Leonard is?'

A closed look came over his face. 'Everything went fine and when I phoned the hospital a short while ago, they told me that Leonard has had his operation and is as well as can be expected. I doubt if he'll ever be well enough to return to active service though.' He looked slightly embarrassed then as he explained, 'I'm sorry I can't say more, but you've probably realised that the work I do is very hush-hush.'

'Are you a spy?'

He grinned as he lifted a sausage. 'Sort of, but that's about as much as I can tell you.'

'It's all right, I understand.' They ate in silence for a few moments until she asked, 'Will you be goin' to see your family before we go back? You said they lived in London, didn't you?'

He kept his eyes on his plate. 'Yes, I did, and no I won't. I'm afraid I'm going to have to leave you for most of today and we'll be returning to France late tomorrow evening. But I do have most of tomorrow free, so if there's anything you'd like to do I'd be happy to oblige. I'm afraid many of the theatres are closed but we could perhaps do a little sightseeing?'

'Oh, I'd love that!' Annie's eyes lit up, and he thought again how beautiful she was.

Their eyes locked for a moment and something seemed to spark between them until Alex turned his attention back to the meal, feeling guilty.

'Right you are, it's a date . . . Well, not a date exactly . . .'

He looked so embarrassed that she giggled. 'I understand what you mean,' she assured him, but felt strangely disappointed. Perhaps he didn't feel the attraction she did? After all, he had never been anything other than a perfect gentleman when he was with her. Only time would tell.

Chapter Eighteen

After Alex left later that morning, Annie went shopping. Alex had thoughtfully left her some money as she hadn't thought to bring any with her, which she assured him she would pay back. It had been a long time since she had been able to do any window-shopping, and she enjoyed wandering around the large emporiums that seemed to sell everything a woman could wish for. She sighed at the sight of the expensive evening gowns and thought how wonderful it must be to have places to wear them. She fingered real silk underwear and thought how Belle would have loved it, but all she bought were a couple of cheap novels and magazines to pass the time when she got back to the hotel.

Alex had ordered a light lunch to be served in their room for her when she got back and she tucked into fresh-baked rolls and cheese and ham before settling down to read for a while. It had been a very long time since she had been able to relax so she had another long bath and then had a sleep. She woke feeling refreshed and to find that Alex had returned.

'Oh, you're back,' she greeted him. Reaching for her purse, she handed back the remainder of the money he had left for her.

He frowned. 'I was hoping that you'd treat yourself to something nice.'

'An' where would I wear it back at the 'ospital?' She smiled at him.

'Well, I'm not sure about there, but this evening I'm taking you out to dinner.'

'Oh!' She looked dismayed as she thought of the outfit she had brought with her. It was very drab and out of date. 'But all I have with me is what I'm wearing and a rather old skirt and blouse.'

'You would look beautiful in anything,' he assured her, causing that warm glow in the pit of her stomach again. 'But don't worry, we needn't go anywhere too fancy if it would make you feel uncomfortable. And now if you'll excuse me, I'm going to have a bath.'

Later that evening he took her to a fish restaurant not too far from the hotel, where they dined on fresh fish with a delicious white wine sauce. Alex was dressed in civilian clothes and as he pulled her chair out, Annie was aware of the glances he received from women.

Once they'd finished, he smiled warmly at her. 'Now, how about we go for a stroll along the banks of the River Thames to walk off some of that dinner?'

It would have seemed churlish to refuse so she tucked her hand into the crook of his arm, suddenly very aware of the heat of him through his jacket. The streetlights were dimmed in case of attacks from the air but it only served to give the city a romantic atmosphere as they strolled along looking at the moon reflected in the water.

'Have you decided where you'd like to go tomorrow? I have the whole day free before we go back in the evening.'

'Oh, I'd love to see Nelson's Column and the Tower of London,' she told him without hesitation. 'St Paul's too if we have the time.'

He chuckled. 'And how about we make a little time for some shopping?' he suggested. 'I meant what I said earlier. I'd really like to treat you to something nice after what you've done for me and Leonard.'

'I was only doing me job,' she pointed out.

He shook his head. 'That's as maybe but not many would have risked what you did. You're a very brave young woman and I'm pleased I met you.'

He stopped abruptly and turned her gently to face him, gazing down into her deep blue eyes and for one wonderful moment, she thought he was going to kiss her. But then he seemed to change his mind and abruptly drew her on leaving her feeling strangely cheated.

Once back at the hotel, Annie took her nightclothes into the bathroom to change while Alex ordered cocoa to be brought to their room. He was already drinking his when she came out and he pointed to hers on the small table opposite him.

'Thank you for a lovely meal and a wonderful evening,' she said shyly.

He frowned. 'It's no more than you deserve,' he said shortly, and she wondered if she had done or said something to upset him.

Soon after he lifted a blanket and retired to the easy chair saying, 'Get yourself into bed when you've finished. We've got a big day and a long night ahead of us tomorrow. Goodnight.'

'Goodnight, Alex.' She climbed into bed, but she was very aware of his closeness, and it was a long time before sleep claimed her.

The following morning after breakfast, they set off for their sightseeing trip and there followed a day that Annie knew she would never forget for as long as she lived. They visited all the places she had mentioned, jumping on and off the trams, and she didn't stop smiling all day.

On the steps of St Paul's, they bought seed from an old lady to feed the pigeons and at lunchtime they bought faggots and peas from a street barrow and sat and ate them on the side of an ornate fountain. In the afternoon he took her to Madame Tussauds waxworks and an art gallery where she viewed paintings by all the great masters with awe.

It was growing dark by then, and she was disappointed when he said, 'We shall have to leave soon. I've arranged for a car to pick us up and take us to Dover.' He wasn't looking forward to the crossing, the weather had changed for the worse during the afternoon and thunder was grumbling in the sky above them. Suddenly the heavens seemed to open and grabbing her hand he dragged her into the nearest shop doorway to shelter from the rain.

She was shivering as she leant against his chest, and when he suddenly lifted her chin and his lips came gently down on hers, she did nothing to stop him. As the kiss deepened her arms snaked up and around his neck and she wished that it could go on forever. But suddenly Alex stiffened and, taking both her arms, he pushed her away, his face stricken. 'I . . . I'm so sorry, Annie. I shouldn't have done that!'

Annie felt bemused. It had felt so right and she certainly hadn't minded.

'B-but I liked it,' she told him in a wobbly voice. 'You've nuthin' to apologise for!' The raw pain in his eyes made her feel even more confused.

He turned away and said sharply, 'Come on. We don't want to miss the car.'

Annie had no choice but to follow him, almost having to run to keep up with his long strides. Soon she was breathless and had a stitch in her side but at last he pointed to a car parked outside a warehouse. 'There it is.'

They crossed the road and he opened the back door to let her in before slamming it closed and climbing into the passenger seat in the front. Inside, Annie was crying; somehow something that had seemed so wonderful had turned into a disaster, but she didn't know why. Even so she had her pride and remained tight-lipped as the car pulled away from the kerb and headed to the hotel to pick up their bags before heading out of the city.

The drive seemed to take forever but at last they turned down the narrow lane leading to the small cove they had arrived at. As soon as they had got out, the driver turned the car round and disappeared back the way they had come, leaving Annie and Alex to wait for the boat in the bitterly cold evening air. It was still raining, and she felt cold and miserable, although she would never have admitted it.

Alex led her to the shelter of a small tree but she noticed that he waited well away from her, so she too stood quite still staring across the choppy waves, getting wetter by the minute. At last, after what seemed like a lifetime, they heard the sound of a boat's engine and as it pulled into the cove Alex strode to the shoreline and waited to lift her in.

'It's all right. I'm not afraid of gettin' wet, thank you,' Annie told him curtly. With that she held her small bundle above her head and waded into the freezing waves. Once aboard she headed for the scant shelter at the back of the boat and sat there feeling miserable and humiliated. Alex joined her eventually, but she said nothing as he squeezed into the space at the side of her.

'Look, Annie . . . I . . . I feel I should explain.'

He looked so miserable that she felt herself softening a little.

'The thing is . . .' He was obviously struggling to find the right words. 'The thing is, I shouldn't have kissed you back there because . . . I'm not free to. I . . . I have a wife and child.'

Annie felt as if all the air had been sucked out of her lungs as she stared at him horrified. 'Why didn't you tell me before?'

'I suppose it was because I was so attracted to you, and the more I got to know you the more I felt for you.' He shook his head. 'I should also tell you that my wife and I . . . well, let's just say that we would have parted long ago if it wasn't for Lucy. She's my daughter and she's four years old. Perhaps you'll understand that I could never leave her. She's such a little sweetheart and it isn't her fault that her mother and I aren't compatible. I was quite happy buzzing along the way things were. After all, I'm not home that often and when I do go home it's only to see Lucy. But then I met you and from that very first time I couldn't get you out of my head. That doesn't excuse what I did, of course. I should have told you sooner. But I just want you to know that had I met you first . . . Oh, there's no point in going down that road. What's done is done. But if things had been different . . .'

Annie swallowed the lump in her throat as she avoided his eyes. 'Aw well, thanks fer bein' honest wi' me. At least I know now.' Inside she felt dead. This was the second time she had cared for a man who couldn't return her feelings, and she began to wonder if she would ever get it right, but at that moment the pain she was feeling was so great that she wasn't sure she'd ever want a man again.

Suddenly she remembered something Monty had said to her before he left for war. *We'll have all the time in the world!* He considered her to be his girl but now she knew that she didn't feel for him what she felt for Alex so perhaps it would be kinder to tell him when next they met. She had survived on her own up to now and she was determined that she would carry on doing so.

The journey back was fraught, and she and Alex sat as far apart as they could on the narrow seat, but eventually, as they passed out of a thick sea mist, they caught a glimpse of the coastline. As they neared the beach the boatman killed the engine and they bobbed on the waves while Alex took out a pair of binoculars and began to examine the coastline.

Then suddenly everything seemed to happen at once.

'*Turn around!*' he shouted to the driver in French.

Squinting, Annie could see dark shapes looming ahead of them on the sand. German soldiers. Her heart skipped a beat as she realised they were being fired at.

Within seconds the boat was heading back out to sea, and Alex threw her none too gently into the bottom of the boat and dropped on top of her.

'*Go man, go!*' he screeched as bullets hit the water at either side of them. Annie had never been so afraid in her life and held her breath until at last the mist surrounded them again and the sound of gunshots receded into the distance.

Alex spoke rapidly to the Frenchman again, issuing instructions, before helping Annie back up onto the hard wooden bench. She was bruised from the fall but otherwise none the worse for wear, although she was aware that things could have turned out very differently.

'I've instructed the boatman to take us to our other safe harbour,' Alex told her. 'Someone must have tipped the Germans off. Are you all right?'

She nodded, wrapping her arms about herself. 'Fine, thanks.'

He swiped his hand across his brow and sighed. 'Good grief, that was a little too close for comfort. If anything had happened to you, I . . .'

When his voice trailed away, Annie assured him shortly, 'But it didn't. We were lucky.'

Some twenty minutes later, the boat pulled into another cove and this time all went without a hitch. The Frenchman and Alex dragged the boat onto the beach then led her to a small cottage. From there they would arrange a lift to get Annie back to the hospital.

'I have to go now but, Annie . . . Thank you and take care.'

She nodded numbly, very aware that she was speaking to a married man, and averted her eyes so that she wouldn't have to watch him leave. And then he was gone, swallowed up in the darkness and she had to bite her lip to stop herself from crying, wondering if she would ever see this wonderful man again.

Chapter Nineteen

The sky was lightening by the time Annie struggled out of her sodden clothes and clambered into the bed beside Belle's. The journey back had been long and arduous, and the roads had been so rough that at times she had thought they would never make it back. She crawled into bed, still shaking with shock after her near encounter with the Germans, and though she was chilled to the bone, her forehead was feverishly hot.

I'll feel better after a few hours' sleep, she told herself and fell into a fitful doze.

The next thing she was aware of was Belle leaning over her and gently shaking her arm. 'Annie, Annie are you all right?'

'Wh-what?' Annie tried to lift her head but it seemed to be stuffed with rocks. Her lips were cracked and dry from all the salt in the sea spray and her head was pounding. It hurt to breathe too.

'Right, that's it. Just stay where you are. I'm going to fetch the sister.'

She was vaguely aware of being lifted as dreams filled her head. Charlie was telling her he was in love with a man, then suddenly Alex was there telling her about his family. She tried to push the dreams away – they were just too painful and she never wanted to feel for another man again. And then the darkness came, a welcoming darkness where nothing hurt and she slipped gratefully into it.

'Sister . . . I think she's coming round!'

The voice seemed to be coming from a long way away, and as Annie's eyes slowly blinked open, the pain flooded back.

Belle was leaning over her looking anxious and upset. 'Oh, you've given us a right old scare I don't mind telling you,' Belle said in a choked voice, stroking the damp hair from Annie's forehead. 'I was afraid you weren't going to wake up.'

Annie was disorientated. The last thing she could remember was arriving back at the camp and slipping into bed, then there was nothing.

'Wh-where am I?' she asked groggily.

'You're in the hospital tent. You've been really ill, but don't worry we'll soon have you right now you're awake,' Belle soothed.

The sister appeared at the side of her to take Annie's temperature. 'Welcome back, Nurse Lilburn.' The woman smiled. 'How are you feeling?'

Belle lifted Annie's head and held a glass of water to her lips.

Annie drank thirstily; nothing had ever tasted so good. 'I . . . I ache all over,' she said as Belle laid her back on the pillow.

'I'm not surprised. You've had pneumonia and it was touch and go for a while,' the sister informed her.

Annie was confused. 'How long have I been here?' she croaked.

'A week today. But lie still and rest now. Do you think you could eat anything?'

Annie tried to shake her head but that set it thumping so she lay still again. Her chest felt as if it had a tight band around it.

'Wh-when will I be able to get up and back to work?'

The sister patted her hand. 'I'm afraid there's going to be no work for you for some time, young lady. Once you're well enough we're going to get you shipped back home and, depending on how you are, you can either go to a hospital there to recover or home to your family – if they're able to look after you, that is. Then, when you are better, it will be entirely up to you whether you decide to come back to France. No one would think badly of you if you didn't. You've already gone over and above your duty.'

Annie nodded. At that moment she felt so ill and miserable that she didn't care what happened to her. Once she returned to England, she would never see Alex again and it was almost more than she could bear, although she had accepted that it couldn't be otherwise.

'Meanwhile Nurse Malton will continue to take good care of you,' Sister went on with a smile at Belle. 'She has barely left your side.'

Annie smiled weakly back, but it was getting harder by the second to keep her eyes open and she drifted back off to sleep.

Two days later, Belle approached the bed with an excited grin on her face. 'You've got a visitor.'

Annie frowned. No one here had visitors and she couldn't imagine who it might be.

'You dark horse,' Belle giggled. 'You kept him quiet.'

Seconds later a face she thought she would never see again swam in front of her eyes and Annie felt her heart rate quicken.

'H-hello, Alex. It was good of you to come. 'Ow did you know I'd been ill?'

He smiled and tapped the side of his nose. 'You above all people should know that I make it my business to know what's going on.' His face became solemn as he pulled a chair to the side of the bed. 'How are you now, Annie? The sister told me how ill you've been and I've felt so guilty. That crossing and what happened on the beach was horrendous and I should never have subjected you to it. If anything had happened to you, I wouldn't have been able to live with myself. I'm so sorry . . . for everything.'

'Don't be. I chose to come with you, no one forced me,' she pointed out.

'I, er . . . hear that you're going to be shipped home when you're a little better.'

When she nodded, he dropped his eyes and wrung his hands. 'In that case, I'm glad I had this chance to see you one last time.

And may I just say . . . had I met you in another time and another place things could have been very different.'

A tear made its way out of her eye and ran down her cheek and he reached out and tenderly wiped it away just as the sister bore down on them. 'Right, Captain Gordon, I'm afraid I shall have to ask you to leave now. I can't have visitors upsetting my patients.'

'Of course.' He rose from his seat and stared down at her one last time. 'Goodbye, Annie, and thank you again.'

Her throat was so full she couldn't answer him and could only watch as he turned and strode away without once looking back. And yet she found comfort in the fact that he had admitted he had feelings for her too. They were just two people who had met at the wrong time.

Later that day Annie found out that while she'd been ill, Belle had been given some driving lessons and had taken her place driving the truck each night.

'Please be careful,' Annie pleaded one evening. 'The Germans don't always keep to their promise not to fire when the stretcher-bearers are busy.'

'Oh, don't you get worrying about me. I'm as tough as old boots. It would take more than the Jerries to knock me down.' Even now, as she was about to leave to do one of the worst jobs imaginable, Belle had her lipstick on and a smile on her face. Yet despite her brave words a terrible sense of foreboding came over Annie as she waited for her to come back.

Despite feeling as weak as a kitten and being desperately tired, Annie fought to stay awake until Belle returned later that evening, minus her lipstick and covered in blood. She looked as if she'd been in a battle herself.

'Crikey, before I started, I didn't realise how hard this job was. And the sights you see . . . it's enough to break your heart. There were so many injured today we didn't have time to look for any bodies; we've had to leave the poor buggers where they fell. No doubt the mud will have swallowed them up by this time tomorrow, but the Germans started firing at us and we didn't dare risk going back for any more.'

It was so strange to see Belle without a smile on her face that Annie felt sad for her. She knew first-hand what a horrible job it was. 'At least you made it safely back, that's the main thing.' She squeezed Belle's dirty hand. They had become close friends in the time that they had been there and Annie didn't think she would be able to bear it if anything happened to her. 'Why don't you let someone else take a turn driving tomorrow?'

Belle stubbornly shook her head. 'No, I volunteered for this and I'll see it through for as long as I'm needed. Now you get some rest while I go and try to clean up a bit. I just hope I'll be able to get the stench of blood out of my nostrils.'

The next morning, when the sister came to check Annie's temperature, she was pleased with her progress. 'I've written to your parents this morning to inform them that all being well you will be being shipped home sometime next week. Whether the letter will get there before you do is another matter entirely. Once you're home, you'll be able to recharge your batteries.'

'Thank you, Sister.' Annie had never told anyone there except Belle that Levi and Maggie weren't her real parents; she had seen no reason to. And now she began to feel a little excited at the prospect of returning home. She wondered how they all were. She guessed that Charlie would be heartbroken at losing Peter – that is if he even knew – but she was looking forward to seeing him again all the same. She was looking forward to seeing everyone, apart from Reggie. Hopefully he'd have joined up by now so wouldn't be there to bother her.

Once again that evening she forced herself to stay awake until Belle returned, but the clock kept ticking long after she and the rest of the stretcher-bearers should have been back, and the feeling of foreboding that had hung over her like a black cloud increased. And then suddenly she heard a ruckus at the end of the ward and looking towards it she saw a soldier covered in blood speaking to the sister. The man was clearly traumatised and Annie watched the sister race out of the tent.

After what felt like a lifetime she returned, clearly very upset and, Annie was shocked to see, looking even paler than some of the patients. Annie struggled up onto her pillows and tried to catch the sister's eye, but the woman was clearly avoiding looking at her until at last she realised it could be put off no longer and she slowly advanced down the ward.

'Nurse Lilburn . . . Annie . . . I'm afraid I have some very bad news for you.' There was a catch in her voice and Annie could have sworn she saw a tear in her eye. The woman had always been so professional and had never addressed her by her Christian name before, so Annie knew that it must be something very bad and she had an awful idea what it might be.

'Is it Belle . . . Nurse Malton, Sister?'

The woman took a very deep breath and tried to pull herself together. 'I'm afraid it is. While the stretcher-bearers were carrying the injured to the truck, the Germans opened fire and it seems that many of them were shot.'

'I-including Belle?'

'We don't know for sure yet. Some of the soldiers and doctors have gone back out there. We should know more when they get back.'

She turned and walked away and the terrible wait began. Only four of the twelve stretcher-bearers were brought back alive, but they had all suffered injuries. The rest of them, including Belle, were dead.

Annie sobbed for most of the night for the friend she would never see again and now more than ever she longed to go home and for this hateful war to be over. Belle had been so beautiful; so young and full of life with her whole future ahead of her and it all just seemed so pointless.

Belle had always spoken very lovingly of her parents and Annie could only guess how heartbroken they would be when they received the telegram telling them of Belle's death. She promised herself that as soon as she was home and well enough, she would go and see them personally, and with the sister's blessing she would return the few personal items Belle had brought with her. It was the last thing she would ever be able to do for her friend.

Chapter Twenty

The following week the ward sister came to say goodbye to Annie as the patients who were being shipped home were loaded into the back of the ambulance that would take them to the ship. 'Goodbye, Nurse Lilburn, and thank you for all your hard work. You truly have gone far beyond the call of duty and you will be missed. I do hope you decide to come back.'

Annie gave her a weak smile. She was much better but still far from fully recovered and she just wanted to be back home now. The loss of Belle and Alex had affected her badly.

Luckily the crossing was comparatively calm compared to the last one she had made with Alex, and Annie slept for most of the way, only waking when they arrived at the dock where she was transferred to an ambulance that would transport her home. Again, she dozed and when she woke it was to find she was almost home.

'Not long to go now and you'll be back with your family,' the kindly nurse who had accompanied her told her. 'We've just got to drop Private Higgins here off in Bedworth and then we'll be taking you.'

The young private in question had barely spoken a word the whole journey, as he wondered how his young wife and family would react to seeing him with only one leg. But as it happened, it appeared he needn't have worried. When they rushed out to greet him, they were just grateful he was still alive.

''E'll find it hard to adjust,' Annie said sadly.

The nurse nodded in agreement. 'Happen he will but at least he's come back, unlike many of his friends.'

The next stop was Swan Lane and as the nurse went to knock on the door, Annie chewed her lip, wondering what sort of reception she was going to get. There was no one looking out for her, which told her they probably hadn't received Sister's letter. Through the open back of the ambulance, she was surprised to see Peggy answer the door and when the nurse told her why, her face lit up in a wonderful smile.

'Annie . . . she's *really* home . . . oh, this is wonderful.' She was down the path in a second and climbing into the back of the ambulance where she showered Annie with kisses as tears streamed down her cheeks. 'Eeh, pet, we've been so worried about you. What's 'appened?'

'I'll explain everything once we're inside,' Annie promised as the ambulance men lifted her down and carried her into the house.

Maggie was in her usual chair, rocking to and fro, and didn't even look up as Annie said goodbye to the men and the nurse, and thanked them for getting her safely home. Then came the questions. Annie explained that she'd had pneumonia, although she was careful not to speak of how she had caught it.

Peggy couldn't stop smiling. 'Aw Levi, Eve and Ellie will be tickled pink when they get in to find you 'ere,' she gushed. 'Now let me go an' get yer a nice hot cup o' tea. An' how about a bite to eat?'

Although she had slept for most of the journey, Annie was still worn out and she sank back in the chair as Peggy rushed away to get a warm rug to tuck about her legs. 'Just a drink please, Peggy,' Annie answered, wondering why Eve and the others would be coming there after work. And why hadn't she mentioned Charlie?

Peggy filled her in on everything that had gone on while Annie was drinking her tea. 'We 'ad to close the shop an' Maggie weren't copin' very well. Then things got worse after Charlie disappeared, so I agreed to move in and take over runnin' the house. He took the news o' Peter's death really hard an' just upped an' left wi'out a word. So, I just work part-time at the munitions factory now so Maggie ain't left on 'er own fer too long, and it seems to be pannin' out all right. Oh, and did I mention that we're expectin' a new addition? Eve is pregnant, the little 'un is due in April. Although the sparkle's gone from it cos she got a telegram to say that Davey were missin' in action.'

'Oh no, poor thing, she must be worried sick,' Annie said sadly. 'And 'ave you 'eard how the others are? Barney, Harry and Monty?'

'Not for a while, but they were all right the last we 'eard of 'em. Oh, an' there's sommat else yer should know.' She glanced towards Maggie and lowered her voice before going on, 'Susan 'ad a little girl back in June but there's only me an' Levi as knows about it as yet. She didn't tell Maggie. Even Theo didn't know about it. She came 'ere to stay till she were too far along fer him to make her get rid of it. But then he went an' done a bunk cos he were afraid o' bein' called up, an' as far as I know he's still missin'.'

'Good grief.' Annie could hardly take it all in. She looked over at Maggie. 'And how about her?'

Peggy tutted. 'She ain't good, as yer can see, bless 'er. Now, you just finish that drink an' get some rest. You ain't as far through as a line prop an' I'm gonna get you right, my girl.'

As Peggy had predicted, Levi, Eve and Ellie were thrilled to find her there when they got back, although they were concerned when they heard how poorly she had been.

'At least I'm on the mend now which is more than I can say for my friend Belle,' Annie told them, breaking down in tears again.

It was almost three weeks before Peggy deemed Annie fit enough to visit Belle's parents and pass on her belongings, and although they only lived just along the road it required a tremendous effort on Annie's part. She had started to do little jobs about the house to help Peggy but she soon tired and was beginning to realise just how ill she had been.

Belle's parents were devastated at their daughter's loss, particularly as their son was now missing too and when Annie left them her heart was heavy.

Christmas was quiet that year, as those with loved ones away fighting didn't feel much like celebrating, but Peggy did them proud with the Christmas dinner she cooked and they all made an effort for Ellie. The New Year was much the same, but in January things got worse. Until then the army had relied on volunteers to fill the ranks. Over two million men had enlisted but as the war dragged on and the casualties piled up, more were needed, so the Commons passed the controversial Conscription Bill, making serving in the armed forces compulsory for all single men between the ages of eighteen and forty-one.

'Huh! I don't reckon this will go down very well wi' Reggie next door,' Levi commented as he read it in the newspaper.

'Why should he not 'ave to do 'is bit when all our lads are away fightin'?' Peggy responded as she rolled out pastry for a pie. She had little time for Reggie, particularly as he'd started to bother Annie again. It seemed that every time she so much as set foot out of the door, which wasn't often, he was there.

Although there had been no news for some time from Barney or Harry, Annie did have a letter from Monty, and she was relieved to hear he was safe. She was also concerned about what might happen when he came home, for since her kiss with Alex she had realised that although she cared for him, the love she felt for him was more like that she might feel for a brother, whereas when she had spent time with Alex she had somehow felt more alive. Just a smile from him had been enough to set her heart pounding, and she had tingled from head to foot every time he touched her. And that kiss . . . She sighed as she thought of it and what might have been had he not already been married. Nothing could ever come of the feelings she had for him, but it was time to be honest with Monty. It wasn't fair to keep him hoping that she felt the same as he did.

In his letter he had told her he had been with the British Expeditionary Force that had been fighting in Gallipoli since April the year before, but thankfully he and the other allies had been lifted from the beaches of Anzac Cove and Suvla Bay safely in December. He wrote that he was now back in the trenches in France, although he couldn't tell her exactly where, as all the soldiers' letters were heavily edited before they were posted.

'At least we know one of 'em is safe – or at least he was when he wrote that letter,' Levi commented. 'Oh, an' by the way, I 'eard on the grapevine that Weddington Hall is goin' to be made into a military hospital fer the duration o' the war. They've begun on it now by all accounts.'

Annie's ears pricked up. If the hall was indeed to become a hospital they would need nurses. Perhaps this could be an alternative to going back to France? She knew it would be hard to go back there now that Belle was gone. She said as much to Peggy.

'Don't you even *think* o' goin' back to work yet, my girl,' she warned with a glare. 'You still ain't completely better an' until you are you'll do as yer told!'

'Yes, Peggy,' Annie agreed meekly, but already she was seriously thinking about it.

Finally, by the start of February, Annie felt well enough to think of working again, and so one rainy cold day she set off for Weddington Hall. On arrival there she found people buzzing around carrying beds and equipment inside.

'Who should I see about coming to work here?' Annie asked a young woman in a nurse's uniform as she was walking past with an armful of blankets.

She nodded towards the enormous hallway. 'Try Matron's office. First on the left just inside,' she called over her shoulder as she headed for the staircase.

Annie paused to straighten her hat and make sure her hair was neatly tucked away before tentatively tapping on the door she'd been directed to.

'Enter,' a voice called and stepping inside Annie found herself in a large office. The matron, a plump middle-aged woman in a stiff white apron and cap was busily scribbling away at an enormous leather-topped desk and she glanced up to ask, 'May I help you?'

'I'm 'opin' so.' Annie told her why she was there and what she had been doing in France.

When she had finished the woman nodded her approval. 'Excellent, we need as many people like you as we can get.'

Annie beamed. She hadn't realised how easy it would be. 'When do you think the 'ospital will be ready to open?'

The matron waved her hand airily. 'That's irrelevant, my dear. We need as many hands on deck as we can get right now. That's if you don't mind working to get everything ready for the first influx of patients?'

'I don't mind,' Annie assured her.

'Good, in that case would tomorrow be too soon?'

'I reckon that'd be all right.'

'Then welcome aboard. Report to the housekeeper tomorrow morning at eight o'clock sharp.'

Annie walked out with a smile on her face. It would be nice to feel she was doing something useful again. She hurried home to tell Peggy the good news, but had only just entered the kitchen when the back door opened behind her and Susan appeared carrying a child in her arms.

'Sus—' The joyous welcome died on Annie's lips as she stared at Susan's face. One of her eyes was black and blue and completely closed, her lip was split, and she had another large bruise on her cheek.

'Good grief, yer look like you've done ten rounds in a boxin' ring,' Peggy muttered as she rushed forward to take the baby from Susan's arms. She was ghastly pale and looked like she might collapse at any minute.

Annie quickly led Susan to a chair and pressed her gently down into it before rushing away to fill the kettle and put it on to boil.

Even Maggie, who usually seemed oblivious to everything going on around her nowadays, looked concerned.

'So . . . what's gone on?' Peggy asked.

Susan started to cry, great gulping sobs that took her breath away. 'I-it was Theo,' she choked. 'But it was my fault.'

Peggy scowled. She couldn't abide men who beat their women. 'And what did you do that were so bad to give 'im licence to do this?'

Susan hung her head. 'As you know, I didn't tell him about the baby until it was too late to get rid of her. But then when I got home, he'd disappeared and I didn't see him for months. And then he just turned up out of the blue. I think he wanted somewhere to hide once he found out that all single men were going to be called up. Anyway, when he saw the baby, he just went mad and told me it was either him or her. He wanted me to take her and leave her on the steps of the workhouse . . . but I couldn't do it.'

'And nor should you 'ave to,' Peggy declared indignantly, staring down into the sleeping baby's face. She was certainly a bonnie little girl with the look of her mother about her, but she also saw there was something a little different about her.

'Anyway, when I refused, he . . . he . . . Well, as you can see, he lost his temper. I waited until he was asleep and snuck out. He said that she should have died at birth . . . that she wasn't normal. I just hope he doesn't think to come here looking for me.'

Peggy's eyes flashed fire. 'Let the bugger come, that's what I say! An' I promise yer if he does, he'll go out quicker than he come in wi' my foot up his arse, the bloody *coward*.' Her face softened as she looked down at the infant. 'An' does she 'ave a name?'

'Constance.'

Annie came over to look at the baby and smiled. 'Oh, she's adorable. No wonder you couldn't think of getting rid of her. I know what it's like to be left at the workhouse an' I wouldn't wish it on anyone.' As the memories of the loveless years she had spent there began to press in on her, she hurried away to make the tea.

'I was hoping that Levi might let me stay here for a while,' Susan went on. 'The trouble is, I've brought very little with me. I just had to grab what I could and get out of there while I had the chance.'

'Oh, don't worry about that,' Peggy told her. 'We've still got clothes that'll fit the pair of you at the shop. We've 'ad to close it fer a while, see, cos o' the war. When Eve gets in this evenin', I'll get her to pop round there an' sort yer some things out. They won't be quite what yer used to o' course, but beggars can't be choosers, eh?'

'I'll be glad of anything just so long as Constance is safe,' Susan said humbly. 'But why are you and Eve staying here? And I thought you were away nursing in France, Annie.'

They spent the next hour catching up on all that had happened since they had last seen each other.

'Crikey, so our Maggie and Levi have been rattling around in this place and now suddenly it's full again. Are you sure there's room fer me and Constance? I can pay my way, I promise you.'

Peggy patted her shoulder. 'It would be fuller still if we gave in to Flo and let her in, but Levi knows that she just wants to come an' be waited on and get free lodgin's,' she chuckled. 'And don't forget we're only 'ere till this war is over an' then me, Ellie an' Eve will be goin' back to our own places. But I'm pretty sure Levi will say you're welcome to stay 'ere fer as long as yer want. You are family after all.'

They were distracted from their conversation by the sight of Maggie leaning over the chair where they had laid Constance. Her face was animated and she was gently stroking the baby's cheek.

'Well, I'll be . . .' Peggy was shocked. Recently Maggie had been oblivious to everyone and everything around her, but she certainly seemed to have taken a shine to Constance.

The little girl woke shortly after and Peggy went to make her some pobs, but when Susan went to feed them to her, Maggie asked quietly, 'May I?'

'Of course.' Susan handed the dish to her and propped the baby up amongst the cushions, then watched closely as Maggie lovingly fed her.

'She'll need a clean binding now,' Maggie told them when the child had cleared the dish. 'Did you bring any with you, Susan?' It was the most she had said for weeks.

'Er . . . yes, I grabbed a few before I left. I'll just get one for you if you're sure you want to do it?'

'Of course I am.' Maggie grinned as she lifted Constance onto her knee and the baby smiled up at her. She really was a placid little soul.

Peggy and Maggie exchanged a glance as Susan rushed away to get the binding. Peggy silently prayed that this might be a turning point for Maggie. Not that she was holding her breath just yet. Maggie had been the same with Ellie when she had first brought her home from the workhouse and look how that had turned out. Still, she could hope.

'Right, young lady, while Maggie sees to the little 'un, let's get yer face cleaned up a bit, eh?' Peggy said to Susan when she returned with the binding. 'An' then we'll go up an' sort a room out fer you an' the baby. I think Ellie's old crib is still up in the loft, so I'll get Levi to fetch it down after he's had his dinner this evenin'.'

Susan smiled her thanks. She was broken-hearted at the way Theo had treated her but at least she and Constance would be safe here – for now at least. Despite what she had said to Peggy when she first arrived, deep down she was hoping that Theo would regret his actions and come looking for them before he had to go and fight, but only time would tell.

Chapter Twenty-One

Bright and early the next morning, Annie set off for her new job. She was looking forward to having something to do again. On arrival she reported to Matron who directed her to an enormous room that was being transformed into a ward. Rows of beds had been placed along either side of it and it would be Annie's job to get them all made up with crisp white sheets, pillows and blankets. Two of the downstairs rooms were being turned into operating theatres and men were busy carrying in operating tables, large lights and all manner of medical equipment. The drawing room downstairs would become a day room overlooking the lawned gardens, but there would also be one on the first floor for the less mobile patients.

Annie finished work at five o'clock and set off for home feeling as if she had achieved something, but her happy mood disappeared as she turned the corner into Swan Lane and saw Reggie Taylor-Lloyd walking towards her with a miserable face and his hands thrust deep into the pockets of his smart overcoat. Annie briefly thought of crossing the road but it was obvious he had seen her, so she put her chin in the air and marched on.

'Not going to speak then?' he said sarcastically as she drew abreast and made to pass him. 'Not even to hear the news about Monty.'

Annie stopped abruptly and faced him. 'What news?' she asked bluntly.

He smirked. 'I thought that'd stop you. Mother had a telegram this afternoon. Apparently, your mate is being shipped home with serious injuries.'

The breath caught in Annie's throat. 'Wh-what sort of injuries?'

He shrugged. 'All we know is he's been shot. They'll be taking him to a military hospital in Southampton when he's fit enough to travel. *If* he survives, that is.'

He looked at Annie's shocked face and grinned. 'I hope you'll be as concerned if the same thing happens to me. I dare say you've guessed that I'll be going next. No choice in the matter. I've told them I'm a conscientious objector, so they'll be using me as a driver or a stretcher-bearer.'

Annie knew very well he was just a coward but was too polite to say so. Instead, she said shakily, 'Would you ask your mother to let me know when Monty is back, please? I'll try to go and see him when he's well enough for visitors.'

'Hmm, can't promise she'll do that,' he chuckled. Then he walked on, whistling.

Annie's shoulders sagged. Poor Monty; he was such a kind soul and she dreaded telling him that there was no future for them. Still, at least he wasn't dead, she tried to comfort herself.

When she arrived back at the house, she found Maggie down on the rug in front of the fire playing with Constance, who was happily kicking her plump little arms and legs in the air and giggling contentedly. The smell of cottage pie filled the kitchen, making Annie's stomach rumble with anticipation, and Peggy was in good spirits, although Eve and Susan still seemed sad. They were both thinking of the men they had lost.

'How did it go, pet?' Peggy asked as she entered the room and hung her cape on the nail at the back of the door.

'Very well; I've been makin' beds up all day but I'm afraid I've just 'eard some bad news about Monty.' She told her what Reggie had said.

Peggy sighed. 'I dunno, it seems to be allus the good 'uns that cop it. What did he say were wrong wi' him?'

'He didn't,' Annie said worriedly, and then, 'Do yer think I should go round an' ask Mrs Taylor-Lloyd?'

'Ooh, I don't know about that, pet.' Peggy scratched her head. 'Yer know that woman 'as no time fer the likes of us. She'll likely just send yer away wi' a flea in yer ear.'

Annie chewed her lip. Peggy was right, but even so, Monty was very dear to her and she was gravely concerned about him.

'I'm gonna risk it anyway,' she decided, and before Peggy could say another word she was up and out of the door.

She went to the back door of the Taylor-Lloyds' house as she guessed that the lady of the house wouldn't take kindly to her knocking at the front, and the timid little maid answered it.

'I, er . . . was wonderin' if I might 'ave a word wi' yer mistress?' Annie wasn't feeling quite so brave now, but she stood her ground.

'I'll go an' ask, miss.' The maid closed the door and when it opened again, Mrs Taylor-Lloyd was standing there.

'What do you want, girl?' she asked abruptly.

'Reggie told me Monty's been injured,' Annie said quietly. 'I was wonderin' if yer knew what had 'appened to 'im?'

The woman sucked in her breath, her back as straight as a ramrod. 'Reginald had no right to speak about our private business,' she said tartly. 'And what has happened to Montgomery is no concern of yours, so please leave.' And with that she slammed the door in Annie's face. It was no more than Annie had expected, so she slowly crossed the yard and went home again. All she could do now was hope that Monty would write to her.

By the beginning of April, the hospital was almost ready to take its first patients. There were now five wards housing fifty-five beds on the first floor, although because there was still room for many more these would be added to as the need arose. They were each named after the people who had contributed to funding them. There was the Griff Ward, the Arley Ward, the Hall and Philips Ward, the Birch Coppice Ward and the Haunchwood Ward.

Dr Wolfendale and Dr Nason would be the doctors responsible for the patients' care and the Red Cross commandant

Mrs Fowler would be the matron. It was she who had encouraged Annie to continue her training before going to France and now that she had all her certificates, Annie hoped she would be an asset to the hospital

Meanwhile life was becoming more difficult for everyone. Although Nuneaton was as yet untouched, there had been Zeppelin raids on eight counties, killing twelve people, and now everyone lived in fear, wondering when it would be their turn.

Food prices were rising alarmingly – bread was now tenpence a loaf – and there were often queues outside grocers' shops, where it was a case of first come first served. As well as the food shortages the newspapers reported that there were to be no more imports of spirits, pianos or motor cars until the war was over.

Luckily, Peggy was well able to produce healthy meals from almost nothing and everyone who lived in Swan Lane counted themselves lucky to have her.

Abroad there were concerns about the rising number of venereal diseases being reported, as the camps were known to be frequented by prostitutes. The young men, lonely and far from home, were easy targets and drugs were being shipped out to them to try and combat the disease.

Annie often thought of Alex and wondered if he was safe. She wondered about Charlie, Harry and Barney too, but there had still been no word from them. She could only pray that wherever they were they were safe.

On a brighter note, the arrival of Constance seemed to have had a wonderful effect on Maggie, who was slowly becoming much more her old self, although there were still times when she would chatter away to Penny. And then one evening, shortly after arriving back from a hard day's work at the hall, Annie noticed that Eve was flushed and very quiet.

'How are you feeling?' she asked as she poured herself a cup of tea.

Eve had been forced to quit her job in the munitions factory the month before because of severely swollen ankles. She was the size of a house and hadn't slept well for days.

'Oh, I'm all right.' Eve gave her a weak smile as she rubbed at her back and tried to get comfortable on the chair. 'It's just a bit of backache. It's all this extra weight I'm carryin', I expect. I've forgotten what me feet look like.'

Annie and Peggy exchanged an anxious glance. Peggy had assisted in more than a few births when she lived back in the courtyards, where most people couldn't afford doctors or midwives, and it looked to both of them that Eve's time was very close. They were both concerned when they thought back to what had happened to Eve's last baby. But they didn't want to alarm her, so they said nothing but kept a close eye on her.

Much later that evening, as Peggy and Annie were clearing the table after dinner, Eve gave a little gasp and clutched at her stomach.

'Oh dear.' She looked embarrassed. 'I reckon me waters 'ave just broke!'

'It's looks like it, me girl,' Peggy told her calmly, glancing down at the little puddle on the floor. 'But as yer know, it's nuthin' to panic about. Let's get yer upstairs an' get yer comfortable, eh?'

She grinned as she looked at Levi, who had turned a sickly shade of white.

'Oh dear . . .' Eve gulped. 'But I don't feel ready yet.'

Peggy chuckled. 'Well, ready or not if it wants to come it'll come. It stands to reason what goes in must come out. Now come on, let's get yer up them stairs right now.'

Eve had gone as white as a sheet as she thought of the baby she had once lost. Unlike this one, that baby had been forced upon her by Mr Taylor-Lloyd, who she had worked for. She had fled to live with Susan in London to escape him before returning to live with Peggy shortly before the baby was born. And then when the child was born, she had blamed herself for its death because she hadn't wanted it. She had lived with that guilt ever since. The only good thing that had come from that time was the fact that she had met Davey in London and he had turned out to be the love of her life. But now, she wondered, would she lose this child too? She didn't think she would be able to bear it if she did.

Peggy and Annie followed close behind Eve as she mounted the stairs, but only halfway up Eve had to stop and grip the banister as another contraction took her breath away.

'What if I lose it?' she gasped.

Peggy gave her a gentle prod in the back. 'Just cos it happened before don't mean it's gonna happen this time,' she said sensibly. Once in her room, Annie laid wads of newspaper on the bed before they gently lowered Eve onto it.

'Ow, I'd forgot 'ow much it hurt,' Eve wailed as they helped her into a nightgown. Peggy turned to Annie. 'I want yer to start timin' 'ow far apart the pains are. This is her second baby an' they tend to come quicker than the first, but there's no point in sendin' fer the midwife till she's nearer her time.'

Levi, meanwhile, was downstairs prowling up and down like an expectant father.

A long hour later Eve was having contractions every three minutes. 'Right, go down an' tell Levi to get some water on the boil an' ask Susan to bring up as many clean towels as she can find. Then you nip an' tell Nurse Borne she's needed, there's a good gel,' Peggy instructed.

Annie shot away as if the hounds of hell were snapping at her heels. Despite her training, she had never delivered a baby and she didn't want to start now.

The midwife lived in Fife Street and was a regular sight thereabouts as she visited new and expectant mothers on her bicycle. But that evening Annie was out of luck when her husband opened the door and told her apologetically, 'I'm sorry, me duck. She just got called out to another delivery. She could be hours yet. Shall I ask her to come round when she gets back?'

'Y-yes please.' Annie was panicking now, so after giving him the address she made for the doctor's house but got the same response there. 'I'm sorry, he just finished his evening surgery and he's out doing house calls now. He could be anywhere and I've no idea how long he'll be.'

Annie thanked her and hurried back to Swan Lane where she found an anxious Levi still pacing the floor.

'Is the midwife on 'er way, pet?'

She shook her head. 'I'm afraid not. At least not fer some time. I left messages fer both 'er an' the doctor so let's just 'ope Eve don't 'ave this baby anytime soon.'

She rushed back upstairs and told Peggy the news. Peggy shook her head. 'Looks like we'll 'ave to deliver it ourselves. She's almost there an' this baby ain't goin' to wait to be born for no one!'

'*Us* deliver it?' Annie was horrified.

'Well, I don't see nobody else 'ere who can help us.' Peggy patted her hand before rolling her sleeves up. 'Don't worry, I'm sure you've seen enough blood an' guts while yer were workin' abroad. This'll be easy-peasy. It's the most natural thing in the world so long as there's no complications.'

Eve let out an agonised wail and they both turned to her. Sweat stood out on her forehead and she gasped, 'I feel like I wanna push.'

'Then let's do it, pet,' Peggy told her as she hoiked Eve's nightgown up to her waist and bent down to look how far along she was. 'Ah, wonderful, I can see the baby's 'ead crownin'. Now on the next pain give me a long hard push. That's a good girl.'

Annie watched in fascination as Eve put her chin on her chest and pushed for all she was worth.

'That's it, that's it,' Peggy encouraged as Eve gripped Annie's hand. 'An' again on the next one, yer doin' just fine. This baby'll be 'ere afore yer know it.'

Ten minutes later Eve's son was born, and tears of joy ran down their faces. He was the picture of health, screaming lustily, and the absolute double of his father.

'Oh Eve, he's just *beautiful*,' Annie told her emotionally as Peggy deftly cut the umbilical cord and wrapped him in the towel Annie held ready. He was then passed to his mother as Peggy waited for the afterbirth to come.

Eve looked radiant as she gazed down at her wonderful son. 'He looks just like his dad,' she said in awe.

'An' so he should.' Peggy was thrilled for her. 'Have yer thought of a name yet?'

'I was hopin' that Davey would be 'ome an' we could choose one together,' Eve said with a catch in her voice as she thought of how proud Davey would have been.

Neither Peggy nor Annie knew quite how to respond so they remained silent. They could only imagine how Eve must be feeling. It was such a precious moment and she loved Davey so much.

Eve clung on to the baby while Peggy and Annie cleaned her up and changed the bed and her nightgown before suddenly announcing, 'I'm gonna call him Jack, an' his middle name will be David like his dad's.'

'It suits him,' Peggy told her, just as the door flew open and Nurse Borne appeared.

She gaped at the sight of the new mother and Annie giggled, 'Thanks fer comin', Nurse Borne, but yer a bit too late.'

'So I see, but now I am here I may as well give mother and baby a check-up to make sure everything is all right.'

Minutes later the nurse departed after confirming that everything was just as it should be, and Levi and Susan were allowed upstairs to see the new addition to the family. They all fell in love with the little chap instantly, especially Susan, who said he would make a wonderful playmate for Constance when he got a little older. Even Maggie made her way upstairs to meet the baby, and stared down at him with tears in her eyes.

Eve had a glow about her, although her happiness was marred by the fact Davey wasn't there to meet Jack, but all the same she thanked God that this time the birth had gone well. Whatever happened now she would always have a piece of Davey with her.

Chapter Twenty-Two

The following afternoon, as Annie was arriving home after her shift at the hospital, she was shocked when Mrs Taylor-Lloyd, who had just got out of a cab, approached her. Normally the woman avoided the Lilburns and anyone connected to them like the plague as she considered them too far beneath her to bother with, but today she had a smug expression on her face.

'Have you heard that my Reginald is to become an officer?' she asked.

Annie blinked. He'd told her that he'd had no choice but to sign up and was going to become a stretcher-bearer.

'He's training at Sandhurst,' Mrs Taylor-Lloyd went on. Annie didn't much care what happened to Reginald, although she wished him no harm. She was only concerned about Monty.

'His father and I have bought him a commission,' the woman went on. 'I wish we had done the same for Montgomery, but he insisted on doing it his way.'

Annie was at a loss what to say as the woman sailed past her and she hurried along the side of the house to the kitchen where she told everyone what Mrs Taylor-Lloyd had just said.

Peggy guffawed. 'God help any poor sods he's in charge of. He couldn't organise a piss-up in a brewery. He's half-cut most of the time if he's still anythin' like he used to be. An' one thing's fer sure, he'd never have made an officer if his mammy an' daddy hadn't paid for it. Still, the good thing is 'e won't be 'ere to bother you anymore.'

Levi nodded in agreement.

'How are Eve and the baby?' Annie asked as she slipped her cape off.

Peggy beamed. 'Absolutely lovely, the pair of 'em. Would yer believe Eve wanted to get up today! I told her, you're stayin' there fer at least five days, me girl. But what sort o' day 'ave you 'ad?'

'We're just doin' all the last-minute jobs before the patients start to arrive. We've been told today that they'll be coming towards the end of next month. I reckon I'm gonna 'ave a couple o' weeks when I won't be needed, so I was thinkin' I might get out on Dobbin and see if I couldn't do a bit of collectin'. We're still payin' rent on the shop and if I only collect a fraction of what we used to, at least it'll give us a bit more stock for when we can open again. A trot out will do Dobbin good as well, he's gettin' fat bein' out in the paddock all the time.'

Levi sighed. 'There's no need for you to do that. It could be years till this war finishes an' we can open again, despite what they said at the start of it. Things are just goin' from bad to worse if yer can believe what yer read in the papers. Why don't you just take a couple of weeks off an' rest up, pet?'

Annie shook her head. She had never been one for doing nothing, besides, it left too much time for brooding, as she'd discovered when she'd been convalescing. During those long weeks, she'd started thinking obsessively about how her birth family were faring during the war. It was funny, while she'd been in France, she hadn't given them much of a thought – she hadn't had the time. But once she was home, she had again taken to looking through the possessions that had been left with her on the steps of the workhouse. The need to find them was strong, although she still didn't have a clue how she might go about it. But even so, she would sit late at night, holding the beautiful shawl and wondering what the woman who once wore it might have looked like. Was she short or tall, dark or fair? They were all questions that plagued her, but she knew she might never find out.

At the beginning of May the nurses at the hospital were told they would not be needed again until the twenty-fifth of the month when the first patients were due to arrive. It was over three weeks away, so bright and early one morning Annie donned her old breeches and harnessed Dobbin to the cart.

Maggie had always been horrified when she had worn trousers – she didn't even approve of the new straighter ankle-length skirts women were favouring – but Annie put them on regardless. They were so much more practical for hopping on and off the cart and she had never been a vain person.

However, this time when she came downstairs in them Maggie barely raised an eyebrow. She was too intent on feeding Constance her breakfast. Eve had been up and about for some time now and with two babies to see to each morning it was always hectic. But the good thing was, Maggie was never on her own anymore, which was a relief to everyone.

Peggy was due at the munitions factory for one of her shifts later that morning and as Annie passed her on her way to the stables, she gave her a wink and followed her out.

'Things must be lookin' up.' Peggy grinned. 'Her ladyship didn't even bat an eyelid when yer appeared in them old breeches. Anyway, good luck, pet. I'd best be off else I'll be late an' me supervisor is an old tartar. Ta-ra fer now.'

Annie clambered up onto the bench seat of the cart and set old Dobbin in motion and soon they were rattling up Tuttle Hill towards Mancetter and Atherstone. Dobbin was much slower than he used to be and despite her urging tended to go at his own pace, but he was so much older, so she supposed it was to be expected. She had no doubt that if and when the war was over, they would have to retire him and look for a younger horse. This made her think of Spirit, and her eyes filled with tears. It was doubtful that she or any of the other horses that had been taken to work in the war would ever return. The papers regularly reported that many were being killed in battle, and it hurt her to think of such a gentle horse having to endure such vile conditions.

When she finally reached Mancetter she began door-knocking. Surprisingly, she did far better with her collection than she had expected. At the bigger houses the women who were slaves to fashion were discarding the full-length, fuller skirts for the more modern style, so by mid-afternoon she had quite an assortment on the back of the cart.

Peggy oohed and ahhed over them when she got home. 'We can alter a lot o' these,' she decided. 'We can make some o' the dresses into shorter, straighter skirts, an' make the tops of 'em into blouses. Then when we finally open the shop again, we'll have some fashionable stuff to sell.'

Levi thought it was an excellent idea. He missed doing his rag-and-bone rounds dreadfully but like the rest of the men who were too old to be called up, he was more than willing to continue his driving job and feel that he was doing his bit.

The next three weeks flew by, and Annie found she had colour in her cheeks again after being on the cart in the fresh air each day. Soon, though, the morning of the twenty-fifth dawned and she dressed in her Red Cross uniform ready for duty again.

The first lot of patients arrived at Weddington Hall mid-morning and were stretchered inside to the wards. Some of them had been sent to convalesce while others were in need of operations. Suddenly the previously empty rooms rang with chatter and the sounds of footsteps. During the day the male orderlies would help those fit enough to get down the stairs and outside to sit on the lawns in the sunshine. Matron, who was a cheerful, kindly soul, encouraged patients' visitors to come whenever they wanted, insisting that a visit from a loved one could work more magic than any tonic, and very soon everyone was enjoying the calm, easy atmosphere of the place.

In the day rooms the fitter men played cards and chess or read books from the selection that had been placed in there for them. Many of the younger ones flirted shamelessly with Annie, but while she always had a ready smile, none of them interested her.

Her heart still belonged to Alex, and she began to wonder if it always would.

One night she arrived home to find a letter waiting for her and her heart began to thump as she recognised the handwriting. It was from Monty.

'Come on now, don't keep us in suspense, gel?' Peggy urged impatiently. 'What's 'e have to say?'

Annie grinned. 'If you'll just let me get in, take me cape off an' sit down I'll open it an' tell you.'

They all clustered around as she took a seat and slit the envelope before withdrawing a single sheet of paper. She cleared her throat and read aloud.

Dear Annie,

I don't know if or when this note will reach you but I guess you will have heard that I've been injured by now, and I didn't want you to worry. I was injured some time ago and spent a lot of time in a field hospital, but I am now in the military hospital in Southampton and improving. I know it's a big ask, but if you aren't still in France, I would welcome a visit. It can get pretty lonely here. Mother and Father came to see me last week but to be honest Mother cried so much I felt worse when she left than when they arrived. I pray every day that you are safe and well and of course I shall understand if you can't get to see me. Perhaps you could write instead if you can spare the time? Anyway, that's enough of me rambling on. I shall look forward to hearing from you one way or another. Take care.

With much love,
Monty xxx

'Huh! that didn't tell us much!' Peggy snorted in disgust. 'He didn't even tell yer where he was shot or 'ow bad it is.'

'You know what Monty's like – 'e wouldn't want to worry us.' But Annie was worried. She'd dealt with enough patients to know that only the worst of them were sent back to hospitals in England.

'So will yer go an' see 'im?'

Annie chewed on her lip. Monty was very dear to her but she knew that sooner or later she would have to tell him that she didn't want to be his girl anymore. Even so, she had a soft heart, so eventually she nodded.

'I've got the day off on Sunday. If I got a train Saturday night I could find somewhere to stay overnight then visit 'im in the mornin' and set off back 'ere fer work on Monday in the afternoon.'

Peggy and Levi nodded their approval. They were both fond of Monty and hated to think of him being injured.

'If I could get petrol for the car, I'd drive yer there, but it's as rare as hen's teeth at the minute,' Levi said.

'I'll be fine on the train, I promise.'

Levi wasn't altogether happy about her going all that way on her own, but then, he was always worrying about her, and Southampton was a lot safer than France!

The following Saturday Annie took a change of clothes to the hall with her and as soon as her shift was over, she put on her civilian clothes and set off for the train station. Later, as the train click-clacked along the tracks she wondered what state she might find Monty in the next day.

It was very late that night by the time she arrived in Southampton, and she was stiff from sitting on the hard seats for so long. Gripping her small carpet bag in one hand, she left the station and made for one of three cabs that were waiting outside.

'Could you tell me where I might find a cheap room fer the night?' she asked the elderly cab driver.

He smiled at her. 'It just so happens I can. Me sister runs a small boarding house not far from 'ere, though she ain't had much trade lately. Hop in an' I'll take you round there.'

Soon the cab drew up outside a small house in a terrace whose front doors opened directly onto the street. It wasn't grand but Annie noticed that the lace curtains and the front doorstep were scrupulously clean.

The driver banged on the door and it was opened by an elderly lady with her hair in metal curlers wearing a nightgown with a shawl about her shoulders.

'What you doin' here at this time o' night, our Fred?' she scolded. 'I'd just gone to bed.'

'Stop moaning, Mabel, I've brought you an overnight lodger here. A young lady. You wouldn't want to see her walkin' the streets now, would you?'

She peered at Annie and shook her head. 'I suppose not. You'd best come in, me dear.'

Fred turned to leave but Annie caught his arm to thank him and to ask, 'How much do I owe yer?'

He waved his hand. 'Ah, forget it. It's only a hop, skip an' a jump from the station.'

'Thank you, you're very kind.'

'I've got a granddaughter about your age an' I would hope that someone would do the same for her,' he muttered, clearly embarrassed. ''Tain't safe for young women to be wanderin' the streets at this time of night, especially in places they don't know. Goodnight, me dear.'

Annie watched him gee the horse up and move off before following the woman into the little house.

'Now, dear, would yer like a hot drink an' a sandwich before I show you up to your room?' Mabel offered.

Annie had been travelling all day and she stifled a yawn as she shook her head. 'Thank you, but I'd rather just get some sleep, if yer don't mind.'

The woman nodded and led her up the stairs to a room that overlooked the street. It was small but cosy, and a bed had never looked so inviting. A pretty flowered bedspread covered it and floral curtains hung at the window.

'Will this do yer, dear? I'm afraid the privy is in the backyard and we don't have an inside bathroom, but I'll bring you up a jug of hot water in the morning and there's a chamber pot under the bed.'

'That's fine, thank you.' Annie gave her a grateful smile.

'In that case I'll leave you to it. I can see you're jiggered. I'll be back in the morning with hot water, and breakfast will be at eight o' clock, if that suits?'

'That will be perfect,' Annie assured her as she put her bag down and the woman left her to get ready for bed.

Annie was excited and apprehensive all at the same time at the thought of seeing Monty the next day and doubted she would sleep a wink despite being tired, but within minutes of her head hitting the pillow she fell into a deep sleep and only woke when the landlady knocked on her door the next morning.

'Sleep all right, dear?' the woman asked as she handed Annie a steaming jug of water.

'Like a log, thank you.'

'Good, good, well, get yourself washed and come down when you're ready. Breakfast will be in about twenty minutes.'

The meal was excellent, there were fat juicy sausages, mushrooms, crispy slices of bacon, fried eggs and as much toast as Annie could eat, along with a large pot of tea.

'Good grief.' Annie stared at it in amazement. 'I haven't seen a breakfast like this since before the war.'

The landlady winked and tapped the side of her nose. 'Aw well, rationing doesn't really affect us around here. We look after each other, if you know what I mean.'

As soon as she'd finished Annie went to her room to pack her few possessions and after paying Mabel, the kindly lady drew her a little map to help her find the hospital.

'Normally you could catch a bus at the end of the street that would take you almost straight to the hospital, but being a Sunday I'm afraid there aren't any running. It's not so far as the crow flies, though, especially on a lovely morning like this.'

Annie chewed her lip. She hadn't taken into account the fact that perhaps the trains wouldn't be running on a Sunday either. When she asked Mabel about it the woman shook her head.

'I doubt there will be any trains at all today, dear,' she told her. 'But you're more than welcome to come back here if you need to and you can catch one early in the morning.'

'I'll have to, and thank you.' Annie's heart sank. It would mean she wouldn't get back into Nuneaton until well into the afternoon the next day and Matron wasn't going to be too pleased, but there was nothing she could do about it. She would just have to explain to her and hope she understood. 'In that case will it be all right if I just leave my bag here? There's no point taking it with me if I'm comin' back.'

'Of course, give it here, I'll go and put it back in your room,' Mabel said kindly. 'And I'll do you an evening meal as well. It's no bother as I'll be cooking for meself anyway.'

It was indeed a beautiful morning and under other circumstances she would have felt like she was on a little holiday with the seagulls dipping and diving in the sky above her and the smell of the sea air. But she still had no idea just how badly hurt Monty was so she was too apprehensive to enjoy the walk. She just hoped that whatever his injuries were, they wouldn't be something life-changing like a lost limb.

Chapter Twenty-Three

She got lost a couple of times on the way to the hospital, so it took her almost an hour to get there, but at last she saw a large stately home, not dissimilar to Weddington Hall, perched high on a hill overlooking the sea, and she quickened her steps. The house was surrounded by rolling lawns and she could see some of the patients sitting outside in bath chairs enjoying the sunshine.

In the foyer, a nurse was sitting at a desk making notes and Annie went over to her.

'Good morning, I've come to see Montgomery Taylor-Lloyd.'

The nurse gave her a friendly smile as she lifted a book from a drawer in the desk and looked through a list of names.

'Ah yes, here he is. Take a seat, miss, and I'll go and find out where he is for you.'

'Thank you.' Annie did as she was asked, and watched the nurses scurrying about. It was a very bright and airy house and Annie couldn't imagine anywhere better for a patient to convalesce.

The nurse returned a few minutes later. 'Second Lieutenant Taylor-Lloyd is in the garden, miss. Would you like me to take you to him? And then I'll organise a tray of tea for you.'

'Thank you very much.' Annie gave the nurse a smile and followed her through a labyrinth of corridors until at last they reached double doors that led out to the lawns.

The nurse paused and scanned the men outside before pointing towards a large oak tree. 'There he is. He's sitting in the shade.'

Annie thanked her again and set off across the grass, feeling self-conscious as some of the other patients watched her progress. Monty was sitting in a bath chair in his dressing gown with a rug tucked about his knees as he stared pensively out to sea, so he didn't see her approach until she was almost upon him and said gently, 'Hello, Monty.'

His head whipped about and a radiant smile lit his face. 'Why, Annie, what a lovely surprise. No one let me know you were coming.'

She smiled as she bent to peck his cheek, noting how pale he looked. He had lost a lot of weight too, but she didn't comment on it. 'I didn't get your letter until a few days ago so there was no time to write back and tell you. How are you feeling?'

He sighed. 'Not too bad. I've had a couple of operations and another scheduled for tomorrow, but I'm getting there.'

She was relieved to see that at least all his limbs appeared to be intact.

'What happened?'

He grinned ruefully. 'Afraid I got peppered with a land mine. They've got most of the shrapnel out now, apart from one or two pieces.'

'Why didn't they get it all out at the same time?' Annie frowned as she sat down on a chair close to him.

'Apparently it was too risky till I got a bit stronger. The pieces that are left are very close to my heart but hopefully tomorrow that'll be all of them gone and I can get properly better.'

'Let's hope so. An' I couldn't 'elp but 'ear the nurse call you second lieutenant. Well done for climbing the ranks so quickly.'

He chuckled. 'I could have been an officer if I'd let my parents have their way. They wanted to buy me a commission, but I wanted to earn it myself. They told me that they've bought one for Reggie, so who knows, if I ever get back out there, I might find I'm under his command, God forbid!'

Annie chuckled too. 'I know what you mean. I pity the poor chaps he's put in charge of . . . er, sorry, I shouldn't 'ave said that.'

Monty shrugged. 'You're only telling the truth. Our Reggie is very good at dishing orders out but not so keen on doing anything himself, yet Mother thinks he can do no wrong. But anyway, that's enough about that. Tell me what you've been up to. I've missed you so much!' He took her hand and gazed at her lovingly.

Annie flushed and told him about her time in France, although she omitted to tell him about her sea crossings for the Resistance. The less anyone knew about that the better, even Monty.

'I dare say I'd still be there if I hadn't been ill.'

The nurse arrived just then with a tea tray and a plateful of shortbread straight out of the oven.

'Looks like they feed you all right here,' she commented as she strained the tea into two cups.

He nodded. 'They're marvellous, actually. How long are you here for?'

She grinned. 'I made a blunder. I intended to go back on the last train this evening, not realisin' they wouldn't be runnin' on Sundays, so now it looks like I'll 'ave to go back first thing in the mornin'. Matron isn't going to like it, but never mind. I'll make the time up to her.'

'Actually, Mother and Father are coming to see me this afternoon. You could perhaps have a lift back with them in the car? I don't know how they've managed to get hold of any petrol.'

'Oh, I don't think they'd be too keen on that idea,' Annie said quickly. 'Your mother wouldn't even tell me 'ow you were when I asked.'

Monty flushed. 'I'm sorry. I know what a snob she is. Now tell me what's going on with everyone else next door. Any word from Barney or Harry yet?'

The next hour flew by, and they were both surprised when the nurse appeared to say, 'Sorry to disturb you, sir, but lunch is ready. Would you like me to wheel you in? And would you care to join him, miss?'

'Oh no, no thank you,' Annie answered hastily. Monty's face fell and she felt guilty. She'd been hoping to tell him how she felt, but the right moment hadn't presented itself and now it was too late. 'I really ought to be goin'.'

'Will you be coming back later?' he asked hopefully, catching her hand again.

Annie patted the back of it. 'I don't think that would be a very good idea if your mam an' dad are comin'.'

'I suppose not,' he said glumly. 'But when will I see you again?'

'Hopefully when you've 'ad all your operations and they send you 'ome to recover. I'm working at Weddington Hall now, so we'll be next door to each other again.'

He released her hand reluctantly and the nurse began to wheel him back towards the hospital. Just before he went inside, he turned to wave and she waved back, then with a sigh she set off back for the town.

The next morning Annie was on the first train bound for home. She had spent a pleasant afternoon and evening with Mabel, who seemed glad to have someone to talk to, but now she was keen to get back and face Matron. Annie couldn't imagine that she was going to be too pleased with her.

When she entered the house, little Jack was crying as Eve prepared to feed him and Constance was demanding to be picked up by Maggie, who was still besotted with her little niece. Peggy and Levi were at work, and Susan looked relieved when she walked in. 'Oh, here you are,' she said. 'We were expecting you back last night and were gettin' worried.'

'Sorry.' Annie explained about the trains not running and headed for the stairs. 'But I can't stop, I'm just goin' to change then I'm going to work. I've got an 'orrible feeling Matron is going to be cross because I didn't turn in this morning.'

'I'm sure she'll understand when you tell her where you were,' Susan told her.

When Annie arrived at the hospital, she was proved to be right.

'Very well, Nurse Lilburn. You weren't to know that the trains weren't running but don't let it happen again. Now hurry along, you're on Griff Ward today, and be prepared, we've had some new patients in, so it's rather busy.'

Annie was surprised when she opened the door of the ward to find there were at least twice as many patients as there had been the last time she'd been there.

'Ah, extra help, wonderful,' the ward sister greeted her. 'And just in time to serve afternoon tea. Could you see to that please, Nurse?'

Annie hurried away feeling like she was being thrown in at the deep end, but at least it would mean she was kept busy. A lift had been installed to help those in wheelchairs and trolleys to get from the ground floor to the first, and soon Annie pushed the tea trolley into it and headed back to the ward.

'What will it be? Tea or coffee?' she asked the patient in the first bed cheerfully. 'An' 'ow about a lovely slice of Cook's delicious sponge cake, or there are jam tarts if you'd rather?'

The poor chap's head was so heavily bandaged that he looked like a mummy. Only his lips and eyes were visible. *Another burn victim by the looks of it*, Annie thought sadly. Once she had served him, she moved on to the next bed, glancing at the patients' name charts hanging on the ends of the beds as she went. She was about halfway down the other side of the ward when she again glanced at the bed's occupant's name chart and a shiver ran up her spine. *First Lieutenant Leonard Fairbrother*. Shock coursed through her as she thought back to the night she had crossed the Channel with Alex and a patient who had suffered a serious leg wound. But surely this couldn't be the same Leonard Fairbrother?

One glance at his ashen face told her that it really was him and she gasped. 'Lieutenant Fairbrother.' Her voice came out as a squeak, and he opened his eyes to look at her. 'D-do you remember me?' She was whispering now and as he stared at her he looked as shocked as she did.

'Of course I do. I'm not likely to forget that night in a hurry,' he responded quietly.

'But I saw Alex before I left France an' he told me you were recovering in a hospital in London?'

'I was, but I managed to get well enough to return to Belgium. Then a damned infection set in. If they can't clear it up this time it looks like the old leg is going to get chopped off and that'll be the end of my career.'

'That will be a last resort,' she told him as she started to pour him a hot drink. She was so flustered she hadn't even thought to ask him what he preferred. 'The doctors here are brilliant, so you're in very good hands.'

'Alex told me you'd been ill and were coming back home,' he said. 'But I didn't expect to see you here.'

'I live in Nuneaton.' She placed his tea down, along with a sizeable slice of cake. Then as she caught the sister watching her, she quickly turned. 'I'd best get on. Sister 'as 'er eagle eye on me and she won't want to see me givin' preferential treatment to anyone. I'll try and get back for a chat after my shift.'

Her heart was hammering. There was so much she wanted to ask him. Had he seen Alex lately? Was he all right? But it would have to wait until later.

After tea duty it was Annie's turn in the sluice room, a job that none of the nurses liked. Still, it had to be done so she donned some rubber gloves and got on with the pile of dirty bed pans. It was only then that she allowed herself to admit how often she thought of Alex. She could see his face as clearly now as she had on the first night she'd met him. Not that it could ever come to anything. He had a wife and child and he was an honorable man so would never leave them. With a sigh she finished her job and went to see what the sister had lined up for her to do next.

Chapter Twenty-Four

'You're quiet tonight, hinny,' Levi commented that evening as Annie sat with Peggy altering some of the clothes she had collected for the shop. 'Not worrying about young Monty, are you?'

'No, not at all. As I told yer I reckon he's gonna be fine.'

'Hmm, and no doubt eager to get home to you,' Levi teased. 'A blind man on a gallopin' hoss can see that he adores the ground yer walk on.'

'I'm sure that ain't true,' Annie said more sharply than she'd intended, and instantly felt guilty as Levi's face fell. 'Sorry, I'm just a bit tired after all the travellin' an' work an' what not. I reckon I might go up now. I've got another early start tomorrer an' I don't want to upset Matron again.' There'd been no chance to speak to Leonard again without drawing attention to the fact that she knew him, and that was the last thing she wanted. To the people in the hospital, he was just another wounded soldier, and for his and Alex's safety they must keep it that way. Even so, she was longing to ask for news of Alex and barely slept that night for thinking of him.

There were bags under her eyes when she came down to breakfast the next morning and Peggy peered at her.

'Are you feelin' bad again?' she asked, placing her hand on Annie's forehead. 'I reckon yer doin' too much. If you ain't at the hospital yer out on Dobbin tryin' to get stock fer the shop.'

'I'm fine. I just didn't sleep very well.' She grabbed a quick cup of tea and minutes later was out of the door.

'Now that's what I like to see, Nurse,' the matron said approvingly as she entered the hospital earlier than usual.

Annie smiled and hurried on. Hopefully she would have time for a quick word with Leonard while the night shift was changing over to the day shift.

'How are you feelin'?' she asked when she reached his bed. He was having very strong doses of painkillers and was having the wound washed out regularly with antiseptic. She thought he looked slightly better.

He nodded. 'Not too bad, all things considered, although I have to say you don't look too chipper.'

She grinned and before she could stop herself rushed on, 'I was wonderin' . . . 'ave you seen anything of Alex recently?'

'I last saw him a few months or so ago. We were working in Belgium,' he confided. 'But this damn knee started flaring up again, so I got shipped back.'

'And is he well?'

'He was the last time I saw him. He mentioned how ill you'd been in France and said that he'd been to see you before you got sent home.'

He gave her a knowing look and she felt colour flood up her neck and into her cheeks. Besides working together, Leonard and Alex were good friends. Leonard had guessed some time ago that Alex had feelings for this girl by the way he spoke about her and now he sensed that Alex's feelings were returned. But he also knew that Alex would never desert his wife and child. It was a bloody shame. Alex's wife was a right little flirt and he deserved better, but that was only his opinion.

'I, er . . . I'd better get on. Is there anything I can get you?'

When he shook his head, she hurried away, hoping she hadn't made a complete idiot of herself.

She was still thinking of Alex when she got home after her shift, but the second she walked through the door she knew something dreadful had happened. Peggy was sitting in the chair rocking to and fro with a bleak expression on her face, and when Annie raised her eyebrow enquiringly, Susan pulled her to one side and told her in a low voice, 'Peggy had a telegram earlier on. Her youngest, Tom, has been killed in action, bless him. She's heartbroken.'

'Oh no. She's only just beginning to get over losing Frank.' Annie's heart ached for Peggy as memories of all the young men who she had nursed and lost in France flooded back. There would be no family funeral for them or Tom. He would be laid to rest in a row of graves in France amongst all the others with just his name on a small wooden cross.

Crossing to Peggy, Annie gently laid her hand on her shoulder and whispered tentatively, 'I'm so very sorry, Peggy. There's nothing I can say to ease what you must be feeling but, well, we're all here for you.'

The words had barely left her lips when there came a banging on the back door and they all started.

'All right, all right, keep yer 'air on I'm comin',' Annie shouted as she rushed to answer it. A tall, good-looking man almost exploded into the room and Annie gasped. 'Theo!'

Susan's head snapped up as she heard his name and a mixture of emotions crossed her face.

'Th-Theo!'

Without a word he crossed to her and took her hands. 'I thought you'd be here. I . . . I had to come; I couldn't keep away any longer. I've been *such* a fool, Susanne. Can you ever forgive me?'

Tears started in Susan's eyes as she stared back at the love of her life. She so desperately wanted to believe him, but he had hurt her so many times in the past and now she had Constance to think of.

'But you . . . you told me that I either got rid of our daughter or we were over.' Her voice came out as a croak.

Seeing her distress, Annie quickly stepped in. 'Why don't you two go into the front room where yer can talk in private? I'll keep me eye on Constance.'

Susan gave her a grateful smile and led Theo through the hall door.

Eve and Annie glanced at each other. 'I 'ope the lousy swine don't talk 'er into goin' back wi' 'im,' Eve said bitterly. 'I wouldn't trust that bloke as far as I could throw 'im.'

The back door opened yet again and this time Flo breezed in.

'I'm afraid now ain't a very good time, Flo,' Eve said shortly. She couldn't stand Flo at the best of times let alone right now when there was so much going on. 'Peggy's 'eard today that 'er Tom 'as been killed an' Susan is in the lounge with Theo.'

'Ooh, so he's turned up 'as he?' Flo's eyes grew round in her plump face – she loved a good bit of gossip. The only trouble was that anything she learnt would be all around the town in no time. 'An' I'm sorry to 'ear about Tom, ducks.' She patted Peggy's hand, but the poor woman was in shock and didn't seem to register that she was there. 'I reckon a cup o' 'ot, sweet tea is what she needs,' Flo commented. 'An' I wouldn't say no either if yer makin' one.'

Annie sighed and went to put the kettle on, while Flo took a seat. She was sure the woman's skin was as thick as that of a rhinoceros.

'What's 'is Lordship come for?' Flo asked as Annie laid out some cups and saucers.

'I 'ave no idea,' Annie said curtly. 'And it's none of my business, which is why I said they should go into the front room to speak in private.'

'Ooh, 'ark at little Miss La-Di-Da!' Flo sniffed, but showed no sign of leaving. 'An' 'ow is our Maggie?'

'As you see.' Annie nodded towards Maggie, who was dozing in the chair with Constance fast asleep on her lap. As she poured out the tea, she kept an eye on the door leading into the hallway; all was quiet but she couldn't help but feel nervous. Theo had been off the scene for some while now and Susan had appeared to be settling, but would his visit reignite the feelings she might still have for him?

After a moment's quiet, Flo dropped the next bombshell. 'I, er . . .' She slurped at her tea. 'I find meself in a bit of a pickle,' she said cautiously. 'An' I were wonderin' if any of yer could see yer way clear to lendin' me a few bob? The thing is, that no good 'usband o' mine 'as gone an' got the sack an' I need some money to pay the rent see?'

Eve tutted. They all knew what a waster Flo's bloke was. 'Then you need to tell 'im 'e'll just 'ave to get off 'is fat, idle arse an' get hisself another job, won't yer?' She'd seen how Flo constantly scrounged off the family but for her to even think of doing it today of all days, when Peggy had received such dreadful news, was unforgivable.

Flo tutted indignantly. 'Chance 'ud be a fine thing. He's buggered off an' left me, just like that!' She clicked her fingers. 'Wi' not a thought of 'ow I'm supposed to manage.'

'In that case *you'll* 'ave to get up off yer fat idle arse an' I'll see if I can get yer on at the munitions factory where I work,' Eve said unsympathetically. She had gone back to work part-time shortly after Jack was born and ever since, she and Peggy had worked opposite shifts so they could share the childminding between them.

'*Me* go to *work*!' Flo looked as if Eve had told her she had to face a firing squad. 'But who'd look after the 'ouse if I were to do that?'

'Lot's o' women 'ave 'ad to go to work wi' their men away fightin'. Me included, an' I don't even know if my man is gonna come 'ome!' There was a catch in Eve's voice. Davey was still classed as missing but while that lasted, she clung on to hope.

Flo looked hopefully towards Annie, but she too shook her head. 'I can't 'elp, Flo. Till the shop opens again I'm livin' on what I saved afore the war and me nurse's wage, sorry.'

'In that case don't be surprised if I end up on yer doorstep 'omeless.' Flo slammed her cup down on the table, splattering tea everywhere. 'It's a poor look out when families can't 'elp each other!' And with that she rose and left, slamming the door so loudly behind her that it danced on its hinges.

Annie anxiously bit down on her lip. It seemed that everything was happening at once.

'Now don't you go frettin' over Flo,' Eve said angrily. 'We've got enough troubles of our own at the minute wi'out tossin' hers into the pot. She'll manage. Her sort allus do, one way or another. But I stand by what I said. She should get up off her fat, idle arse an' get 'erself a job. We've all 'ad to.' Her voice broke and tears welled in her eyes, and Annie knew she was thinking of Davey.

The hall door opened and Susan appeared looking flustered. 'I, er . . . wondered if you'd keep your eye on Constance for me for a while?' she said timidly, wringing her hands nervously. 'Theo has booked into the hotel in town and he wants me to go back there with him so we can have a good talk.'

'Yer can do that 'ere, can't yer?' Eve frowned, and Susan flushed. 'Don't you go lettin' 'im sweet talk yer into goin' back to 'im now, will yer? He's never showed a scrap of interest in Constance an' you'll just be lettin' yerself an' the little 'un in for another load o' heartache, you just mark me words. Leopards don't change their spots!'

'Actually, I think he has changed. He's really sorry for the way he's treated me, but I promise I won't make any rash decisions till I've heard everything he has to say.'

'Go on. I'll keep an eye on Constance,' said Annie.

Susan's face lit up and she hurried away to fetch her bonnet and coat.

Eve shook her head. 'Things are goin' to end badly if she takes 'im back, you just see if I ain't right,' she sighed.

Chapter Twenty-Five

Peggy was having a lie-down when Levi returned from work, and his heart broke for her when he heard of her loss. He went upstairs straightaway to see if she was all right, but she didn't answer his knock, and sensing she wanted to grieve in private, he returned to the kitchen, only for Annie to tell him of Theo's visit.

'Has she forgot the state she were in when she came back last time?' He frowned.

'It seems she 'as.' Eve began to dish up the meal. 'But she's a grown woman, so all we can do is advise 'er. Now let's eat an' then me an' Annie 'ave got to get the nippers ready fer bed. Fer some reason I ain't expectin' Susan back any time soon. Oh, an' by the way, Annie, I forgot to tell yer: be on yer guard. Reggie is 'ome fer a few days afore he gets drafted abroad. I seen 'im earlier on struttin' about like a peacock in 'is smart uniform.'

Annie groaned aloud but said nothing. Hopefully she wouldn't have to see him.

Late that evening, when Annie retired to bed, Susan still hadn't returned, so Eve took Constance into her room to sleep with her and baby Jack. Annie had offered to have her but as Eve pointed out, she would need to be up early the next morning for her shift at the hospital.

'Anyway,' she grumbled. 'I'd expect 'er to come back this evenin' even if she's late. Yer can't just clear off overnight when you've got a baby to look after.'

Annie hoped she was right and eventually fell into a deep sleep.

The next morning, once she had washed and changed into her uniform, Annie went downstairs to find Susan and Theo already in the kitchen deep in conversation over a pot of tea.

Not wanting to interrupt them she said, 'Can't stop, early shift today. I'll see you both this evening. Ta-ra fer now,' and hurried out. She had almost reached the end of the road when she saw Reggie striding towards her with a newspaper tucked under his arm. She groaned. He did indeed look very smart and handsome in his officer's uniform, but she still found him completely unappealing. There was no point trying to avoid him, though, so lowering her head, she quickened her steps, hoping he would let her pass without comment. But on that she was sorely disappointed, as he said pleasantly, 'Morning, Annie. Off to work, are you?'

She swallowed before answering quietly, 'Yes I am, an' I don't want to be late, so you'll 'ave to excuse me.' She moved past him and was annoyed when he turned and fell into step beside her.

'I hear you went to see our Monty.'

'Er . . . yes, yes, I did. Have you heard how he is?' She forced herself to be civil.

'According to Mother, he'll be coming home quite soon. She can hardly wait. But I'm afraid his army days are probably over, whereas mine are just beginning. I've got two more days off before I'm shipped out to Belgium.'

'But I thought you said you were a conscientious objector and would only go as a driver or a stretcher-bearer?' Annie smirked.

'Ah . . . Well . . . that was before my parents offered me the chance to be an officer.' He puffed his chest out with importance.

'Gave you the chance to show off, you mean. But anyway . . . I hope all goes well for you.' Annie was hoping he would leave her then, but he continued to walk at the side of her making her feel increasingly uncomfortable, especially as he was being so friendly.

'I was wondering . . .' He licked his lips before going on, 'If I couldn't tempt you to come out with me either tonight or tomorrow evening?'

'I'm afraid I'm really busy at the moment.' Annie quickened her steps but still he kept pace with her.

'I'm only asking you out for an evening, I'm not asking you to marry me!' There was a sharp note in his voice but Annie remained firm.

'And as I explained, I'm rather busy at present, but I'm sure there are any number of girls who'd be willing to go out with you. I'm just not one o' them. Bye, Reggie.'

He stopped abruptly, and she was painfully aware of his eyes burning into her back as she hurried away. She made it to the hospital in record time and reported to the ward early.

'Ah, Nurse, could you administer some painkillers to Lieutenant Fairbrother; I'm afraid he's had rather a restless night.'

'Of course.' Annie fetched the trolley containing the medications and wheeled it to Leonard's bedside. She found him looking pale and listless.

He smiled weakly as she passed some strong painkillers to him with a drink of water.

'Bad night, was it?'

He nodded. 'Yes, but the doctor just came and said it's to be expected. I just want to get out of here and back to work.'

'All in good time.' She smiled at him. 'There's no point leaving until we've got you right, otherwise you'll just have more problems and be back to square one.'

'I know that but it's so damned frustrating lying here. Me and Alex were a team, and he must be struggling on his own.'

'I'm sure he'll manage,' Annie told him, and hurried away with the trolley.

It was particularly busy that day, with an influx of patients who all had to be assessed, and Annie's feet barely touched the ground as she rushed from one job to another. Lunch was out of the question – there was far too much to do – but eventually at three o'clock the sister told her, 'Get yourself off to the staff room and have a break, Nurse. Everything is under control now.' Yet more beds had been brought into the ward and the new patients were now as comfortable as they could make them.

When she returned after having a welcome cup of tea, the patients' visitors were beginning to trickle into the ward and she noticed someone sitting with Leonard. Her heart began to thump so loudly that she was afraid someone might hear it. She could only see the visitor from behind but the way he held himself and the broad shoulders looked very familiar. The man was in uniform, although he had removed his peaked hat, and she moved towards them, trembling slightly. And then she was next to him, and as he looked towards her, her heart did a somersault.

'A-Alex. How are you?' She was afraid she might be dreaming but she blinked and when she opened her eyes again, he was still sitting there.

'Annie, Leonard told me in his last letter that you were here. I was hoping I'd see you.'

Her mouth had suddenly gone dry and she couldn't think of a single word to say.

'How about you go and fetch us both a cup of tea, Nurse?' Leonard suggested with a grin to break the awkward silence.

Only too glad to escape, Annie nodded. 'Of course, and perhaps when I come back, we could get you into a wheelchair and take you along to the day room where you can speak more privately.'

'Excellent idea,' Alex said.

By the time she returned bearing a tray of tea and cake, Alex had already located a wheelchair and manoeuvered Leonard into it. Annie led them along the seemingly endless corridors until they reached the day room. There were a few other patients with their visitors in there but the room was large, so she led them towards one of the huge bay windows overlooking the sprawling lawns.

'Right . . . I'll, er . . . leave you to it.' Annie placed the tray on a small table between them.

Alex nodded. 'Thank you, Annie. Could we have a word before I leave?'

'It's rather difficult while I'm on duty,' she answered truthfully.

He nodded in understanding. 'Then what time do you finish? I could perhaps walk you home, or better still I could take you for a meal somewhere.'

'I finish my shift at six o'clock but I'll still be in my uniform,' she said nervously. 'But we could perhaps go and sit in the park for a while?'

'Sounds perfect.' The smile he gave her made her go weak at the knees, and she turned and hurried back to the ward.

The rest of the afternoon seemed to pass incredibly slowly, but at last it was time to leave.

Alex was waiting outside the main doors for her and when he saw her his face lit up. He took her hand and tucked it through his arm.

'Right, Nurse Lilburn, if I can't tempt you into coming out for a meal with me, you'd better show me the way to the park.'

Annie was very conscious of the warmth of his arm through his jacket as they walked. And it was then that the hopelessness of their situation hit her afresh. She had fallen for someone she could never have and the thought of him with his wife brought jealous tears stinging to her eyes.

'So, how have you been? Are you completely recovered now?'

His voice brought her back to the present and with an effort she pulled herself together and blinked back the tears.

'Yes, thank you. I'm quite well now,' she answered primly.

'Good . . . actually I'm glad I managed to see you for more reasons than one,' he said tentatively.

She raised an eyebrow in query.

'The first, obviously, is that I've been worried about you and I wanted to see you,' he began. 'But the second reason is because I have a proposition to put to you.'

'Oh?'

He cleared his throat. 'The thing is, I'm still making those undercover trips with injured agents across the Channel, and to put it bluntly I haven't been able to find another nurse willing to risk it, which has resulted in . . . well, let's just say some of the injured men haven't fared so well. So, I was wondering, would you consider coming back to work in France? You needn't necessarily go back to the hospital. The French Resistance would hide you in one of their safe houses and, believe me, you'd be invaluable to them, and to me.'

Annie looked shocked and he hurried on, 'I know it's a big ask and I'll quite understand if you don't feel you can do it. I'd be a liar if I told you there was no risk involved because you know there is. And I don't need to tell you what happens to members of the Resistance if they are caught. But what I will promise is I'll do all I possibly can to keep you safe. So, will you at least consider it?'

Annie couldn't have been more stunned. This was the last thing she had expected and as she thought back to the trips she had made in the small boats in pitch darkness and rough seas, she shuddered.

'I-I'm not sure.'

'Of course, it's something you have to sleep on, and as I said I'd quite understand if you didn't want to come . . . But I really hope you will.'

'But what would I tell my family?'

'We would tell them you're going back to the hospital as a Red Cross nurse. I shall be leaving in two days' time, and should you decide you're willing to do it, you could come back with me. No one is going to take any notice of a nurse and an army officer travelling together, and once we are back in France you would be taken to the safe house.'

'All right, I'll sleep on it.' Annie's mind was in turmoil. She wanted to say yes just so she could see Alex from time to time, but would that be setting herself up for even more heartache? Not to mention the risk she'd be taking working for the Resistance.

They walked on in silence until they reached the Leicester Road bridge that crossed Trent Valley Railway Station. Alex drew her to a halt to look down at the trains below and they watched the passengers come and go for a moment. Most of them were soldiers lucky enough to have a few days' leave, others were just setting out to join the war with no idea of the carnage that lay ahead of them.

'Poor young sods; you'd think they were going on holiday, wouldn't you?' Alex sighed. He knew the majority of them would never return.

After a walk in the park, Alex took Annie home, promising he would see her again the next day at the hospital. She had an awful lot of thinking to do and not a lot of time to do it, she thought as she watched him walk away. It was going to be a long night.

Chapter Twenty-Six

The next morning, Annie woke from an uneasy sleep still nowhere nearer to reaching a decision. There was still no sign of Peggy who was usually up first, so Annie made a pot of tea and took a cup up to her.

Levi sensed that something was amiss the second he set foot in the kitchen. 'Bad night?' he asked, looking at the dark shadows under her eyes.

She nodded. They were the only two people up and she decided to confide in him. She knew that whatever she said to him would go no further.

'Hmm!' He stroked his chin when she had finished. 'I have to admit I don't like the idea of you puttin' yourself at risk again,' he admitted. 'But you're a plucky young thing. Just promise me you'll give it careful thought and don't go makin' a decision you might regret.'

'I promise.' She reached across the table and squeezed his hand. At that moment Susan appeared with Constance in her arms looking worried and their conversation came to an end.

'What's the trouble?' Annie asked. They had all noticed that Constance wasn't developing as quickly as other children her age, but they adored her none the less.

'She was a bit breathless in the night.' Susan dropped a kiss on the baby's broad forehead. 'The doctor did warn me that she had a heart murmur when she was born. It's common, apparently, with children born with this condition, but I think I'll get her checked out today just to make sure it hasn't got any worse.'

Levi nodded in agreement before glancing at the brass clock on the mantelpiece and hastily finishing his tea. 'I'd best be off else I'm going to be late.'

'I think I'll get off as well,' Annie said as she too rose from the table. 'I'm a bit early actually, so I might just call into the shop on me way and make sure everythin's all right.'

Annie entered the shop through the back door in the yard and after having a quick check around to ensure that everything was as it should be, she made for the kitchen to leave the way she had come in.

She had just closed the door leading into the shop behind her when she gasped with shock to see Reggie standing in front of her. His eyes were bloodshot and he was dishevelled, and by the looks of him he had been up all night.

'What the *hell* are you doing here creepin' up on me like that?' she barked angrily. Even from where she was standing, she could smell the stale stench of beer on his breath.

He scowled. 'How else am I supposed to get a moment alone with you?' he leered. 'I asked you out nicely but that wasn't good enough was it Miss La-De-Da! You should be flattered that I'd even look at a wench from the workhouse! Why, I could have any girl I wanted.'

'Then I suggest you go and bother one of them.' Annie was livid. 'I 'ave a job to get to. What are you doing here at this time of the mornin' anyway?'

'I was at a card game that went on all night and saw you coming in. Unfortunately, it didn't go the way I planned, so now I'm going to have to go home to Mater and get her to dig me out of a hole. The person I lost to isn't the sort you'd want to upset.'

'Serves you right!' Annie spat. 'Now get out of here. I've got to get to work.' Annie made to move past him but he caught her arm in an iron grip and swung her around to face him.

'Not so fast. I'm off to fight for my King and country tomorrow and I think the least you could do is be nice to me before I go! How about a little kiss to see me on my way?'

Annie was incensed as she struggled to free her arm. 'I'd rather kiss the devil 'imself,' she stormed. The first flutters of panic were beginning to churn in her stomach and the smell of his stale breath was making her gag.

'Let me go *right now* or I'll scream so bloody loud the whole of Nuneaton will hear me!'

'I don't think so.' Suddenly his free hand clamped across her mouth and his leg came out to smack into the back of her knees making her tumble to the ground with him on top of her.

For a moment she was winded but then she began to fight for all she was worth. It was like fighting against the tide, though, and terror pulsed through her as she realised her strength was no match for his.

His wet lips were sucking at her face and neck and the heavy hand across her mouth was making it difficult to breathe as his other hand tugged her skirt above her knees. Somehow, she managed to raise one of her arms to scrape her nails down the side of his face, but this just seemed to excite him more.

'I like a lass who puts up a bit of a fight,' he gasped as his hand reached inside her drawers.

She tried to shake her head as tears spilled down her cheeks, but Reggie seemed oblivious to everything apart from what he intended to do. She could feel the cold air on her legs above her stockings, and he was fumbling with his flies. She finally realised there was nothing she could do to stop him. Her drawers ripped as he pulled them to one side and she felt his manhood press against the top of her leg. Vomit rose in her throat, but the sheer weight of him kept her pinned to the ground. Suddenly there was a searing pain as he forced himself into her and began to buck up and down. He was making horrible gasping, guttural noises, and in that moment, she wished that death would come and claim her, because she knew after this, she would never want another man to touch her ever again.

The pain seemed to go on forever, but suddenly, he let out a strangled cry and became rigid before dropping heavily onto her, panting and laughing.

'There,' he said breathlessly. 'You didn't know what you were missing, did you?'

At last, he rolled off her and Annie curled into a ball and yanked her skirt down.

She was petrified that he would do it again but thankfully after a few moments he rose unsteadily and nonchalantly pulled his breeches up and buttoned his flies.

'That wasn't so bad, was it?' He chuckled as he tucked his shirt in. 'I bet you wish you hadn't kept me at arm's length all this time now.' And with that he turned and sauntered out, leaving the door swinging open behind him.

Annie lay there for some minutes as her heart settled into a steadier rhythm before dragging herself up onto her knees and being violently sick all over the floor. Somehow, she forced herself to clear the mess up before crossing to the sink and grabbing a piece of huckaback. She soaked it under the tap and began to scrub at her most private parts but no matter how much she scrubbed herself she still felt dirty. More than anything in the world she wanted to run home and lock herself in her room. But she knew she couldn't do that. Peggy would guess something was wrong immediately if she saw her in this state and Annie couldn't bear that. She would die of shame and humiliation if ever anyone found out what had happened.

And so, with a superhuman effort, she pulled herself together and tidied herself as best she could before locking the shop and setting off for the hospital. She ached everywhere and was sure she must be covered in bruises from Reggie's rough treatment, but she forced herself on. Hopefully the bruises would all be in places that didn't show, so no one need ever know.

Her courage deserted her for a moment when the hospital came into view, but she took a deep breath, put her chin in the air and moved on. She supposed she must be slightly late for her shift but with luck the ward sister wouldn't have noticed.

From the moment she entered the ward she was rushed off her feet and she was glad of the fact because it gave her no time to dwell on what had happened.

Around mid-afternoon, as she was serving afternoon tea, Alex arrived and Annie's heart dropped as she quickly avoided his eyes. She wondered how she would face him now – she was no longer the girl he knew. But then common sense took over. What did it matter? Alex was a married man and after what had happened with Reggie she doubted she would ever want to be intimate with any man again, even Alex.

When she reached Leonard's bed, Alex gave her a broad smile as she served him and Leonard with tea and cake.

'Have you given any more thought to what we talked about last night?' he asked quietly.

Suddenly, Annie made her decision. 'Yes, I have. I've decided to do it.'

'Wonderful. Shall I wait for you when you finish work and we'll discuss the arrangements? You do realise that we'll have to leave early in the morning the day after tomorrow?'

'I understand,' she said far more calmly than she was feeling. 'But I shall have to speak to the matron and explain that I'm going back to France. I can't just disappear.'

'Of course.' He looked delighted. There was something about this young woman that drew him to her like a magnet, even though he should have been running the other way from her. He had realised some time ago that he had never felt about his wife as he did about Annie. Still, what was done was done and he would have to be content to just be close to her, until the end of the war – if they both survived it.

As Annie got on with her tasks her mind was working overtime. What had made her make such a rash decision? But deep down she knew. Anything was better than having to stay here and face the people who cared about her. They knew her too well and the chances were if she stayed, she would break down and tell them what Reggie had done to her, and goodness knew what Levi might do. He was a placid, kind man but also fiercely protective of the people he cared about, and she knew she wouldn't be able to bear it if he did something rash and got into trouble over her. No, it would be better if Levi never found out. *I've made the right choice*, she consoled herself. All she had to do now was tell Matron that tomorrow would be her last day, then go and break the news to the family. It wouldn't be easy but hopefully it would ensure that she wouldn't have to face Reggie again for a very long time.

Chapter Twenty-Seven

'Are yer quite sure about this, hinny?' Levi asked on the morning of her departure. She was to meet Alex at the station where they would take the train to Euston and then another on to Southampton where they would board the army ship that would take them to France.

'I'm sure,' she told him quietly.

His heart ached as he saw the look in her eyes. There was something wrong, he could sense it. She hadn't been herself for the last couple of days, but whatever was bothering her, she was keeping it to herself.

'I'll write whenever I can,' she promised.

Eve and Susan stepped forward to give her a hug. Maggie was still in bed and Peggy had already left for work after saying her goodbyes the night before. Annie had confided in her about what Reggie had done. She hadn't had much choice; Peggy could read her like a book and had known something was seriously amiss. She'd hoped not to have to tell anyone, but she would have trusted Peggy with her life and knew her secret would go no further, although Peggy had been baying for Reggie's blood. Annie was relieved he'd left to join his regiment as there was no saying what Peggy might have done if he hadn't.

'You two be sure and look after these little ones now,' Annie said as she planted gentle kisses on Jack and Constance's cheeks.

'Shouldn't you be wearin' yer Red Cross uniform?' Eve asked as Annie lifted her carpet bag.

'Oh, I, er . . . it's in here.' Annie had to think quickly as she patted the bag. 'I'll get changed into it when I get to Southampton.'

Alex had specifically asked her not to wear it. Once they arrived in France, she would be staying with members of the Resistance at a safe house close to the coast with easy access to the boats. To all intents and purposes from then on, she would be French, like her hosts, and Alex had warned her, the less she was seen the better.

Now, as she tearfully left for the station, she couldn't help but be nervous. She was wearing a long-sleeved blouse to hide the bruises Reggie had inflicted on her and an ankle-length skirt with a simple shawl about her shoulders. In the bottom of her bag was the beautiful shawl she had been wrapped in when she was left on the workhouse steps. For some reason she hadn't wanted to leave it behind this time. It was far too precious to wear every day, but it was all she had of the mother who had abandoned her.

She thought about the letter she had written to Monty the night before and felt guilty. In it she had told him that she didn't want to think of being romantically involved with anyone until the war was over but wished him well. She knew she should have told him how she felt before, rather than take the coward's way out but she hadn't been able to bring herself to do it. Their relationship had gone no further than a chaste kiss and holding hands, but Monty had wanted more, and she felt bad about it. Even so, she knew she had done the right thing. She shuddered to think of what might happen if Monty ever found out what his brother had done to her. It didn't bear thinking about.

Alex was waiting on the platform looking smart and handsome in his officer's uniform. 'I shall change into civilian clothes on the boat,' he told her as they waited for the train to arrive. He too had noticed how quiet Annie had been but had put it down to nerves about the new part she was about to play in the war. They both knew only too well what became of the Resistance members who fell into German hands, and he didn't know how he would be able to live with himself should anything happen to her.

The train arrived soon after, and he helped her aboard. They found seats in a carriage crowded with subdued soldiers returning to the front following their leave. This limited the conversation they were able to have but Annie was quite content to sit and watch the passing countryside.

It was late afternoon when they arrived in Southampton and they had some hours to spare before the ship was due to sail.

'Come on, we'll get something to eat.' Alex took her arm and frowned when she winced. 'Sorry, did I hurt you?'

'Oh . . . no, I, er . . . just knocked it at the hospital and bruised it,' Annie answered quickly, colour rising in her cheeks.

'I see.' From the way Alex looked at her she could tell he didn't believe her, but thankfully he didn't press the issue and soon they came to a small café.

'Not very salubrious I'm afraid but it looks clean enough.' Alex peered through the steamed-up window before holding the door open for her.

She found a seat by the window while he went to the counter to order and soon steaming bowls of vegetable soup and thick slices of crusty bread and butter were placed in front of them.

'Sorry, there wasn't an awful lot of choice on the menu.'

Annie smiled as she lifted her spoon. She had only just realised how hungry she was, for she had scarcely eaten a thing since the terrible incident with Reggie.

'Don't apologise, it looks delicious,' she assured him, and it was. Soon both their dishes were clean.

Annie felt slightly better with some food inside her and now all they had to do was while away the time until they were able to board the ship for Boulogne.

Much later that night they finally went aboard. Most of the passengers were soldiers on their way to the front along with some Red Cross nurses. Many of the nurses were new recruits and as she glanced at their excited faces, Annie felt sorry for them. The poor souls could have no idea of the horrors that lay ahead for them.

On deck there was a special room reserved for the officers and Alex led Annie towards it. 'It will be quieter in there and I can explain a little more about what you'll be doing.'

He was right, there were only two other officers present, and they were both at the other side of the room smoking cigars and reading newspapers.

Once they were seated at a table next to a porthole, Alex made her comfortable before hurrying away to change out of his uniform.

'I need to be as inconspicuous as I can once we reach dry land,' he explained.

When he returned, he could easily have been taken for a working-class Frenchman. He was dressed in an old corduroy jacket and thick trousers with a beret perched on his thatch of hair. Under different circumstances, Annie would have found it amusing – he looked so different out of uniform – but right now she could find little to smile about. She still ached from Reggie's attack and as she looked back on it, she had another reason to be afraid. What if he had planted his seed in her? The thought terrified her.

Alex took a seat opposite her and after a moment asked gently, 'Annie, is it just what you're about to do that's making you so quiet or is there something else on your mind? I understand how nervous you must be, but you really haven't been yourself for the last couple of days.'

She lifted her chin and forced a smile. 'I'm perfectly fine.'

He shrugged. 'In that case I'll tell you about where you will be staying. You'll be living with Monsieur and Madame Moreau in their cottage at the coast. They have two children, a daughter called Amelie, who's slightly younger than you, and a son, Lucien, who is slightly older than you. They are all members of the French Resistance and have been invaluable to us, but they risk their lives by helping us every single day.

'To all intents and purposes, they are a poor family. Monsieur Moreau and Lucien are fishermen and Madame Moreau and Amelie run a smallholding. They keep chickens, goats and pigs. The Germans tend to leave them alone because they supply them with fresh fish and eggs, which is why their property is still standing, unlike many in their village who were not so fortunate. They have already put the word about that Madame's sister and husband have been killed and their niece will be coming to stay with them – that's you, and while you are with them you will be known as Celeste Leroux.

'The Moreaus do speak English and that is acceptable while you are inside in their company. But you *must* remember to try and speak French at all times should you leave the cottage. It would be preferable if you ventured out as little as possible. The Moreaus also speak German so are able to converse with the soldiers who call to collect their supplies. Are there any questions you would like to ask?'

Annie swallowed as she tried to take in all he had told her. It suddenly seemed very real and she was only too aware of the danger she would be putting herself in.

When she shook her head, he went on, 'From time to time injured members of the intelligence service will be brought to the cottage and hidden in a secret room until I am able to secure a boat to bring them home. I hope that you might be able to offer help to the injured until I can get there. Do you think you can do that?'

Annie nodded. 'Yes, just so long as you understand I'll be limited in what I can do. I'm not a surgeon.'

'I do realise that, but still, you have more medical skills than most.' He paused and frowned as he removed the beret and ran his hand through his hair. It was a habit that Annie had noticed he adopted when he was worried or nervous. 'If you have any reservations at all, Annie, I can arrange for you to return home on this very ship tomorrow and I wouldn't think poorly of you.'

Her chin jutted and her eyes flashed as she shook her head. 'No, I'm prepared to do this an' I'll do the best I can,' she assured him.

He reached out and took her small hand in his large one and she felt tingles run up her arm. As their eyes locked, they might have been the only two people in the room. 'You really are a quite remarkable young woman,' he muttered. 'If only—' He stopped abruptly and withdrew his hand as if the feel of her skin was burning him. 'Anyway . . .' He cleared his throat. 'I think that's about all I can tell you for now. So, shall I try to find us both a hot drink? Then perhaps we might be able to catch a little sleep.'

It was the early hours of the morning when the boat docked at Boulogne and even in the darkness Annie could see the devastation the Germans had wreaked on the city. Trucks were waiting to take the troops to the front and the nurses to the hospitals, but Alex led her beyond them to a horse and cart with a middle-aged man in the driving seat. He was dressed as a typical Frenchman, portly with a kindly face and he climbed down as they approached, glancing around him all the time.

'Monsieur.' He shook Alex's hand heartily and after removing his beret he bowed to Annie. 'Mademoiselle.'

'This is Celeste,' Alex introduced her. 'Celeste, this is Monsieur Moreau, your host for the foreseeable future.'

The man clicked his heels together and nodded to the back of the cart. Alex helped her up into it before joining Monsieur Moreau on the seat at the front.

There was an overpowering smell of fish and Annie wrinkled her nose as she sat down and tried to get comfortable on a pile of fishing nets.

Alex and Monsieur Moreau talked in French as the horse clip-clopped through the streets, which were mostly deserted once they had left the docks. Annie was dismayed to see the piles of rubble where people's homes had once stood and she wondered where the people were now, or if they had been inside the buildings when they were attacked. It hardly bore thinking about.

The streets were in darkness save for the light of the moon and eventually they gave way to lanes surrounded by forests and fields. Annie was jostled about as the lanes became rougher, which did nothing to help her bruises, but she suffered in silence and clung to the sides of the cart. Eventually they turned into an even narrower lane that led downhill through woodland. She could see the sea above the tops of the trees and smell the salt in the air. Eventually they turned again and soon after a cottage came into view. This, she supposed, was to be her new home, and a shudder ran up her spine. There could be no going back now!

Chapter Twenty-Eight

'Monsieur, take Celeste into the kitchen,' Monsieur Moreau told Alex when he drew the horse and cart to a halt. 'Odette will be waiting for you both. I have to stable the horse.'

Alex helped her down and they padded across the yard towards a door. Alex tapped on it before opening it and ushering her inside. Annie blinked in the sudden light of the oil lamp which stood on a pine table that appeared to be almost white after so many scrubbings.

A short, plump woman was filling a large brown tea pot with boiling water. Her dark hair, which was showing signs of grey around her ears, had been swept back into a bun and she had piercing blue eyes. She was wrapped in a voluminous white apron that covered most of the dark-blue serge gown she was wearing, and her smile was kindly.

'Greetings, Monsieur Gordon, Mademoiselle Celeste. It is nice to meet you.' She shook their hands warmly before ushering them towards the table where a large slab of cheese, a crusty loaf and a pat of butter were laid ready for them. 'I am thinking you will be hungry after your journey. You will stay tonight, Monsieur Alex, *oui*?'

'If it's no trouble, madame.'

She smiled. 'It is no trouble at all and you must not worry, your friend will be well looked after during her stay.'

'I have no doubts on that score.'

Annie could see they got on well and started to relax a little. Both the monsieur and his wife were warm, friendly people so perhaps it wouldn't be so hard staying there after all.

'My son and daughter are in bed asleep,' Madame Moreau informed Annie. 'But in the morning, you will meet.'

She nodded as she took a seat at the table next to Alex, who was carving slices from the loaf. The food, although simple, was delicious and the atmosphere relaxed. By the time they had finished eating Annie was stifling a yawn and the kindly little woman lifted the oil lamp and pointed towards a door that led to a steep staircase.

'Go up and rest,' she urged. 'Amelie is asleep in the first bedroom you come to but there is another bed in her room prepared for you. Do not worry about waking her. Once Amelie is asleep nothing would rouse her.'

Annie smiled her thanks and after bidding them all goodnight she went up the stairs while Madame Moreau stood at the bottom of them to light her way with the lamp.

Amelie's gentle snores reached her as she entered the room and she tiptoed towards the other bed. She had forgotten to take her bag up with her but she was too tired to go back down for it, so she quietly stripped down to her chemise and slipped between the cool cotton sheets; minutes later she was sound asleep.

A cock crowing woke her early the next morning and as she blinked awake, she stared around, disorientated. The other bed was empty, so she rose and dragged on her clothes. As she crept downstairs voices reached her, and she entered the kitchen to find Madame and Monsieur Moreau sitting at the table deep in conversation with Alex. A young woman was making them a pot of coffee and Annie was sure she must be one of the prettiest girls she had ever seen. This, she guessed, must be Amelie. Her thick brunette hair hung down her back in shining waves and her eyes were the colour of warm treacle. She was very small and dainty, but her smile seemed to light her face as she shyly held her hand out to greet her new roommate.

'Bonjour, mademoiselle.'

'Oh please, just An—er . . . Celeste will do.'

Amelie nodded. '*Oui*, and I am Amelie. I 'ope I did not disturb you when I got up?'

'Not at all,' Annie assured her as the girl carried the coffee pot to the table. There was bacon sizzling in a pan on the stove and it smelled delicious.

'My brother Lucien will be in shortly to meet you,' Amelie informed her. ''E is out collecting eggs for breakfast. You like bacon and eggs, *oui*?'

'Oh yes, thank you,' Annie assured her, remembering to speak in French. She had just joined the others at the table when the door opened and a tall, broad-shouldered young man appeared. He was very handsome with the same colour hair and eyes as his sister, and he too gave her a friendly smile.

Breakfast was a light-hearted affair but as soon as it was over Alex rose and lifted his kitbag. 'I'm afraid I must leave you,' he told Annie regretfully, and her stomach turned over. Now that the time had come to part, she felt nervous again.

'W-when will I see you again?' she asked in a slightly shaky voice.

He shook his head. 'It could be tomorrow, in a week or a month's time. There's no way of knowing. But don't worry, you're in safe hands. I would trust the Moreaus with my life. In fact, I frequently do.'

He embarked on a hasty discussion with Monsieur Moreau before saying his goodbyes and heading for the door. And suddenly he was gone, swallowed up by the morning mist that had come in from the sea, as if he had never been there.

'Now, Celeste, we will talk,' Madame Moreau said quietly, seeing that Annie looked a little unnerved. 'During your stay with us you will address me as Tante, Basile will be Oncle. It sounds better when the Germans visit for supplies, *oui*?'

Annie nodded. This new identity was going to take some getting used to.

'When we 'ave washed up, Lucien will show you where we keep any soldiers who need our 'elp. Thankfully we 'ave no one at present but that changes from day to day.'

Half an hour later, Lucien led her across the yard as indignant chickens pecking amongst the cobblestones hurried out of their way. Outside a large barn he lifted a wicker basket and explained, 'Whenever you come in 'ere you must carry this in case anyone is watching. That way if they question you, you can say you were looking for eggs, *oui*?'

She nodded and they entered the gloomy interior, blinking as their eyes adjusted to the gloom. A ladder halfway across led to what looked like a large hay loft and Lucien began to climb it with her following close behind. There were huge piles of hay stacked all around it and he led her behind one such stack and nodded towards the back wall. It consisted of sturdy planks of wood and she was surprised when he gently pressed the end one and it slid soundlessly back behind the others revealing a small room beyond.

'This is a false wall with this room beyond it,' he explained. 'And this is where we keep anyone who is trying to escape from the Germans. Some are men who have been shot down and have parachuted to safety. If they are well, Alex arranges a boat to take them back to their homeland, but if they are wounded you will be needed to accompany them.'

She nodded as she glanced around. Bunk beds stood against one wall and a single bed against another with a small table and chairs between them. The only light was from a small skylight in the ceiling and Annie guessed that she might feel very claustrophobic if she had to spend any length of time in there. Still, this was what she had agreed to, and she had every intention of keeping her promise.

Over the next few days, she grew to know and like the Moreau family. She discovered that their fishing was just a ruse to fool the

Germans. Only one of the men would ever go out to sea to catch fish while the other went to work with the Resistance. She was full of admiration for them as they were only too aware of what the consequences would be should the Germans ever discover what they were doing. She got on particularly well with Amelie, who took it upon herself to improve Annie's French even further.

And then one day, as the girls were cleaning out the pig sties, a truck drove into the yard and two German officers climbed down and strode towards the kitchen.

'Stay 'ere and try to keep out of sight,' Amelie hissed, then hurried across the yard to them. '*Bonjour*, gentlemen,' she greeted them. 'You 'ave come for some supplies, *oui*? Good, good, my *pere* 'ad a good catch yesterday. The fish are being smoked in the smoke 'ouse. I will fetch some for you. We also 'ave eggs and some pork. My *pere* killed one of the pigs a few days ago. Come, I will gather everything together for you. My *mere* is in the kitchen.'

The tallest of the Germans snapped his heels together and gave a little bow before following her into the kitchen while Annie slunk down out of sight in the sty. It wasn't the most comfortable place to hide and stunk to high heaven, but anything was preferable to conversing with the enemy. After what felt like an eternity the Germans reappeared, followed by Amelie and Madame Moreau, who loaded provisions into the back of their truck. And then at last they pulled out of the yard and Annie sighed with relief as she climbed out of the sty.

Madame Moreau's face was set in grim lines as she spat on the ground. 'Murdering swine,' she cursed. And then with a sigh she said, 'Come along, *mes filles*, let us go an' 'ave some coffee. I need to get the taste of those scum out of my mouth.'

It was the first time the Germans had visited while she was there, and Annie had to admit it had shaken her, but she admired Madame Moreau and Amelie for the way they had handled it. They were truly brave people.

Another quiet week passed, but then, late one evening, as they sat in the kitchen, there was a hammering on the door.

Madame Moreau put a warning finger to her lips as she hurried to answer it. Annie gripped the arms of her chair, wondering who it could be. There was a hurried conversation with a small wiry-haired man in rapid French. Annie recognised him as Francois, one of the fishermen who'd had taken her over the Channel before. After he'd raced away, Madame Moreau shut the door.

'We must prepare the secret room. An English plane 'as been shot down. Both men inside parachuted out before it burst into flames, but one of them is badly injured and they are bringing 'im 'ere now. Francois thinks that 'is leg is badly injured and 'e is in a lot of pain. It will be up to you to do what you can for 'im, Celeste. Meanwhile, I will get word to Monsieur Gordon to return as soon as 'e is able to, to arrange a boat back to England. You will need to go with 'im, Celeste.'

'Of course.' Annie's heart was beating like a drum. Apart from the one visit from the Germans it had been quiet and she had been lulled into a false sense of security, but now she realised the danger they would all be facing while the escaped prisoners were with them. 'Do you know where Alex is?'

Madame Moreau patted the side of her nose and shook her head. 'Yes, but it is better if you do not know.'

Annie nodded. And now she wondered if her heart was beating through fear or the thought of seeing Alex again. Could he know by looking at her that she might be carrying a child? She'd had no course since that day, and the fear that she might be carrying Reggie's baby haunted her. But there was nothing she could do about it, so she tried to put the worry to the back of her mind and steeled herself to face Alex again.

Chapter Twenty-Nine

Some hours later, Francois returned with the two airmen. One of them was being carried on a makeshift stretcher, and one look at his grey pallour told Annie of the agony he was in.

'Get him into the barn quickly,' she instructed.

He was bleeding profusely, and once inside the secret room, they laid him on the bed and Annie cut his trouser leg off, drawing in a ragged breath when she saw a bone protruding through the skin halfway between his knee and his ankle.

'I'm going to need hot water and some pieces of wood to make a splint,' she said urgently, and Amelie hurried away to fetch what she needed.

She turned back to the patient, who had bitten down on his lip so badly that it was bleeding. 'I'm so sorry but I'm goin' to 'ave to try and pull yer leg back into position an' it's gonna hurt like hell!' she said, wishing with all her heart that she was a surgeon. What if she did more harm than good to the poor soul? But then she had seen enough doctors and nurses do the exact same thing when in the field hospital and his leg couldn't be left like this. She would just have to do the best she could.

'I will fetch some brandy,' Madame Moneau said, and disappeared.

Soon after Madame Moreau appeared with half a bottle of brandy, which the other airman started to pour down his mate's throat. The poor chap coughed and spluttered but at last he seemed to relax a little and, grim-faced, the other man nodded to Annie.

'I reckon he's as ready as he'll ever be.'

She nodded as she gently began to bathe around the wound and tie a tourniquet above his knee to try and stop the bleeding. 'I'll need you to 'old his shoulders down while I try to straighten 'is leg and get the bone back into position.'

Gritting his teeth, the airman stood behind his injured friend and tightly gripped his shoulders.

Annie took a deep breath and, grasping his ankle, she twisted his leg as far as it would go. The poor man screamed with pain then thankfully passed out, leaving Annie free to apply the makeshift splints as best she could.

At last, it was done, and she wiped the sweat from her brow. 'That's the best I can do,' she told them in a shaky voice. 'We just 'ave to hope it's not infected an' 'e doesn't develop a fever. An' obviously the sooner we can get 'im to a hospital where they'll be able to set it properly the better.'

The airman, whose name was John Swallow, did develop a fever and for the next two days and nights Annie and Michael Jones, the other airman, took it in turns sponging him down with cool water and trickling water between his cracked lips.

At last, on the third day, Alex appeared and Annie almost cried with relief.

'How is he?' Alex asked, staring down at the patient.

Annie shrugged. 'Not good to be honest. I've done the best I can but 'e really needs to be in a proper hospital.'

'I've arranged a boat for tomorrow night. You've done a grand job,' he praised her.

'So will you be staying 'ere tonight?' she asked.

He shook his head. 'No, the least I'm seen in this area the better, but if you could be ready for when it's dark tomorrow Monsieur Moreau will meet me at a cove we use for a quick getaway. That's if there are no Germans about, of course. If there are we'll have to bide our time.'

Annie frowned. 'I 'ope it is tomorrow, because despite our best efforts we can't get 'is fever down. I'm concerned 'e's got an infection an' we don't 'ave the right medicine to treat it 'ere.'

'You can only do your best.' He patted her hand and made for the door. 'Until tomorrow.' And with that he was gone, leaving her feeling strangely bereft.

Annie slept little that night as the young airman's condition worsened. She was frustrated because there was nothing else she could do for him, but eventually, when he seemed slightly more relaxed, she dropped into a doze in the chair next to his bed, holding his hand. Amelie woke her when she arrived early the next morning with breakfast for them all in a wicker basket.

'How is 'e?' She placed the basket down on the table and bent to look at the airman before straightening again and saying in a croaky voice. 'I . . . I fear 'e 'as gone, Celeste.'

Michael hurried to stand by the bed, as Annie jumped out of the chair and stared down at her patient. He was still holding tight to her hand, but she noticed instantly that his was cold and a sob broke through her.

'Oh no, no! I shouldn't have fallen asleep. The poor chap!'

Amelie put her arm about her as tears coursed down Annie's cheeks.

'It is not your fault, *mon cherie*. There was no more you could 'ave done for 'im, an' at least he died with someone 'olding 'is 'and. But now I must go an' tell my *pere* 'e will 'ave to get word to Monsieur Gordon. It looks like you will not be needed now, Celeste.'

Annie was devastated. She felt that she had let the poor man down although she didn't know what more she could have done for him.

'Wh-what will happen to 'im now?' she asked.

Amelie sighed. 'Because 'e was 'ere with us, Monsieur Gordon might decide to take 'im with them tonight and return 'is body to 'is family in England. At least that way he will be able to be buried in his homeland and 'ave a proper funeral, poor man. If that is not possible then *mon pere* will bury 'im in the orchard.'

Michael put his arm about Annie's shaking shoulders and said soothingly, 'Please don't blame yourself. You've tended to him round the clock. There was absolutely nothing more you could have done.'

Annie had seen many deaths during her time in the field hospital, but she had never been solely responsible for caring for any of them, as she had for this poor man, and the guilt weighed heavily upon her. In a strange way she was also sad that she wouldn't be needed to accompany Alex. She had been looking forward to spending a little time with him, although she couldn't admit to that. So instead, she wiped her wet cheeks with the back of her hand and gently pulled the sheet up over the dead man's face. At least he wasn't suffering anymore.

That night, Monsieur Moreau and Michael loaded John Swallow's body into the back of the cart and set off to meet the boat, while Annie and Amelie cleaned the hidden room for the next people who might need it.

The next few weeks passed peacefully until mid-August when there was yet another pounding on the door in the middle of the night.

Annie and Amelie started awake and heard Madame Moreau plod down the steep stairs to answer it.

Both girls hurriedly rose and pulled on their dressing robes before rushing down to join her. The sight that met Annie's eyes shocked her. Monsieur Moreau was helping a man who was no more than skin and bone, and hardly able to stand to sit at the table, while his companion leant heavily against the wall.

'Th-the Germans are after us,' he gasped in English. 'We were taken prisoner by them over a month ago and they were taking us to a prison camp when we managed to escape through the forest. If they catch us, they will shoot us and possibly you as well, so if you want to send us away, I'll understand.'

'We will do no such thing!' Madame Moreau was outraged at the very thought. 'But come, we 'ave not a moment to waste. We must 'ide you. Celeste, come with us.'

'Put all the lights out and go back to bed. Lucien and I will join you presently,' Monsieur Moreau instructed as he and Lucien helped the weaker of the two men to stand and between them, they half carried and half dragged him to the barn.

With her heart in her mouth Annie lifted an oil lamp to light the way and hurried ahead of them across the yard to the hidden room. 'We must go back now so that if the Germans come they will suspect nothing,' Monsieur Moreau told them. 'And please, do not make a sound.'

Her face creased with fear, Annie nodded as they deposited the ill soldier onto the bed. And then all they could do was wait.

'What's wrong with yer friend?' Annie asked in a low voice to the second soldier who was sitting on the bottom bunk with his head in his hands. He looked dishevelled and exhausted. His British army uniform was in tatters and he was painfully thin.

'The bastards treated us like animals.' He screwed his eyes up as the memories rushed back. 'They kept us in huts so crammed together that we couldn't move around and we had to sleep on the cold floor and had no toilet. We were on starvation rations, one drink of dirty water and a stale crust of bread each a day.' He shook his head. 'No washing facilities, nothing. And if anyone complained they were dragged outside and shot! It didn't take long before we all learnt to keep our mouths shut, I can tell you.'

Annie pursed her lips at the picture he had conjured up, then she extinguished the lamp and they sat in silence, their ears straining into the darkness.

There was no way of knowing how long they sat there before they heard the roar of at least two trucks driving into the farmyard.

Annie felt sick and gulped deep in her throat as the second soldier gently squeezed her hand, sensing her fear. They could vaguely hear raised voices and the sound of footsteps in the barn below them. They were German voices and although they couldn't hear what was being said they were obviously angry. They heard barrels being overturned and next the horrifying sound of someone walking about in the hay loft barking orders.

They all held their breath as they silently prayed the secret door would not be discovered. If it was, none of them would see daylight again. And then at last they heard the footsteps going back down the ladder and the faint voices coming from the farmyard again before the German soldiers entered the house.

After what seemed like an eternity, they heard the trucks start up and leave, and finally they dared to breathe.

'It's all right . . . I think they've gone,' the soldier assured Annie.

'What should we do?' she whispered. Her eyes were wide with fear and she was shaking like a leaf.

He shook his head. 'Nothing. This might be a trick. They could have left someone behind to see if we surface after they've gone. Just sit tight till someone comes to tell us it's all clear.'

They sat on until at last they heard someone climb the ladder. Dawn was breaking by that time and a thin light was filtering through the dirty skylight.

The door slid back to reveal Madame Moreau with a basket of food on her arm. She gave them a weak smile. She was clearly badly shaken up. 'It is all right, the German bastards 'ave gone now,' she assured them. 'But they 'ave caused 'avoc in the 'ouse. The sooner we can get you away from 'ere the safer we will be so Lucien 'as gone to take a message to Monsieur Gordon. In the meantime, you must eat and try to get your strength back.'

She set the basket down and the soldier gave her a grateful smile as he selected a chicken leg and handed it to his friend, who was barely strong enough to hold it.

'Thank you . . . for everything.' There was a slight catch in his voice. 'If you hadn't taken us in when you did . . .'

His voice trailed away but they knew what he meant. The Germans would undoubtedly have caught up with them and they would both have been dead by now.

'It is God's will that you 'appened upon us,' Madame assured him in a kindly voice. 'And now we must do all we can to get you back to your 'omeland. Come, Celeste. What these men need is food and sleep.'

The women left, closing the door gently behind them and when they entered the house a few minutes later Annie gasped with dismay. The Germans had ransacked the place, and broken pots and overturned furniture lay everywhere.

'Oh, Tante, look what the lousy swines 'ave done to yer lovely 'ome.' Annie had grown accustomed to calling the woman aunt now and they had grown close, though not as close as her and Amelie.

Madame Moreau shrugged as she righted a chair and set it back at the table. 'It does not matter. We will soon put everything to rights. Come, we must go and get some rest. All this can be done later.'

Annie would happily have pitched in to help there and then but seeing the sense in what she said, she nodded and headed for the stairs, grateful to be alive.

Amelie was just climbing into bed when she got upstairs and seeing Annie's pale face she asked, 'Are you all right?'

And then the tears came thick and fast until Annie felt as if she was choking. Amelie was back out of bed in a flash and wrapped her arms about her.

'It is all right, the danger is over now,' she soothed.

'Not all of it,' Annie choked, feeling that if she didn't confide in someone soon, she couldn't carry on. Apart from telling Peggy, she had kept the horror of what Reggie had done to her to herself, but the fear that she might be carrying his bastard was suddenly too much to bear anymore. As the whole sorry story came spilling out, Amelie listened without a word.

"'E is a very bad man,' Amelie said quietly when Annie had finished. 'But you must not think the worst yet. You 'ave told me you 'ave only missed one course up to now an' that could be because of the trauma you 'ave suffered. Just be patient an' all might be well. But now you must rest. You 'ave 'ad another bad shock tonight. We all 'ave, but 'opefully Monsieur Gordon will be able to get the men away very soon.' Then seeing the expression on Annie's face at the mention of Alex she said softly, 'You 'ave feelings for Monsiuer Gordon, *oui*?'

'Yes, I do,' she admitted. 'But nothing can ever come of them. He is married and I might be carryin' an illegitimate baby! I should never've let Reggie anywhere near me. I *knew* what 'e was like! He'd tried it before.'

'No.' Amelie shook her head. 'What this Reggie did to you was not your fault. But now you must rest.'

Annie nodded and slid into bed, but sleep evaded her and when she rose later in the day to begin the clean-up operation there were dark shadows beneath her eyes.

Chapter Thirty

'What do yer mean, yer goin' home?' Peggy looked aghast at Susan, who hung her head. 'But I thought when he come 'ere an' you sent him off wi' a flea in 'is ear you'd made yer mind up?'

'I had,' Susan admitted as she cuddled Constance to her. 'Or at least I *thought* I had. But Constance needs to grow up knowing her father and he's promised in his latest letter that things will be different when I go back.'

'Huh! An' pigs might fly,' Peggy scoffed with a shake of her head. 'It's the money you earn him he's missin' more like, than you an' the little 'un. Think of it, gel, what if he wants you to go back on the game again? Is that the sort o' thing you want Constance to see? An' what if she takes bad again an' you ain't there? Who'll look after 'er. The doctor's told you she's got a dicky ticker, bless 'er.'

'There are doctors in London, you know,' Susan said defensively. 'And if I'm out Milly can look after her. I'll get her to live in so that Constance is never alone. But I won't be doing that again anyway. Theo promised me I needn't. I think we could end up getting married very soon.'

'An' what about 'er?' Peggy nodded towards Maggie, who was sitting in her usual place in the chair. 'Yer know 'ow she dotes on that little girl. She'll be devastated if you take 'er away.'

Susan glanced guiltily at her sister. 'Yes, I know she'll miss her,' she admitted. 'But I can't live my life for Maggie.'

Peggy sighed as she rubbed her hands down the front of her apron. 'In that case there's nuthin' more I can say to get yer to change yer mind. I just 'ope yer don't live to regret it – *again*! It's that little 'un I feel sorry for. Fer all yer say he's changed, I didn't see Theo pay 'er much heed the last time 'e were 'ere. Still, yer yer own woman an' you'll do as yer please. When were yer thinkin' o' goin'?'

'I, er . . . thought tomorrow.' Susan licked her lips. 'There's no sense in delaying. I'll just stay to say goodbye to Levi this evening and I'll get off in the morning.'

Eve and Peggy exchanged a worried glance. Eve wasn't entirely surprised at Susan's decision; she'd been like a cat on hot bricks ever since Theo had returned to London. He could play her like a fiddle. But then, as Eve knew all too well, when you loved someone, it didn't just stop. Only Susan could decide if the life she would lead with Theo was the one she wanted. She still had her fancy flat and her maid to go back to, so at least they would know she and Constance weren't living in squalor. She actually envied her up to a point. She would have given the world for just a word from Davey but they had received no further news of him. It was as if he had vanished from the face of the earth and all she could do was pray that he was still alive somewhere.

Levi and Peggy were worrying about Annie too. She had written to tell them she was safe and well but there was never any forwarding address for them to write back to her. Monty was out of hospital and home now, and from what little Peggy had seen of him when one of the maids wheeled him out into the garden to get a little sunshine, his spirits were low. He had repeatedly asked them for an address where he could write to Annie but all they could tell him was that she was working at a field hospital somewhere. The poor chap. Peggy felt for him; it seemed his mother was driving him mad, constantly fussing over him. But at least Reggie had gone to join his regiment – and it was a good thing he had. She knew he was part of the reason Annie had decided to go back to France, and when Annie had told her what Reggie had done to her, she had wanted to take a knife to him. But Ellie needed a mother and he wasn't worth dangling at the end of a rope for. But even so, she knew if she saw him, she'd have difficulty controlling herself. Hopefully he would get his comeuppance on the battlefield.

She was still grieving for Tom, and then there was Harry and Barney to worry about! There was still no news from them either and she knew Levi had sleepless nights wondering where they were and what they were doing. There was so much to be concerned about and still no end to the war in sight. So much for those who had said it would end quickly, she thought bitterly. The shop still stood empty and she knew that Levi missed doing his rag-and-bone rounds desperately. Flo didn't help matters either; she was still constantly coming round begging for money and food. Peggy knew Levi slipped her what he could, but money was tight and the food shortages were affecting everyone. She was just grateful for the lovely vegetable plot Annie had planted before she went away.

She sighed and her hands stilled as she glanced at Maggie. She had been calmer and not so prone to talking to her dead daughter since little Constance had been on the scene, but would she revert to how she had been before when Susan took Constance away from her? Nothing felt right anymore. But one day hopefully, when this damned war was finally over, she and Ellie would return to the cottage in Abbey Street. The thought brought her no joy, for some time ago she had been forced to admit to herself that she had strong feelings for Levi and she suffered endless guilt for it. She had never told him, nor ever would. He was her best friend's husband and although his and Maggie's marriage had become something of a sham, she would never betray Maggie. For now, though, all they could do was plod on and pray that all those they loved would be home safe and sound and that things might return to some sort of normality one day.

Chapter Thirty-One

August 1916

Alex appeared mid-afternoon the day after the Germans had paid the Moreaus a visit. Annie had continued to care for the weaker of the two injured men but it had soon become apparent that both men were severely malnourished. So far, there had been no more sign of the Germans, but they were all painfully aware of the risk they were taking while the two men were at the farm.

Annie heard Alex speaking to Monsieur Moreau in the hayloft, and her heart skipped a beat. When they entered the room a few moments later she kept her eyes downcast before muttering her excuses and skittering away. She had been feeling unwell all day but was unsure whether it was nerves after the Germans' visit or something else.

'I-I think I'll just go for a bit of a lie-down,' she muttered to Amelie, who had come to bring the men some food and drink.

Amelie nodded. 'Of course. You 'ave 'ad 'ardly any rest.' She watched her go and sighed before turning her attention back to what Alex was saying.

'I've made arrangements to get you both away this evening as soon as it's dark,' Alex informed the soldiers. 'There's no guarantee the Germans won't come back, so the sooner we can get you out of here the better.' Then addressing the weaker of the two he asked, 'Do you feel you need Celeste to accompany us on the journey to help you?'

The soldier shook his head. 'Not at all. There's no point, I'm just weak, but a few o' my missus's home-cooked meals will have me right in no time!'

Alex nodded and stepped out of the room into the hayloft with Amelie. Once they were alone, he asked, 'Is Celeste all right? She doesn't seem herself at all.'

Amelie frowned. She had a feeling that Alex was more than a little fond of Celeste and she knew Celeste felt the same about him.

'Shortly before she came 'ere she suffered a trauma,' she confided. She hated to break Annie's confidence, but she had come to care deeply for her and hoped that if she told him what Reggie had done to her, he might be able to help her, especially if Annie's worst fears were confirmed and she discovered that she was carrying Reggie's child.

'Go on then, tell me,' he urged and he listened intently to what she had to say.

Annie went to her room and lay on the bed, and eventually she slipped into an uneasy doze. She was awakened sometime later by terrible cramping in her stomach, and she staggered down the stairs and out to the toilet. She cried with relief when she found that her course had finally come. She leant her forehead on the wall. Now at least no one else need ever know what Reggie had done and she would not have to face the shame of giving birth to an illegitimate child, but she would never forgive him or forget what had happened.

Eventually a tap came on the door and Madame Moreau asked gently, 'Are you all right in there, Celeste? You 'ave been a very long time.'

'I'm fine, Tante. It's just my monthlies.'

'Ah, then come inside, *ma cherie*, an' I will find you some rags.'

Annie didn't see Alex again that day and after darkness fell the two soldiers were smuggled away to the cove where a boat was waiting to take them to safety. They had only been gone a matter of minutes when two trucks rattled into the yard setting the chickens squawking indignantly as they scattered out of their way. Amelie and Annie were sitting darning socks and Annie had no time to hide as Madame Moreau answered the pounding on the door. Three German soldiers burst into the room.

Annie had no idea what they were saying as they snapped at Madame Moreau in rapid German. She sat so still she might have been turned to stone as terror ran through her veins like iced water.

For a terrible moment she thought that they were going to tear the house apart again but after a cursory glance around they eventually left and Madame Moreau sank onto a chair, her hands shaking.

'They asked if we 'ad seen the escaped prisoners yet an' when I tell them no, they wanted to know where Basile and Lucien were. I tell them they 'ad gone night fishing and thank goodness they believed me. They also asked who you were and I told them you were our niece.'

Amelie hurried away to pour some coffee for her as the woman mopped her brow. She had been as cool as a cucumber while the Germans were there, but now she was a bag of nerves.

'I just pray that Lucien and Basile will not meet them coming back from the cove without any fish,' she said worriedly as she took the coffee from Amelie and gulped at it.

Annie was full of admiration for her. This woman and her whole family risked their lives daily for people they had never met before, and she suddenly felt very humble. *From now on I'll try even harder to do them proud*, she promised herself.

It was nearing the end of August before Annie was called on again to help.

Alex turned up unexpectedly when the men were out fishing one day. He was dressed as usual in his old beret and jacket and looking every inch the Frenchman, but his expression was troubled as Madame Moreau ushered him into the kitchen.

'I have a badly injured soldier at one of our safe houses in the village,' he told the women without preamble. 'And he is too ill to move at present. One of our men found him on the edge of the front line after dark. The stretcher men must have missed him when they went out collecting the dead and the injured. So, the thing is . . . and I know this is asking an awful lot, but, Celeste, would you be prepared to come and nurse him until he is well enough for me to try to get him back home?'

Before Annie could answer Madame Moreau frowned. 'But surely you realise this would put Celeste at even more risk than she is already? I think I know where 'e is, and if I am correct, they have a room concealed beneath the floor in the kitchen.'

When Alex nodded, she sighed. 'I am sure I do not 'ave to tell you that this particular family is being watched closely by the Germans. And should they discover where the injured man is being 'idden it would be certain death for all of them.'

'I know.' Alex swept his beret off and ran his hand distractedly through his hair. 'But I do have my reasons for asking this of Celeste. You see, the young man's name is Barney Lilburn. I believe he is connected to you, Celeste.'

Annie gasped. 'Y-yes, he's my brother.'

Alex nodded. 'I thought as much, and that is why I thought you might be willing to help.'

She nodded without having to think about it. 'Of course I will, but what's the matter wi' 'im?'

'I'm afraid he's terribly burnt from the gas that the Germans are using now. It's lethal stuff with terrible side effects. Some don't survive it. Barney was lucky, I suppose, but his wounds are quite bad. It's mainly his hands and one side of his face that have been affected, but he's also having trouble breathing, so he's in quite a bad way.'

Annie took a deep breath and nodded. Poor Barney, he must be in considerable pain but luckily, she had learnt a lot about treating burns in the field hospital.

'I'll come with you now if you like.'

Alex looked relieved while Madame Moreau looked worried. ''Ow long do you think she will be gone for?'

'I promise I'll get her back just as soon as he's in a fit condition to be moved,' Alex assured her as Annie went off to pack a small bag. She was back in the kitchen in no time and went to kiss Madame Moreau's cheek.

'Don't worry, I'll be careful,' she promised, and turning to Amelie she kissed her too. They had all grown to be close in the time she had been there.

Five minutes later she and Alex set off, taking the quieter route through the trees to the next village and keeping their eyes peeled for German soldiers.

'Should we see any, take hold of my hand immediately,' he instructed her. 'And I will tell them that we're a courting couple seeking a little time on our own.'

They were deep in a thicket some minutes later when Alex paused and produced a small pistol from his pocket.

'This is for you,' he told her gravely. 'Do you know how to use it?' When she shook her head, he began to show her how to load it.

'I-I'm not sure that I could shoot someone,' she faltered.

He stared at her intently. 'This is not meant for that, Annie.' He could use her real name while they were alone. 'It's meant for you and your brother should the Germans discover where you are. I don't think I need to tell you what they would do to you, do I?'

She shuddered as she thought back to the morning Reggie had raped her. The Germans had raped and pillaged throughout every village they had attacked and she knew she couldn't go through that again.

'I understand,' she answered in a small voice, tucking the small pistol into her pocket.

The house he led her to was not unlike the Moreaus' but unfortunately the Lecroix family spoke only a smattering of English.

Alex introduced her to the lady of the house immediately but there was little time for niceties, and after a brief greeting, the woman and her son pushed aside the large scrubbed table in the middle of the room, rolled back the carpet and opened a trap door that led down to a cellar.

'You will knock when you wish to come out?' she asked Alex, and he nodded. Annie followed him down the steep stone steps into a surprisingly comfortable room.

Two beds were placed on either side of it. Between the beds stood a table with a glowing oil lamp on it and mismatched chairs arranged around it. Pushed against the other wall was a chest of drawers with jugs of cold water and a selection of bandages and dressings standing on it in readiness for bathing the wounds. Next her eyes went to the first bed and she gasped with dismay. One side of Barney's face was badly blistered as were his hands, which lay limply on top of the blankets, and his breathing was laboured. He looked so different with his lovely black hair shorn to the army regulation short back and sides, that had she not known it was him she might not have recognised him.

'Oh Barney, you *poor* thing. Let me try an' make yer more comfortable,' she soothed. Then to Alex she said, 'Will yer help me lift 'im to get more pillows be'ind 'im please? His breathin' will be easier if we prop him up.'

'Of course.' Alex hurried to the other bed and fetched the spare pillows and soon they had Barney in a more upright position.

'Is there anything else I can do to help before I go?'

Annie shook her head. 'No, I'll manage thanks.'

'In that case I should leave. Madame Lecroix will bring food and drink down at regular intervals throughout each day, and I believe there is a chamber pot for you to use behind that screen over there. When you think Barney might be well enough to travel tell her and I'll arrange to get him away. And, Annie, I think you're very brave.'

She glanced up and seeing the softness in his eyes her heart started to thud.

'I'm not as brave as you. You risk yer life to 'elp these people every single day,' she said, turning her attention back to Barney.

'It's what I'm paid to do, amongst other things. But I must go. Goodbye for now.'

She said nothing as she watched him climb the stairs and tap on the floor and moments later, he disappeared through the hatch and she and Barney were alone.

Chapter Thirty-Two

Over the next twenty-four hours Annie was kept busy bathing Barney's burns with cool water and wrapping them loosely in bandages so as not to burst the blisters, although she feared that when they eventually healed, he might still be scarred. It was such a shame, he had been such a handsome young man, but the scars were irrelevant for now, saving his life was her main goal.

Throughout the day she had two visits from the Lecroix's two young daughters. Yvette was a pretty, vivacious fifteen-year-old, tall and slender with brunette hair and big brown eyes, while her sister Marie at two years older was dainty and delicate with fair hair and blue eyes. They were friendly girls who spoke more English than their parents, so Annie didn't feel quite so isolated and could speak to them in her native tongue when she was alone with them. She got on particularly well with Marie and found herself confiding in her about her past and about what Reggie had done to her and the fact that she had come to France to get away from the memory of what had happened. But no matter how far she ran, the memory was as fresh as if it had just happened, and her hatred of Reggie only grew.

In the cellar, time had no meaning. She had no way of knowing if it was day or night and was grateful for the small selection of books she found down there. Admittedly they were written in French, but she was more than fluent in the language now.

The family brought food down three times a day and emptied the chamber pot for her, and because Barney slept a lot of the time, she was always glad of the company. On the evening of the second day, when Barney's breathing had become a little easier, he finally opened his eyes and blinked up at Annie.

'M-Mercy . . . is that you?'

She smiled and patted a section of his arm that wasn't burnt. 'No, it's me . . . Annie.'

'Annie?' Slowly things began to come back to him and after a time he asked, 'Where am I?'

'You're somewhere safe but you've been injured so yer still in France,' she explained gently. 'But don't worry, you're gonna be all right an' when you're a bit better you're gonna be sent 'ome.'

As he made to turn his head he winced with pain and his hand came up to touch his face. 'What's 'appened to me, Annie?'

'You were burnt by mustard gas.'

He shuddered. 'Am I disfigured?'

Annie wasn't sure what to tell him, but decided she couldn't lie to him. 'One side of your face is burnt and so are yer 'ands, but they won't look so bad when they've 'ealed. The main thing is that you're alive.'

'Unlike many o' me mates.' His eyes filled with tears as he recalled the horrors he had seen. 'We were on the field an' one of 'em stood on a landmine. It blew 'im clean in 'alf an' all across the field, poor bugger. They filled another of 'em so full o' lead that—'

'*Stop!*' Annie held her hand up. 'It can't do no good to think about things like that right now. You just 'ave to concentrate on gettin' strong enough to get back 'ome. Think 'ow chuffed yer da an' yer ma will be to see yer. Why, they'll likely give yer a hero's welcome.'

He looked confused as something occurred to him. 'But what are you doin' 'ere? I thought you were workin' in the field hospitals.'

'I was,' she admitted as she gently began to change the bandages on his hands. 'But I'll explain more later.'

'An' Harry? Have yer heard how he's doin'?' He was getting agitated.

She shook her head. 'Not yet, but I'm sure he'll be fine. Now try an' get some rest, eh?'

He nodded and was soon asleep again, and the room fell silent, aside from his laboured breathing.

That evening, when Yvette carried a tray of food down and saw that Barney was awake she blushed prettily. She was just at the age when she was beginning to notice men and boys and she could see that Barney must have been quite handsome before he got burnt.

'*Ma mere* 'as made for you onion soup and boeuf bourguignon,' she told them shyly.

Annie smiled at her. '*Merci beaucoup*, Yvette.'

Annie started to feed some of the stew to Barney but he only took a few mouthfuls before waving his hand weakly for her to stop. It wasn't much but Annie was hopeful this was a good sign. She had been far more concerned about the effects the gas might have had on his lungs than the burns. She made him comfortable before starting her own meal. She certainly couldn't fault Madame Lecroix's cooking.

Over the next few days Barney grew steadily stronger and was soon able to sit propped up with pillows. Annie was hopeful that soon he might be well enough to travel. But then one evening, as they were settling down for the night, she heard the distant sound of trucks pulling into the yard and her heart started to thump. She put a warning finger to her lips to convey to Barney that he must be silent and extinguished the oil lamp.

They heard the sound of a door banging open, and then German voices shouting and heavy footsteps stamping over the floor above them. It sounded as if the furniture was being overturned and she could hear the two young girls screaming and pressed her hand to her mouth to stop herself from crying aloud. If the Germans discovered their hiding place they would all be dead in no time.

She fumbled in her bag until her hand closed around the small pistol Alex had given her. With difficulty she loaded it with bullets and cocked it ready to fire, and then all she could do was wait. If the trap door opened, she would use it first on Barney and then on herself, but she could do nothing to help the Lecroix family, and her heart ached for them as she heard the madame scream. The sounds of pots smashing and furniture thumping on the floor seemed to go on for a very long time, and then suddenly there was silence and the overpowering smell of petrol.

'Good God, I reckon they're gonna set fire to the place,' Barney whispered, and the words had barely left his lips when four gunshots rang out, one after another.

'*Oh no!*' Annie felt sick. Minutes later they heard a whoosh from above and they knew the cottage was on fire and there was no way out for them.

'At least they ain't found us so just sit tight,' Barney warned, and she nodded in the darkness as she pictured all Madame Lecroix's treasures going up in smoke.

Soon the heat in the cellar became almost unbearable and smoke started to fill the room. Thankfully there were airbricks and somehow Annie managed to get Barney over to them so at least they could lean against them and get some fresh air. She had no idea how long they sat there but at last they heard the roar of the trucks leaving and all they could do was wait, hoping the Lecroix family had survived and would come to let them out.

But no one came and after a long time the smoke began to filter through the airbricks.

'I'm goin' to try an' push the trap door open,' Annie told Barney eventually, when there was no sound from above. 'You just get back on the bed.'

She felt her way blindly about the room, cracking her legs painfully on the sparse furniture as she went, until at last, she felt the bottom stair and started to crawl up. It was then that she found out what had saved them. The kitchen floor was made of solid stone, hot to the touch but it had blocked the fire. However, when she put pressure on the heavy trap door it showed no sign of movement and for a moment she panicked.

But then common sense took over. Alex knew they were here, so eventually, when he had no word, he would come and find them. He had to.

Fumbling and sliding her way back down the stairs she made her way to the table and after feeling about for the matches, she managed to relight the oil lamp. The flickering flame cast dancing shadows across the walls and looking towards Barney she saw he was watching her.

'What if they come back?' he asked quietly.

'Don't worry.' She patted the pistol in her pocket. 'I'll never let them take us, I have this and I'll use it rather than let that happen.'

'I believe yer would an' all.'

'Here.' Annie poured them both some wine from the carafe Madame Lecroix had sent down for them. 'Have a little of this, it'll steady our nerves.' And then she asked in a small voice. 'Those gunshots . . . do you think—'

'Think of something else,' he ordered. Shock was setting in and she was shaking now and suddenly their roles had reversed, and it was him looking after her. And so they settled down to wait, the only sound from above the hiss of the dying flames and the crash of the walls as they caved in.

At last they heard voices and Annie quickly put out the oil lamp in case it was the Germans returning. She took the gun from her pocket and gripped it tightly as they listened to the sound of rubble being shifted and the trap door being opened. Daylight poured in and Alex appeared on the stairs.

With a sob Annie ran to him and threw herself into his arms. 'Oh, Alex, I was so afraid. But the Lecroix . . .'

He gripped her tightly to his chest and there was a catch in his voice as he answered, 'Don't think of them for now.'

'B-but we heard gunshots and when they didn't come to let us out, we thought . . .'

He nodded. 'They have been shot. The Germans lined them up and killed them like the low-life cowards they are. Thankfully, Marie managed to escape into the forest and made her way to me but by the time we got here . . . Well, we won't dwell on that. For now, I just need to get you and Barney to a safe place.'

'But the Lecroix . . .'

He sighed as he gently put her from him. 'My men are up there burying them; may God bless their souls. They were brave people.'

'And what will happen to Marie now?' Tears were streaming down Annie's pale cheeks.

'She is being taken to a safe house in Paris where she will stay until the war is over.'

Behind him two other men began to clatter down the stairs and, nodding towards Barney, Alex told them, 'Get him wrapped up and into the cart. The sooner we're away from here the better. Have you done what I asked upstairs?'

The man nodded, his face grim, before approaching Barney. After wrapping a blanket about him he lifted him as if he weighed no more than a feather, saying gently, 'Come on, matie.'

Alex urged Annie to follow the two men up the stairs. Her first glimpse of the Lecroix's kitchen as she emerged from the cellar made her cry out with dismay. Most of the furniture was nothing but ash and glancing up she could see the stars through the roof. Smoke was still rising from the debris as Alex ushered her on.

'We must get away as quickly as possible. There's no saying the Germans won't be back and if they do come . . .'

He had no need to say more. Annie was only too aware what would happen and she kept her hand on the little pistol in her pocket.

Outside, Alex hoisted her into the back of a cart next to Barney, who was groaning with pain. Sacks were thrown across them and then the horse moved on.

At last, feeling bumped and bruised after being rolled about in the back of the cart, it came to a standstill and Annie heard Madame Moreau's voice ask, 'Did you manage to save them?'

The sacks were removed and she and Barney were lifted from the cart and carried straight to the hidden room in the barn.

'Aw, *ma cherie*, we 'ave been so worried about you,' the kindly French woman said as she gave Annie a hug. 'And this must be your brother, Barney?'

When Annie nodded the woman sighed and turned back to Alex. 'They will stay 'ere, *oui*?'

He shook his head. 'No, madame, only until I can arrange a boat, hopefully for this evening. It's too much of a risk to you for them to be here now. I'm afraid the Lecroix . . .'

'Oh no!' Tears started to her eyes. She had known the family well and would miss them.

'I . . . I'm so sorry,' Annie whimpered.

Madame Moreau wagged a finger at her. 'It was not your fault, Celeste. Like us they knew the risk they were taking and they were willing to die for the cause.' Then turning to Alex, she asked tentatively, ''Ave they been buried?'

'Yes, madame, I made sure of it. But now you must excuse me. I have arrangements to make to get these two away as quickly as possible. The Germans must have been tipped off that the Lecroix were sheltering English there and they might come here as well.'

'I understand,' she said bravely. Like the Lecroix she was willing to die for what she believed in and once again Annie was full of admiration for her bravery.

Then Alex was gone again and, as she held tight to Barney's hand, all they could do was wait.

Chapter Thirty-Three

That very same evening, Monsieur Moreau helped Barney into the back of his cart and after saying a tearful goodbye to the family Annie scrambled in beside him. The Germans could be heard pillaging and burning nearby villages and there was no time to waste. Every minute they stayed there put themselves and the Moreaus in grave danger.

'What will 'appen to Barney when we get to England?' Annie dared to ask once the horse was trotting along.

Alex was holding a rifle and looking from side to side as they went.

'He'll be taken to a hospital in Dover until he's well enough to travel on to his family,' he told her. 'Meanwhile we will get word to them and they'll be able to visit him. So will you.'

'What do you mean? I'll be coming back with you, won't I?'

She was staring at the back of Alex's head because he was sitting up front with the driver.

'I don't think that would be a good idea. I've already put you in terrible danger and I can't ask you to take any more chances.'

'But I *must* come back!' she said heatedly. 'Who else will 'elp you get the injured back across the Channel if I don't?'

'Look, let's just concentrate on getting safely to the boat, shall we? If the Germans stop us on the way the chances are none of us will be going anywhere.'

Annie lapsed into silence, Barney leaning heavily against her. Although balmy, the night air had affected his breathing and every breath was laboured. She just prayed he would survive the journey and that the crossing would be relatively calm.

They eventually pulled up to the same little cove she had sailed from before and within minutes the boat appeared through a sea mist and drew as close to the shore as it could.

'The mist is good,' Monsieur Moreau told her as Alex waded through the shallows with Barney in his arms to place him in the boat. 'There will be less chance of you being spotted until you are clear of the coast. May God go with you, *ma cherie*. You 'ave been brave indeed.'

'But I want to come back,' Annie said with a catch in her voice. 'There is so much more I could do to 'elp.'

'You 'ave done enough.' He squeezed her hand fondly as he handed her the bag she had brought with her. 'And almost lost your life in the process. No, you go back to nursing in England.'

Alex splashed his way back to her and made to lift her, but she slapped his arms away. 'I can do it myself,' she said stubbornly, and after planting a kiss on Monsieur Moreau's cheek she waded out to the boat. She would continue her argument with Alex on the journey.

Annie could feel the tension as the boat pulled away from the shore but thankfully the sea mist obscured the craft and there was nothing to indicate that the Germans had heard them depart. They were some way out to sea before Alex sighed and took a seat beside her and Barney, who was once again leaning heavily on Annie. Thankfully the sea was calm so the crossing shouldn't take too long.

'I-if Annie is going home then I want . . . to go with 'er,' Barney stated breathlessly.

Alex frowned. 'But we have arranged for you to be taken to the nearest hospital, you need treatment.'

Barney stubbornly shook his head. 'We 'ave hospitals in Nuneaton an' I wanna go 'ome.'

Alex stared at him for a moment. It was dark but he could just make out their faces by the light of the moon. 'Very well, if you're sure that that is what you want, I will instruct the ambulance to take you to Nuneaton instead, so long as you think you're up to the journey?'

Barney nodded and soon after slipped into an uneasy sleep.

'I *don't* want to go home. I want to come back to France wi' you!' Annie said after a moment's silence.

Reaching out to her Alex took her hand. 'Do you realise that you could have been killed back there? How do you think I could have lived with myself if you had been? When Marie got word to me that the house was on fire and her family had been shot, I was sick with dread that I would find you dead as well. No, you have done more than your fair share. It's time for you to go back to nursing in England – if that's what you want to do.'

'I want to come back and carry on wi' you,' she said stubbornly.

Alex sighed and fell silent – there was little more he could say.

The small boat approached the shore as dawn was breaking, and as Alex had promised, an ambulance was waiting for them. While the ambulance men transferred Barney into the back of it, Annie turned to Alex with fire flashing in her eyes.

'So, is this it? You're really sendin' me 'ome?'

'It's for your own safety,' he told her regretfully. 'But you must be sure to tell people that Barney ended up in the field hospital you were working in and never mention that you've been working with the Resistance.'

Her shoulders sagged as it dawned on her that this might be the very last time they would ever see each other. Alex had awakened feelings in her that she had never known she had and although she knew he was a married man a tiny part of her had always hoped that someday they could be together. She pulled herself together sharply. What was the point of daydreaming? There could never be any future together for them. They were in the middle of a war and the chances were that one or both of them might not even survive it.

She took a shuddering breath and held her hand out. 'This is goodbye then. Thank you for what you've done for Barney. If it wasn't for you . . .'

He reached out and pulled her into his arms, kissing her lips tenderly. When it was over she nestled momentarily against his broad chest, feeling as if her heart would break. Damn this war and damn his wife!

Alex gently put her from him and, turning, he splashed his way back to the boat while Annie clambered into the back of the ambulance with Barney.

Late that afternoon they drew up outside the house in Swan Lane, and France and all that had happened there suddenly seemed a very long way away.

They were given a royal greeting, especially by Maggie, who was overjoyed to have one of her sons back home.

While Barney was put to bed, Annie was filled in on all that had been happening. So much had changed since she went away. She was particularly shocked to learn that Susan had returned to London with Constance. She just hoped that Theo would treat them better this time.

'What will you an' Barney do now?' Peggy asked late that night when everyone else had gone to bed and she and Annie were enjoying a cup of cocoa.

'Barney will be sent back if he recovers from the gas. It'll depend if it's done any lastin' damage to his lungs. If it has, there'll be no more fightin' for him. The burns on his hands and face should heal nicely, but the doctors will decide. And as for me . . . I think I'll probably go back to the 'ospital in Weddington, if they still want me.'

'Oh, I've no doubt they will,' Peggy told her. 'The place is bulgin' at the seams wi' injured soldiers arrivin' daily.'

Annie nodded. 'And 'ow is Monty?' she asked eventually.

Peggy sighed. 'Well, he's 'ome from 'ospital, poor love. He sits out in the garden fer a lot o' the time. No doubt to get outta the way o' his mother fussin' over 'im.'

'I'll keep my eye out for him tomorrow. No point in goin' round to ask if I can see 'im I don't suppose. Mrs Taylor-Lloyd would probably give me a mouthful an' send me packin'. An' has there been any news o' Davey?'

'Not a dicky bird. Poor Eve. But she won't give up 'oping that he's alive somewhere. I reckon it's only havin' little Jack to look after that's kept 'er sane.'

Annie sipped at her drink. It felt strange to be home again and she wondered what Alex was doing. Was he safely back in France? And if so, how long for? Giving herself a shake she tried to turn her thoughts to other things.

The following day, shortly before lunchtime, Annie saw Monty sitting in the garden next door and she wandered over to speak to him. His face lit up at the sight of her and she was pleased to see that he looked somewhat better than the last time she'd seen him.

'Mother heard you and Barney were back,' he greeted her, holding his hand out to her. 'Are you here for good now?'

'For the foreseeable future at least.' Annie bent to peck his cheek. 'Now tell me 'ow are you? Will you be goin' back?'

His face fell as he shook his head. 'I'm afraid not. They managed to remove one of the pieces of shrapnel the last time they operated but it was still too tricky to remove the other pieces, so they've had to leave them.'

When Annie raised an eyebrow, he shrugged. 'It's all in the lap of the gods now. Someday they could move of their own accord and if they move towards my heart . . . Anyway because of that I'm classed as unfit to go back to my regiment. I shall probably go back to my office job when the doctor allows it. At least that isn't strenuous.'

'I don't understand. If the shrapnel moves towards your heart what happens?'

He grinned ruefully. 'If it moves towards my heart I won't know much about it, because I'll be a goner. We just have to hope that if it does move it goes the other way and then they'll finally be able to get it out. To be honest, I just wish it would hurry up and do it. At least then, if I do survive, I wouldn't have to take it easy all the time. But tell me how Barney is.'

They continued chatting for a few more minutes until Annie eventually turned to leave. 'Sorry, I must go. I'm goin' back to the 'ospital to see if they still need me. I can't just sit about, I'd go mad.'

He nodded in understanding. 'I know exactly what you mean and I'm sure they will want you back. There's been some terrible stories of the poor chaps that have been taken there with mustard gas burns. I'll come back out here for a while later this afternoon and perhaps we can have another chat?' he ended hopefully.

'I'll try.' Annie smiled before hurrying away to get ready to go to the hospital. She didn't want to give him false hope.

Some days later Barney went for his medical and was told that because of the damage to his lungs he would not be allowed to return to the front.

'So what will yer do now?' Annie asked gently.

'I'm goin' back to the circus,' he told her.

It came as no surprise. She knew how much he had loved that way of life and he had become increasingly unsettled since returning home. 'But will they still be performin' wi' the war on?'

He shook his head. 'Probably not, but there's still the animals to tend to and jobs to be done. It'll be better than sittin' around doin' nuthin' all day. An' anyway, I want to be there when Mercy comes home from prison.'

'Then I wish yer well,' she said sincerely. They would all miss him, but she knew he was doing the right thing.

Chapter Thirty-Four

Annie had been working back at the hospital for a few weeks when, in September, a new weapon that everyone hoped would break the deadlock of trench warfare was used for the first time with startling results. Codenamed The Tank the armoured monster roared over the muddy battlefield of the Somme on its tracks, spitting bullets and spreading panic through the German lines. Some German soldiers fled shouting, 'The devil is coming.'

Within two hours of its appearance the attacking British and Canadian troops had taken more than 2,000 German prisoners.

'This could be a turnin' point fer our lads,' Levi said with satisfaction as he read the piece in the newspaper out to them at home that evening.

'Let's 'ope so, there's been far too much bloodshed,' Peggy agreed sadly. Even the end of the war would not bring her son back to her, and she still suffered nightmares thinking of him lying in a lonely grave amongst hundreds of others in a strange country.

'It's frantic at the 'ospital,' Annie agreed. 'Some poor bloke come in today wi' his face blown off. I doubt he'll still even be alive when I go in to me shift tomorrow.'

Levi shook his head. It seemed a world away since he had taken Dobbin out on his rag-and-bone rounds, and he still missed it. 'I heard the shop next to ours is goin' up fer rent,' he told them. 'Another small business bit the dust, more's the pity. What wi' all the young men away fightin', the women can't manage to keep 'em open. Soon there'll be nothin' much fer the young men to come 'ome to. Those that do come 'ome,' he ended soberly.

'We 'ave to stay positive,' Annie said quietly, ever the optimist. 'I'm personally lookin' forward to gettin' our shop open again when this is all over, an' I've got lots o' plans fer it.'

Levi stared at her for a moment. Annie never failed to amaze him and he often wondered how she had become such a strong young woman. She had been left as a newborn on the steps of the workhouse, never knowing who her real parents were and once she'd come to them, Maggie had never been the mother she deserved. When she was old enough, she had happily joined him in his business when his own sons had no wish to, and she had begun to build the business up before the start of the war. Since then, she had risked her life in France and now here she was talking of her plans for the business when the war was finally over. She truly was a remarkable young woman, and he couldn't have been prouder of her if she was his own flesh and blood.

''Ow is Monty?' he asked.

Annie sighed. He had recovered enough to go back to his office job but he was still having to be careful. The shrapnel that was lodged close to his heart could move at any time and he was living constantly under the shadow of death. 'He's much better than he was,' she answered. 'To tell the truth I reckon 'e were glad to get back to work to stop 'is ma fussin' over 'im.'

'I can understand that.' Levi scratched his chin. 'He's a good lad is Monty, none better, an' he'll make someone a fine 'usband one o' these days.'

Annie smiled at his obvious attempt at matchmaking. She and Monty were still good friends and she knew he still had strong feelings for her. But although she was very fond of him, she didn't love him. His touch didn't set her pulses racing as Alex's had. And anyway, even if she did decide to marry Monty, she wondered how she would cope with having Reggie as a brother-in-law. Just the thought of it brought her out in a cold sweat! No, as fond as she was of Monty she was better off alone – for now at least.

The next evening, after dinner, Annie and Monty went for a stroll. Before the war they had often visited the picture house or the Prince of Wales Theatre for an evening out, but they had been closed for some time now and there was little hope of them opening again until after the war was over.

As they headed for Tuttle Hill before taking the lane down to the canal they trod across a carpet of russet and gold leaves that were fluttering down from the trees.

'Had a good day, 'ave you?' Annie asked conversationally.

Monty shrugged, his hands tucked deep into his coat pockets and his head down. 'Same old,' he answered quietly. 'I just wish I could go back to the front and do my bit. I feel a fraud being here while all the other chaps my age are away fighting.'

'You know that's not possible,' she scolded gently. 'And from where I'm standing you've done more than your bit. You could 'ave been killed.'

'I sometimes wish I had been,' he muttered despondently. 'I can't even have a game of football or do anything strenuous, and my mother fusses over me to the point that I feel like screaming.'

Annie glared at him. 'That's not the way to talk. Feelin' sorry for yerself ain't goin' to help anyone, an' much as me an' yer mam don't get on, I can understand 'er bein' as she is. She's bound to be worried.'

'I just wish this damn shrapnel would move one way or another and be done with it!' Monty kicked at a loose stone sending it skittering along the pavement in front of him and for a while they continued in silence.

They were strolling along the canal towpath when Monty asked, 'How are you enjoying being back at the hospital? Do you like it more than doing the shop and the rag-and-bone rounds?'

Annie thought about it for a moment. 'I suppose I do enjoy doin' what I'm doin' now. But I must admit it were nice doin' the rounds wi' old Dobbin. I were me own boss then, wi' no one to tell me what to do. I did consider goin' into nursin' full time after the war but I've changed me mind. Soon as I'm able I'll be back in me old trews an' out collectin' again. I've also got some ideas fer the shop. The shop next to ours will be comin' up fer rent and I'm thinkin' o' talkin' Levi into takin' it on.'

Monty looked confused. 'But what would you want more than one shop for? Surely you have room in the one you have?'

She nodded. 'Yes, we 'ave, but I'd like a shop that sells new things as well, not just second-'and clothes. When this war is over people will want to buy reasonably priced clothin' an' we could sell shoes an' hats an' all. An' o' course there's the added benefit o' the rooms above the shop. I could live in them. I'm grown up now an' I can't stay with Levi and Maggie forever.'

'Hmm.' He stared at her with a wry grin before saying cautiously, 'Or of course you could always marry me and then you need never work again. I'd buy us a house of our own to live in.'

'Oh Monty, you know I think the world o' you, but I still ain't ready to marry anyone just yet. An' even when I do, *if* I do, I'd still want to work. I've worked all me life. Why, they set me on cleanin' at the workhouse just as soon as I were big enough to hold a broom. I think I'd go mad just sittin' about all day wi' nowt to do but keep the house tidy.'

She tucked her arm into his and they carried on walking. Monty smiled sadly. Her answer was always the same, but it wouldn't stop him trying and who knew, one day she just might say yes. He hoped so because he had known since the very first time he had set eyes on her that she was the only girl for him.

Could he have known it she was beginning to wonder if, despite the thought of having Reggie as a brother-in-law, marrying him would be such a bad idea after all. He was solid and dependable, kind and considerate, and he could have had his pick of young women if he'd had a mind to. Perhaps love would grow if she gave it a chance? It was something that she was seriously considering, for there was no future with Alex.

She had always wanted to have children of her own one day, children who she would shower with love. She was determined that they would never know the heartache she had suffered as a child, and Monty would make a wonderful husband and father.

If only Alex's face didn't flash in front of her eyes every time she thought about it.

Chapter Thirty-Five

Before they knew it, it was November. Levi, who read the newspapers cover to cover each day, kept them informed of the progress of the war.

'Things are lookin' grim,' he said one night after dinner. 'Despite the tanks on the battlefields the terrible weather conditions at the Somme are makin' attack impossible fer our lads. The poor buggers are dyin' in thick cloyin' mud an' they reckon we've lost at least forty-two thousand of our chaps, an' the French 'ave lost another twenty thousand o' theirs. All them young lives snuffed out like candles in the wind! So, I reckon it's safe to say the war ain't goin' to be over any time soon.'

They all became silent as they tried to imagine the carnage; it didn't bear thinking about.

With so much bad news, British spirits reached an all-time low, and all too often the dreaded telegraph boy could be seen pedalling furiously down far too many streets. Continued rain had turned the battlefields into quagmires and the idealism of the young men who had so bravely and eagerly marched off to war had died. All they wanted now was for the war to be over so they could be back home with their families for Christmas, but they knew there was little chance of that happening.

Monty and Annie were discussing the situation one evening as they walked home after he had met Annie from her shift at the hospital. Now that the nights had drawn in, he wasn't keen on her walking home in the dark, and met her whenever he could, although Annie insisted there was really no need. It was another show of his devotion to her, and she couldn't help but be touched by it.

They had gone some way with their breath hanging on the air like lace ahead of them when he told her, 'Mother had a letter from Reggie today.'

Just the mention of his name made Annie cringe. It was just as well Monty had no idea of what Reggie had done, because despite his condition he would have set about him.

'Oh yes . . . what did 'e 'ave to say?' She supposed she had to make an effort to sound interested.

'Reading between the lines it sounds to me like he's happy to sit tight in the bunkers while he sends his men up onto the battlefield to be slaughtered,' he said with disgust. 'Can you believe he was actually bragging about how comfortable he is, while the men have to lie in mud with rats crawling over them.' He shook his head. 'An officer should lead his men, but you know Reggie.'

Annie did, all too well, but she couldn't tell him that. 'Perhaps the officers are allowed to do that?' she ventured for want of something to say.

He shook his head. 'Not while I was out there, they weren't. The officers were first up and leading their men, but not our Reggie. If Mother hadn't paid for this commission, I reckon he'd have turned tail and gone AWOL long before now.'

Monty was getting agitated and Annie squeezed his arm. 'Calm down, yer know yer not supposed to get yerself into a tizzy.'

Monty sighed. It was very frustrating not being allowed to be as energetic as he had once been.

They continued in silence for some way and Annie's thoughts, as they often did, turned to Alex. Deep down she had hoped he would be in touch. She knew he had her address and every morning before leaving for the hospital she checked the mail. But then, she supposed she shouldn't be surprised; he was an honourable man and would remain loyal to his wife and child. That was just as it should be, but it didn't stop her yearning for him, even if a future for them was out of the question.

'It'll be Christmas again before we know it.'

Monty's voice brought Annie's thoughts sharply back to the present. 'Sorry?'

'I said it'll be Christmas again soon.' He smiled. 'You were miles away then. What were you thinking about?'

'Oh, nothing much,' she said quickly, glad that the dark would hide the colour that had crept into her cheeks.

'Hmm, I suppose it's too cold to ask you if you fancy going for a proper walk tonight?'

She nodded and stifled a yawn. 'I'm afraid it is. I just want a hot meal and my bed. I did an early shift today and I've been runnin' about for fourteen hours solid. But why don't yer come in an' have a drink before you go home?'

When they arrived back, Peggy informed them they had received a letter from Susan that day.

'Really?' Annie was surprised. 'And what did she have to say for herself?'

'She asked if her and Constance could come an' join us fer Christmas.'

Annie raised an eyebrow. 'That's strange, ain't it, if she's supposed to be makin' a go of it wi' Theo?'

'That's what I thought,' Peggy agreed as she started to mash some potatoes. 'But Levi told me to write back an' tell 'er they'd be welcome. I reckon it would certainly cheer Maggie up no end.'

'And where is Levi?'

Peggy nodded towards the window. 'He's out there beddin' old Dobbin down.' Then turning to Monty she asked, 'Are yer joinin' us fer dinner, lad? There's plenty to go round an' yer more than welcome.' She couldn't help but notice how peaky he looked, but he hadn't looked well since he'd returned from the hospital.

'Thanks, Peggy, but I won't. Mother will have something ready. Or should I say the cook will, and you know what a stickler my mother is for the family eating together. I'll just have a cup of tea if it's no bother, then I'll be off.'

An hour later Annie retired to bed with a hot-water bottle. Already a thick pattern of frost had formed on the inside of her bedroom window and the sheets were icy cold when she crept between them. But she knew from the casualties that were arriving at the hospital daily that this discomfort was nothing compared to what the soldiers in the trenches were having to endure. Trench foot, caused through standing in icy, dirty water for hours on end, was common. So were respiratory problems, rheumatism and frostbite. Only the day before, as she had attempted to clean a young man's badly affected feet, one of his toes, which had turned jet black, had come off in her hand and it had taken all she had not to scream. Another young man, who had suffered horrific burns across his body, had died in her arms calling out for his mother. Every morning, before arriving at the hospital, she had to steel herself for what the day ahead may bring. All the nursing staff did their very best but there were too few of them and too many patients.

Shivering, she wondered what Alex was doing at that moment, and his face was the last thing she saw in her mind's eye before she fell into an exhausted sleep.

At that moment in a cold, wet, rat-ridden trench Alex was making his way to the officers' quarters. He had been travelling all day and was bone tired, but he would not rest until he had imparted the information he had gleaned to the right channel.

The fighting was over – for that day at least – but weary men were smoking and leaning against the muddy walls of the trench keeping watch for any unexpected attacks.

After some way Alex saw a makeshift shelter with a tin roof ahead. Crude as it was, it was luxurious compared to what the soldiers were used to. A roughly hewn wooden door stood at one end of it and Alex opened it without knocking.

Two young officers were lying on bunk beds, reading and drinking brandy. They looked up in surprise at his entry and the younger of the two snapped, 'Who the hell do you think you are walking in here without permission?'

Alex eyed him coldly. 'I am Captain Alex Gordon. I'm with the intelligence service and I have important information for headquarters back in London.'

'Oh, er . . . right. You'll need to use the radio then.' The man's attitude changed immediately. Captains were of far higher rank than they were. He motioned to a radio standing on a makeshift table in the far part of the small room and crossing to it, Alex sat down and began to tap his message out in code. When he was done, he leant back in the chair and sighed wearily.

'How has it gone today?' he asked the men.

'Could have been better,' the officer told him with a shrug. 'Lost a lot of men apparently. I believe the stretcher-bearers are still out on the field bringing them in.'

'What do you mean, you *believe*? Why aren't you out there supervising? Some of those men could have been from your regiment!'

One of the officers hastily put his tunic on and made his way out of the door, leaving Alex with the remaining man.

'Well, er . . . yes some of them probably were.' The officer was flustered. He had barely left the shelter for days apart from to use the toilet.

'*Probably* were? Weren't you up there with them?'

He flushed. 'Not for a while I've, er . . . been indisposed. Jippy tummy, you know?'

'So, your men were sent over the top with no one to lead them? What do you think headquarters would think of this?'

The man scowled. He didn't like being talked down to but before he had chance to reply Alex snapped, 'What is your name?'

He had no doubt this was just another jumped-up little chap whose Mummy and Daddy had paid for his commission.

The man drew himself up to his full height and saluted. 'Second Lieutenant Reginald Taylor-Lloyd . . . *Sir!*'

Alex frowned. The name rang a bell but for a moment he couldn't think why. Then it suddenly hit him and he gasped. It paid to have a good memory in his job. 'I believe you are acquainted with someone I worked with recently, Miss Annie Lilburn?'

Reggie instantly relaxed again and grinned as he made to pour himself another drink. 'Oh, I'm acquainted with Annie all right.' He winked and smirked. '*More* than acquainted if you get my meaning. She was my neighbour back at home.'

Alex felt his hands clench into fists and before he could stop himself, he landed a punch on Reggie's chin that sent him spinning across the room.

'You *dirty* little bastard,' Alex cursed as he remembered what Amelie had told him. This was the swine who had raped Annie.

Reggie clutched his chin and stared up at Alex in shock.

'I know *exactly* what you did to that poor girl,' Alex spat.

Reggie sniggered. 'Oh, came telling you some cock-and-bull story, did she? Well, let me tell you, she was up for it – *gagging* for it, in fact, and she loved it!'

'Annie never said a word about you,' Alex stormed, catching him by the collar and dragging him to his feet. 'But someone she confided in did, and I'm ashamed to see scum like you in an officer's uniform. Let me tell you now, this cushy little life you've made for yourself is about to change. I shall be here to see you personally lead your regiment onto the field tomorrow, otherwise I shall be reporting you!'

The colour drained from Reggie's face but he remained silent as Alex managed to get control of himself again and storm away.

As promised, Alex was back at first light to carry out his threat and Reggie had no choice but to get dressed and join his regiment.

The cry went up and suddenly he was in a tangle of arms and legs as his men scrambled up the rope ladders at the sides of the trenches and rushed forward to meet their enemy with Reggie amongst them for the first time.

A barrage of machine-gun fire met them and all around the men fell like flies, Reggie amongst them. And as he lay there in the cloying mud, he cursed Annie as he sank into darkness.

Chapter Thirty-Six

'Excuse me, ma'am. Sorry to bother yer, but . . .' The little maid gulped. 'But this just came fer you. It's addressed to you an' Mr Taylor-Lloyd.' With shaking hands, she held out the brown envelope that had just arrived.

The colour drained from Mrs Taylor-Lloyd's face. She was at breakfast with her husband and Monty, and she dabbed at her lips and took the envelope from the maid.

'You may go, Dora,' she said.

Mrs Taylor-Lloyd looked at her husband, who nodded gravely, and she slowly slit the envelope. Before even reading the telegram, she had guessed its contents and tears clogged her throat.

'I regret to inform you that your son, Second Lieutenant Reginald Taylor-Lloyd, died bravely on the battlefield on—' The telegram slid from her hand and fluttered to the floor as she began to moan loudly. 'No . . . no . . . this can't be . . .' It was her worst nightmare, just as it was for every other mother in the land.

Monty was around the table in a flash, completely forgetting that he was supposed to take things slowly. He wrapped his arms around his mother. 'Oh Mother, I'm so sorry. But at least he died fighting for what he believed in,' he murmured.

Her eyes flashed fire as she shoved him away from her. 'Fighting for what he believed in? Are you completely *mad*?' she shrieked. 'Reginald only agreed to go if we bought him a commission. If we hadn't, he'd still be here safe and sound. *We* killed him!'

'No, you didn't,' Monty soothed. 'He would have been called up anyway.'

His father had been sitting as if he had been carved in stone, his expression grim, but now he pushed away from the table and picked up the telegram and read the rest of it to himself.

'It says that he will be buried there with the others who fell with him,' he said quietly. 'We must arrange a memorial service for him up at St Mary's.'

His wife sniffed and with an effort pulled herself together. 'Yes . . . yes, that's what we must do. And it must be a grand occasion with a wake afterwards for everyone who knew him. He was a hero after all!'

Monty sighed. He had always known that Reggie was his mother's favourite. His father had always been fairly indifferent to both his sons, if truth be told, but now suddenly his mother seemed intent on turning Reggie into a hero. He could live with that; his brother was dead, and although they had never been the best of friends, he was sad to hear it. It felt strange to think that he would never see him again. Slipping quietly away he hurried next door hoping to catch Annie before she left for work. He was in luck and caught her going down the drive that divided the two houses.

'You're an early bird today,' she said as she pulled her cape more tightly about her. It really was bitterly cold. Then as she noted his glum face she asked quickly, 'Is everything all right, Monty?'

'It's Reggie . . .' There was a catch in his voice.

Annie stopped walking to stare at him, her heart thumping. 'What about him?' She was praying that he wasn't going to say Reggie was coming home. Just the thought of having to see him again filled her with dread.

'He's dead. Mother just got a telegram.'

'Oh!' She knew she should say she was sorry but somehow the words seemed to stick in her throat and all she could feel was relief. For weeks after he had raped her, she had lived in fear, terrified that she might be carrying his child, but now she would never have to fear him again.

'I . . . I don't know what to say,' she mumbled. 'Perhaps we could talk this evenin' when I get back from work? I'm sorry but if I don't get off now, I'm gonna get it in the neck from Matron.'

'Of course, you go on,' he urged. 'I'm sorry. I just wanted to see a friendly face.'

'I'm always 'appy to see yer.' She squeezed his arm. 'Come an' meet me tonight an' we'll talk more, eh? In the meantime, try an' keep yer chin up.' She gave him a quick peck on the cheek and hurried away.

The day dragged abominably slowly as Annie battled with her emotions. She could feel nothing but relief that she would never have to see Reggie again, and yet she felt guilty because he was Monty's brother.

At last, her shift was over and after collecting her cloak from the nurse's station she stepped outside and saw Monty waiting for her.

'How are you?' Hurrying over to him she slipped her arm through his.

'Oh, you know, coming to terms with it. And perhaps feeling a bit guilty because I'm not as upset as I should be,' he admitted. 'I mean, I know Reggie was my brother, but we were never close. I always thought he resented me coming along because until then he'd been the only child. Not that my coming changed anything. He was always Mother's blue-eyed boy.' He shook his head. 'I'm telling you this memorial service she has planned would be fitting for royalty.'

'I suppose she's bound to want to do something in his memory,' Annie answered.

'Yes, I agree. But most of the poor chaps that have fallen from the town get their names read out in church on the following Sunday. Reggie's having a long, drawn-out service all for him, telling everyone of his many virtues and what a hero he was. Then she's hired caterers to lay on a spread fit for royalty at the Bull Hotel. You will come, won't you?'

Annie shook her head. As much as she wanted to support Monty, she couldn't bring herself to be a hypocrite. 'I'm sorry, but I don't think yer parents would be too pleased if I were to show me face. You know what they think of us lot.'

He sighed. He knew she was right, but he was dreading the whole thing. 'You don't need to apologise, I understand. Anyway, what have you got planned for this evening?'

'I think Levi said he was goin' to pick a Christmas tree up tonight, so I've no doubt I'll be helpin' Ellie to decorate it. Why don't you come round an' help too? At least it'd get you out o' the house fer a while.'

'I might just do that,' he agreed.

Annie received another surprise when she entered the house shortly after when she saw Susan.

They hugged each other warmly, and searching the room Annie's eyes settled on Constance. She was nestled on Maggie's lap and had grown considerably since the last time Annie had seen her.

'So how 'as she been?' Annie asked as she removed her cape.

Susan shrugged. 'She's fine at the minute.' Her eyes were sad as she stared at the child she adored. 'She's not really doing much else but the doctor did warn me that children with her condition take longer to develop.' It had brought it home to her after seeing little Jack, just how far behind in her development Constance was.

'And Theo?'

Susan's eyes clouded. 'Same as ever. He's gone walkabout again and I didn't fancy spending Christmas on my own with the little one, so thought I'd come and join you all. How is our Flo doing?'

'Oh, she, er . . .' Annie didn't quite know how to answer. Word had reached them from more than one source that Flo was actually doing quite well for herself. 'Fine as far as I know. She hasn't been round for a couple o' weeks unless she's come while I've been at work.'

Peggy shook her head. 'No, we ain't seen her.'

'Is she working now?' Susan asked innocently.

Peggy chuckled. 'Aye, she is by all accounts, if you can call layin' flat on yer back workin'.' She was never one to mince her words. Then remembering that Susan did the exact same thing for a wealthier clientele, Peggy had the good grace to blush. 'Not that I wouldn't do the same if it were the only way to pay the rent,' she added hastily.

Luckily Susan had a sense of humour and smiled, and the awkward moment passed.

Soon after Levi arrived, dragging a rather splendid Christmas tree behind him.

Jack and Constance cooed and gurgled happily at the sight of it, and after dinner Monty joined them and he, Annie and Ellie set to decorating it with the tiny glass baubles that Maggie had collected over the years.

Ellie was now twelve years old and growing into a very pretty girl. She was tall and slim with thick brunette hair that had a tendency to curl. Her nature was as pleasant as her looks and she was much loved by all of them, apart from Maggie, who was still indifferent to her. Even so, Maggie had improved in as much as she no longer spent half her time talking to her dead daughter and Levi lived in hope that one day, the happy, loving woman he had married would return to him.

Jack was now eighteen months old and was into everything, much to their amusement. Constance, however, was showing no signs of being mobile, and whereas Jack constantly chattered away in his own little language, Constance merely cooed and clapped her chubby little hands.

Within minutes of the tree being finished, Jack began to take all the baubles off again, but no one had the heart to stop him. He was such a cheerful little chap and the absolute double of his father, which brought Eve a great deal of comfort. She was still clinging to the hope that Davey was alive somewhere and prayed daily that one day he would meet his son.

After everyone retired to bed, Annie and Monty found themselves alone downstairs. He had been quiet all night despite her best attempts to cheer him up, but she supposed that was to be expected.

'How are you feeling?' she asked gently, handing him a cup of cocoa.

He shrugged. 'I just wish it was me that had died and not Reggie,' he said quietly. 'And I get the distinct impression that my mother does too.'

Annie squeezed his hand. 'Look, you're bound to feel low at the minute, you've just lost yer brother an' you ain't well, but it won't always be like this. You're handsome and clever an' someday soon yer goin' to meet a girl who'll love you to bits.'

He shook his hand loose and stood up. 'When are you going to get it into your head that I don't want anyone else but you, Annie? But don't look so worried. I've got the message now. You don't want me!'

'No, you're wrong.' She shook her head. 'It ain't that I don't want *you*, Monty. I don't want anybody just yet. I ain't ready to settle down. I've got plans fer the shops when the war is over an' I want to make somethin' of me life.'

He stared down at her for a moment before turning and leaving, closing the door quietly behind him.

Annie felt guilty. She wished she could love him. He was everything she had said he was, and one day he was going to make someone a wonderful husband. Tears pricked at the back of her eyes as a picture of Alex's face swam in front of her. It was just her luck to give her heart to someone who was unattainable. She had no doubt that had she not met Alex she and Monty probably would have wed. Would it be such a bad thing? she wondered. Could love grow in time? With a sigh she rose and went to lock the door before retiring to bed.

Chapter Thirty-Seven

November 1918

The last two years had passed painfully slowly for everyone. Susan and Constance had long since returned to London and there had been nothing but the odd letters from Charlie and Harry to let them know that they were at least still alive. Annie felt as if all she had done was work and sleep. Then one cold November day she was changing a dressing on a soldier's leg in Griff Ward when the double doors were flung open and a young Red Cross nurse appeared, her face alight with joy.

'*It's over!*' Her voice echoed around the room as nurses, doctors and patients alike swivelled to look towards her. 'The war – it's *finally* over. The armistice has just been signed!'

A cheer went up and suddenly everyone was laughing and crying as they tried to take it in.

'Are yer quite sure, pet?' A patient with his arm heavily bandaged asked.

The nurse giggled. 'Absolutely sure! We won! Matron just heard it on the wireless and our boys will be coming home.' And then her face became solemn as she ended, 'Or at least . . . some of them will.'

The man who Annie had been tending grabbed her and placed a smacking kiss on her lips and Annie laughed for what felt like the first time in a very long while. It had been a hard year for everyone, not least the men fighting abroad.

That morning at eleven a.m. on the eleventh day of the eleventh month the fighting on the battlefields had finally ceased. The end had come more swiftly than the Allies had expected when two German generals and a senior minister in the new German government had put their signatures to the armistice document shortly before dawn in a railway carriage in Compiègne. The Germans had been ordered to hand over 5,000 heavy guns, 30,000 machine guns and 2,000 war planes, as well as their U-boats.

Suddenly the sound of church bells ringing reached them and a tidal wave of joy swept through the hospital. Even Matron and the surgeons were seen laughing and shaking everyone's hands. But the war had exacted a heavy cost. Over three-quarters of a million young men from Britain alone would not be returning home and Annie couldn't help but think of them and their families as tears streamed down her face.

'I can't believe it,' one of the young nurses cried with glee as she swung Annie about, nearly lifting her off her feet. 'My sweet'eart will be comin' 'ome an' we can finally get married.'

For the rest of the day there was an almost party atmosphere in the wards. 'It's just a pity this didn't come a couple o' weeks ago afore this happened,' a young man who had had both his legs blown off told Annie ruefully as she dressed his wounds. 'I'm not so sure my girl will want me now.'

'At least you came back and if she truly loves yer she will,' Annie told him as she gently dressed the stumps where his legs had been.

'Hmm, we'll see.' He didn't look too sure but even so the happy atmosphere was so infectious that soon even he was smiling again.

'Ain't it wonderful news?' Peggy cried the moment Annie walked in that evening.

'We can start gettin' back to the life we knew now wi' a bit o' luck,' Levi piped up joyously.

'Yes, and if my Davey is bein' held prisoner somewhere they'll release 'im.' Eve still couldn't envisage the rest of her life without Davey and clung on to hope tenaciously.

Monty appeared shortly after, and he too was thrilled about the news.

'So what will 'appen at the hospital now?' Levi asked Annie.

'We'll be working there until the patients have been discharged, so I could still be there fer a good few months yet, unless not so many of us are needed once the numbers go down. What about you, Levi? Will yer carry on wi' yer drivin' job?'

'Fer the time bein',' he answered. 'Though there won't be so much call for the deliveries now, so soon as I ain't needed I shall go back to doin' me rounds. That's sayin' old Dobbin is still up to it. I'll be in trouble if he ain't, cos I reckon the chances o' gettin' another younger horse at the minute will be slim. The poor young buggers all got took to be war horses, including our poor little mare.'

'Yes, an' it goes wi'out sayin' that the munition factories will close soon, so me an' Eve can go back to workin' in the shop,' Peggy pointed out.

Little Jack pottered over to Annie and she lifted him and gave him a cuddle. He had picked up on their good moods and was smiling from ear to ear.

Over the next few months, many men who had fought so bravely began to return, but they were no longer the men who had left so light-heartedly. Many of their faces were haunted by the terrible sights they had seen and the conditions they had been forced to live in. Even so, they were given heroes' welcomes by their womenfolk who waited anxiously for their return on the train station platform. Soon after Harry's wife and Levi received curt notes telling them that he would not be returning. He had fallen in love with a young French woman and would be making his life with her in France. Levi was upset but not surprised. Harry had never made a secret of the fact that he hadn't wanted to get married.

In the spring of 1919, the munitions factories closed down and Levi's driving job came to an end. By that time many of the patients at the hospital had returned home, so Annie's nursing came to an end too, and they decided it was time to try and get their rag-and-bone business back on track.

Annie was saddened at the sight of the town centre. Many of the small businesses had gone to the wall and so many shops stood empty with their windows boarded up. But at least that stood her in good stead when she negotiated rent for the empty shop next to theirs and got it at an unbelievably low price.

'They'll probably put it up when things start to get better,' she told Levi. 'But hopefully by that time we'll be into profit an' able to meet it. Meantime we can give it a clean an' get it ready fer openin'. I know things are gonna be a bit tight wi' none of us bringin' any wages in at the minute, but it shouldn't be fer long. We'll just 'ave to tighten us belts.'

Levi was only too happy to leave the organising of everything to Annie. She was so much better at it than he was. And so, they all set about painting and scrubbing the new shop. After gaining permission from the owner of the shops, Levi put a door through from one to the other and Annie began to plan what they should sell.

'Peggy, when we open, I reckon you should stay in this side wi' the second-'and clothes, you're the one that gets 'em ready fer sale after all,' Annie said thoughtfully. 'An' I think Eve should be in the new part wi' the new ready-made ones. Nuthin' too fancy, mind. Money is goin' to be tight fer everyone fer a time so we need to stock good serviceable things. An' you an' me, Levi, can go out on the cart an' start collectin' again. It might be a good idea if yer get Dobbin used to goin' out regular again an' see if the old chap is still up to it.'

'In that case I reckon it's time me an' Jack came back to live in the rooms above the shop,' Eve decided. 'There ain't much in the place worth robbin' at the minute but there will be once we start to restock, so it'll be wiser to 'ave someone on the premises.'

Levi frowned. 'Are yer sure you'll both be all right, pet?' He had grown very fond of them both.

Eve smiled. 'We'll be fine. Jack can be downstairs wi' me when I'm workin' in the shop. But thank you fer puttin' us up fer all this time. I don't know 'ow I would 'ave coped wi'out you all.'

They had all noticed a change in her over the past few weeks. She had been so sure that Davey would come home but as the weeks passed with no news or sight of him, her hope was finally beginning to waver.

When they returned to the house in Swan Lane that evening, they found Maggie had taken a major step backwards. She had been on her own all day and was sitting chatting to Penny again. She had been slowly regressing since Susan had taken Constance back to London a few months before.

Levi shook his head in despair. 'You've got to stop this nonsense once an' for all, pet,' he scolded.

Maggie looked up at him from tear-filled eyes. 'But she's still here with me, lad,' she said with a catch in her voice.

Annie looked at her sympathetically, then stifled a gasp as, just for an instant, she was sure she saw the outline of a small child standing at the side of Maggie. She remembered the child she had seen once before upstairs and now she began to wonder if there was something in what Maggie said, and if there was anything she could do to help.

Much later that evening, Annie set off for the vicarage of St Mary's. She knocked on the door and the vicar's housekeeper ushered her into the hallway, and pottered off to see if the vicar had time to see her.

'Miss Lilburn, how can I help you?' the elderly vicar asked when she had been shown into his study. He had been busy preparing a sermon but always made time for his parishioners.

'Well, I, er . . .' Annie licked her lips, hoping he wouldn't think she was stark staring mad. 'As yer know, Mrs Lilburn 'as suffered wi' mental 'ealth problems ever since the death of 'er little girl.'

He nodded. 'Yes, I am aware of that, it was quite tragic. I actually went to visit Mrs Lilburn after a visit from her sister Susan. But it clearly didn't help.'

Annie shook her head and went on to tell him of how Maggie had started talking to Penny again, although she omitted to tell him that she too had seen the child. 'Anyway, I read in a book I got from the library some time ago that sometimes people who die aren't aware they've passed on an' they don't know how to move on to the next life. So, I were wonderin' . . . is there anythin' you could do to 'elp?'

She held her breath as the vicar steepled his fingers and stared at her thoughtfully for a time. 'Are you suggesting that the child's ghost is still earthbound?'

Annie shrugged, feeling foolish. 'I don't know,' she admitted. 'But I do know that Maggie thinks she is.'

'I see. In that case there is a service I could perform, although I can't guarantee success,' he said eventually.

Annie sighed with relief. 'Oh, thank you. When would be the best time to try it?'

'It might be better if we attempted it when Mrs Lilburn and anyone else is out of the way,' he suggested.

She nodded. 'Perhaps late one evenin'?'

'Yes. I have come across this situation once before but as I said I can't guarantee that I'll be successful, especially if this is all a figment of Mrs Lilburn's imagination.'

'But I'm sure it ain't!' Annie blurted out, then blushed furiously.

'Then in that case we shall try to send the poor child to a better place,' he said gently. 'How about tomorrow evening?'

Annie nodded and after thanking him she left. It was growing dark and she hurried past the leaning gravestones with the hairs on the back of her neck standing to attention. After seeing the apparition for the second time she felt shaken. What if Maggie really was seeing her dead child? The poor woman, it was no wonder that she seemed to be going mad. Hopefully if the vicar was successful and could help Penny's ghost on her way, Maggie might finally find some peace.

Chapter Thirty-Eight

True to his word, the vicar arrived late the following evening. Everyone had gone to bed by then except for Annie, who was nervously waiting for him.

He entered the room and stood for a moment looking around before taking a bottle of water from his bag.

'I blessed this earlier on,' he told her. 'May I?' Seeing how nervous she was he went on, 'There is no need to be afraid. This isn't an exorcism or anything like that. If there is a spirit here it isn't a bad one, just a poor soul who doesn't realise it's time to move on. Sometimes a little gentle persuasion is all that's needed.' He began to walk about, liberally sprinkling the water here and there before taking his Bible from his bag and saying solemnly, 'Penny, if you are here, it is because you haven't realised that it's time for you to go to the light. Go. You will feel peace there.'

Next, with a nod at Annie, he began to say the Lord's prayer and she joined in:

Our Father who art in heaven . . .

When they had finished, he nodded to Annie again and began to recite Psalm 23: 1–6

'The Lord is my shepherd, I shall not want.
 He maketh me to lie down in green pastures: he leadeth me beside still waters.
 He restoreth my soul: he leadeth me in the paths of righteousness for his name's sake.
 Yea, though I walk through the valley of the shadow of death, I will fear no evil for thou art with me, thy rod and thy staff they comfort me.

Thou preparest a table before me in the presence of mine enemies: my cup runneth over.

Surely goodness and mercy shall follow me all the days of my life: and I will dwell in the house of the Lord forever.'

He closed his Bible quietly and suddenly Annie sensed a change in the room as if someone were watching her. The oil lamp on the table dimmed, leaving them in shadow, and over by the window a faint light started to glow. She saw the priest smile.

'I sense you are with us, Penny. Go towards the light now, my child, and find eternal peace.'

Just for a second the light seemed to grow brighter as a small shape moved towards it, then suddenly it was gone and the oil lamp flared again.

Annie let out a deep breath as the vicar mopped his forehead.

'I-is she gone?' Her voice came out as a croak.

'I can't say for sure but let us hope so. We'll have to wait and see. But now I'm away to my bed if you don't mind. It's been a long day.'

Annie helped him into his coat. 'Thank you, Father,' she said sincerely, handing him his hat.

He sighed. 'The death of a child is always hard to bear,' he said quietly. 'But if she has moved on, she can rest in the arms of the Lord now and hopefully her mother will finally find a measure of peace too. Goodnight, Annie.'

When he had gone, Annie slipped the bolts on the door and leant against it as she stared around the room with a huge lump in her throat. She had done all she could to help Maggie, and hopefully, she would start to get better.

The next morning, for the first time in a very long while, Annie appeared at breakfast in her old breeches and coat and Levi smiled. It was almost like old times, although none of them would forget the horror of the last four years.

'I don't think we'll 'ave any problems wi' old Dobbin,' Levi assured her. 'His prolonged rest seems to 'ave given 'im a new lease o' life, but I reckon we'll just go as far as Witherley an' Fenny Drayton today; break 'im in gently, eh? I'll drive an' you can do the door knockin'.'

'Sounds good to me,' Annie agreed and soon after they set off.

The first day didn't go quite as well as they had hoped. People had had to make do and mend throughout the war because of shortages and were not yet in a position to throw their old possessions away, but even so they collected a fair few things, which Annie thought could be sellable with a little work.

'We're not just collectin' rags an' bones now,' she had informed Levi. 'I'll take anythin' – furniture, pots, pans, rugs, anythin' at all that can be resold an' might make a bob or two. Look at this console table. It's solid mahogany but it's got a wonky leg an' they were gonna chuck it out. If you can mend it, I'm sure it'll polish up a treat.'

After examining the table Levi agreed, and after the evening meal, he took it outside and made a start on it while Annie went to help Peggy sort through the rest of the things they had collected. By the end of the week, the first shop had a fair amount of goods in it and on Saturday Annie set out to source some affordable ready-made clothes. There were quite a few clothes warehouses in Coventry and she selected some sensible gowns that would appeal to the women of the town.

'These are actually quite nice,' Peggy praised when Annie arrived home that afternoon. 'And some of 'em could be prettied up for Sunday best. What I mean is, I could put lace collars on 'em and fancy buttons, what do yer think?'

Annie nodded her approval and by Monday they were ready to reopen. The men of the town were still drifting home after the war and a Salvation Army Hostel had opened to house those who were now homeless. During the day some of them had taken to sitting on the pavements with begging bowls, and it broke Annie's heart to see them. There were some with arms and legs missing, and others who were so badly burnt that they were unrecognisable. Some of them wandered around muttering to themselves, their eyes vacant, their minds gone after the atrocities they had lived through. Money was still very tight, but Annie found it hard to pass by these men without dropping at least a few pennies into their bowls.

And then one day she saw a new figure huddled in a shop doorway. He was sitting hugging his knees with a hat pulled low over his face and a heavy coat with the collar pulled up, despite the warm weather. Annie had come to know a lot of the men by name and she paused to speak to him. It was evening and she was going to help Peggy load the clothes they had ready onto the rails in the shop.

'Good evening . . . are yer all right?'

There was no reply from the man, so Annie rummaged in her pockets for some money. It was then that he glared up at her and her stomach turned over. She had seen and nursed many burn victims but this man's face was almost gone. There was a gaping hole where his nose should have been and what she could see of his face was covered in scar tissue. Most of his top lip was burnt away too, exposing his teeth and gums. She had no idea how old he might be but was shocked he had even survived. She had seen many men die with far less severe wounds than he had.

'I don't want your money!' he growled, and Annie took an involuntary step back. The man clearly didn't like anyone to look at him so after a mumbled apology she hurried on.

When she entered the shop Peggy noticed that she looked shaken and frowned. 'What's up, pet? Yer look like you've seen a ghost.'

'I just saw some poor soul out there in a shop doorway with the worst burns to his face I've ever seen,' she said in a shaky voice. 'No amount o' surgery will ever put that right.'

Peggy continued to sort through the clothes and nodded. 'I reckon I know the one yer mean. He's been hangin' around fer a few days. I went out to offer 'im a drink o' tea yesterday an' he almost snapped me 'ead off. But don't get frettin' over someone as yer don't even know. We've got enough to worry about if we're to get this place up an' runnin' again.'

Annie knew Peggy was right, but for some reason she couldn't get the sight of the poor man's face out of her mind.

When she got home later that evening, she found Maggie greatly agitated and pacing the floor.

'I can't find Penny. I've been looking for her all day,' she told Annie.

Her stomach did a little flip. Could it be that the vicar had been successful in sending the child on her way?

'She's been like this ever since I got in,' Levi told her, looking worried.

'Let's go and sit in the garden for a moment,' Annie suggested gently, taking Maggie's elbow.

Maggie stared at her for a moment before agreeing meekly. Outside, Annie led Maggie to a bench beneath the apple tree. Maggie was plucking at a loose thread in her skirt as Annie told her softly, 'Maggie, I know that you've seen Penny ... I've seen her too.'

Maggie's eyes stretched as her head snapped around to look at her. 'You have? Then you don't think I'm mad like the rest of them do?'

'No, I don't,' Annie assured her. 'But the thing is, because you've still been able to see her, I don't think you've allowed yourself to accept that she's gone. Penny is dead, missus, and has been for a long time now. I think she's finally moved on, to heaven hopefully, and in future, if you want to be near her, you'll 'ave to visit 'er grave. I don't think she's 'ere anymore.'

Maggie's eyes filled with tears and she looked stricken, but she didn't argue, which Annie hoped was a good sign. Maggie had never been the loving mother that Annie had hoped she would be to her, and yet she couldn't help but feel compassion for her. She had obviously doted on her daughter and had struggled to come to terms with her loss for all these years.

'Tell yer what, after dinner we'll go for a walk to the churchyard, shall we?' she suggested kindly, and after a while Maggie nodded.

They picked some flowers from the garden and after Annie had washed and dried the dishes following dinner, they set off for the churchyard.

Levi had offered to go with them, but Annie suggested it might be better if they went alone. The grave looked neglected and untended. Maggie had hardly ever visited it because that would have been an admission that Penny was really gone, but now she stood for a long time staring at the little marble headstone with Penny's name on it, before stooping to lay the flowers in front of it. She said nothing, and it was hard to see her expression, but the peace of the place did seem to calm her.

'Do you think she'll be happy in heaven?' Maggie suddenly asked.

'I think so, and one day, 'opefully a long time from now, you'll be together again if what the vicar tells us is true.'

Annie discreetly left Maggie to say her farewells and went to stand by the lychgate. Eventually, a very subdued Maggie joined her, and they made their way home in silence. Annie hoped that Maggie would finally accept that Penny was dead and find some peace.

Levi looked worried when they returned, and Annie couldn't help but notice how pale he looked. He hadn't seemed himself for some time, not that he had complained, and she was concerned about him.

Maggie went straight upstairs to change out of her gown. That was one thing that hadn't changed: she still insisted on looking her best every time she set foot out of the house, which hadn't been often over the last few years.

'Do yer think she's finally accepted that Penny 'as gone?' Levi asked, his voice weighed with sorrow.

Annie nodded. 'I think so. Hopefully she might start to get better now, but we'll have to wait and see. What about you? Yer look a bit peaky to me. Are yer feelin' all right?'

'Aye, I'm fine.' Levi raised a smile just as Monty appeared to ask Annie if she fancied going for a stroll. She'd had a long day and had been looking forward to putting her feet up but seeing that he looked a bit down too, she agreed.

They had just reached the end of the road when they saw a hunched figure shuffling towards them and recognising it as the man with the terribly burnt face, Annie whispered, 'I think that's the poor chap that's been hangin' around by the shop. He's horrifically burnt, the poor soul.'

'Him and a few thousand others,' Monty answered. He looked towards the man and frowned. 'That's war for you, but at least he came home.'

Annie could think of no answer to that, so she held her tongue as they turned up Tuttle Hill and headed for the canal.

Chapter Thirty-Nine

Trade was slow to pick up in the shops. People were still struggling with shortages after the war, and money was tight, but Annie doggedly went on, determined to make it work. There had been no more word from Harry since the letter they had received saying that he was staying in France, and Becca had informed them that she was now seeking a divorce.

But Charlie had written to assure them that he was well and back in his home in London.

Slowly but surely, as they moved into the autumn, Annie's determination began to pay off. The women particularly were sick and tired of having to make do, and soon the ready-made dresses became very popular, so much so that Annie was making frequent trips to Coventry to visit the warehouses and restock.

At home they had all noticed a change in Maggie. She no longer chatted to Penny, but the sparkle had gone out of her, and she still insisted that Levi sleep in his own room. They had also noticed that Levi had changed. He was quieter and seemed content to leave Annie to organise everything.

'I'm worried about 'im,' Peggy confided to Annie one evening as they unloaded the cart. 'He ain't seemed 'imself fer some time an' I swear he's lost some weight.'

Annie wasn't sure how to answer. She had her concerns as well but didn't want to voice them and worry Peggy even more. 'I think everyone's a bit down at present,' she said instead.

Eve, who was helping them, nodded in agreement. 'Too true. The war's goin' to take some gettin' over. I had one lady in the shop yesterday who's 'usband just got back an' she says he's a changed man. The poor woman hardly dare open her mouth else she gets her 'ead bitten off.'

'There's a lot like that,' Peggy agreed. 'But it's no wonder, is it? Not after what the poor blighters 'ad to go through.'

Eve blinked back tears and thought of Davey. There was still no news from him and every morning when she opened her eyes, she prayed that this day would be the day he came home. Jack was growing like a weed and it broke her heart that his father had never even met him.

Luckily Peggy changed the subject when she said, 'That poor bugger wi' the burnt face is still hangin' around 'ere.'

'I know, I've seen him.' Annie shuddered at the thought of him. There was something about him that frightened her, although she couldn't say what it was. Since the first time she had met him they hadn't spoken a word but every time she hurried past him, she could feel his eyes boring into her back. 'I was thinking of making a start on the rooms above the shop next door,' Annie told them. 'After all, I can't stay with Levi and Maggie forever. It's time I became a little bit more independent.'

Eve nodded encouragement. 'I'd love havin' you next door. We could be company fer each other. Why don't we go round there an' 'ave a look at what needs to be done when we've finished up 'ere?'

'I'm afraid I'll 'ave to leave you two to do that.' Peggy straightened her back and yawned. 'I ain't no spring chicken anymore an' I'm lookin' forward to puttin' me feet up in front o' the fire now the nights are turnin' colder.'

After Peggy had set off for home, Eve and Annie climbed the stairs to look at the rooms above the second shop. The shop below them had sold hardware and Annie was delighted to find there was quite a bit of stock left up there. Buckets, bowls spades and all manner of odd tools, which she was sure they could resell.

'It'll need redecoratin',' Eve said glumly as she stared at the stained walls and filthy floorboards. 'But I dare say we could pitch in an' do it together on a Sunday. There's quite a few pieces downstairs that you've collected on yer travels to furnish it an' all. There's a couple o' fairly decent armchairs fer a start. Admittedly they don't match but they'd do yer till yer could afford somethin' better. There's rugs an' curtains as well.'

Annie felt a little bubble of excitement start in the pit of her stomach. She had only ever lived in the workhouse or with Maggie and Levi, but be it ever so humble, this would be her first home to call her own.

And so the following Sunday, Annie, Eve and Peggy set to emptying the rooms. Levi pitched in to help too, carrying the heavier things downstairs for them, and when they had finished, Peggy went downstairs with him to sort out what was sellable while Annie and Eve began the job of scrubbing the place. By the end of the first day it was ready for a coat of whitewash, although that would have to wait until the following weekend because they were too busy to even think about it during the week.

As they set off for home Annie noticed how tired Levi seemed and asked worriedly, 'Don't yer think yer should get yerself off to the doctor's? He might be able to give yer a tonic or somethin'.'

'I'm fit as a flea, just gettin' a bit older that's all,' he insisted, so Annie held her tongue.

They arrived home to find Maggie had cooked them a meal. She had started to do a little more about the house now, and she'd become a lot softer towards Annie too, which was a pleasant change. Now that Maggie no longer talked to Penny, Annie had noticed that she was visiting her grave in the churchyard more, so she seemed to have accepted that she really was gone.

It was a shock when Maggie seemed quite upset when she told her she would be moving out. She had never shown her any affection so

Annie wondered if it was because she would miss what she did about the house or whether she would genuinely miss her.

'We'll have the 'ouse all to uselves when young Annie goes, pet,' Levi told Maggie over their meal with a cheeky wink. 'It'll be the first time since all the kids grew up an' flew the nest. It'll be like a second 'oneymooon.'

'I don't think so,' Maggie responded primly.

Levi sighed. He was beginning to wonder if they would ever share a room and live as man and wife again, but he was too afraid of her relapsing back into her melancholia to say anything.

The following Sunday, the decorating began in Annie's new rooms, and by teatime it was ready to start bringing the furniture upstairs. Peggy had polished an old brass bedstead until it gleamed, as well as sorting out no end of bits and pieces that Annie would need.

'I've mackled you a set o' cutlery together. Admittedly, it don't match, but it'll do the job, and I've scrubbed them two old armchairs an' they've come up a treat. I've even sorted out some pretty cushions to go on 'em. There's some saucepans an' all, but you'll have to share the kitchen downstairs wi' Eve.'

'I don't mind that at all.' Annie was getting quite excited now.

'If Levi can carry the chairs an' the bed upstairs in the week, me an' Eve can get the rest ready while it's quiet in the shop so 'opefully next Sunday it'll be ready fer you to move in.'

For the rest of the week Annie was so busy that she had little time to think of her new home, but early the following Sunday she and Peggy went to view the rooms.

Annie had expected to find there was still a fair amount to be done but when she climbed the stairs and opened the door to her little sitting room, she gasped with pleasure. 'Oh . . . it looks *wonderful*!' Annie stared around in amazement.

There were pretty flowered curtains hanging at the gleaming windows and cushions in the same material on the two old wingchairs, which looked entirely different now that they'd had a good clean. Peggy had even found her a small, highly polished table where she could sit and eat in comfort, and either side of it were two ladderback chairs. Rugs were scattered about the scrubbed wooden floorboards and it looked cosy and inviting. There was even a fire laid ready in the small fireplace.

'Go an' 'ave a peep in the bedroom,' Peggy urged with a smug smile on her face, clearly enjoying herself.

Annie didn't need telling twice. She stared at the brass bed, which was now made up with clean sheets, warm blankets and a patchwork quilt. There was a china jug and bowl standing on a slightly chipped marble-topped washstand, as well as a chest of drawers and a small wardrobe. The same pattern of curtains that hung in the parlour were hanging at the window in the bedroom and Annie was momentarily speechless.

'I got Levi to 'elp us up wi' the heavier stuff,' Peggy explained.

Crossing to her, Annie planted a sloppy kiss on her cheek.

'Get off, yer daft ha'porth,' Peggy laughed, blushing with pleasure. She had come to love Annie like a daughter over the years and there was nothing she wouldn't have done for her.

'Oh, it looks just lovely, I don't know how to thank yer,' Annie breathed, her eyes shining. 'I never *dreamt* it could look this good.'

'It's amazin' what yer can do when yer set yer mind to it, but I can't take all the credit. Eve an' Levi 'ave done their share an' all. All you've got to do now is fetch yer clothes and yer bits an' pieces an' settle in.'

'In that case I might as well go an' make a start.' Annie suddenly became solemn. 'Do yer think Maggie will be all right? What I mean is, she'll be on her own fer a lot o' the time now when Levi is at work.'

'I don't think you should worry about that,' Peggy answered. 'You've done more than yer fair share in that 'ouse over the years an' it's time fer you now. Maggie 'as started to do a bit more now that we ain't all there to do it for 'er. But when you've gone, she'll have to pull her socks up, won't she? I do 'ave to say, though, I reckon it's time yer started thinkin' o' makin' a family of yer own. You've certainly got more than yer fair share of admirers. Monty bein' the main one.'

'I'm not sure I'm ready to settle down yet.' Annie looked away, because this wasn't strictly true. She still thought of Alex every day but had resigned herself to the fact that nothing could ever come of her feelings for him. Even so, there was a yearning inside her now for a family of her own. She loved her friends and her adopted family, but she longed to have someone who was related to her. She had never stopped wondering about her mother and father, but the older she got, the more unlikely it seemed she would ever meet them. So, for now she was keen to make something of herself, to build the business and make Levi proud of her. After all, he was the nearest thing to a father she had ever known, and she thought the world of him, to the point that she felt slightly guilty about moving out.

When she got back to the house, Levi insisted on helping her pack the rest of her things. She had already done most of it so it didn't take long, and soon she was ready to go.

'But who'll cook the dinner if I go now?' she fretted.

Levi smiled sadly. 'That ain't for you to worry about anymore,' he answered. 'Me an' Maggie will get by.'

The kitchen door opened as he was speaking, and Monty walked in.

'Now, young man, yer just in time to 'elp Annie carry the rest o' these bags round to her rooms.'

'Gladly.' Although Monty smiled, he too was sad that Annie was going. Admittedly, she wasn't going far, but it wouldn't be the same as having her right next door.

Downstairs, Annie crossed to Maggie, who had just come back from the Sunday service.

'Ah, so you're ready to go.'

Annie nodded, not quite knowing what to say. 'But you'll see me again in the morning when I come to collect Dobbin and the cart.'

'Right then, er . . . take care of yourself.' Maggie held her hand out and Annie dutifully shook it. Then Maggie shocked them all when she suddenly enveloped Annie in a warm hug and muttered, 'I'm sorry I didn't turn out to be the mother you hoped for Annie. But I *do* care about you. I'm just not very good at showing it anymore.'

Finally, after all the years they had lived together, Maggie was showing her some affection and it touched Annie deeply.

Levi was fighting to hold back tears as Annie went to him and hugged him too. 'Thanks fer all you've done fer me,' she whispered huskily.

'It should be me thankin' you, hinny. You've been a godsend to this family over the years. An' never forget, I'm allus here if yer need me.' He put her from him and noisily blew his nose. 'Now go on, get off wi' yer an' enjoy the rest o' yer life.'

Annie and Monty lifted her bags and she set off for her new home with a huge lump in her throat.

Chapter Forty

Barney hammered in the last of the guide ropes to secure the big top and then stood straight and wiped the sweat from his brow. The circus had arrived in Nuneaton early that morning and now as dusk approached everyone was tired. They had been working non-stop to ensure that everything would be ready for the first performance the next day, but Barney was used to hard work and never complained. It was the way of life he had chosen.

His boss had left early that morning in the horse and cart and hadn't been seen since, which Barney found strange. Usually, he was there barking orders at everyone and making sure that everything was done to his satisfaction, but for some reason he had seemed on edge for the last few days and had cleared off that morning without telling anyone where he was going or what time they might expect him back. Even Charity seemed to have no idea where he was.

As Barney made to move away, he glanced across the field and paused. It looked like the boss was on his way back, but there was someone with him. Someone with long dark hair. Barney's heart started to hammer. He had been counting the days until Mercy's release from prison and knew it must be soon. Could it be that the boss had gone to fetch her?

Suddenly he forgot how tired he was as he dropped the heavy mallet and started towards them. Yes, it was Mercy. He felt as if his heart would burst out of his chest with joy. Charity had spotted them too and was running towards them with tears streaming down her face. Eventually the horse drew to a halt and Barney was shocked at the change in the girl he adored. She was stick thin and her once lustrous hair was straggling like rats' tails down her back. She was dressed in a drab grey shapeless gown with a faded shawl about her shoulders and her eyes were dull and listless.

'Oh, my *poor* baby!' The horse had barely stopped when her mother helped her down and wrapped her arms about her. Even on such a happy occasion, Luca refused to look at his wife and moved on to stable the horse. 'Whatever have they done to you? You should have been home months ago!' Charity said to her daughter.

'I . . . I was ill and they kept me in the prison infirmary,' Mercy said tonelessly.

Barney just stood there. He wanted to snatch her into his arms and tell her how much he had missed her, but the time wasn't right, and he didn't want to intrude.

'I had pneumonia,' Mercy told her mother as Charity led her away.

Barney watched them go feeling wretched. He had imagined their reunion to be a joyous moment but Mercy looked nothing like the girl he had known. But then neither was he the same as she would remember him. He was no longer the handsome man he had once been. His hair had grown again, which hid the worst of the scarring, but it was still visible, although it was healing far better than he'd thought it would. He'd wondered often over the years if Mercy would still want him. But it seemed he would have to wait a little longer to find out. Still, he supposed it was to be expected. She had spent years cooped up in prison, so it would probably take her some time to recover. He could only hope so because he hadn't even had a casual dalliance with any other girl since she had gone and he knew that if he couldn't have her, he'd not settle for second best.

The following Sunday evening Barney visited his old home in Swan Lane and was surprised to find only his parents there.

Levi told him that Annie was now living above one of the shops and Eve above the other.

'It's working well,' Levi told him. 'But come on now, son, tell us what you've been up to.'

Barney shrugged. 'Just the same as usual, really, though there's nowhere near as many performers or acts in the circus now. A lot o' the chaps who left to go to war didn't come back, poor buggers – oops, sorry, Ma. Anyway, on a slightly happier note Mercy is home, but she ain't too well, so I ain't seen much of her. Her mother's lookin' after her an' will hardly let her out of her sight.' He glanced at his mother and asked cautiously, 'An' how 'ave you been, Ma?'

Maggie laid aside her knitting and rose to put the kettle on. 'I'm fine, especially now I've seen you. You will stay for a cup of tea, won't you?'

After she'd bustled away, Barney lowered his voice and asked his father, 'How is she really?'

'Much better,' Levi assured him. 'I took her for a spin in the car earlier an' it perked her up no end. I'm able to get a bit o' petrol from time to time now. I'm surprised the car still goes, seein' as it's just stood out there for the whole o' the war.'

'An' what about Harry an' Charlie?'

Levi shook his head. 'Charlie is back in London, but Harry is stayin' in France. But there's still no news on Eve's Davey, an' between you an' me I'm beginnin' to think that he won't come back. I ain't said as much to Eve, obviously. The poor soul still clings on to the hope that he'll turn up out o' the blue one o' these days.'

Barney stayed for another hour and when he left, he bumped into Monty coming down the drive that divided the houses.

'Barney.' Monty shook his hand. 'It's good to see you. I was just going to pay Annie a visit. Why don't you join me?'

Barney shook his head. 'Thanks, I'd like to, but I've got to get back to bed the animals down.'

They parted when they reached the town and Barney carried on towards Pingle Fields, although he didn't hold out much hope of seeing Mercy. They hadn't been able to have a single word alone with Charity standing over her like a guard dog; it was as if she was afraid that should she take her eyes off her someone would spirit her away again. Barney supposed he could understand it – her time away hadn't been easy for any of them. He had hoped that it might bring Luca and Charity back together but Luca still avoided his wife like the plague. It seemed unlikely they would ever be reconciled, but as it was none of his business, he kept well out of it. But oh, he hoped he would be able to speak to Mercy soon! Being so close to her and not being able to see her was torture and he just hoped that she still felt the same way about him.

Monty arrived at the shop to find Annie downstairs sorting out the things she had collected that day.

'Don't you ever rest, woman?' he teased when she opened the door. 'You know the saying "all work and no play?"'

'I do.' She smiled. 'But things can't sort themselves and Peggy's gone home with a raging toothache.'

'In that case I'd better give you a hand and then perhaps you'll make me a cup of tea?'

They worked side by side for a time, picking out anything they thought would be sellable and taking the rest to the yard where Levi would claim what he could for scrap. Very little ever got thrown away.

When they'd finished, she led him into the kitchen where she loaded a tray with a pot of tea and some biscuits, then took him up to her little sitting room.

'So how are you enjoying being independent?' he asked as she poured the tea.

'Very much except . . .' She paused and bit her lip.

He frowned. 'Except?'

'It's probably just me bein' a bit paranoid. But do yer remember that chap I pointed out to yer? The one wi' the badly burnt face an' hands?'

Monty nodded.

'Well . . . I've noticed him loiterin' outside the shop a few times now. Mainly in the evenin', an' it's unnerved me a bit.'

'I see. Would you like me to have a word with him the next time I see him?'

'And say what?' She passed him his tea. 'He ain't actually *done* anythin' or even *said* anythin' if it comes to that. Like I said, it's probably just me bein' nervy. I ain't quite used to livin' on me own yet.'

'Hmm, well if he does come back be sure to tell me.' He went on to tell her about Barney's visit. 'I was thinking we could perhaps visit the circus on Sunday. It's about time you had a bit of fun,' he suggested.

'We'll see,' she said vaguely.

Monty sighed. Annie was very difficult to pin down, and sometimes he despaired of her. The trouble was, in his eyes no one else could hold a candle to her, so all he could do was wait and hope that one day she might see him as more than a good friend – if the shrapnel in his chest didn't move the wrong way, that was.

Luckily his job as an accountant didn't involve hard manual work but sometimes he almost wished it did. He was tired of living under a cloud, having to take it easy, all the while wondering each morning if he would be alive to see the sun set. And when he thought like that, he felt guilty. Reggie hadn't been given a choice and his mother was still grieving for him.

When Barney got back to the circus he was surprised and delighted to see Mercy and her mother sitting outside on the steps of the wagon with their shawls about their shoulders.

He hurried over to them. 'It's nice to see yer out an' about again, girl.' He smiled at Mercy.

'I thought a breath o' fresh air would do her good,' Charity told him. She stood and turned to go back into the wagon. 'I'll let you two have a few minutes on yer own but don't yer get goin' off, mind. I want yer where I can see yer, my girl.' She winked at Barney and disappeared inside.

Barney stared at Mercy, and was heartened to see a faint glimpse of the girl she had once been returning – no doubt thanks to her mother's care. Her long hair was shining again, and she had gained a little weight, so she didn't look quite so gaunt, although she still had a long way to go. She was dressed once more in one of her colourful skirts and tops, and to him she looked beautiful.

'So how are yer feelin'?' he asked softly.

She smiled. 'I'm on the right road now, though I'll never forgive meself fer what I did.'

'You just 'ave to remember yer were only defendin' yerself,' he pointed out. Then before he could stop himself, he blurted out, 'I've missed you somethin' terrible an' I still love yer, Mercy.'

'I still care about you too,' she confided, so quietly that he had to bend to hear her. 'But your poor face. Ma told me that you'd been burnt but you're still the most 'andsome man I've ever seen.' She leant over and tenderly stroked the scars on his cheek. 'Just give me a little time an' we'll see where it goes, eh?'

Suddenly Barney felt as if he was walking on air and the future looked bright again.

Chapter Forty-One

October 1920

On a cold and blustery day in October, Eve and Peggy were working in the shop when the bell above the door tinkled and what at first glance appeared to be an old man stepped inside. He was dressed in an ill-fitting suit, the fabric worn and shiny, and he was so stick thin that he looked as if a puff of wind would blow him away. A kitbag was slung across his shoulder and his hair was snow white.

Jack, now a mischievous four-year-old, was playing on the floor with a wooden fire engine. He was a friendly child with a ready smile for everyone, but the man's eyes were fixed on Eve, who hadn't looked at him, assuming that he had come in to browse. He stood as if he had been turned to stone as he drank in the sight of her, before saying huskily, 'Eve!'

Her head snapped around and she frowned as she peered at him. 'Yes . . . may I help you?' Then she gasped and her hand flew to her throat. 'D-Davey . . . is that you?'

'Aye, it's me, love,' he croaked. 'I-I've come home.' And then the kitbag landed with a thud on the floor as they covered the distance between them and were soon locked in each other's arms.

'I- I had a telegram,' she choked through her tears. 'It said you were missing presumed dead.'

He nodded as he stroked her shining hair. 'I wished I was at times,' he admitted. 'I was taken prisoner and in a camp in Germany. It was hell on earth. So many of my friends didn't survive it. We were starved and beaten to within inches of our lives. But somehow the thought of coming back to you kept me going, although I feared after all this time that . . .' His voice faltered and she stared up at him expectantly. He swallowed and went on, 'I feared that you'd have found someone else.'

'*Never!*' she told him staunchly. 'You should've known that there'll only ever be one man for me. I will admit that as time went by I thought I'd lost you forever. But look at you, you're as thin as a bone an' your lovely hair . . .'

He raised his hand self-consciously to shift a straggly lock from his forehead. 'I know I must look a mess. It were some months after the war finished afore our lads came to set us free an' we got by by scavengin'. We even resorted to settin' rat traps an' cookin' them over a fire. Then we were put in hospitals till they felt we were well enough to travel. One o' the nurses wrote to you for me to tell yer where I was and when you didn't reply . . .'

As his voice trailed away she shook her head. 'I never got a letter.'

'Ah, I wondered why you didn't write back. But never mind, that's enough about me. Look at you! You're even more beautiful than yer were when I went away.'

'Oh, get off wi' you.' Eve blushed prettily and as her eyes settled on Jack, she smiled. 'There's someone else 'as been longin' fer you to come 'ome an' all.'

He raised an eyebrow. 'Oh yes, an' who would that be?'

Jack wandered up to her and stared up at the stranger intently. 'This little chap 'ere is Jack, Davey . . . He's your son.'

'My . . .' Davey's eyes were almost popping out of his head as he tried to digest what she was telling him.

'I found out I was expectin' soon after you left an' Jack were the result.' She knelt to Jack's level, and with an encouraging smile she told him, 'Say 'ello to yer daddy, Jack.'

Jack looked up at him solemnly as Davey hunkered down with tears in his eyes. 'Hello, matie. I hope you an' me are gonna be the very best o' friends.' He tenderly stroked the boy's hair before lifting him from the floor and hugging him.

Peggy, who had been watching the tender reunion with tears in her eyes, cleared her throat. 'Right, seein' as this is such a special day, I'm goin' to put the closed sign up an' make us all a celebratory cup o' tea. Yer look as if a decent meal wouldn't go amiss either, me lad. Yer certainly need fattenin' back up.' She bustled over to the door, locked it and turned the sign before hurrying off to the kitchen. She would make them all a drink and leave the family to it. Father and son had a lot of time to make up and she didn't want to be in the way.

The following day Eve insisted on the doctor calling early to check Davey over. With his emaciated frame and silver hair, he no longer resembled the young man who had gone away to war, but she supposed it was no wonder after the horrors he had been forced to endure.

Their first night back together had not been without its problems as Davey frequently had to dash down to the outside toilet. He cried out in his sleep too and flailed his arms at something or someone Eve couldn't see.

Thankfully after giving him a thorough examination the doctor folded his stethoscope and smiled. 'He's severely malnourished and dehydrated and has a nasty case of dysentery,' he told Eve. 'I can give him something for the runs, but it'll be up to you to feed him up and hopefully in time he'll be as good as new. It looks like a good haircut wouldn't go amiss either, young man,' he teased Davey.

Davey self-consciously fingered his long locks. They reached down almost to his shoulders and stood about his head like a wild halo. 'We didn't have access to a barber where I've been,' he told the doctor, who patted his shoulder.

'No, I wouldn't imagine you did, lad,' he said gently. 'But well done for surviving and welcome home.'

'Thank you, sir.'

The doctor took a phial of liquid from his bag and instructed Eve on how much she was to give him every four hours before taking his leave.

Davey looked worn out and Eve pointed to the small sofa where Jack was waiting patiently for him to join him.

'You go and put yer feet up,' she ordered. 'I'm goin' to take Jack round to Peggy's then I'll come back and make you some bacon and eggs.'

'Ah, do I 'ave to go to Peggy's today, Mammy?' Jack pouted. 'I want to stay 'ere an' play wi' Daddy.'

Eve laughed as she ruffled his hair. 'You can do that when you get home and for the rest of your life,' she told him. 'I've got a lot to do today so run and clean yer teeth there's a good lad.'

Jack reluctantly did as he was told, and once he'd left the room Davey said, 'I suppose I should go an' get me hair cut like the doctor said.'

'You're going nowhere till you've got yer strength back a bit,' Eve told him firmly. 'You're goin' to stay here an' rest. Later on, I'll get the bath out fer you an' sort some o' yer clothes, although they're goin' to hang off you at the minute.' She gave him a smile and bustled away to get Jack ready, leaving Davey to rest.

Levi and Annie popped up to see Davey before their rounds and were clearly delighted that he was home.

'Don't even *think* o' comin' back to work fer a while.' Levi wagged a finger at him. 'Yer need to get yer strength up first.' He shook Davey's hand so hard that he feared it might drop off before he and Annie set off to work with broad smiles on their faces.

'I must say you've got your rooms very comfortable,' Levi commented as he urged Dobbin into a gentle trot.

'I really love living there. I thought I'd be a little nervous at first,' she admitted. 'But actually, with Eve in the rooms next door I've been fine.'

'Good.' Levi nodded, although he was still missing her dreadfully. Ever since she'd moved out he and Maggie seemed to have been rattling around the big house in Swan Lane, and it felt as if the heart had gone out of their home. Still, he was aware that chicks must fly the nest eventually and Annie was a sensible young woman, and had proved that she could manage just fine.

Late that evening Annie went down to the kitchen to make herself a mug of cocoa before going to bed. She had just put a pan of milk on the hob to warm when she thought she heard something in the yard outside, so she crossed to the window and peered out into the darkness.

Must have been a cat or a fox, she thought when she saw nothing untoward. She had just turned back to the stove when there was an almighty crash and a brick hurtled through the window catching Annie a glancing blow on the forehead. She screamed as she raised her hand to feel her head and when she lowered it, she was shocked to see that it was covered in blood. Everything felt hazy and before she could do anything else, she crashed onto the cold quarry tiles.

'Come on, pet, wake up.'

Annie's eyes blinked open and through a fog she made out Eve kneeling over her. 'Wh-what happened?'

The back door was wide open and a cold draught was flooding into the room.

'Someone lobbed a bloody brick through the winder an' it caught yer head. Davey's out there now seein' if he can spot who it was. We heard the ruckus an' rushed down. Come on, let's get you upstairs an' then I'll make yer a cup o' hot sweet tea while Davey boards the winder up.'

'B-but why would anyone do that?' Annie muttered.

'No sign of anyone out there now. Whoever did it is gone,' Davey told them, coming back inside.

He and Eve helped her to her feet and somehow between them got her up the steep, narrow staircase to her rooms. She felt light-headed and dizzy but after bathing her head, Eve assured her that although she had a lump the size of an egg on her forehead the cut wasn't too bad. She left her sitting by the dying fire while she went to make her some tea and Davey boarded up the window.

Almost an hour later, after drinking the tea, which Eve had added a splash of brandy to, Annie felt much better.

'You two get off now, I'll be fine,' she assured them.

But Eve was having none of it. 'No way am I leavin' you on yer own tonight,' she told her firmly. 'Just in case the bugger that did it comes back again. Davey, you go round an' stay wi' Jack. I'll sleep 'ere tonight wi' Annie.'

Annie protested weakly but in truth she was grateful for Eve's company. The incident had unsettled her more than she cared to admit, especially as she had no idea who she might have upset.

'You probably ain't upset anyone,' Eve assured her when Annie said as much. 'It were probably just some drunk on his way 'ome from the pub who were hopin' to break into the shop.'

Annie nodded but deep inside she had a bad feeling that she couldn't shift.

Chapter Forty-Two

The following morning the glass in the window was replaced and Levi set off on his rounds without her. He had insisted she should take at least one day off, even though she assured him she felt fine.

'I'll be perfectly all right on me own fer one day,' he told her, leaving her under Eve's watchful eye.

Later that morning Ellie called in to see them while she was in town buying some embroidery silks for her new mistress. She was now sixteen years old and had been fortunate enough to get a position as a lady's maid to the mill owner's wife in their smart house on the outskirts of the town.

She was horrified when Peggy told her what had happened the night before, but full of her new position.

'Eeh, it's grand workin' there,' she told them after a hasty cup of tea. She didn't want to be gone too long and blot her copybook. 'The mistress is lovely to me an' when I ain't needed I can go down an' talk to the other staff in the kitchen. I still can't believe she chose me cos I'm so young an' hadn't been trained fer the job. But she says I'll learn as I go along an' she likes young people around her. It's a shame she only had the one son, Master Nicholas. Now he's away at university she misses him sommat dreadful.' She giggled. 'The mistress says she's gonna get me some ele-elecu . . . Oh, I can't remember the right word but basically someone to teach me to talk proper. She says it'll be better when she has visitors.'

'Ooh, we'll be havin' to make an appointment to see yer soon,' Peggy teased. She'd missed her dreadfully since she'd left home.

Ellie shook her head and squeezed her hand. 'That'll never happen,' she promised. Peggy had brought her up as her own and couldn't have loved her more if she tried, and her love was returned.

Ellie drained her cup and rose to leave. 'Right, I'm off now.' She smiled at Eve. 'And I'm chuffed to bits that Davey's come 'ome.' She kissed each of their cheeks and breezed out.

Peggy sighed. 'I don't know. It don't seem a minute since she were a babe in arms,' she said sadly. 'An' now 'ere she is all grown up.'

'She's a credit to you,' Eve told her. 'And thanks to you her future is bright.'

Peggy shrugged and went back down to the shop, and after making sure that Annie had everything she and Davey needed, Eve went to join her.

Despite her assurances that she was fine, the incident the night before had unnerved Annie badly, but she would never have admitted it. She was made of stern stuff and was determined to get back to work as soon as possible.

As it turned out that happened even sooner than she expected because that very afternoon when Peggy brought her up a cup of tea, she looked shaken.

'I've got to leave Eve in charge o' the shop,' she told Annie, not wanting to worry her.

'Oh yes, why's that?' Annie raised her eyes from the book she had been trying to read. She wasn't used to sitting about and had barely got past the first few pages.

'Er . . .' Peggy sighed. 'I just 'ad a message that Levi's been took bad so I'm goin' round to Swan Lane to see what's up.'

'What do yer mean he's took bad?' Annie was instantly anxious.

'You know as much as me, pet. Young Jimmy Trent brought the message from Maggie.'

'In that case I'm comin' with you,' Annie told her, rising from the chair.

'You'll do no such thing, you need to rest,' Peggy said sternly but her words were wasted, Annie was already dragging her coat on.

Minutes later they set off. Annie still felt a little shaky from her bang on the head, but she bravely kept up with Peggy and soon they were entering the kitchen at Swan Lane to find Maggie pacing the floor, her silken skirt swirling about her legs.

'What's goin' on? I got yer message,' Peggy asked.

Maggie shook her head. 'A gentleman found Levi collapsed on the cart and he kindly brought him home. The doctor is in the parlour with him now.'

'And where is Dobbin an' the cart?' Annie asked.

'I think the man said he found him up Tuttle Hill so he must still be there,' Maggie said tearfully.

'Right, I'll wait to see what the doctor says then I'll go an' fetch him an' the cart back,' Annie volunteered.

Peggy scowled. 'You shouldn't even be out yerself yet.'

Annie didn't argue, but Peggy knew her well enough to know that once she'd made her mind up to do something she'd do it no matter what she said.

A few minutes later, the doctor emerged looking grim-faced. 'I'm afraid Levi has had a seizure, a sort of stroke,' he informed them solemnly. 'It's affected him all down his left side. He should really be in hospital but I don't feel he's well enough to be moved at present. Can you manage to nurse him here?'

Maggie looked horrified. 'But he will get better, won't he?'

'I think the next forty-eight hours will determine that. If he can get through the next two days, there's a good chance he'll recover, but there's no guarantee. He's going to need round-the-clock care – can you manage that?'

Maggie gulped, but Peggy assured him, 'Yes, we can, doctor. I'll move back in to 'elp so Maggie won't 'ave to do it all on 'er own. We'll manage between us, but what can we do to 'elp 'im?'

The doctor snapped his bag shut. 'Keep him warm and quiet. He mustn't have any sort of stress, and make sure that you get some liquid into him. He probably won't be able to eat anything just yet but we don't want him dehydrating. Oh, and it might be a good idea if you could bring a bed downstairs for him to make him a little more comfortable. I'll call back first thing in the morning, but of course if he should take a turn for the worse, or if you need me, I shall come immediately.'

When Maggie lifted her purse to pay him, he shook his head. 'Don't worry about that for now, Mrs Lilburn,' he said kindly. 'Let's see how the next couple of days go first, shall we? Good day, ladies.'

He had barely left the house before Annie shot through to the parlour like a bullet from a gun. Her first sight of the man who had been like a father to her brought tears to her eyes, but she bravely blinked them back and forced a smile.

'I don't know – I can't leave you alone fer a minute, can I?' she said softly as she gently took his hand. One side of his face seemed to have dropped, giving him a lopsided appearance, and he was drooling, but there was recognition in his eyes. He tried to speak but all that came out were a few guttural sounds.

'Quiet now while me an' Peggy go an' fetch a bed down for you,' she ordered. 'Then when we've got you all tucked in I'll go an' fetch Dobbin 'ome an' get 'im settled in 'is stable.'

A look of relief flitted across Levi's face. Annie knew he would be more worried about Dobbin than himself.

Between them, she and Peggy brought down the single bed from Barney's old room and set it close to the front window where he could watch the world go by, then Annie left Maggie to get him changed into his pyjamas while she went to find Dobbin.

Luckily, he was where the man had said. Annie knew that normally Levi would have been much further afield at that time of day so perhaps he had been coming home early because he felt unwell. Dobbin pawed the ground and snickered at the sight of her and, after giving him a fuss, Annie climbed onto the cart and led him home.

An hour later, when Dobbin was happily back in his stable with a warm blanket across him and his nosebag on, she went back in to check on Levi. He seemed to have shrunk since the last time she had seen him, and he looked old and frail. Maggie was almost beside herself, weeping, wailing and wringing her hands, but Annie suspected it was more because she was afraid of the hard work that might lie ahead rather than concern for her husband.

'How am I going to cope?' she cried. 'He can't do anything for himself and he's much too heavy for me to move about.'

'I told you I'll move back in to 'elp,' Peggy said with an encouraging wink at Levi. 'Just till he's on the mend again, an' that won't be long will it, me man?' Taking Maggie's elbow, she firmly propelled her out of the room and into the kitchen.

'What the 'ell are yer thinkin' of, woman?' she said angrily. 'Don't yer the think the poor bugger is scared enough wi'out you making things worse fer 'im? Didn't yer hear what the doctor said? This next forty-eight hours will be crucial. We've got to make 'im feel that he's goin' to be well again. Yer know 'ow proud an' independent he is. If you go on like yer just did, he'll think he's dyin' an' give up. Now pull yerself together.'

Maggie dabbed ineffectively at her cheeks with a sliver of lace handkerchief. 'So what do you want me to do?'

'You can start by makin' a pan o' chicken soup. We need to try an' tempt 'im to eat wi' things that'll be easy to digest that he don't need to chew.'

'And what can I do?' Annie had followed them into the room and she looked almost as ill as Levi did. She couldn't begin to think of what life would be like without him and she didn't want to.

'You can make 'im a nice jug o' lemonade while I go an' make the fire up in the parlour. We'll need to keep one burnin'. Yer heard what the doctor said about keepin' 'im warm, an' it's turned cold now.'

Annie hurried off to do as she was asked while Maggie reluctantly started on the soup.

When Annie took the drink through to him, she gently lifted his head and trickled some liquid into his mouth, but he had difficulty swallowing it and most of it dribbled out onto the cloth tucked under his chin.

'Don't worry about that,' she soothed. 'Now 'ow about I read yer a bit from the newspaper, eh?' She sat down with a smile on her face and started to read, although inside she was crying. She had barely read more than a few words when his eyes drooped and he fell asleep.

After gently pulling the blankets up to his chin and throwing some more coal on the fire she stole away to join Maggie and Peggy in the kitchen.

'He's asleep,' she told them.

'Who's going to bring the money in if he can't work?' Maggie fretted.

Annie and Peggy exchanged a glance. Trust Maggie to think of that at a time like this.

'Well, I can do the rounds on me own,' Annie said. 'Davey ain't recovered enough to help yet, but I'll manage. Eve will probably cope in the shops on 'er own fer a while. Then me an' Peggy can go round to 'elp her sort through stuff of an evenin' if you can watch 'im while we're gone.'

Maggie nodded and without any of them saying a word they each knew that a difficult few months lay ahead – if Levi survived.

As promised, Peggy went home shortly after to fetch some clothes while Annie went back to the shop to tell Eve what was going on.

'Oh bless 'im.' Eve was upset to hear what had happened.

'You can't do the rounds all by yourself,' Davey told her. 'I'll come out with yer tomorrer.'

'You most certainly will not!' Eve rounded on him. 'You still ain't built yer strength up an' we don't want to 'ave to nurse two of yer. No, you'll stay 'ere an' perhaps manage the shop each day fer a couple of hours while I nip round to the yard to see what needs doin' there. Peggy can't do it if she's helpin' to look after Levi. We'll manage just fine if we all muck in together.'

Annie flashed her a grateful smile. At least Peggy and Eve could always be relied on.

Chapter Forty-Three

Thankfully Levi did survive the first forty-eight hours, although by November he still hadn't shown any signs of recovery. Annie was just relieved that they hadn't lost him and spent as much time as she could with him, which wasn't as much as she'd have liked because she was doing the rounds alone.

The nights were dark and the weather had turned bitterly cold, but between her, Peggy and Eve they were able to keep everything ticking along. Monty had stepped up to the mark as well and spent at least an hour every evening with Levi reading him snippets from the newspaper and trying to keep his spirits up. Levi had lost all feeling in his left leg and left arm and Annie could see how frustrated this made him. He had never been an idle man and having to lie about all day was torture to him.

And then out of the blue something happened that seemed to perk him up a little.

It was a cold, rainy night and Annie had just arrived after checking stock with Eve and stabling Dobbin. She was trying to get her hands warm by the fire before going to see Levi when the door suddenly opened, letting in a blast of icy air, and there was Charlie, large as life.

'*Charles!*' His mother flew up and flung her arms around him. 'Why didn't you let us know you were coming? I could have aired your room for you.'

Peggy and Annie looked on in surprise. It was the first they had heard or seen of him since the day he had left home following Peter's death six years before. It was so strange to think that he had once been her idol and she had envisaged spending the rest of her life with him, but a lot had happened since then and meeting

Alex had shown her what true love felt like. No one before or since could ever hold a candle to him and she suspected they never would. He was still the first person that she thought of when she opened her eyes each morning and the last one she thought of when she closed them each night, even though she had long since accepted that there could never be anything between them other than friendship.

'Are you home for good? Oh, *please* say you are!' Maggie implored as he extricated himself from her arms and removed his hat.

He smiled a greeting at Annie and Peggy before answering, 'I could well be, Mother. We'll have to see. But tell me what you've all been up to.'

Maggie haltingly told him about his father's stroke.

Charlie frowned. 'I must go and see him,' he said. 'Is he upstairs in bed?'

'No, he's in bed in the parlour. He can't manage the stairs and it's easier for us to care for him down here.'

Peggy glanced at Annie in amusement. Maggie had done very little caring – not that she minded. She had even slept in the chair by his bed since the stroke while Maggie went about her day-to-day routine almost as if nothing had happened, more than happy to leave Levi's care to Peggy or Annie.

'First you must tell us what you were doing in France – you'd told us you didn't want to go and fight,' his mother persisted, and he sighed.

'Actually, I did join the army but not to fight.'

'Really?' His mother smiled. 'So what did you do?'

'It's not something I can really talk about,' he said somewhat shortly. 'Let's say it was all a little hush-hush.'

'What? You mean you were a spy?'

'I wouldn't say a spy exactly, but I did work closely with the intelligence and the French Resistance,' he admitted. 'And that's about all I can tell you.' He looked at Annie. 'As it happens, I think you and I have a mutual acquaintance. Does the name Alex Gordon ring any bells? I told him you were my sister and he mentioned that he'd met you.'

Annie felt heat rise into her cheeks. 'Y-you know Alex? Er . . . how is he?'

'He was very well when I saw him a couple of weeks ago. In fact he said he might drop by and see you if he's ever down this way.'

Annie tried to hide how elated she was. 'Oh . . . that would be nice. But do you want to come through to the parlour now? I'm sure seein' you will be the best medicine Levi could have.'

She was right. Levi's eyes lit up at the sight of his son and he raised his one good arm to give him a hug.

'Ugh . . . ugh . . .' He was desperately trying to talk and Annie could see his frustration.

'Now don't you go gettin' yerself all worked up,' she scolded. Then with a nod she made for the door. 'I'll leave you two to have a catch-up while I make yer both a cup o' tea.'

Charlie chuckled as he looked down at his father. 'I see nothing changes here. A good cup of tea seems to be the cure for all ills in England.'

Later that night, as Monty accompanied her back to her rooms, Annie found it hard to keep her mind on what he was saying because she couldn't stop thinking of Alex. She wondered if he would drop by to see them, or whether it had just been polite conversation. Half of her hoped he would while the other half wanted him to stay away. After all, there could be no point in raking up her feelings again.

Monty had been walking her about after dark ever since the night of the smashed window, and Annie had made no objection because she was still feeling vulnerable, although there had been no further incidents. She was hoping it had just been a group of boisterous kids or a drunk on the way home.

'I'll come up with you, shall I?' Monty asked when they arrived at the shop doorway.

She shook her head. 'Not tonight if you don't mind.' She squeezed his arm, hoping to take the sting out of her refusal. 'I've been up an' on me feet since five o'clock this mornin' so I reckon I'm just goin' to have an early night.'

'As you like.' As he leant in to kiss her, she quickly turned her cheek to him.

'Night, Monty, an' thanks fer walkin' me back.'

'Night, Annie. I'll see you tomorrow.'

A thick fog had come down making it hard to see her hand in front of her and as he walked away it swallowed him up as she hastily let herself into the shop, closing the door firmly behind her.

Once upstairs she was comforted to hear the soft drone of Eve and Davey's voices through the wall. She wearily removed her old breeches and overcoat, and within half an hour she was tucked up in bed fast asleep.

The following morning Annie went in to check on Levi as she always did before getting Dobbin ready to begin their rounds. As usual, Peggy was bustling about taking care of him. Maggie was still in bed, of course.

Once Dobbin was ready, Annie set off. It was a dark, dismal day, with black rain clouds scudding across the sky, and before they had gone very far the heavens opened and within minutes she was soaked to the skin. She briefly thought of turning for home, but decided to battle through. Things had picked up in the shop now and they were back into profit, and Annie's share of what they made, even after paying Peggy and Eve's wages and the other outgoings, were mounting up nicely, so she needed to keep collecting.

Even so, by mid-afternoon she was so cold that she had lost all feeling in her hands and feet, and poor Dobbin's head and ears were down. He looked so sorry for himself that she decided to call it a day and turned for home. Once back she took Dobbin into his stable and dried him down with a towel before throwing a warm blanket over him and settling him in his stall with a nosebag, before going into the kitchen.

Peggy had seen her arrive and had a steaming mug of coffee ready for her – Annie had developed a taste for it since living in France.

'I thought you might be back early,' she greeted her. 'I just wonder why you stayed out so long. It ain't fit for man nor beast to be out in this weather.'

'I've just thrown a tarpaulin over the back of the cart. I'll sort through today's collection tomorrow.' Annie gratefully lifted her drink and took a huge gulp, even though it burnt her tongue and throat. 'How 'as Levi been today?'

Peggy smiled as she stirred the dish of beef stew she had simmering on the stove. 'As yer know I've been doin' exercises on his bad side to try an' build the muscles back up, an' for the first time today he was able to move 'is fingers so I'm takin' that as a good sign.'

'Well done.' Annie beamed at her. 'And is Charlie settling back in?'

'I ain't seen too much of 'im to be honest. He shot off straight after lunch to see if 'e could get his job back wi' his old firm, so that tells me he's probably plannin' on stayin' fer a time at least.'

Maggie strode into the kitchen holding a fashion magazine. She had it delivered weekly and followed the trends religiously. She hardly even noticed that Annie was in the room as she crossed to show Peggy a picture in it. 'Look at this. I've only just got used to wearing ankle-length skirts and now calf-length is coming in. It's very daring, don't you think? And look how straight the skirts are. It says in here that women should be cutting their hair off too, to this shorter length bob style here. I'm not sure that I'm brave enough to do that just yet.'

Peggy snorted. 'I can't be doin' wi' all that malarky!' She shook her head. 'All I possess is me old clothes I work in an' a Sunday best dress. Why would anyone need any more than that? The only time I ever 'ave anythin' new is if sommat wears out.'

Maggie looked Peggy up and down. 'You really should take more care of yourself,' she said. 'You could still be quite attractive if you did.'

Peggy wasn't sure if this was meant as an insult or a compliment and she laughed. 'What you 'ave to remember is, them women in those magazines are models. They just stand around posin' all day an' get paid fer it. They don't 'ave to scrub floors an' cook and clean as we do . . . Well, *I* do at least.'

Despite her words Peggy was happy to see Maggie taking an interest in herself again. She no longer talked to Penny and had started to go out a little more, which Peggy could only think was a good thing, although they suspected that she rarely went further than Penny's grave.

Maggie spotted Annie then and asked, 'Has rain stopped play?'

'I'm afraid so. I'm soaked to the skin so I'm just goin' to go through an' 'ave a word wi' Levi then I'm goin' 'ome to get changed.' Her clothes were beginning to steam in the warm kitchen and Maggie wrinkled her nose as she caught a whiff of them.

'Hmm, I suggest you do and perhaps you can find time to give them a wash. They certainly smell as if they need it. It's bad enough that you insist on wearing baggy old men's trousers but when they start to smell . . .'

'If you saw some o' the stuff I 'ave to lug about you'd understand why they smell,' Annie answered, as she walked towards the kitchen door. She was used to Maggie's ways, so she hadn't taken offence. In fact Maggie had been a lot kinder to her lately.

When she entered the parlour, Levi's eyes lit up.

'How yer feelin'?' she asked as she stroked his hand, and he nodded. His smile was still lopsided, but Annie was sure it wasn't quite as bad as it had been. He was managing to say the odd word now, too, but they were still somewhat slurred. Even so, Annie was hopeful that he was on the mend, and it was no wonder after the way Peggy nursed him.

Annie told him about her day and the appalling weather and soon after she set off for the shop where Davey and Jack were keeping Eve company.

'It's been really quiet today. I reckon the weather 'as put everybody off comin' out,' Eve told her.

'Why don't you close up early? Go on, you get yourselves away. I'll finish off whatever needs doin' an' lock up.'

'If yer quite sure.' Eve looked around doubtfully at the pile of clothes she'd been sorting.

Annie undid the string belt around her old coat and waved her away. 'Go on now, before I change me mind.'

The little family trooped away to their rooms and Annie continued with the sorting. The afternoon was already darkening and she decided that as soon as she'd finished, she would close early. Glancing up a short time later, she saw someone standing staring through the window, and her stomach turned over as she realised it was the man with the badly burnt face. He hadn't attempted to enter the shop, but she crossed to the door anyway and after securely locking it and turning the sign to closed, she hurried into the kitchen, her heart hammering. She hadn't seen him for a few days and had hoped that he'd moved on, but that clearly wasn't the case and she felt strangely unsettled. There was something about the look in his eye that struck terror into her heart, although she couldn't for the life of her think what she might have done to upset him.

After a time, she peeped round the kitchen door and was relieved to see that he had gone, so she went back into the shop, extinguished the lights and hurried upstairs to her room. The fire was burning low so she raked it back into life and threw some coal on it before crossing to the window to peer into the street below. The streetlights had just come on, throwing a yellow glow over the wet pavements but thankfully there was no sign of the man, so she went back down to the kitchen to make herself a cup of tea.

She went to bed early that night and after reading for a time she fell asleep.

It was the smell of burning that woke her sometime later and she lay blinking for a moment. Pulling herself into a sitting position she knuckled the sleep from her eyes and it was then that she spotted it: a plume of smoke coming under her door from the sitting room. Panicking, she leapt out of bed, trying to think what to do. If there was a fire in there, it could come into the bedroom if she opened the door, so how was she to get out? Suddenly it came to her and, snatching up her boot, she began to hammer with all her might on the wall that separated her rooms from Eve and Davey's.

'*Help . . . Help . . . there's a fire!*' The smoke was starting to make Annie cough. She desperately looked around for another way to escape. One window in her room looked down on to the back yard, and the front window looked down on to the street, but there was no way she could escape from either of them – the drop to the ground was too great. Suddenly she heard a noise from the other side of the wall and she sobbed with relief as she began to hammer on it even louder. '*Help . . . Help!*'

Minutes later she heard Davey's voice from the yard. 'Stay where y'are, Annie. Don't open the door. I've sent Eve fer the fire brigade.'

She could see him filling buckets of water from the tap in the yard and throwing them into the kitchen, but all she could do was watch, wait and pray. The smoke was so dense by that time that she kept losing sight of him, but knowing he was there gave her hope. Once the fire engine arrived, they had the fire under control within minutes, and shortly after she heard the sound of footsteps pounding up the stairs and a fireman appeared.

'Are you all right, miss?'

She nodded as he lifted a towel and threw it to her. 'Put this over your nose and mouth and stay close to me.' He gently took her elbow and propelled her towards the stairs. Thick, acrid smoke was still belching upwards and as she stumbled down close behind him her eyes began to water.

The second she fell into the yard she gulped at the fresh air as Eve caught her to her.

'Eeh, are yer all right, pet? How could this 'ave happened?'

Annie mopped at her streaming eyes with the thin shawl she had thrown about her shoulders. 'I don't know.' But she wasn't telling the complete truth, because she had an idea.

Chapter Forty-Four

The following morning, at first light, they were able to survey the damage and thankfully it wasn't as bad as they'd feared. Someone had clearly set a fire against the back door and it had gone into the kitchen, but apart from the clothes smelling vaguely of smoke, the shops were untouched, which Annie supposed was something.

'Who do yer think might 'ave done it?' Eve asked fearfully.

Annie chewed her lip, wondering if she should voice her suspicions. 'I, er . . . 'ave no idea, unless . . .'

'Unless what?'

'Well, shortly before I closed the shop I saw the man wi' the badly scarred face, do yer know who I mean? He were standing outside watching me through the window an' it unnerved me a bit. I've seen him hangin' around outside an' watchin' me a few times now.'

Eve frowned and shook her head. 'But why would he want to hurt yer? We don't even know 'im. Per'aps he were just lookin' to see if there were anythin' interestin' in 'ere.'

Annie stayed silent. Every instinct was telling her that he had something to do with the fire, but she had no proof, so she decided it was best to say nothing to anyone else.

The police questioned her about the fire shortly after, and when they asked if she had any idea who might have a grudge against her, she stayed silent. After all, as Eve had quite rightly pointed out, the man didn't even know her so why would he have done it? She was worried her imagination was running away with her, and although the damage wasn't as bad as it could have been, her blood ran cold when she thought of what might have happened if she hadn't woken up when she did. They might have all been burnt in their beds.

'I don't want Levi to know about this,' Annie told Eve when the police had gone and they were clearing up the mess. 'It could set him back if he starts worryin' an' he's only just startin' to show signs o' gettin' better.'

Eve agreed. 'He won't hear nowt from me,' she promised.

Davey had gone to buy a new back door, which was beyond saving, but luckily it was just smoke damage in the kitchen, so after cleaning the walls and windows, the place looked respectable again by lunchtime.

'I suppose I should check the stock and open the shop this afternoon if everythin' is all right,' Eve said wearily, wiping some soot from the end of her nose. They were both filthy and reeked of smoke.

Annie shook her head. 'No, let's leave it today. If anything smells of smoke we can leave the back door open to try and clear it.' She was still more shaken by what had happened than she cared to admit but Davey had promised to fix a strong padlock on the back gate, which would hopefully keep any intruders out.

'In that case I'm going to get the copper on the boil fer some hot water an' 'ave a nice bath,' Eve said. Then grinning, she added, 'You look like you could do with one an' all.'

By mid-afternoon they were both squeaky clean and Annie began to feel a little better.

'I think I'll pop round an' see how Levi is,' she told Eve, slipping on her coat, and soon after she set off for Swan Lane.

She was delighted to see Levi looking better than he had for weeks. Peggy had got him propped up on pillows and he smiled at her as she entered.

'H-he-llo, hi-hinny.'

Monty was there reading the newspaper to him. 'You look very nice,' he said admiringly. 'How about I take you out tonight?'

She opened her mouth to refuse but thought better of it. Perhaps a night out would do her the world of good, so she nodded. 'Sounds good to me.'

That evening Monty took Annie to a small restaurant and then to the pictures. She'd made an effort with her hair and clothes, and as always Monty was good company, so she found she really enjoyed herself. It was a welcome relief to take her mind off the fire and the scarred man.

At the end of the evening, Monty walked her to the door and this time when he leant in to kiss her, she didn't stop him.

'I know you said you're still not ready,' he said tenderly, gently stroking her cheek. 'But you must know I'd marry you tomorrow if you'd just say the word.'

He expected her to turn him down again but to his surprise and delight she didn't. Instead, she said quietly, 'Just give me a little more time, Monty. I am very fond of you.'

His face was like a ray of sunshine and when he had seen her safely inside, he set off for home with a spring in his step.

Annie watched him go through the window. Would it be so bad being married to Monty? He was kind and considerate, and handsome into the bargain. He could have had his pick of the girls, but he had never had eyes for anyone but her. More than ever now she was longing to have a family of her very own and she knew without doubt that Monty would never let her down. Never having known who her real parents were, and not having a mother who loved her, Annie had always craved a proper family. Unbidden, a picture of Alex flashed in front of her eyes, but she shook her head to clear it. There was no sense pining for someone she could never have, and she didn't want to spend the rest of her life alone.

She was pensive as she made her way upstairs to her room. That night, sleep evaded her as she tried to decide what she should do.

There was just two weeks to go until Christmas when Dora, Mrs Taylor-Lloyd's maid, entered the morning room looking worried. 'There's a gentleman 'ere to see yer, ma'am.'

'Oh, who is it?' The woman looked annoyed; she was expecting friends for a morning coffee shortly and could have done without the interruption. 'Can't you tell them to come back later?'

'I tried, ma'am, but 'e said yer'd want to see 'im. Shall I show 'im in?'

Mrs Taylor-Lloyd frowned. 'No, I'll come through and see him. Where is he?'

'He's in the kitchen. I couldn't stop 'im comin' in,' Dora said.

'Oh, very well.' She followed the maid out of the room and along the hallway and as she entered the kitchen, she stopped abruptly as she saw the man standing by the door. He looked like a tramp and his face was so badly disfigured that she couldn't even guess how old he might be.

'Yes, may I help you?' She stared at him coldly.

He removed his hat and gave a sad grimace of a smile. 'Well . . . I expected a better welcome than that, Mother dearest.'

Shock coursed through her and she leant heavily on the back of the nearest chair. 'Mother . . .?' She gulped deep in her throat. 'R-Reginald – is it really you?'

When he nodded, her clenched fist flew to her mouth. 'B-but we were told you were dead . . . We had a memorial service for you up at the church.'

He shrugged. 'I sometimes wish I had died.' The burns had affected his vocal cords as well as most of his body and his voice was gruff, but even so, as she stared at him, she saw her son's hair, badly in need of a decent cut admittedly, but she knew with a mother's instinct that it was him.

'Oh, my *poor* dear boy, what has happened to you and where have you been all this time? Why didn't you come home when the war ended?'

'I've been back for some time living in the refuge and on the streets,' he admitted. 'I didn't think you'd welcome me back looking like this. But it's so cold and . . .'

When his voice trailed away, she flew across the room and threw her arms about him. 'You *silly* young man. You're still my son and you should be proud of your scars. You got them fighting for King and country and you're a hero! Oh, I can't believe you're really alive. It's like a miracle.'

She led him to the table and pressed him down onto a chair before snapping at Dora, who was watching open-mouthed, 'Dora, go and tell the gardener to fetch my husband and Montgomery from work immediately. We have some celebrating to do. Our hero has returned from the dead.'

'You're not going to believe what's happened,' Monty told Annie and Charlie when she arrived back in Swan Lane to stable Dobbin later that afternoon. He had been out filling the coal bucket. 'You know that man with the badly burnt face? Well it's only our Reginald, and he came home today.' He shook his head. 'I thought there was something familiar about him.'

Annie felt the colour drain out of her face.

Charlie didn't look much happier about it. 'A-an' how 'as your mother taken it?'

'*Huh!* She's over the moon. I suppose it's to be expected. But why did he wait until now to come home? He says he didn't think we'd accept him because he's so disfigured but that doesn't sound like Reginald.'

Annie bit her lip. She couldn't pretend to be pleased after what he had done to her, but thankfully Monty still didn't know about that, and it was more important than ever that he never did.

'Can you believe she's throwing a big welcome home party for him?' He scratched his head. 'And she's already had a tailor out to measure him for new clothes. You'd think no one else had ever been injured in the war, and that he'd won it single-handed.' He looked guilty and gave a wry smile. 'I sound like a jealous brat, don't I?'

She squeezed his arm as she led Dobbin to the stables. 'No, yer don't. Let's just hope that he's come back a better person than what he were when he went away, eh?'

She told Peggy and Maggie the news as soon as she went into the kitchen. They too looked shocked.

'Well, I can't pretend to be pleased to 'ear he's back,' said Peggy as angry colour flooded into her cheeks. 'He allus were a nasty piece o' work. Admittedly I can understand his mam bein' pleased to 'ave 'im home, whatever state he's in. Yer kids are yer kids at the end o' the day but personally I wish he'd stayed away.'

Annie went through to Levi to tell him the news. One thing was for sure, now that she knew Reggie was back, she would be keeping a very wary eye out for him. He certainly had a motive to have set the fire, and she was scared he'd do something else.

The following week, Mrs Taylor-Lloyd threw a welcome home party that would be the talk of the town for a very long time to come. Monty had asked Annie to accompany him, but she wisely told him that she wouldn't feel comfortable there, and he accepted that. If truth be told he would rather not have gone himself, but it would have looked strange if he didn't. Now that Reggie was back, Annie never ventured out after dark unless Monty was with her, and she kept her eye out for him loitering about. Having him back was like having a big black cloud hanging over her, but she kept her worries to herself. She shuddered to think what might happen if Monty ever found out how she had suffered at his brother's hands.

Charlie, who had been a close friend with Monty when they were boys, also refused the invitation, and on the night of the party, he dropped a bombshell when he told them, 'I've been thinking; I believe it's time for me to get back to my own place in London. I've been making enquiries and heard about a good job that I've applied for so I shall be leaving in the next couple of weeks.'

Annie frowned; she was pleased that Charlie felt ready to move on, but it had been wonderful to have him home, and she would miss him – they all would.

Chapter Forty-Five

Christmas passed pleasantly. Eve and her little family had decided to spend Christmas alone, which was understandable, but Annie stayed at the house in Swan Lane on Christmas Eve to help Peggy with the cooking and Levi's care. He was now able to get up for short periods each day to sit in a chair by the window and his speech was slowly improving. He seemed to be getting stronger by the day and they all hoped that eventually he would make a full recovery.

In the week leading up to Christmas, the shop had been unbelievably busy, and Annie was thrilled with how business was going. If things continued as they were, she would have to think about getting another horse and someone else to work with her on the rounds, because she could hardly collect enough to keep the shop stocked. The new clothes were selling like hot cakes, too, and she'd had lengthy discussions with Peggy about adding new items to their collection in the new year.

Peggy had collected bunches of holly with shiny green leaves and bright red berries and had scattered them about the rooms in vases, which gave the house a festive feel, and on Christmas morning they exchanged small gifts after breakfast, after which Maggie went off to the morning service at St Mary's Church while Annie helped Peggy with the dinner. Maggie came back in a quiet, pensive mood and after removing her bonnet she went to spend some time with Levi, which surprised Peggy and Annie, but it was a good sign.

As always, the meal was excellent, but even so they were glad when it was over. Maggie had chosen to have her dinner in the front room with Levi and with only Annie, Peggy, Ellie and Charlie round the table, it felt strange.

Monty joined them in the afternoon, and things improved a little as they settled in front of the fire in Levi's room. Monty and Annie played chess, while Maggie read to Levi and Peggy and Charlie dozed by the fire.

'I don't suppose you fancy a stroll, do you?' Monty eventually asked hopefully.

Annie squeezed his hand and gave him an apologetic smile. 'Sorry, but I've decided I'm going back to work the day after tomorrow, so I want to get some rest. Besides, it's freezing out there. I wouldn't be surprised if we don't get some snow. But how are things at home?' She'd noticed he looked down.

He shrugged despondently. 'Same as always. Mother is fussing over Reggie. I half expected her to start feeding him his dinner, and of course Reggie is lapping up the attention.'

They went into the kitchen to make everyone a hot drink and afterwards, Monty returned home while Annie tackled the pile of dirty pots.

Luckily, the snow held off, although it was bitterly cold, and the day after Boxing Day, Annie harnessed Dobbin to the cart and set off on her rounds. The warehouses where she purchased the new clothing wouldn't be open until the day after New Year, so until then she wanted to collect as much second-hand stock as she could to keep Peggy going in the shop.

Late that afternoon, after dropping the collection off to Peggy in Abbey Street, she returned to Swan Lane to stable Dobbin. When he was comfortably settled, she went into the house to check on Levi. The first thing she saw when she entered the kitchen was Maggie sitting at the kitchen table quietly crying and she hurried over to her.

'Maggie, is Levi all right?' she asked anxiously.

Maggie sniffed and nodded. 'He's fine, he's been out of bed for quite a while today and seems a lot stronger.'

Annie breathed a sigh of relief as she tentatively touched Maggie's arm. 'So why are yer cryin' then?'

Normally Maggie would have shrugged her hand away but today she laid her own gently on top of it. 'I suppose I've taken a long hard look at myself and I don't much like what I see,' she said quietly.

'What do yer mean?'

Maggie took a deep breath as she mopped at her wet cheeks with a handkerchief. 'I'm afraid I've been very unfair to you, Annie.' When Annie opened her mouth to protest, Maggie held her hand up to silence her. 'No, don't deny it, I have. For years I treated you as little better than a skivvy and you were worth so much more than that. You've held this family together over the last few years and I don't know what we'd have done without you. So . . . I suppose what I want to say is . . . I'm sorry.'

Annie didn't know what to say so she remained silent and eventually Maggie went on, 'I think you know, don't you, that seeing Penny wasn't *all* in my imagination?'

Annie licked her lips nervously and nodded. 'There, er . . . were a couple of times when I thought I saw a little girl,' she admitted.

Maggie sighed. 'She was here with me, but now she's gone, and I don't know how I can go on without her,' she said brokenly.

'But you have Levi and your other children who need you,' Annie pointed out gently.

'They have each other but Penny is all alone now, wherever she is.'

Annie couldn't help but feel sorry for her. They had all hoped she was getting over Penny's death but it was apparent that she was still grieving badly and she suspected she would be worse when Charlie moved to London in the new year.

'Look, we're on the brink of a brand-new year,' Annie said. 'Let's try and stay positive. Time is a great healer and I'm sure Penny is happy and in a better place.'

Maggie sadly shook her head and standing up, she quietly left the room, leaving Annie with a feeling of dread.

Annie celebrated the New Year quietly in her little rooms above the shops as she made plans for the next step in the business. Davey had already agreed to go with her to look for another horse and insisted he was quite well enough to start doing the rounds again. Annie personally thought it was still a little early but Davey was adamant, and so a few days later they visited the cattle market where they found just what they were looking for.

Raven was ten years old and as black as coal, and Annie fell in love with him on sight. He belonged to a farmer who she thought was asking a little too much for him, but after some bargaining with Davey they finally settled on a price they were all happy with. She and Davey led him back to the stables at Swan Lane to introduce him to Dobbin.

'He's a beauty,' Davey said happily, stroking his silky mane. 'And after working on a farm he'll be used to hard work.'

They were just leading him up the drive when Reggie appeared and immediately the smile slipped from Annie's face.

'Been off spending the old man's money, have you?' Reggie said caustically, eyeing the horse. 'It's perhaps as well, old Dobbin looks as if he's on his last legs.'

Annie bit back the retort that sprang to her lips and stared at him frostily. She'd had the misfortune of seeing him a few times since his return – far more often than she would have liked, in fact – and each time he had done his best to intimidate her. She had managed to ignore his jibes, however, and now she marched past him with her nose in the air. But there was angry colour in her cheeks, and once they had reached the stables, she let out a deep breath.

'I swear one of these days I'll lose my rag with him,' she muttered.

Davey frowned. 'It would be better if yer didn't. You'd be the one in trouble if it came to blows. But come on, cheer up. We've got Raven here to settle down. I can't wait fer Levi to see him. I just 'ope he approves of our choice.'

'I'm sure he will,' Annie said, feeling better now Reggie was out of the way.

Charlie left for his new apartment that same week after promising to come back to visit often, and as they had all feared Maggie's depression worsened.

By the end of January Levi was pottering about again with the use of two stout walking sticks that Annie had collected on one of her rounds, and very slowly he was getting stronger. The same couldn't be said for Maggie who seemed to be sinking deeper and deeper into a dark depression.

'I wonder if we shouldn't get the doctor in to 'ave a look at 'er,' Peggy fretted one day when Annie called in to see Levi after doing her rounds.

Maggie was sitting in the chair rocking to and fro, and she looked ghastly.

'Let's just give 'er a few more days, eh? Susan's comin' tomorrow fer a visit an' yer know seein' Constance always perks her up.' Annie couldn't deny that Maggie was getting progressively worse by the day, but she feared that if they called the doctor, he would have her put into Hatter's Hall again and she was sure that would do more harm than good.

Peggy shrugged. 'If yer think that's best, but I 'ave to admit I don't like leavin' 'er alone for any length o' time.' She looked towards Maggie and frowned. 'She's been sayin' some really odd things lately an' they've bothered me.'

'Such as what?'

'Things like she wishes she could go to be wi' Penny. Yer don't think she'd do owt daft, do yer?'

'Of course not,' Annie answered quickly, but deep down the same concern had occurred to her. 'Let's just wait an' see 'ow she is once Susan an' Constance get 'ere, eh?'

Susan arrived the next day with Constance close beside her. She had lost her glow and looked older and tired. Constance was her whole world and had already outlived the doctor's predictions, but her heart condition was becoming steadily worse, and she lived in dread of anything happening to her.

She had been behind in everything – walking and talking especially – but even so she had two features that made everyone she met fall in love with her. The first was her thick, gleaming long hair, which was the exact colour of her mother's, and the next was her loving, sweet nature. Constance loved everybody, which meant that Susan had to constantly watch her because she was so trusting that she would have gone off with anyone.

'So 'ow have yer both been, pet?' Peggy asked, putting her arms around Constance, who had ambled over to give her a hug.

'Oh, you know, you keep going, don't you.' Susan dropped the two heavy bags she was carrying onto the floor and sunk tiredly onto the nearest chair. She looked towards Maggie, who didn't even seem to realise that her sister and niece had arrived.

'She's not so good then?'

Peggy shook her head as she gently put Constance away from her and went to fill the kettle. 'No, an' if truth be told she's gettin' worse. I was only sayin' to Annie yesterday that I think we should be callin' the doctor in, but Annie wanted to wait until you got 'ere.'

'And Levi?'

Peggy smiled. 'Gettin' better by the day, I'm pleased to say. Annie and Davey are still doin' the rounds fer now but Levi is hopin' to be able to do Annie's again soon so as she can concentrate on the shops.'

As if by speaking of him he had been conjured up, Levi appeared in the hallway door leaning heavily on his sticks. At the sight of him, Constance rushed across the room and threw her arms about him, almost knocking him off his feet.

'Now that's a nice welcome, hinny.' Levi affectionately ruffled her hair.

'Well, you seem much better,' Susan told him with a warm smile.

He nodded. 'I am much better. Hopefully I'll be back to me old self soon.' His speech was mostly back to normal, but he did hesitate and have to choose his words carefully. He glanced towards his wife, who was rocking to and fro, and the smile slid from his face. Once Levi was well enough to move back upstairs, she had allowed him back into their bed and he had loved being close to her.

He looked at Peggy and when she shook her head, he sighed and went to take a seat next to Susan while Constance made a fuss of the old ginger tom cat that had casually strolled into the kitchen one day some months before, and had rarely left since.

'How are things in London?' Levi enquired.

Susan shrugged. 'Oh, much the same.' She had long since given up on her dream of a cottage with roses around the door with Theo, although she still loved him. But she loved Constance even more and she was her reason for living now. She still had her clients, although she was very selective and only worked enough hours to keep herself and her daughter in comfort. Theo had never been the best at helping to provide for them, but she was used to it and didn't expect he would ever change now.

'Susan . . . why don't you an' Constance leave London an' come an' live 'ere wi' us?' Levi offered. 'Me an' Maggie rattle around this place an' you'd be good company fer 'er when I'm back at work.'

Susan smiled wryly. 'I might just do that one of these days,' she said quietly.

Chapter Forty-Six

June 1921

As summer returned, Levi started to go out on his rounds again, although at Annie's insistence, he was only working two days a week. She was worried that if he did too much all at once he would have a relapse, so she was being quite strict with him.

With a little more time on her hands, Annie started making plans for the shops again. Over the past few months, they had got busier, as suddenly the women who had not had the opportunity to think about their clothes during the war were taking a pride in their appearance again, and the fashions were changing rapidly. Cloche hats and calf-length skirts were in vogue and Annie intended to take full advantage of the fact.

One day, as Annie explained to Levi how she intended to buy in more fashionable clothes, he gave her an indulgent smile. 'An' where would yer sell 'em?' He couldn't fault her energy and enthusiasm.

'It would have to be in one of the shops we already have for now,' she admitted. 'Although eventually I'd like to rent another one where we could concentrate on selling just new things. Up to now we've catered for the working classes but I'd like to go a bit more up-market for the wealthier women who can afford the latest designs. There's nowhere in the town that caters for them really and they have to go to Coventry, Birmingham or Leicester. It would be a more select shop with proper fitting rooms. What do yer think o' the idea?'

Levi smiled as he scratched his chin. 'Well . . . things are pickin' up now,' he admitted. 'But don't yer think we might be takin' on a bit too much, hinny?'

Annie shook her head. 'The war is over an' things are slowly going back to normal. The women from the big houses are gettin' rid of the clothes they'd hung on to during the war, and they want the latest fashions. Peggy or Eve could run the shops we 'ave with their eyes shut and Peggy is so good with a needle. I'm thinkin' we might offer an alteration service. I'm sure she'd be capable. I could run the new shop an' you 'ave Davey to help you wi' your round. Oh, *please* say you'll at least think about it, Levi!'

He nodded slowly. 'Aye, I'll think about it,' he agreed. 'But that's all I'll do fer now so don't get runnin' away wi' yerself.'

'Thank you.' She leant over and planted a sloppy kiss on his cheek before skipping away and he watched her go with a smile.

Monty, too, thought it was a good idea, when she told him about it that evening, although he wished she would slow down. She was still no closer to committing herself fully to him and he was beginning to get a little frustrated. Most young women her age could think of nothing but settling down and having babies but that seemed the furthest thing from Annie's mind. Still, he loved her enough to wait until she was ready – forever if need be.

It was a beautiful balmy evening and they were sitting on a bench in the garden enjoying the sound of the birds in the trees, when suddenly the roaring of an engine broke the tranquility.

Monty frowned. 'That'll be Reggie coming back in his new car,' he commented. His parents had bought it for him the week before and ever since he had been racing around the town showing off in it like an idiot. Monty was surprised he hadn't broken his neck yet.

Since coming home, his mother had spoilt him shamelessly and Reggie was taking full advantage of the fact. Unfortunately, his smart clothes and shiny car didn't make him any more attractive to the opposite sex, which for Reggie, who was used to young ladies falling at his feet, went severely against the grain. Even so, he wasn't short of female company. Rumour had it that he was now a regular visitor to the whore house on the outskirts of town. Under other circumstances Monty would have felt sorry for him, but because he was such a bully he no longer cared what his brother got up to, so long as he left Annie alone.

They heard the engine stop and a moment later Reggie came strutting up the drive. He sneered when he saw them but said nothing as he strode past and disappeared into the house.

Monty shook his head then turned his attention back to Annie. 'How is Maggie today?'

Since Christmas, their concern for her had grown. She was barely eating or drinking enough to keep a bird alive. It was heartbreaking to see and Levi was afraid to leave her alone for fear of what she might do, which was why Annie was there to keep an eye on her that evening while Levi was at the yard sorting his metal ready for a visit from the scrapman. They all took it in turns to be with Maggie as much as they could.

Annie sighed as she rose from the bench. 'No better – worse if anything. In fact, I'd better get back inside and check she's all right. I only came out for a breath of fresh air. Will you come in for a drink?'

He nodded and followed her inside and she went to fill the kettle at the sink. The kitchen was empty, so she asked Monty, 'Would you mind going to check if she's in the parlour and tell her there's a cup o' tea comin' up.'

Monty headed for the hallway as Annie began to prepare the teapot. But she stilled with alarm when she heard him gasp, a horrible premonition coming over her.

She turned quickly as Monty rushed back in and stood in the doorway, his face chalk-white.

'Get a sharp knife and come quickly!' He fled back the way he had come while, all of a dither, Annie grabbed a knife and raced after him. When she reached the door she froze at the sight before her. Maggie was dangling from a thick rope tied about the banister halfway up the staircase, her feet swinging from side to side like the pendulum of a clock.

'Get up the stairs and cut through the rope as quickly as you can,' he shouted, grasping Maggie's feet to try and take the weight from her neck.

Annie's legs had turned to jelly but she stumbled towards the staircase to do as she was told. Minutes later she had managed to saw through the rope and Maggie's lifeless body slid into Monty's waiting arms. He laid her gently down but one look at her distorted features told them that Maggie was beyond help. Her eyes were bulging and her tongue lolled out of the side of her mouth.

'Stay here with her, I'm going to fetch Levi and the doctor.' Monty was on his feet again and Annie gently lifted Maggie's head onto her lap and stroked her hair back from her face.

'I'm *so* sorry, Maggie,' she sobbed brokenly. 'I only popped outside for a few minutes, but I should *never* have left you.' Her tears fell onto Maggie's pale cheeks as guilt consumed her. It was all her fault; she should have watched her more closely. If she hadn't gone out for a bit of fresh air Maggie would still be alive. But what was done was done and she didn't know how she was going to face Levi.

It seemed like an eternity before Levi, closely followed by the doctor and Monty, appeared again, and at sight of his wife Levi groaned, tears springing to his eyes.

'Aw, hinny, what've yer done?' he cried as he dropped to his knees and gathered her into his arms.

Monty led Annie into the kitchen and began to organise the tea. Annie was shaking uncontrollably and looked like she could do with one. Peggy huffed into the kitchen then and leaning heavily on the back of a chair she gasped breathlessly, 'Where is she?'

Monty nodded towards the hallway and with her face grim Peggy went to her oldest friend.

The next two hours passed in a blur for Annie. Every time she closed her eyes, she could see Maggie dangling at the end of the rope, and she knew she would never forget the sight for as long as she lived. The doctor left eventually after stating on the death certificate that Maggie had taken her own life while the balance of her mind was disturbed.

'Well, he got that right,' Peggy commented, while they waited for the undertaker. 'She ain't never been right since the day she lost Penny an' I reckon Susan takin' young Constance away again just tipped her over the edge. I just 'ope that if there really is an afterlife Maggie and Penny are together again now.'

Monty handed her another cup of tea. They had drunk so much tea in the last few hours that Annie felt as if she was drowning in it. Levi was still in the hall with Maggie, flatly refusing to leave her, and it was heartbreaking to see his grief. Eventually the undertaker and his assistant arrived bearing a plain wicker coffin and Peggy asked him worriedly, 'Will she be able to be buried in consecrated ground? I know the church don't look kindly on suicides.'

'Because of how the doctor has worded the cause of death I think it may be permitted,' he assured her. 'Just leave it with me and rest assured I shall do my very best to try and have her buried as close to her daughter as is possible.'

Peggy inclined her head as the two men passed through to Maggie and Levi. It seemed a long time before the men solemnly bore the coffin away to the chapel of rest. Once they'd left Levi joined Annie, Peggy and Monty in the kitchen looking utterly broken.

'I-it's my fault,' Annie sobbed. 'I went out to get a bit of air and . . . I'm so sorry. I had no idea what she was planning to do.'

Levi shook his head and sank onto a chair. 'Don't blame yerself, pet,' he mumbled. 'None of us could 'ave been with 'er every moment of every day.'

It was funny, Annie thought, that over the last few months she and Maggie had been closer than they had ever been in all the time they had lived together. And now looking back she could see all the signs that this was what Maggie had wanted. She had intended to join Penny the only way she knew how and had just been waiting for the right moment.

She looked at Monty and frowned. The poor chap was as pale as putty and looked quite ill, which was understandable after the shock he'd had.

'Why don't yer get yerself off 'ome lad, an' get some rest,' Levi suggested. 'We don't want you bein' ill an' all.'

'I think I might if you're sure there's nothing else I can do,' Monty said quietly. He just wished he could have done more.

'I'll see yer home.' Annie rose and followed him outside.

'Do yer think Levi will be all right on his own tonight?' he asked when they reached the drive.

'Don't worry, he won't be alone,' Annie assured him. 'Me an' Peggy will stay wi' him. But you get yerself in now.'

He pecked her on the cheek and went on his way as she turned and went back to Peggy and Levi.

Maggie's funeral took place the following week on a beautiful day with not a cloud in the sky. Annie felt it was wrong somehow for anyone to be put in the earth on such a beautiful day. Susan had come from London with Charlie, leaving Constance with her nanny. Even Barney had managed to get there in time. Flo was also there looking more like she was going to a party than a funeral in a gaudy, brightly coloured dress and hat. The only one who hadn't come to see his mother laid to rest was Harry who as far as they knew was still living with his new love in France.

Surprisingly it was mainly Maggie's old neighbours from the courtyards who attended the service at Chilvers Coton Church. Monty was there but there was no sign of his mother, although that didn't really surprise any of them. She had never accepted Maggie nor even tried to hide the fact, so Annie was glad she had kept away.

When the funeral was over, Maggie's coffin was carried to a grave very close to Penny's in the churchyard and Annie wept as it was lowered into the ground. The vicar was halfway through reading the prayers when she glanced up and her breath caught in her throat, for there beneath the branches of a yew tree was Maggie. She was smiling and clutching the hand of a little girl who looked like a miniature version of her mother, and Annie knew in that moment that Maggie was where she wanted to be, and the thought gave her some comfort. As she watched, Maggie and Penny turned and walked away, their images growing misty before they faded completely.

Annie stared down at the coffin but she knew now that Maggie wasn't there. She had gone to a better place and was reunited with the daughter she had so adored.

Chapter Forty-Seven

October 1921

Levi took Maggie's death very badly. Annie had feared that the shock of losing her as he had would bring on another seizure, but thankfully it hadn't, although all his sparkle and wit had gone. Peggy had been marvellous, ensuring that he had a meal with her in the cottage each evening after he had finished his rounds. She worried that if she didn't, he wouldn't bother to eat. Annie was spending as much time as she could with him round at Swan Lane too and it was one evening when they sat sharing a cup of tea that he told her, 'I'm thinkin' o' puttin' this place up fer sale.'

Annie wasn't surprised. The house was far too big for one person, or even two if it came to that.

'The thing is, it has no happy memories fer me now,' he said sadly. 'An' every time I walk into the hall I . . .' He gulped and shut his eyes for a moment before going on, 'I thought this place would be the makin' o' Maggie. She'd allus had dreams o' livin' in a house like this but it couldn't make up fer the loss of our Penny. Nuthin' could. I just hope if there is an afterlife that they're together again now.'

'I'm sure they are.' Annie reached across the table to gently squeeze his hand. 'But where will yer go?'

He shrugged. 'I ain't thought that far ahead.'

Peggy came in at that moment. She often popped round of an evening to keep him company when he wasn't at hers, and when Annie told her of his decision she nodded.

'I thought yer might decide to do that,' she told Levi. 'So when the house is sold, why don't yer come back to share the cottage wi' me?'

Levi raised an eyebrow. 'Crikey, can yer imagine what people would say if I did that? The gossips would 'ave a field day.'

'So let 'em.' Peggy stuck her chin in the air. 'It'd be a nine-day wonder, an' while they were busy talkin' about us, they'd be leavin' some other poor buggers alone. But I ain't suggestin' anythin' immoral! I've got a spare bedroom an' you've got your yard an' the stablin' back there fer the horses. You've been runnin' backwards an' forwards between the two ever since yer moved in 'ere an' it is still your cottage, so it makes sense from where I'm standin'.'

'I agree,' Annie chipped in. At least if he did as Peggy was suggesting she wouldn't have to worry about him being on his own so much.

'Another thing is, if yer moved back to the yard, yer overheads would be so much less,' Peggy pointed out sensibly. 'You could afford to retire old Dobbin an' let Davey do the rounds, especially if Annie does get a shop of 'er own to run. Me an' Eve could keep the other shops goin' an' you could concentrate on keepin' the yard sorted.'

Levi nodded. He knew it made sense and looked around sadly at all the beautiful furniture Maggie had bought over the years. 'Well, if I did, I certainly wouldn't need all this lot. It wouldn't even fit in the cottage.'

'Then sell the house fully furnished,' Peggy said.

'Hmm, I suppose I could do.'

Sensing that he was going to say no more on the subject for now Peggy and Annie went on to speak of other things until it was time for them to leave.

Monty arrived shortly after to see Annie back to her rooms above the shop. She still didn't like venturing out after dark while Reggie was about, and on the way back, she told him what Levi was thinking of doing.

'It might be for the best,' Monty said quietly. 'I don't think Levi has ever been truly happy there. In fact, I think he only ever bought the place because it was what Maggie wanted. But on a different note, are you still looking around for another shop?'

She nodded. 'Yes, I am, but the trouble is, the one I really like in Bridge Street is for sale and not to rent and I couldn't afford it yet.'

He opened his mouth to say she could if she agreed to marry him, but quickly clamped it shut again. Over time, he'd learnt the hard way that Annie wouldn't do anything until she was good and ready, but sometimes it felt like he had been waiting forever.

The very next morning Levi arranged for an estate agent to come and value the house on Swan Lane. Now that he'd made his mind up there seemed no point in waiting and by the end of the week a 'For Sale' board had been erected at the end of the drive, much to Mrs Taylor-Lloyd's delight.

'The Lilburns were never suited to living in this neighbourhood,' she simpered to the ladies that came to her coffee morning. 'I just hope someone a little more genteel moves in.'

Much to Levi's surprise, the house sold very quickly and he made a handsome profit on it, even after agreeing to leave all the furniture. House prices had risen since the end of the war and a barrister from London who was due to retire had bought it to be closer to his relatives who lived in the Midlands.

'It should all be sorted before Christmas,' Levi told Peggy.

'Good . . . an' 'ave yer decided where yer goin' to live yet?'

'I 'ave actually.' He took his cap off and twisted it in his hands. 'I'd like to take you up on yer offer o' comin' back to the cottage if yer still o' the same mind. I wouldn't be bringin' a lot wi' me, just a few clothes an' odds an' sods so I wouldn't take up too much room.'

'You can bring back whatever yer like,' Peggy told him. 'If anythin' it should be me that's leavin'. It is still your cottage after all.'

'Oh no, I don't want yer to do that,' Levi protested quickly. 'I'm sure we'll muck along just fine together.'

'In that case, I'd best start gettin' the stables cleared out. I've been usin' 'em for storage since yer moved 'ere, but I can 'ave 'em right for the horses in no time.'

The next few weeks passed in a blur as Annie and Peggy helped Levi sort out anything personal that he wanted to take with him, and at the beginning of December it was time for him to hand the keys to the solicitor. On a cold and frosty morning, he took a walk through the house with tears in his eyes. He had hoped that this place would be the start of happier times for him and Maggie, but it hadn't worked out that way. With a sigh he locked the door for the last time and left without looking back.

It felt strange to be back in his old cottage. It seemed incredibly small now that he had become accustomed to larger rooms, especially as he was in the smaller bedroom. Peggy slept in the room he had shared with Maggie. She had offered to move into the other one, but he said not to.

'Aww well, if yer change yer mind just give me the wink an' we'll swap over,' she told him.

Levi now had the sort of bank balance he had only ever dreamt of and he began to plan what he would do with the money. He had written to Charlie in London to tell him he was now back in the cottage but he had no forwarding address for Barney or Harry and was concerned about what would happen if they came to visit and he wasn't there.

'That's easily solved,' Peggy told him. 'Fer a start off if they do go to Swan Lane there's plenty as knew yer there who'll tell 'em where you are now. An' even if they didn't if they come an' you ain't round at Swan Lane the first place they would come next would be 'ere.'

Levi saw the truth in what she said and nodded.

*

They were planning a quiet Christmas at the cottage with just the two of them and Annie. Ellie had to work, Eve and Davey were staying in their rooms again and Charlie had written to say that he would be staying in London. He sounded happier and had obviously settled there so although they would miss him, they were pleased for him.

Annie set off for Peggy's bright and early on Christmas morning, looking forward to a relaxing day and to seeing Monty, who had agreed to join them in the afternoon. The pavements were white with hoar frost and she was so intent on not slipping over and wondering what Alex would be doing that day that she failed to see the figure coming towards her until it stopped directly in front of her, blocking her path.

Startled, she looked up and her heart did a flip as she found herself staring into Reggie's disfigured face. Had he been anyone else she would have felt nothing but pity, but because it was him, all she felt was repugnance. He was leering at her and she straightened to her full height and stared back at him. Her pride would never allow her to show how afraid she was of him.

'I thought I'd catch you if I came early enough. I think it's time we had a little chat.'

'And why would I want to chat with you?' She clutched her gifts to her and stared at him defiantly.

He grimaced. 'Because I'm about to do you a favour.'

'*Really?* And what favour could I *possibly* want from you?'

'Respectability for a start.'

It was her turn to frown now.

'The thing is,' he went on in a softer tone. 'I know I'm not the good-looking chap that went off to war, but then you're not such a catch either, are you? What I mean is, you're a bastard. You don't even know where you came from, but I'm prepared to overlook that. You clearly don't want my little brother or you wouldn't have kept him dangling on a string for so long, and so I'm prepared to make an honest woman of you. Think of it: you'd live in the lap of luxury with servants to wait on you and you'd never have to work again. What do you think?'

'I think you must be mad to think I'd even *consider* it,' she spat, angry now. 'Why . . . Monty is worth a dozen or more of you and I wouldn't marry you if you were the last man on earth. Is that clear enough for you? Now get out of my way and let me pass.'

He reached out to touch her but she slapped his arm away so fiercely that she almost dropped one of the gifts. As she rushed away, his voice carried after her.

'You're going to live to regret what you've just said, you just wait and see! That dimwit little brother of mine is the walking dead because when that shrapnel moves he'll be gone – and good riddance! And then just think how vulnerable you'll be, living all on your own . . . anything could happen!'

In that moment Annie was convinced that it had been Reggie who had set the fire at the shop but she didn't wait to hear any more and it wasn't until she'd turned into the ginnel that led into Peggy's yard that she paused to lean against the wall and get her breath back. How could Reggie think even in his wildest dreams that she would ever consider marrying him? She loathed everything about him, and it was nothing to do with his disfigured face. After what he'd done to her she couldn't bear to be around him. And now she was certain he had something to do with the fire that could have killed her, not to mention the awful things he had said about Monty . . . It wasn't definite that the shrapnel would move towards his heart, it could move the other way. Just thinking about it made her shudder.

Eventually her heart settled into a steadier rhythm and after straightening her hat, she plastered a smile on her face and moved on.

Chapter Forty-Eight

Warmth and the delicious smell of roasting turkey wrapped itself around Annie like a blanket as she entered the cottage.

Peggy looked up from where she was sitting in the chair opposite Levi and smiled. 'Ah, here you are, pet. We were just sayin' we wondered how long yer'd be. I hope yer hungry; that turkey Levi bought is so big I could barely get it in the oven and I reckon it'd feed the whole street. But are yer feeling all right? Yer look a bit pasty.'

'I'm fine,' Annie told her. The last thing she wanted was to spoil Christmas Day by telling them about her confrontation with Reggie. 'And yes, I am hungry actually. I didn't have any breakfast.'

Annie looked at Levi and Peggy sitting there, quite at ease in each other's company, and couldn't help but think how well suited they were. They looked like an old married couple.

'Good, then get yer coat off an' come an' sit down while I get yer a drop o' sherry. It is a special day after all.'

Annie removed her coat and hung it on a nail on the back of the door. She had tied the beautiful shawl that had been left with her when she was a baby around her shoulders, and when Peggy caught sight of it, she quickly averted her eyes.

A thought suddenly occurred to Annie. She had worn the shawl only a few times, on special occasions, and each time Peggy had seen her wearing it she had looked uncomfortable, although she had never commented on it. Could it be that because Peggy had worked at the workhouse, she knew more about her parents than she was letting on?

Annie took a seat and accepted her sherry before saying casually, 'I've decided that after Christmas I'm goin' to start tryin' to find out who my real parents are.' She was watching Peggy carefully, but it was Levi who spoke first.

'Won't that be difficult all these years on, pet?'

Annie sipped her drink. 'I dare say it will be, but somebody must know somethin'. Someone who worked there perhaps, or somebody passin' by?'

Peggy said nothing as she hastily rose and went to baste the turkey, so for now Annie changed the subject. It was Christmas Day after all and she didn't want to spoil it.

The meal was delicious and when they were finished, they exchanged presents. There was a warm coat for Peggy from Annie, which she was thrilled with, and a warm shirt and jumper for Levi. Peggy had bought Annie a very pretty skirt, which she loved, and then it was time for Levi to give her his present. He handed her a large envelope and Annie was a little bemused as she opened it with no idea what it could be, although Levi and Peggy couldn't stop smiling.

'I, er . . . don't understand,' she said when she had read through the papers from Levi's solicitor. 'It's about the shop that was for sale in Bridge Street.'

Levi nodded. 'That's right, an' if yer look a bit closer you'll see it's been bought an' is now in your name.' He laughed when she looked more confused than ever.

'I've bought it for you, pet. The shop is yours to do what you want wi'. You've earned it as far as I'm concerned.'

Annie's mouth fell open. She could hardly believe it.

'An there's rooms above it where you'll be able to live an' all, an' a lot more space in 'em than the ones yer livin' in now.'

'B-but I can't accept this . . . it's too much.' Her voice came out as a squeak and Peggy giggled.

'Rubbish,' said Levi. 'I've got more money than I know what to do wi' now that I've sold the house.'

The door opened then and Monty strode in and when Peggy told him what Levi had done, he beamed.

'Congratulations, Annie. You'll be able to sell clothes to the gentry now if that's what you want to do and I'm sure you'll make a success of it.'

Annie was so overcome she could hardly speak, so instead she crossed to Levi and laid her head on his shoulder. 'Thank you,' she said quietly, although the words sounded sorely inadequate for all he'd done for her. 'I promise I'll work hard an' make yer proud o' me.'

'I already am proud of yer.' He kissed the top of her head. 'You've been the glue that's kept this family together over the years an' I can't think of anyone who deserves it more.'

'But what about my share in the other shops?' she asked next.

'Aw well, now yer branchin' out on yer own I thought I'd 'ave the solicitor sign them over to Peggy. I figured you wouldn't need them anymore. I hope yer don't mind?'

It was Peggy's turn to look shocked and she opened her mouth to protest but he held his hand up to stay her words.

'Now I don't want no arguments, woman. Like Annie you've been workin' yer socks off so I figured you deserved your share of the business an' all.'

'I think this calls for a drink,' Monty said, refilling their glasses.

'I think that's an excellent idea,' Annie told Levi with a smile at Peggy. Already her mind was racing ahead to what she would do with her new business, and she could hardly wait to get started.

Once the glasses were filled, they drank a toast to the year ahead, although unknown to each other they were each thinking of Christmases past and Maggie and the loved ones who were no longer with them. It was their first Christmas without Maggie and it had been difficult for Levi.

'Here, I dare say you'll be needin' these,' Levi said when the toast was drunk, handing Annie the keys to her new shop. 'I've no doubt you'll be itchin' to go an' have a look round.'

'I am rather,' she admitted. 'Just as soon as I've helped Peggy wi' the washin' up. There's a mountain o' pots waitin' to be done.'

'Oh, get off wi' you if you've a mind to.' Levi smiled. 'I can give Peggy a hand wi' that.'

Annie needed no second bidding as she raced off to get her coat and minutes later, she and Monty were heading for Bridge Street.

'Who'd 'ave thought I'd ever get to own me very own shop?' Annie breathed, still hardly able to believe it.

Monty smiled. 'I would. I always knew you were going places,' he said quietly.

She glanced at him and was concerned to see that he was looking a little pale. Slowing her steps, she tucked her arm into his. Sometimes she forgot that he was supposed to take his time.

Once they arrived at the shop, she unlocked the door and they began to explore her new property.

'It's in pretty good repair,' Monty commented. 'We should be able to have this ready for opening in no time at all.' The layout was much the same as the other shops, with a kitchen, a yard and a toilet at the back, and stairs leading up to the rooms above.

They headed up there next and just as Levi had said they were larger than the rooms above the other shops, and already Annie could see herself living there.

'Just wait until I tell Eve and Davey about this,' she laughed, clapping her hands in excitement.

Monty grinned. 'Actually, I think you'll find they already know about it. We all did, but Levi wanted to keep it as a surprise for you for today. But what will you do about stocking the shop? I could help out if you like.'

'Thanks, but I have more than enough saved to buy what I need to start with,' Annie assured him as she inspected the bedroom.

'Hmm, don't forget, though, if you're catering to upper-class women, you'll need new clothes to look the part, and the shop will need to be considerably better equipped than the other two.'

'I hadn't thought of that,' she admitted, chewing her lip.

'Don't worry about it, I have money put by if you need it. You can call it a loan if you'd rather and pay me back when and if you can.'

She gave him a grateful smile before saying, 'I'm going to bring the furniture from my other rooms, so I don't have to spend money on more furniture.'

'Good idea,' Monty answered as he stared down at the street below. He'd hoped to propose officially to Annie this Christmas, and there was a diamond ring waiting in his pocket, but now he felt he'd be wasting his time. No doubt she'd be concentrating all her efforts on getting her new business up and running for the next few months at least, and he would have to take second place as always. Still, he consoled himself, it was nice to see her so happy and he'd waited so long already he supposed a little longer wouldn't make that much difference.

Chapter Forty-Nine

Over in Nottingham, where the circus was overwintering, Charity was picking her way across a frosty field to Luca's wagon. Her heart was in her mouth, for they rarely spoke unless it was absolutely necessary, but she felt that what she needed to speak to him about could wait no longer. Once she reached the wagon, she licked her lips and tentatively tapped at the door.

Her husband opened it and frowned. '*Yes?*'

His voice was curt but Charity was not about to be turned away. This was far too important.

'I . . . sorry to disturb you but I need to speak to yer about somethin' important.'

He hesitated for the briefest of moments before standing aside and she stepped past him into the welcoming warmth.

'So what is it?'

She took a deep breath. 'Actually . . . it's our daughter I've come to speak to yer about.'

He raised an eyebrow. 'Oh yes, what about her? She's well, ain't she?'

'Oh yes, she's well,' she assured him. 'At least physically she is. But she's so unhappy an' I think it's time we changed that.'

'An' how can we do that?'

'By givin' her permission to marry Barney.'

He opened his mouth to protest but she held her hand up to silence him. 'Fer once in yer life just hear me out, will yer?'

He was so shocked that she had dared to stand up to him that he snapped his mouth shut.

'A blind man on a gallopin' horse could see how much those two love each other,' she went on quietly. 'Why – he was even prepared to go to prison for her after all that business with Bertie. And yes, I know that it's our tradition to marry our own kind and Barney was a townie when he joined us. But sometimes traditions are made to be broken. You and I broke the rules once, I was from gypsy stock, not circus stock, an' it worked well enough till . . . Anyway, there's no point in goin' over that old ground again. I ain't here to talk about us but our daughter. You might be content to let her pine away but I ain't. You tried to marry her off once afore to a chap she didn't love an' look how that ended! So what do yer say? Are yer prepared to give this young couple a chance or is there sommat you have against Barney?'

'Well, I, er . . . I've nowt against him,' he stuttered. 'He's a good, hard-workin' chap, I'll admit.'

He scratched his chin and stared from the window for a moment before sighing deeply. He'd been aware for a long time how the young couple felt about each other, although he'd tried his best to ignore it. He turned back to her. 'Was there anything else?'

She knew by the set of his mouth and the way he refused to look at her that she was being dismissed so she rose and pulled her shawl more tightly about her. She paused at the door and looked over her shoulder. 'I've got one more thing to say. Many years ago, you punished me for something I didn't do, and you've been punishing me ever since. Our daughter has done nothing wrong, so if you have any love for her don't make her life miserable too.' And with that she left, closing the door quietly behind her.

As Luca watched her cross the field a tear slid down his cheek. Whether he liked it or not he had a lot of thinking to do.

The following day, as Barney was feeding the horses, Luca approached him.

'All right, boss?'

Luca nodded. 'I want to ask yer somethin' an' I want an honest answer. Do you love me daughter?'

Barney blinked. The question was so unexpected, but then he squared his shoulders and turned to face him. The worst Luca could do was send him packing. 'Aye, I love her, allus have done.'

'An' when yer say yer love 'er do yer mean enough to make an honest woman of her?'

Without hesitation Barney nodded. 'I'd marry her tomorrow . . . today if I could.'

'In that case you 'ave my permission to ask her an' see if that's what she wants.'

Luca turned on his heel and strode away leaving Barney with his mouth hanging slackly open. But not for long, for suddenly he began to sprint across the field towards Charity and Mercy's wagon where he banged on the door.

Mercy opened it. 'Whatever's the matter? Where's the fire? We thought you were going to knock a hole in the door.'

'Get yer shawl,' he told her, and she glanced nervously across his shoulder for a sign of her father.

Barney laughed, 'Don't worry about yer da,' he told her. 'He's given me permission to speak to you. Now go an' get yer shawl, woman, an' don't keep me waiting!'

With a smile Mercy did as she was told and he led her to the shelter of some trees.

'I . . . I don't think I need to tell yer how I feel about yer, do I?' he muttered.

She shook her head, looking confused. 'No, yer don't, an' I feel the same about you, but yer know Da is against us.'

'Ah . . . but he ain't anymore!' He took her hands. 'He's had a change o' heart.' The words spilled out of him as he told her of the conversation he'd had with Luca. 'So yer see, there's nothin' to stop us now,' he ended breathlessly. 'We can get wed at last!'

And then she was in his arms laughing and crying all at the same time as Charity peeped at them from the window of her wagon, a smile on her face.

A short time later they went to see Luca hand in hand, and he looked at them solemnly. 'I take it yer in agreement about this match?' he asked his daughter, and she nodded vigorously. 'Then so be it, but there's one thing I ask: I know it's the usual way with our people to have big weddings but I think after what happened wi' Bertie Russell, as a mark o' respect to his people, we should keep this one low-key. Are yer both agreeable to that?'

The young couple nodded in unison.

'And when did yer have in mind?'

'Well, if it's all right wi' Mercy, I'd like to wait till the spring when we go back to Nuneaton,' Barney told him. 'An' that way me family can attend.'

Luca nodded. 'Fine, we'll perhaps just keep it to your family an' ours wi' just a few o' the circus folk if that's agreeable?'

The couple nodded happily and Luca sighed as they turned and walked away with stars in their eyes.

Chapter Fifty

It was late January and Peggy was in her kitchen when a knock came at the door and on opening it, she found Susan standing there. She was sporting a black eye and Peggy ushered her inside. 'Eek, luvvie, what's 'appened now? An' where is Constance?'

The tears came then, spurting out of Susan's eyes so quickly that they barely touched her cheeks as she sobbed broken-heartedly.

'Sh-she died just over two weeks ago,' Susan choked out. 'I buried her three days ago.'

'*Oh no!*' Peggy was deeply sad to hear the news, although it wasn't entirely unexpected. Constance's heart condition had worsened as she got older. 'But why didn't yer let any of us know?'

Susan shrugged as she mopped at her streaming eyes with a scrap of handkerchief. 'There was no point all of you coming all that way.'

'And what's brought this about?' Peggy tentatively touched her swollen eye. 'Theo again, was it?'

Susan nodded miserably. 'Yes, but don't worry, it won't be happening again. I've left him . . . for good this time.'

'And not before time,' Peggy said gently. 'How yer put up wi' him fer as long as yer did, I'll never know, pet.'

'I suppose I always thought he'd change and we'd live happily ever after,' Susan said as Peggy pressed her down onto a chair before hurrying to the sink to fill the kettle. The poor love looked as if she was in need of a good strong cup of tea.

'But look at me, Peggy – I'm not the young girl I once was.'

It was true, Susan was well past the first flush of youth and had been forced to watch Theo recruiting far younger, prettier girls than herself for some time. Her relationship with him had gradually worsened after the birth of Constance and Susan no longer attracted the punters as she once had, so she wasn't so important to him, and he had made sure she knew it. He had never understood her devotion to Constance or the fact that since her birth she had always come first in Susan's affections. And now here she was, racing towards middle-age and she had lost them both.

'Theo didn't even attend Constance's funeral,' Susan said brokenly. 'And on the same evening he came to see me to tell me that he thought it was time he moved me to a smaller flat.' She shook her head. 'I've no doubt he has someone younger and prettier in mind for mine. And that was when I finally realised there was no future for us. We had a terrible row.' She touched her swollen eye with a shaking hand and sighed. 'So here I am. Back to where I started. I wondered if you might perhaps put me up, just until I can find somewhere of my own to rent?'

'Of course I can,' Peggy assured her. 'But you'll 'ave to kip in my room wi' me if you don't mind. Levi sleeps in the second bedroom.'

Levi came in soon after and although he was surprised to see Susan, he greeted her with a peck on the cheek and didn't comment on her swollen eye.

'Susan will be stayin' wi' us fer a time till she can find somewhere round 'ere to rent,' Peggy told him as she ladled some beef stew and dumplings onto their plates.

'In that case I might be able to 'elp.' He hadn't seen Susan since Maggie's funeral and was sad to hear of Constance's death. 'The rooms above the shop where Annie lives will be available soon cos she'll be movin'' into the ones above the new shop.' He went on to tell her about Annie's new business in Bridge Street. 'An' she were only sayin' today that once the shop opens she'll be lookin' fer someone to 'elp, if yer were lookin' fer a job.'

When Susan nodded enthusiastically, he went on to tell them about some happy news. Eve and Davey had told him that day that there was a new baby on the way and Susan sighed as she thought of Constance. 'They do say that family events come in threes, don't they? A birth, a death, a marriage. How wonderful for them. We've had the death, the birth is coming, I wonder who will get married? It's the circle of life, isn't it?'

Levi was half hoping that it would be Annie and Monty, but he didn't say anything. What would be would be.

Susan didn't venture out of the house for the next few days as she grieved for Constance and the loss of all her dreams, but finally one morning, Peggy told her firmly, 'Right, you've shut yerself away fer long enough. Life has to go on. Come on, get yer coat on we're goin' to have a look at how Annie's new shop is comin' along.'

Susan didn't look too happy with the idea but she did as she was told and soon after they set off along Abbey Street. They were both impressed with what they saw when they arrived. Annie and Monty had done most of the painting themselves to save some money, but Annie had paid professional shopfitters to come in to fit the rails that would hold the new clothes and build a very smart fitting room. The walls had been painted a soft shell-pink, and a pale dove-grey carpet was fitted from wall to wall. There were full-length gilt cheval mirrors dotted about where the customers could see themselves in the gowns, and gilded pink velvet chairs where they could sit while they were shown what was available.

'Goodness, this reminds me of some of the upper-class dress shops in London,' Susan said approvingly.

Annie smiled. 'That's what I was 'opin' for. I've just appointed a seamstress who'll do any alterations to the gowns as Peggy'll have 'er 'ands full now she 'as her own business to run. In fact, you might be able to 'elp me there. I'll be goin' to order some stock soon, so per'aps, you could point me in the right direction, cos you'll 'ave more idea about what's fashionable in London at the moment.'

'I'd be happy to,' Susan answered. 'In fact, I can do better than that.' She paused for a moment and Annie saw that her eyes were full of tears. 'I have until the end of next week to empty my flat and I'd like to go and fetch some of my clothes and personal items.

I came away in rather a hurry with very little. Why don't you come back to London with me and we can go into some of the high-class emporiums so that you can see the latest fashions for yourself?'

When Annie hesitated, she hurried on, 'You'd be doing me a favour – I'm not looking forward to going back there alone.'

Annie had been working so hard on the shop and her new home above it that she was feeling exhausted, and added to that Reggie had been hovering around, so perhaps a break would be just what she needed.

'In that case, I'll come,' Annie agreed. 'Just tell me when an' I'll be ready.'

They left on an early train to Euston two days later and arrived in London at lunchtime. Susan was a bag of nerves and Annie guessed she was probably worried about seeing Theo again. Now she had finally found the courage to make the split from him, Annie knew it wasn't going to be easy for her.

Once they arrived at the flat, Susan let herself in with her key and looked around sadly. It had been hers and Constance's home for a long time and it was hard to think that soon she would be walking away from it for good.

Annie helped her do some packing in the afternoon, but it soon became obvious that Susan had far too much to take back on the train. There were so many things of Constance's she wanted to keep as well as her own.

'I'll pack it up and have it sent on,' Susan decided. 'Now, let's go and have a meal somewhere. We can finish this tomorrow.'

They found a small restaurant where they enjoyed a hot meal, and on the way back Annie stopped to stare at the clothes displayed in the shop windows to give her some idea of what she ought to stock in her own. Fashions were changing so quickly and the elegant floor-length gowns were a thing of the past.

During the next few days Annie frequently went out alone to explore the shops while Susan packed up more of her treasures.

She also went to visit Charlie who she was glad to find seemed content and settled in his new job. It was on one such day, as she stood studying a dress on a mannequin in a smart emporium, that Annie heard a voice she thought she'd never hear again. 'Hello, Annie.'

Her heart began to race as she whirled about and came face to face with Alex Gordon. 'A-Alex.' She was aware that her cheeks were flaming and felt a fool. She had thought she might never see him again and yet here he was, as handsome as ever, and dressed in civilian clothes. 'H-how are you?'

'Very well, and yourself? What brings you here?'

'I came with Susan, Maggie's sister, to 'elp 'er pack up her flat and to 'ave a look at what's fashionable. I 'ave me own shop now.'

'Really?' He sounded genuinely pleased for her. 'In that case I think we should go and find somewhere to have a pot of tea and you can tell me all about it. Do you have time?'

'Er . . . yes, I do,' she said in a croaky voice.

He gently took her elbow and steered her through the shoppers. 'So where shall we go?' he asked once they were outside on the pavement. The rain that had been falling when she entered the shop had stopped now and a wintry sun shone in the sky. Annie glanced up and saw the most beautiful rainbow arching across the city and she knew that every time she saw one in the future she would think of Alex and this moment.

'We could find a café, or I'm staying in a hotel just along here. Should we go there and have afternoon tea in my room?'

She nodded numbly, very aware of the feeling of his hand against her arm. They walked for a while until they came to the entrance of a very smart-looking hotel where he paused. 'This is it, but we can go somewhere else if you'd rather?'

'N-no, this will be fine,' she assured him.

So they climbed the stone steps and entered a luxurious foyer. Alex crossed to the desk and had a word with the woman behind it before leading her up a grand marble staircase that curved up to the upstairs floors.

'But why are you staying 'ere? I thought you lived in London?'

'I did,' he agreed. 'But my wife and little girl moved out of the city some time ago to live in Sussex. It wasn't safe for them to be here while all the bombing was going on. I'm only here on business.'

She wanted to ask him what job he did now but didn't like to, so she stayed silent until he paused on a long thickly carpeted landing to fumble in his pocket for his room key. Once inside she stared around. It was a beautiful room with wonderful views over London and as she stood at the window, he came to stand beside her, and her heart began to pound again.

'I've thought about you often, Annie,' he said gently, but before he could say more, there was a tap at the door and a maid entered pushing a tea trolley laden with a silver teapot and plates of dainty sandwiches and tiny cakes.

'I'll be mother, shall I?' Alex joked with a twinkle in his eye as he laid out the delicate china cups and saucers.

They sat down and although the food looked delicious, Annie found that she couldn't eat a thing.

'So tell me what you've been up to.'

And so, Annie began to tell him of everything that had happened during their time apart: of Maggie's and Constance's deaths and Levi buying her the shop, and he listened attentively. Outside, the afternoon was darkening but inside the hotel room was snug and cosy. Suddenly he reached across and took her small hand in his two large ones. 'I've missed you so much, Annie,' he muttered sadly.

'I've missed you too,' she breathed, and then she was in his arms and although she knew he was a married man, she didn't want to stop him as his lips came down on hers.

'Perhaps you should go?' he suggested raggedly when they finally drew apart.

Annie shook her head. 'I don't want to go,' she whispered.

They stared at each other intently, until he took her hand and led her to the bed where he quietly began to undress her. Soon she stood before him naked, but she felt no shame. It was as if this moment was always meant to be and she wanted to belong to him. When he was naked too, they fell onto the bed, his kisses leaving a trail of fire across her body.

He paused just once to stare down at her and ask, 'Are you sure you want to do this, my love? You know I can't marry you.'

'I don't care,' she said, kissing him again. 'This might be the only time we ever 'ave and I want you.'

After what Reggie had done to her, she had thought she would never willingly lie with a man again, but this was so different that it took her breath away. He was gentle and kind, and when she finally lay sated in his arms, with her head on his chest, over an hour later, she had never felt so happy.

There was a catch in his voice when he whispered softly into her hair, 'I wish things could have been different, Annie. If they had I'd marry you in a heartbeat, but this isn't fair to you. It must never happen again.'

'I know,' she said quietly. 'But I don't regret it, Alex, and you'll always 'ave my heart.'

She reluctantly rose and began to get dressed. It was time for her to go back to her life and him to his.

'Shall I take you back to Susan's?' he offered when she put her coat on, but she shook her head.

'No . . . thank you, but I'd rather just go now. As you said, this must never happen again and there's no point in dragging out the goodbyes, but I still don't regret it.'

'Nor do I.' He gently took her in his arms for one last kiss before she turned and headed for the door, and as she let herself out, she heard him whisper, 'I love you, Annie. And in another time . . .'

She nodded. 'I know.'

Chapter Fifty-One

'You're very quiet tonight,' Susan commented later that evening as they sat together drinking cocoa in her flat.

'Am I?' Annie shrugged. 'Oh . . . I'm just a bit tired, I suppose.'

Susan looked around the familiar room that had been her home for so long and hardly recognised it. Everything of sentimental value was now packed away in trunks ready to be forwarded to Nuneaton and the place looked bare.

'We could head back now if you've done what you wanted to do?' Susan said quietly. 'I've only a few last things to pack in the bedroom. We could go back tomorrow if you like.'

Annie nodded. 'Yes, that's fine by me.' They said goodnight and each went to their own rooms and as Annie got ready for bed, she closed her eyes and relived every glorious minute she had spent with Alex. She supposed she should feel sad and guilty about what she'd done, but she didn't. At least now she would always have this precious memory of him to hold in her heart. Even so, she was sensible enough to know she would probably never see him again, and it made her think of her own future. She felt as if she were at a crossroads in her life. She still wanted to begin the search for her parents and have a family – a husband and children of her very own who she would love and cherish. There would be no use in denying herself that because she could never have a future with Alex. He would want her to be happy and so it was time to do some serious thinking.

She and Susan set off for home the following afternoon. Susan was tearful as she left the home she had shared with her daughter for the last time, but she had her memories, and they were precious.

It was evening when the train drew into Trent Valley Station, and because it was raining, they got a cab to Peggy's. She and Levi were sitting by the fire in companiable silence and Peggy hurried away to put the kettle on when they came in. Soon they were sitting with steaming mugs in their hands and Peggy was keen to hear what Annie and Susan had been up to.

Annie told her of all the trips to the shops she had made to study the fashions, and of how content Charlie seemed to be when she'd seen him.

'Good, an' I 'ave to say I'm glad yer back.' Peggy grinned. 'Young Monty's been prowlin' about like a cat on 'ot bricks ever since yer left. I've no doubt he'll be round this evenin' an' all to check if yer back.'

The words had barely left her lips when there was a tap on the door and there he was. His face lit up as his eyes settled on Annie and he rushed forward to kiss her cheek.

'Welcome back . . . I've missed you.'

He sank down beside Annie and took her hand, asking her all about what she'd been up to. The evening passed pleasantly but eventually Peggy yawned.

'Well, I don't know about you lot but I'm jiggered. I reckon I'll get off to bed.'

Susan and Levi rose too.

'I'll walk you home, Annie,' Monty offered.

They said their goodnights and set off through the cold streets. The pavements were almost deserted; many people didn't wish to venture out on such a cold, dark night, and Monty tucked her arm into his as they hurried on. She smiled. It was funny, she thought, that she always felt safe with Monty around. He had always been there for her ever since she had been taken out of the workhouse, and she was more than a little fond of him – loved him, in fact. Admittedly not in the way she loved Alex – that was a once in a lifetime love, but it wasn't meant to be, so now she was going to have to make the best of her life without him.

Once they arrived at the door she asked, 'Fancy coming up for a cup of cocoa before you set off for home?'

Monty didn't need asking twice and followed her up the stairs. He was surprised to be invited up as usually she said goodnight at the door. Once upstairs she put a match to the fire that was laid ready and while the room was warming, she went back downstairs to make them both a drink.

'So . . . I asked you to come up for a reason,' she began quietly once they were sitting together on the small sofa sipping their drinks.

'Oh yes, and what was that?' He put his mug down and stared at her.

Annie felt a blush rise up her cheeks. 'Well . . . while I've been away, I've been doing a lot of thinking . . . I love it in London and I promised myself that one day I'd 'ave a shop there.'

'Nothing wrong with being ambitious,' he acknowledged. That was one of the things she loved about him: Monty would never try to hold her back like some men who still believed a woman's place was in the home.

'But the thing is, I want the best of both worlds.'

He looked a little confused and she rushed on, 'What I mean is, I want a 'ome and children too and so . . .' She stared down at her folded hands. 'And so, if the offer of marriage is still on the table, I'd like to accept it.'

He looked stunned. 'Th-there's nothing I'd like more than to have you as my wife. But it's only fair to remind you that I don't know how long I've got. When this shrapnel moves—'

She held her hand up to stay his words and turned towards him. 'The shrapnel could move the other way and then we'll grow old and grey together,' she pointed out.

'But what if it doesn't?'

'Then I'll be grateful for the time we do 'ave together.'

A look of pure joy spread across his face as he pulled her into his arms. 'I see, and when would you like this marriage to take place?'

'Just as soon as you can arrange it,' she told him solemnly. 'I don't see any point in waitin', although I don't think your mother is going to be too 'appy about it . . . or Reggie if it comes to that.'

'I don't care what they think,' he said. 'I love you, Annie, I always have.'

In the glow from the fire, he kissed her gently on the lips and although his touch didn't set her on fire as Alex's did, she knew she was doing the right thing. With Monty she would build a home to be proud of, with children who would never know the loneliness that she had.

With a happy sigh she laid her head on his shoulder. The rest of her life was just about to begin.

Acknowledgements

Here we are with the second of my Rags to Riches Trilogy, *One Woman's War*! Where does the time go and how do I even start to thank all the people who have been involved in helping it onto the shelves? I am so blessed to have a wonderful team of people behind me at Bonnier. First of all Sarah Benton, our brilliant CEO, my amazing editor Claire Johnson-Creek, Beth Whitelaw, Holly Milnes and far too many others to mention, but you all know who you are and I want you to know how important each and every one of you is to me. Between us we strive to make each book as good as it can be and I couldn't do it without all of you, so thank you for your ongoing support and encouragement. Never forgetting, of course, my wonderful agent, Sheila Crowley from Curtis Brown, always at the end of the phone if needed. And then there's my clever copy-editor, Gillian Holmes, and my excellent proofreader, Jane Howard. The list just goes on and on. I should also, as always, say a special thank you to my family, and especially my husband, for acting as chauffeur, listener and chief tea maker!

Finally, a huge thank you to all my wonderful readers. You'll never know how much your lovely messages and reviews mean to me, so thank you all.

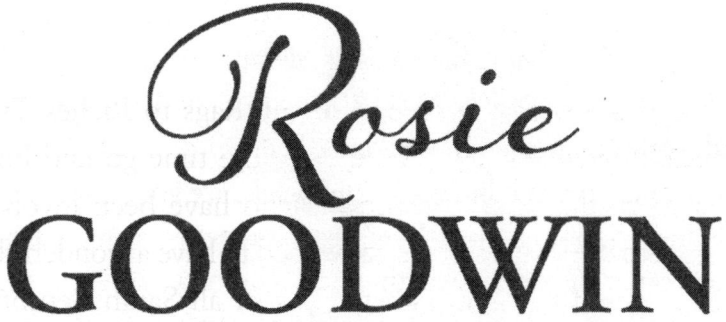

Want to keep up to date with the latest from Rosie Goodwin?

With exclusive content from the author herself, book updates, competitions and more, the Rosie Goodwin newsletter is the place to be if you can't get enough of Britain's best-loved saga author.

To sign up, you can scan the QR code or type the link below into your browser

https://geni.us/RosieGoodwin

MEMORY LANE

Hello everyone,

And just like that Christmas is behind us once again! Where does the time go? I do hope you all had a lovely one with your families and loved ones. I certainly did! It always shocks me after all the weeks and weeks we spend preparing and shopping for it how fast Christmas is over, and then comes the dreary weather and a bit of an anti-climax.

But the good thing now is that spring is marching towards us, so hopefully we'll see some sunshine again before too much longer.

And of course, we now have the release of the second of my Rags to Riches Trilogy, *One Woman's War*, on the shelves! As always my brilliant graphic designer has done a wonderful job of the cover, as I'm sure you'll all agree.

I was absolutely delighted with your responses to *The Rag Princess*. Thank you all so much for your lovely messages and reviews. I was thrilled when she went straight into the bestsellers and hope now you'll love the second instalment as much.

In this one we saw Annie start a new chapter in her life when World War One was declared and she trains to be a nurse. Eventually she goes off to France to work on the front in the field hospitals where she sees sights that will haunt her forever. I can't even begin to imagine how awful it must have been for the doctors and nurses there, not to mention the poor soldiers. But it wasn't all bad for her because while she was there, she also met the love of her life. Sadly, in true Annie form, everything didn't go to plan, and they couldn't be together. I'd love to tell you more but now you can follow the story for yourselves.

· MEMORY LANE ·

Throughout everything, Annie's longing to find her true family never went away. Perhaps she needed to find them to find herself? All will be revealed eventually I promise. In the meantime, I hope you all enjoyed reading it as much as I loved writing it. I can't wait to hear what you all think so do keep the messages coming.

I'm just hoping that this year will be as good for me as last year. It was amazing to see both of my offerings in the Sunday Times bestseller lists and of course I was also shortlisted for The British Book Awards. What an honour that was, and what a brilliant night I had with my wonderful 'Rosie Team' in London! It was certainly one I shall never forget.

So now I'm going to go and leave you all in peace while I'm busily tapping away on the next one, *The Winter Bride*, which will be coming to shelves in September. I can't wait!

I hope you all have a wonderful Mother's Day when it comes, and a lovely spring and summer, and thank you all so much for your ongoing support and encouragement. Please do sign up for my newsletter if you haven't done so already. I love sharing all sorts of bits and pieces there. The link is in the page above this letter. And do also sign up for the Memory Lane Facebook page and newsletter, where you can be kept up to date with what I, and other saga authors, are up to.

Take care.

Much love,

Rosie xx

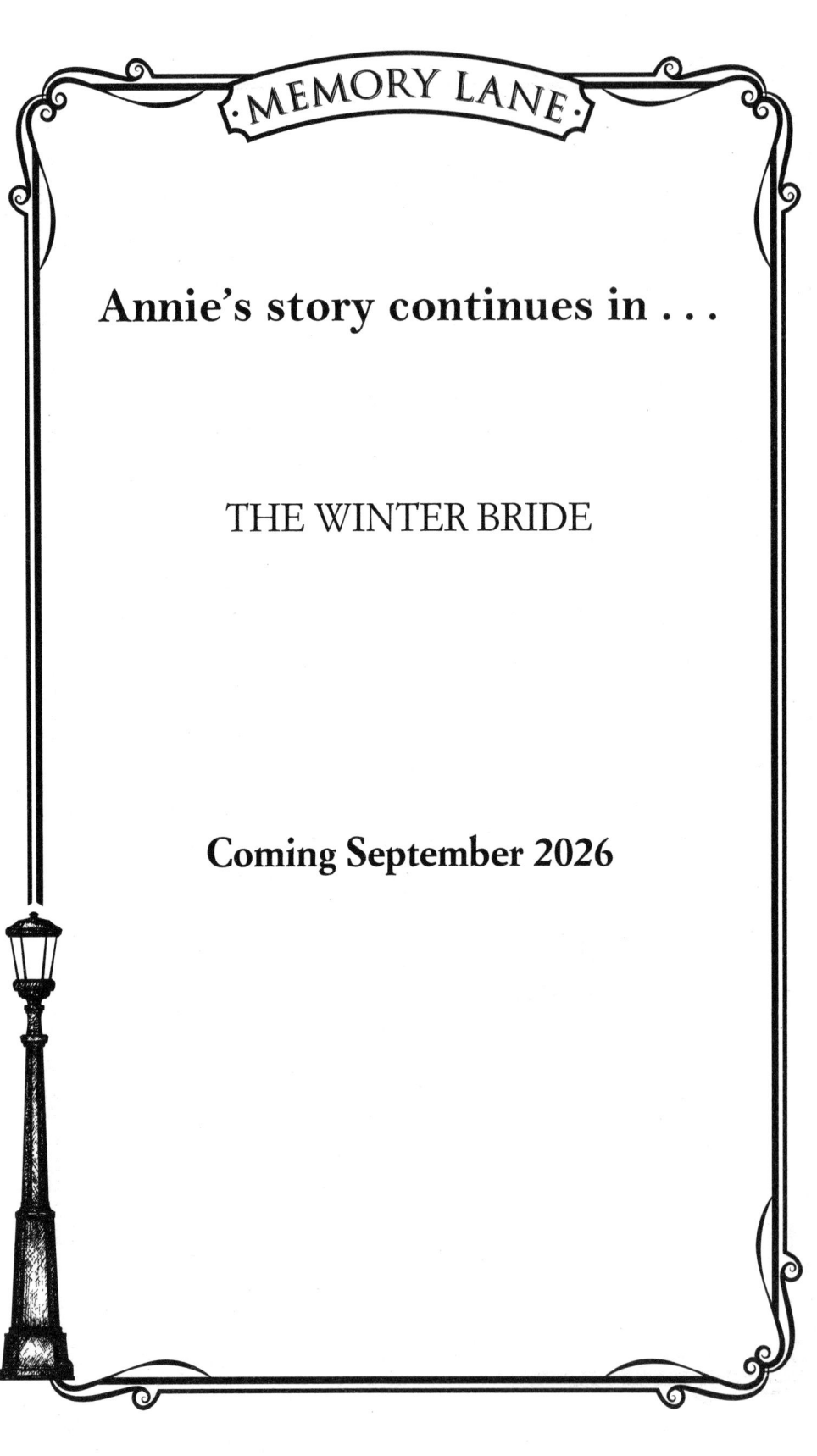

MEMORY LANE

Annie's story continues in . . .

THE WINTER BRIDE

Coming September 2026

The Rags to Riches trilogy

Get to know Annie over the course of three books in a brand-new series from Rosie Goodwin

The Flower Girls Collection

Meet Lily, Daisy and Violet in the new collection by Britain's best-loved saga author, Rosie Goodwin

  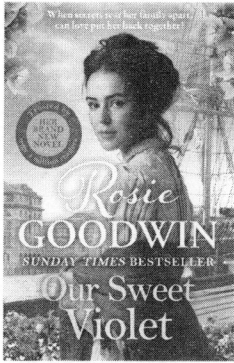

Available now

The Days of the Week Collection

Have you read Rosie's collection of novels inspired by the 'Days of the week' Victorian rhyme?

Available now

The Precious Stones Collection

If you liked Saffie's story, get to know Opal, Pearl, Ruby, Emerald and Amber in the rest of the Precious Stones series.

Available now

The Lost Girl

Can Esme lay the ghosts to rest to save herself and find the life she deserves?

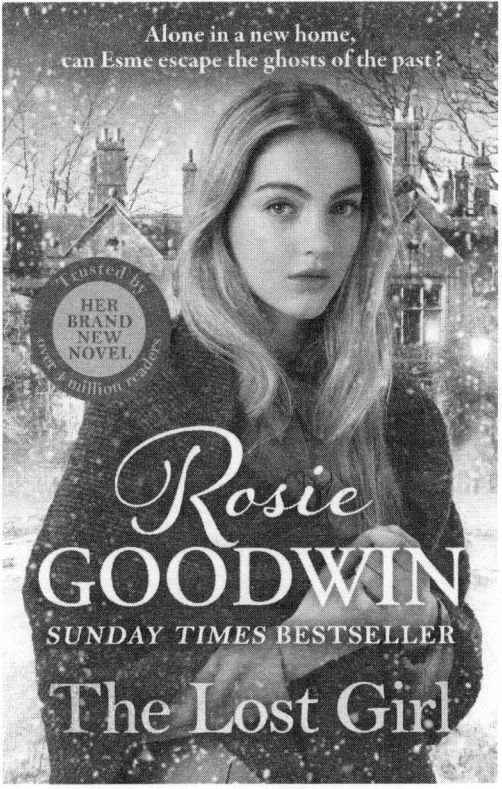

Available now

Loved this book?
Join the Memory Lane Community

A welcoming home for all readers who love heart-warming tales of family, romance and history.

Sign up to our newsletter via the QR code below for book recommendations, giveaways, deals and behind-the-scenes writing moments from your favourite authors.

https://geni.us/memory-lane

Or you can also join the conversation in the Memory Lane Facebook Group.